Map $_{of}$ Stars

Also by Catherine Law

A Season of Leaves
The September Garden
The Flower Book

Map of Stars

of

Catherine Law

ZAFFRE

First published in Great Britain in 2016 by

Zaffre Publishing
80-81 Wimpole St, London W1G 9RE
www.zaffrebooks.co.uk

A CIP catalogue record for this book is available from the British Library.

ISBN: 978-1-785-76047-1

also available as an ebook

1 3 5 7 9 10 8 6 4 2

Typeset by IDSUK (Data Connection) Ltd

Printed and bound by Clays Ltd, St Ives Plc

Zaffre Publishing is an imprint of Bonnier Zaffre
a Bonnier Publishing company
www.bonnierzaffre.co.uk
www.bonnierpublishing.co.uk

For Celeste

PROLOGUE

July 1967

The tender, open-faced rose cupped in Eliza's palm smelt just like butter icing; sugar and cream combined. The petals were dewy, almost without colour, and resembled the bloom on her baby daughter's cheek; the vulnerable translucent pink exactly like her tiny fingernails.

The memory of Stella's birth twenty-five years ago distracted her. She had wanted the baby to mark the end of all that had gone before. To sever the past from the future. She'd made herself believe this was possible in the gasping shock of her appearance, as the doctor cut the cord and she cradled a wailing Stella in her arms. But above that, above exhaustion and unimaginable pain, she'd felt devastating wonder at the fragility of new life that had issued from her body. Her resolution had soon dissolved; it could never be so. For, two and a half decades later, the past and her guilt were still with her, stalking her, tapping her on the shoulder.

Beyond the single flower held in her hand and beyond the merging rose bushes that her late mother-in-law had planted and tended, stood her home. In the glorious light of that summer's afternoon – all shimmering radiance and flickering shadows – the Elizabethan chimneys and gabled end of Forstall Manor comforted her, the half-timbered walls settled solidly into the earth. The house looked exactly as it did 400 years ago and was brimming with secrets, witness to so much. Every so often, it revealed clues to its own mysteries to her: the mummified mice in the wainscots, the marks of the carpenter's chisel on the great beam above the fireplace, the kitten paw prints baked into the bricks by the front door. And Forstall knew all that she had done, secreting its knowledge inside its ancient beams.

Eliza gazed up at the façade, squinting in the hazy sunshine. Behind those drawn curtains flapping in the breeze, second casement along, Stella was sleeping.

Her daughter's sudden arrival home early that morning from London, carrying a battered suitcase and wearing go-go boots, set a black line of irritation scraping down Eliza's spine.

But the balmy afternoon air drifting gently around her worked hard to evaporate her sourness. Here, in the garden created by the grandmother Stella never knew, Eliza cut roses for her daughter; a private gesture of belated welcome. An apology that her daughter did not know she was owed. Stella might like the roses. But then again, she might not even notice.

Holding the stem between her fingers, Eliza leant in with her secateurs. The breeze quickened, stealing for a moment the sweet buttery fragrance. She recoiled. The sharp bite of the thorn drew a bubble of blood. The prick of pain shocked her, sending her attention darting down its dark inevitable path. She popped her finger in her mouth, and tasted old pain: the remorse and misery that Stella's birth had failed to extinguish. She drew a hard breath and mechanically, mindlessly, began to cut the roses.

With her trug full of blooms, she wandered back up the path to the house, pausing in front of the front door. The inscription carved into the threshold at her feet read *Iter meum perfectum est*. My journey is finished. She had read these words a thousand times, and they were a salve to her, were steady and always true.

Inside the dim, cool hallway, the Jacobean staircase rose to the half landing where sunbeams highlighted a rather ambitious cobweb spanning the highest corner. Stella used to sit up there as a little girl, Eliza remembered, on the turn in the stairs behind those thick tapestry curtains. Perhaps she thought herself invisible, spying on what the grown-ups were doing. And yet they could hear her chattering and having funny little conversations with herself.

The clock on the hallstand ticked devotedly and the sound of the Home Service drifted from the radio through the kitchen door. Eliza walked to the sink and filled a vase, her attention drawn through the open window overlooking the back garden. A blackbird hopped across the square lawn and Morris, her father-in-law, was showing her mother a particularly tall hollyhock in his prized herbaceous border. They stood in the shadow of the Stour wing along the east side of the garden and Eliza could hear their soft companionable murmuring. Each of them widowed, they rubbed along easily together at Forstall. She gave them a quick grateful smile.

She and Stella both shared her mother Mathilde's looks: a generous mouth, the lips slightly downturned as if always on the edge of a wry smile. But while she and Mathilde had clear-blue, courageous eyes, Stella's were a muddy green. It was the thick russet hair that linked grandmother to mother to daughter. Mathilde's was now bright and snowy, while her own was inevitably going that way: sprinkled lightly with silver. But over her forehead, a lock of white had appeared, quite suddenly, soon after she gave birth to Stella.

Clutching the vase of roses in one hand and a mug of tea for Stella in the other, Eliza walked across the hallway, passing the mirror. She tipped her head to the side and the shock of white gleamed in her reflection.

On the half landing, near Stella's hiding spot, she put the vase and mug down on the table and made a slow appreciation of the framed photographs. Her parents' wedding, just after the First World War. Her father Richard out of uniform, her mother Mathilde in a gown that showed her ankles. They'd met when Mathilde nursed Richard in a field hospital in France not far from her Picardy home. In the photograph, he is frail, half a man. He'd saved the life of his captain, Morris Staveley, after he'd taken a bullet to the shoulder. Richard had helped Morris into his gas mask before fitting his own. Strictly against orders. The gas killed Richard, eventually. He, the hero, had brought the two families together, and was the reason they were all here at Forstall. And yet Eliza could barely remember him.

Morris and Sybil, older than her parents, had snatched their moment by marrying in 1914, before Morris headed off to France. Sybil was beautiful, bright and slender. She had been fair-headed, just like Nicholas, so very fair. Eliza averted her eyes from the keen face that gazed openly through the lens. She moved on to her brother Martyn. He shone, confident and clear-eyed, out of his photograph, smart and buttoned-up in RAF uniform. His shoulders were set with pride, but even though he was trying to be formal, with leather gloves and Brylcreemed hair, Eliza knew he was perched on the edge of laughter. The Luftwaffe shot him out of the sky over the White Cliffs. When she was little, Stella had not understood. She'd often demanded that Eliza tell her where her Uncle Martyn might be if he was not in the churchyard and not in the sky.

There was no photograph of Eliza and Nicholas's wedding, for that day had been famously broken up by air raids. No evidence of their wedding and, thought Eliza, picking up the vase and mug and walking up the second flight, since Nicholas had been sleeping in the Stour wing for more years than she could care to remember, no evidence of a marriage either.

She stopped outside the door to Stella's bedroom. She listened. The ancient house creaked around her, listening too, heating up and exhaling under the afternoon sun, issuing dry smells of dust and soot and an organic aroma from its corners: plaster, polish and mouse. From Stella's bedroom she caught a faint whiff of patchouli.

Eliza eased the door open a fraction more and peered in. In the dim, curtained light, she could make out the long shape of her sleeping daughter, her hair a dark mass on the pillow. A startling rush of envy switched into outrage. When she had been Stella's age, at the height of the war, it would have been a scandal to be lying in bed in the middle of the day, however long and hard she'd worked through the night. But then Stella had looked so shattered and pale when she arrived home that morning, standing in the hallway with her suitcase at her feet and appearing as delicate as a child. Her suitcase lay open now, spilling its contents onto the tatty sheepskin rug by the kidney-shaped dressing table. When she'd moved to Forstall, Eliza had saved coupons for the furniture in this room and had sewn gingham curtains with her mother, got them wrong and started again.

On a desk beside the dressing table stood Morris's old typewriter, commandeered by Stella, and a rack of LPs. And on the floor, with a picture of the Rolling Stones taped to the lid, the Dansette record player she and Nicholas had bought Stella the Christmas before last.

Eliza took a step in and winced as the floorboards complained under her foot. She gingerly rested the vase of roses in front of the dressing table mirror and set the mug down on the bedside table. Under the candlewick, Stella was curled tight in sleep.

Eliza kept very still; she was loath to wake her daughter just yet. Her attention was captured by the quartet of Alphonse Mucha posters on the wall above the bed. Four mystical woman, each depicting a celestial body, glowed down at her out of the semi-darkness: *The Moon*, shy and enveloped by dreamy constellations; the sleepy *Evening Star*; *The Morning Star*, shielding her eyes from the brightness of the dawn; and *The Pole Star*, fixed and steady, a guiding light.

She'd been enchanted by them ever since Stella had unrolled the posters on the kitchen table a year or so ago, having ordered them especially from a shop in London. They drew something out of Eliza: freedom and hope. A sense of being loved. And, during the time Stella had been away, Eliza had come into the room simply to stare at the posters. Mucha's art nouveau designs, their sinuous lines and intimate half-nudity were back in fashion now that, apparently, London was swinging. New sounds were coming from her radio. 'Psychedelic, Mum,' Stella had pointed out. But Eliza did not relish the hippy movement. Stella told her that she obviously did not approve and Nicholas took pleasure in pointing out to her that she simply did not *understand*. He was right. The younger generation, with their self-proclaimed Summer of Love, made her feel old, tired and jealous. But she never grew tired of Mucha's mesmerising art. She found it hard to fathom that their radiance and ethereal beauty had been created not long before her father and Morris had been fixing bayonets in the trenches.

Eliza tugged at the curtains, letting in a triangle of sunlight and sat down in the Lloyd Loom chair by the bed. Stella stirred, a long pale arm finding freedom from under the sheet and Eliza's impatience melted into tenderness. But she did not reach for her to tap her awake. The roses and the tea were her limit.

Stella screwed up her face, opened her eyes, noticed her mother and began to hoist herself up against her headboard. In the brighter light, her hair looked like it was on fire.

'I thought you might like a cup of tea,' Eliza said. 'It's nearly four o'clock and you can't stay in bed all day. You'll never sleep tonight. Have you dyed your hair?'

'It's henna,' Stella said groggily, settling herself against the pillows, pushing strands of fiery red hair out of her face.

'It's lovely.'

Even as Eliza said this, she flinched with pain, remembering Lewis holding her, whispering into her hair. *Like rich, golden, sweet treacle*, he had said.

Stella reached for the mug. 'It's like piling sticky, smelly earth on top of your head.'

Eliza glanced at the clothes spilling from the suitcase.

'I see you've been shopping,' she said, blandly. 'I like the dress you were wearing when you arrived. Although it is rather too *mini*. You don't get anything like that in Canterbury. Do you go to Carnaby Street? Or is it the King's Road these days?'

Stella merely nodded, answering neither question, taking another draught of tea.

'So what has brought you home so suddenly? I do hope you locked up properly. You know what London is like for petty thieves.'

Eliza heard herself, her worried prattling. She was in danger of boring Stella, wrenching the gap between them even wider. She hadn't seen her in six months. And sometimes felt she did not know her. Silly – she must make an effort.

Stella had left home in January to hole herself up at the Hampstead house to pursue a writing career. She had offered this to her parents as a foil for failed exams, for dropping out of college, for the drag of lost expectations which Eliza had struggled hard not to express. Nicholas had said it was fine as long as Stella was happy and Morris had said that of course Smidgen should do it. And Mathilde was all gentle encouragement. London was the bright, shining Emerald City after all. But Eliza could never be fully happy about it, her ill temper keeping her mute. Stella had left in a cloud of euphoria of her own making, but now she had returned – untimely and unexplained.

'Was it boyfriend trouble?' Eliza persisted in a cool, dry voice. Stella set her tea down. 'Nothing like that.'

'You haven't been taking drugs, have you?'

Stella tipped her head back and her laugh rang out. 'Oh, Mum, really! I'm trying to become a writer. I need to keep a clear head.'

'It's just that it's all over the papers.' She felt foolish. Now she was trying far too hard. 'Your father was only reading about marijuana in *The Times* the other day. They said it might help the creative process.'

'Yes, if you're a famous pop star,' said Stella.

Eliza felt the weight of Stella's intelligent stare, the innocence in her face. She realised then that she wanted to reach for her, perhaps hug her.

'So, then . . .' Her voice was thin with apprehension. 'Why did you come home?'

Stella groaned and shuffled back down the bed, adopting a foetal position. She closed her eyes, thick strands of hair shielding her face.

'Mum, I grew homesick. I just wanted to be here. I know you are wondering why I have not had a bestseller yet.' Her voice was muffled, jaded and raw. 'All I have is a rejected manuscript and a couple of cheques for stories I wrote for the local *Ham & High* rag. London isn't all that swinging, you know, if you don't have any money.' She opened her eyes and Eliza was stupefied suddenly by their colour – so like his.

Stella broke the silence. 'I love Forstall, it's as simple as that. All those stories Gramps would tell me about this place. I kept remembering them while I was alone, knocking around that gloomy London house, supposedly writing. How ancient Forstall is. How Queen Elizabeth the First once slept here . . .'

Eliza cocked an eyebrow and shared her daughter's giggle.

'And I realised, Mum, how important home is to me. And the story of Gramps and Grandpa Richard. How they met in the First War. It's where I come from. How I came to be . . .'

Eliza got up quickly and went to the window, drawing the curtains back and pushing the casement open wider. The rose garden below swam with her unshed tears.

'I wrote all last night. The story of my two grandfathers,' Stella was speaking. 'And when the dawn came, in the middle of the night, it seemed, I looked out across the Heath and didn't think twice. Packed my suitcase and set off home. I got the milk train.'

'It is a bit of a lonely place, isn't it?' Eliza said quietly to herself, willing her tears to retreat. 'I did wonder at the wisdom of you being there all alone.'

She thought of the towering town house in the terrace overlooking the Heath. Of the time she had spent there at the end of the war. Seeking a cure for her sorrow. Seeking comfort from the ghost of Lewis, for if he was to be anywhere, then surely it would be in Hampstead. Trying to mend the breakdown that no one in the family ever spoke of. Desperately alone in a city full of strangers.

'Ha, Mum, I nearly forgot!' Stella, suddenly energised, bounced out of bed, her nightdress billowing. She knelt by her spilling suitcase, scooping back her hair. She rummaged and extracted a battered felt hat and narrow, stained kid gloves. 'Look what I found. They must be yours?'

'No, not mine,' Eliza said on reflex, barely glancing at them. 'We rented that place out for years in the fifties, remember. They could belong to any one of our tenants. They can go to the church jumble.'

'Ah, but what about this?'

Stella plucked something from her purse. She walked over with a ring clasped between her fingertips. The plain, rose-gold band winked aggressively in the sunlight.

'Found it at the back of the laundry cupboard. It's as if it just slipped off someone's finger while they were putting away the towels. Looks like a wedding ring.'

Eliza held up her left hand. 'Well, it's certainly not mine,' she said, desperate to disguise the shock at seeing it again after all these years.

She forced herself to turn away, to pick up the hat and gloves and examine them closely.

'But, on second thoughts, these *must be* mine. Oh, you can smell the mothballs. These gloves would never fit me now. I used to have such delicate, slender hands. I still have slender feet, you know. Your feet don't really change. How old-fashioned this hat is. Who would have thought I could have got away with *this* . . .?'

'I'll ask Dad about the ring, then. He might know.'

Eliza walked away from her towards the door.

'Look, Stella, get yourself up and dressed. Grannie is making cheese on toast for you. Your favourite.'

Keen to leave the room to escape Stella's questions, she started to go.

'Nice roses, Mum.' Stella's words stopped her dead by the door. 'I smelt them as you brought them in. That's what woke me. I was dreaming of Uncle Martyn.'

A sound interrupted Stella. An abrupt sound, like a tap running, a fine pouring of water. It was a welcome intrusion for it meant, for a moment, that Eliza could stop thinking of the house at Hampstead, of the ring. She turned to the window.

'Is it raining?'

But the sky was cloudless, the sun beaming. She followed Stella's stare to the fireplace where a thin trickle of plaster dust was drizzling steadily down from the chimney onto the hearth. Suddenly, the line of dust swelled, joined by chips of masonry and chunks of brick. They fell swiftly, rumbling and rattling like hail, pinging off the floorboards, scattering dirt to the corners.

Eliza shrieked. 'For goodness' sake, we've only just had that chimney swept!'

They both moved swiftly to the door as the appalling crescendo ended in a violent cloud of soot expanding alarmingly through the room.

'Bloody hell!'

'Oh, my gosh, just look at it.'

As the dust faded and settled, Stella walked barefoot towards the fireplace, tiptoeing over chunks of plaster and grit, wincing and wafting her hand through the haze.

'What on earth are you doing?' Eliza fumbled for the handkerchief in her cuff and placed it over her nose. 'You'll hurt your feet. God, I hate dust.'

'I heard something fall.'

'Yes, it sounds as though half the chimney fell!'

Stella squatted down and gingerly prodded at a lump among the debris.

'I believe it's a dead bird.'

Eliza let out a disgusted sigh.

'I think it's a pigeon,' Stella said. 'Hard to tell. Who knows how long it's been up there? It's pretty mummified.'

'This is the limit.'

Eliza went to the landing and called for Nicholas, her shout cracking the delicate peace of the manor's interior.

She waited, agitated, for his faint but affirmative reply, and went back to the doorway to see Stella take the dead bird by the tip of its wing. She clung to the doorpost, revolted, as her daughter lifted it clear of the pile of soot and set it on the hearthstone. It was yet another mystery, another clue to the past, like the mummified mouse, regurgitated by Forstall. Nicholas's footfalls resounded up the staircase behind her. He brushed past and stopped in the middle of the room.

'Crikey, what a mess.'

'Look at this, Dad.' Stella was animated. She excitedly waved him over. 'Look what I've found.'

Nicholas strode forward, unperturbed by the minefield of debris, and bent his tall frame over, his hands resting on his knees. His face was flushed with exertion, the scanty fair hair on top of his nearly bald, vulnerable head rather ruffled. He peered through his glasses then lifted them up to get a better look.

'Goodness gracious! There's a Bakelite phial attached to its leg. Remember them, Eliza? It must be a homing pigeon.'

She pressed her handkerchief more firmly over her face. Breathing gingerly, she took a tentative step closer.

'By Christ, I think it is,' he said, coughing and wafting at the dust. 'Must be one of Castle's. Got lost on the way to his place and stuck in our chimney.'

Eliza protested, 'But that all finished at the end of the war. Can it have been there for so long?'

'Who is Castle?' Stella threw in.

'Don't you remember?' asked Nicholas. 'I suppose you wouldn't.'

'And thank God she doesn't,' muttered Eliza.

'He used to own the farm down the lane near Wickham-breaux,' he said. 'Kept a pigeon loft during the war for messenger pigeons. It was commandeered just as the Stour wing here was being taken over by the War Office. Dead now, of course. And his daughter Jessica, too, we think.'

'You *think*?' Stella asked, but didn't wait for an answer, turning greedily back to the pigeon.

Eliza couldn't draw breath. Her blood seemed to change its course as a long line of bewildering memories paraded through her mind. Her hands turned cold, fingers trembling. She crushed her handkerchief in her fist and forced herself to walk forward, picking her way across the rubble on the bedroom floor to squint at the curious container strapped to the bird.

Stella was eager, pulling the phial from the pigeon's leg, which promptly disintegrated to dust. 'I wonder if there's a message inside . . .'

She dexterously eased off the end of the container to reveal the top of a rolled-up paper. Giving a little sound of pleasure, she began to tease it out.

'Careful now,' Nicholas said. 'It will be old and fragile. It definitely looks wartime to me. What do you think, Eliza?'

She stepped back, silent, unblinking, as her daughter drew the message out of the phial and held it up.

'Bring it to the light, here, by the window,' Nicholas commanded, his voice suddenly high-pitched with excitement. 'Goodness, this takes us back doesn't it? Old Castle's homing pigeons. Messages from the Resistance. How marvellous.'

Eliza's memory sharpened. She whispered, 'The messages . . .'

Stella's bright face turned to Eliza. 'Of course. Mum, you speak fluent French because of Grannie. Were you involved? You must have been. Did you translate them?'

Eliza couldn't bring herself to answer. Her mind had switched to the war, to the long days deciphering communications, when Morse code tapped through the night in the salon in the Stour wing. Intelligence exchanged. Secrets buried. A knife-edge of life or death. Lewis holding her, his hands deep in her hair.

'We were told never to speak of it.' Her words were small and strangled. 'And so I never will.'

Stella, appearing to ignore her, had bent to her task of unrolling the two sheets of stapled paper, using the fingers and thumbs of both hands to stretch it wide across the top of her dressing table.

Eliza stared, recognising immediately what it was that Stella was unravelling. This was no ordinary message chit. This was a document so precious that its loss during the war was deemed a total and utter catastrophe. She'd drafted this document, working on it night after night, and keeping it secure in a safe. Just a handful of people knew of its existence. And all along it had been here, trapped in the chimney of her daughter's bedroom. Only discovered because she'd decided to have the flue swept, getting ahead of herself for the first fires of the autumn. Eliza's skin smarted and a cold sweat broke, drenching her scalp.

Nicholas lifted the paper to examine it. 'Well, isn't this extraordinary.'

The flimsy uppermost layer was a transparent grid covered with a series of dots and codes, joined by lines to resemble a constellation. Visible through it was an ordnance survey map of Kent. And written across the top grid sheet was a message. Faded inked words in a copperplate hand, snaking sideways.

'This writing – it's not in code. Not in French either,' Nicholas said triumphantly, peering closer. 'It's in good old plain English, ah . . .' He sucked his breath back through his teeth and glanced at Eliza, questions in his eyes.

She looked at her husband, her vision swimming. She brought a hand to her throat to stop the sob that bloomed, stifling and hot, up her chest, her neck, her face.

'Do you know what this is?' he asked.

She took it from him and held it with trembling fingers. Her map. Her map of stars. At the end of the handwritten message was one word. Not a signature or a code. Just one word. *Lewis*. She pressed her palm over her mouth.

'He did it,' she whispered. 'He *tried* . . .'

'Who did?' Stella demanded. 'Who, Mum?'

Her core hollowed out and collapsed at appalling speed. Her present shifted bluntly to the past, to the time when she had been loved deeply, passionately, utterly. To that dangerous, glorious time when guilt and desire had caught her in chains of equal length. *She was told never to speak of it.*

The map trembled as she lifted it again to the light and the dead hole inside her filled with wild, futile victory. She read Lewis's message again and again. At last, the truth.

Part I

The Moon
'only shows one face'

Chapter 1

Eliza, 1939

Waiting for the others to catch up, Eliza stepped onto the stile. How well she knew this view, her tapestry of fields and orchards. Taking another rung up and shielding her eyes, she picked out the low meandering course of the Little Stour as it slipped lazily through reed beds and willows. Fluffy hedgerows and treelines marked the routes of field paths, lanes and byways. The white tips of oast houses and brick gables of farmhouses peeped through. Balancing on the balls of her feet, she could make out the distant tower of Canterbury Cathedral, see to the edge of her world.

Closer by, orchards were ready for harvest. Stunted trees, heavy with end-of-summer apples, grew in immaculate rows, the fruit like jewels. In hop gardens, feathery vines draped the frames, shimmering in the breeze. A blackbird called to her from the hawthorn, its song rippling the air. She shared her world with him. And for her it was a world in miniature, as on any given day her journeys were mapped across the same small triangle. She might travel from her home in Nunnery Fields in the shadow of the cathedral, to secretarial college on the outskirts of the city or to Forstall Manor to visit Nick and the Staveleys. Today, Sunday – just like last Sunday – she caught the bus from Canterbury with Maman and Martyn for dinner at Forstall. But there was a kink in her normal routine: even though tomorrow was Monday, Nick's mother Sybil had asked them to stay the night.

Wondering where they had got to, Eliza peered down the bridleway. Martyn was lolloping along, showing signs of boredom already. His shirttails had crept out of his trousers; one hand lazily in his pocket, the other lugging the suitcase which kept knocking his knee. He looked incredibly lop-sided. He'd been to the barber's yesterday and Eliza noted the shaved white line around the nape of his neck and over his ears, which revealed the tan of his long and carefree summer.

Her maman, Mathilde, trailed behind, her floral tea dress dappled with sunlight. In her Sunday best, with her handbag tilted over the crook of her arm, she was as poised as always, even though to walk along the rough footpath in those heels must be a struggle. Her headscarf was rather unbecoming. Eliza preferred her mother hatless and bareheaded, her glorious thick hair on show. For then the years fell clean away.

'Come on, you two,' she called out. 'Maman! Martyn! Nearly there.'

Her brother let out a whistle, trying to mimic the blackbird. He cocked his head, expecting to hear a return and looked angry when none came. He caught Eliza's eye and pretended to stumble, not fooling her for one minute. He switched the suitcase to his other hand, dragging his feet along the wheel rut, his face thunderous.

'Just think, Martyn.' She wanted to put a smile on his face. 'Auntie Sybil might have made her special lemon cake.'

He snapped back, angrily, 'Don't tell me what to think, especially when I'm walking along, minding my own business and doing my *own* thinking!'

'Is he being tiresome?' Mathilde caught up.

'I'm surprised you have to ask, Maman,' Eliza replied and then pressed her brother to reveal exactly what he was thinking, if it was *that* important.

'It's private, but if you must know . . .' His eyes sparkled with outrage, his fringe flopping in his eyes. He'd evidently asked for a short back and sides, long at the front. 'I was wondering just exactly how many times, over all these years, we've walked or stumbled up this blessed track. It always takes aeons to get here. Absolute ages. Endless waiting for the bus in town, the incessant bumping and chugging along boring country lanes. This, the final trudge.'

'Things always seem to take longer when you're a child,' Mathilde assured him, a little out of breath as she reached the stile. She leant against it next to Eliza. 'And you're still a boy – still Tintin in my eyes.'

'But I think it's time you grew up, Martyn,' Eliza threw in quickly, instantly regretting it when she saw that her words had stung him.

She tried to rally him. 'You love it at Forstall, Martyn, you just don't know that you do yet. As much as we all do. You would miss it if you didn't come.'

Her brother lowered his gaze, furious still, and refused to be drawn.

Mathilde looked between her two children, and asked if they would wait while she rested. She dabbed her face with her handkerchief and implored Eliza for the cologne in her handbag.

'I'm not so sure we really need to stay the night, if Martyn doesn't want to,' said Mathilde, patting perfume behind her ears. 'There's a bus from Wickhambreaux at nine tonight that'll get us home.'

Eliza argued gently that while the weather was still so perfect, it would be wonderful to have a night away from town. 'We *want* to stay, surely. We can relax, enjoy ourselves, have a lovely Sunday lunch with the Staveleys. And a nice evening. Then a leisurely trip back tomorrow. It was good of Auntie Sybil to ask us.'

'I just don't like to be a burden,' Mathilde sighed.

Eliza watched her mother wipe her face with the handkerchief and saw sadness in her eyes. There was a permanent cleft down the centre of her forehead, but also much to admire: her skin had the confident deep richness of a French lady, a dusky setting for her fine, wide-set features. She carried widowhood with quiet, nipped-in pride.

'Really, do we have to stay? We come here, *toujours* . . .' Mathilde whispered.

Eliza caught her mother's eye and understood.

She said, 'In that case, I'm sure Nick won't mind giving us a lift back tonight.'

Martyn let out a howl of derision which startled Eliza's black-bird that had been piping gamely from the hedge. It darted out with a noisy shriek and launched itself low over the orchard.

'For goodness' sake, are we going to stay here talking about it, or get on?' His face was thunderous. 'If we decide to go home tonight, what was the point of me lugging this suitcase for you both. All I put in was my toothbrush, so goodness only knows what else is in here.'

Mathilde smiled. '*Martyn*. Sybil and Morris have always been so good to us. I just feel inadequate, unable to return any sort of favour,' she said and turned to take in the view. 'And look at this. Such beauty. How can *this* be so peaceful, when all *that* is going on over there?'

'Come on, Maman, let's not think of it.' Eliza linked her arm, pulled her on. '*This* old landscape won't change. I can assure you of that.'

'But it's inevitable, you ninny,' Martyn leapt in. 'You read the newspapers, don't you?'

'Now, now, Eliza, Tintin . . .' began Mathilde, and then corrected herself. 'You're no longer children so stop behaving like . . .'

'Anyway, we could all be talking German this time next year,' said Martyn.

'*Jamais!*' cried Mathilde, sounding at the edge of despair. 'Don't you dare even speak of it. Not a word! I cannot think of it happening again, not again.'

Eliza's mind bent with worry. Last year, a few months after she'd passed her school certificate, Mr Chamberlain had waved his piece of paper on the tarmac of an aerodrome and announced peace in their time. But now, just as she completed her Pitman's typing and shorthand course at secretarial college, which Mathilde thought would come in handy for a little job somewhere, Germany invaded Poland anyway.

'Never again.' Her mother stuffed her handkerchief back in her handbag with angry force. 'No, not again.'

Martyn mumbled an apology.

'Say no more of it.' Mathilde walked on. 'Eliza, your brother is too careless with his words,' she whispered. 'Does he have to belittle how I feel?'

Hearing the way her mother said *little*, so Frenchly, so precisely, Eliza gave a secret loving smile.

'He is young, trying to act brave, remember,' she said quietly, as Martyn overtook them, sulkily swinging the suitcase through the tall grasses along the hedgerows, scattering their seeds. 'He wouldn't be seen dead showing us the slightest bit of fear.'

'But this is not as it should be,' said Mathilde. 'He should not be *scared* at his age.'

The sadness in her mother's voice filtered through to Eliza as they walked on slowly, and in silence. Was it fair that any of them were frightened of what might happen? At nineteen, she was just two years older than Martyn. And her fear was parcelled away; one bright, brave face shown to the world.

They turned the corner and reached the end of another inevitable journey. Forstall Manor basked in the sunlight amid a froth of trees.

'Hello there!' came a familiar cry and Nick bounded down the garden path through the rose bushes, his long legs brushing past lavender and geraniums, his fair hair lifting in the breeze. He opened the gate and looked at Eliza. 'Whatever is the matter, my dear? You're looking a bit glum.'

'Nothing, just . . . nothing.' She lowered her voice. 'Maman's a bit sad, worried about Martyn as usual.'

'Oh, we can't have that!'

Nick's warm exuberance settled her. She looked gratefully up at his face and happiness lifted inside her, so much so that she wanted him to take her in his arms and kiss her properly, full on the lips, even in front of her mother.

But he leant deftly in to peck her cheek and, in turn, Mathilde's. He pumped Martyn's hand and clapped him on the shoulder while they exchanged sunny 'hello old boys'. He leant in to whisper something to Martyn, who collapsed with laughter.

Nick took Eliza's arm to walk her up the path. 'See, I have cured Martyn's bad mood. He's putty in my hands.'

Laughing with delight, she asked how his parents were.

'Oh, the old 'uns are all right. Ma is preparing a fine Sunday roast with all the trimmings and more. *Rosbif* just for you, Auntie Mat.'

'Well I am honoured,' piped up Mathilde from behind, sounding cheerier. 'But less of the *old 'uns*, Nick. I'm only ten years younger than your mother. Ten years is nothing, my dear, when you get to my age. And I wouldn't want to consider myself an old 'un.'

He laughed in apology and assured them that his father had brought up some splendid '29 from the cellar for her to sample.

'A gesture of defiance from Dad. Roast beef, Yorkshire pud, the best British Sunday lunch imaginable and some Baron de Rothschild claret to wash it down with. Let's get tight if necessary. And it's an *up yours* to you know who.' He made a rude sign to the sky. 'Oh, sorry Auntie Mat, I'm forgetting myself.'

'It's all right, Nicholas. I detest Herr Hitler too.'

Eliza squeezed his arm, giggles of relief bubbling out. Nick looked down at her and gave her his secret smile and she was back in that short, dark day last winter when the moon had set low over the frozen fields and they'd hurtled down the snow-packed slope at the side of the plum orchard on his sledge. It was the only good, fast slope around in a landscape shapeless and colourless under white. She'd laughed so hard, she was scared of wetting herself and Nick had pulled a damp lock of her hair out of her mouth. Her woolly hat had long been lost and he'd held both her hands locked inside his to keep her warm. And, when they'd sat with hot chocolate from the flask under the naked trees, he'd whispered in her ear that he loved her.

Now, standing with him in the cool hallway of Forstall Manor, Eliza felt that love rise fresh in her, like a new, spicy addition to her blood.

'Come right through!' Sybil emerged from the drawing room to greet them, smart in grey slacks and a lemon shirt, her pale hair done up in a tight plait. 'It's such a lovely morning, we've got the French windows open, so we can have our before-lunch sherry either in the armchairs or out in the sunshine. It's up to you, Mathilde.' She glanced at the suitcase that Martyn plonked by the stairs. 'So glad you're staying. I could do with some more benign company. I threw Morris out into the garden as he was driving me mad, pacing the floor, being grumpy. Stoking up his pipe far too early for me.'

Eliza threw a look at her mother to say *see, we are welcome.*

'He's nervous, Ma, that's why he's smoking like a chimney,' said Nick. 'The broadcast is due to start. He always smokes too much when he's agitated.'

Morris must be worrying as much as Maman and perhaps Nick realised this too, thought Eliza, as he began to tease Martyn.

'Well, have you seen your trousers, old boy? They're covered in seeds.'

Eliza watched with pleasure as Martyn looked up to Nick, who was a head taller and a good five years older than him, with quite naked, blushing admiration.

Sybil bustled Mathilde through. 'Come on, dear, no use worrying about what they may or may not say on the radio. It'll be a lot of hot air from these politicians, as usual. It'll blow over. Let's have a snifter.'

She led the way towards the drinks tray in the drawing room and began to decant sherry into tiny glasses, spilling amber drops over her silver tray.

'Well, I'm making a bit of a meal out of this. Despite what I just said, I don't think any of us are exactly the ticket this morning.'

Eliza stepped forward to take over and was surprised at how steady her own hands were.

'Thank you, Eliza, dear,' said Sybil. 'And I need Martyn to sort out the blessed wireless. I think the battery is dangerously low.'

He appeared delighted to have something to do, and bent to the gleaming Bakelite set on the sideboard, turning a knob and releasing a violent crackle into the room.

Eliza handed Sybil a small, delicate glass brimming with sherry.

'Try not to spill it, Ma!' called Nick. 'Perhaps you should have a beaker.'

He was trying for humour, but Eliza saw a new twitch of apprehension in his mild, grey eyes.

'Oh, for goodness' sake, Nick,' Sybil muttered. 'Come on, Mathilde, let's leave the children to it and go out to sit on the terrace.'

Eliza turned to Nick with a smile but he was already distracted by Martyn's efforts with the wireless, so she followed the ladies outside. They settled on garden chairs on the terrace, raising their faces to the mid-morning sun. Mathilde removed her scarf and her thick, russet hair bounced elegantly over her forehead. She managed a tight smile as Eliza caught her eye.

'We thought we'd dig a shelter at the bottom of the garden,' Sybil was saying. 'Morris has ordered corrugated iron and I told him, it's a bloody eyesore. So behind the sheds it goes. I want him to turf it, which of course he'll get round to *eventually*. I'm leaving all of that to him, anyway . . . and they're talking at the church about evacuees, but really, I'm not sure it'll come to that . . .'

'It'll be children from the coastal towns moving inland,' said Mathilde, 'as well as from London . . .'

Eliza sat back in her deckchair, determined to maintain a relaxed demeanour. She idly watched Martyn through the French windows bending to the wireless, blowing on the connector and rubbing it on his sleeve, while Nick hovered around him, speaking in encouraging tones.

The garden was peaceful, voices murmuring. Breezes turned the leaves backwards, flickering them so that they sparkled. The newly cut lawn, Morris's pride and joy, was bathed in light, issuing its new, wet green scent. Maman was right, she decided, how can war happen when there's all this beauty in the world?

Eliza caught the earthy aroma of pipe smoke and saw Morris strolling back across the lawn.

'What a morning for it, I ask you,' he called out. 'That set fixed yet, Nicholas? This broadcast is important. It's the PM, you know.'

Sybil piped up, 'You don't know how important it is going to be, Morris. None of us do. It might have all blown over like last year. Remember Chamberlain and the Munich Conference? Hitler wanted peace then, didn't he? Let's keep a clear head on this until it's done.'

'How much sherry have you had, my dear?' Morris asked.

She waved him away and he gazed at his wife for some moments while he thoughtfully sucked on his pipe, smoke obliterating his face momentarily.

'Ah, and here's my sweet thing.' He stepped forward to greet Eliza with a gentle tap on her shoulder. 'And where's mine?'

'Sorry, Morris.' Eliza got to her feet. 'Forgot about you.'

He laughed. 'How could that possibly be so?' He settled himself into her deckchair.

Once everyone had refills, Eliza retreated to sit on the garden step. The hour of the broadcast was nearly upon them. She glanced

at her mother and saw new fear and deep-rooted memories cours-
ing over her face. Sybil beside her knocked back her sherry and
Morris cleared his throat, his head erect as if to attention, the
shoulder where he'd taken a bullet in the Great War stiff and awkward under his shirt. Nick stood close behind her on the step. She
was aware of his breathing and tried to fix her face with the calmest
expression she could muster. Her stomach was full of flies.

There came a crackling static sound through the French
windows as Martyn at last tuned into the BBC with an inap-
propriate whoop of delight. The grave voice of the continuity
announcer came first and then the clipped patrician tones of
Neville Chamberlain. As he spoke, his words began to cascade
through Eliza's mind – inevitable and unrelenting, changing
their lives forever.

'. . . unless we heard from them by eleven o'clock . . . no
such undertaking has been received . . . We have a clear
conscience . . . you will all play your part . . . I am certain that
right will prevail . . .'

In the silence that followed, as the news of war dropped like
a cold, hard stone into her understanding, Eliza glanced at the
stricken faces of her family, her friends. She reached up for Nick's
hand but he had left her side and darted into the house. He
switched off the set and Eliza watched aghast as he strode back out
across the terrace, past the muted, stunned gathering and straight
towards her. He grabbed her hand and pulled her to her feet.

'Nick, what are you –?'

But he started to run with her across the lawn, Eliza protesting as he pulled her on, her arm tugging painfully at its socket.

They reached the bottom of the garden, breathless. He led her around the back of the greenhouse, out of sight of the terrace, the house and their families. He leant her against a tree, almost placing her there as he would a ladder, and sank to his knees.

She looked down at him in astonishment. His face was white, his forehead coated with a film of sweat, his cheeks ruddy circles. His grey eyes glistened.

'Nick, I can scarcely speak, I'm so out of breath – what are you doing?'

He was breathing fast, his shaking, sweaty hands making a grab for hers.

'Marry me,' he said. 'Marry me, Eliza.'

Her body jerked in shock against the tree. She felt the knobbly bark pressing into her spine.

'I can keep you safe from all of that,' he implored. 'All of the madness. Let's do this together. I will protect you.'

She stared at his earnest face, so familiar, so safe, as the hopeless words from the radio tolled through her head. She had no idea, until that moment, how utterly terrified she was.

'Let's get through this madness together.' Nick's whisper was urgent, his eyes so large they looked like they'd absorb her. 'Whatever that madman brings us, we'll fight it, the two of us. Eliza, say something, will you!' He stood up, his tall frame shielding her, his hands still grasping hers.

A bird was chiming in the branches above her, peeling out clean, clear notes across the morning. A blackbird, singing in the face of it all, singing even as the world was crumbling, defiant under a sky that might soon be black with bombers. Was it the same blackbird as before, the one in the hawthorn? Had it followed her here?

'Eliza!'

'Yes, Nick.'

'*What?*'

'My answer is yes.' She put her hands on his shoulders and pushed him back down to his knees. 'My answer is yes.'

He pressed his face into her stomach and she pushed her hands into his hair.

The garden of Forstall Manor looked exactly the same: flowers in deep borders were soaring and bobbing, leaves rustling, insects bumbling on their merry way. She could even hear the waters of the Little Stour as it coursed past the bottom of the garden. You see, she told herself, nothing changes. This is where I am meant to be.

When at last Nick pulled away, got to his feet and embraced her, she realised her dress was wet with his tears.

Chapter 2

'Seems odd to be popping champagne corks in light of all the to-do earlier, but it's not every day your son gets engaged,' said Morris.

'I'm still shaking from the sound of the siren,' said Sybil, 'let alone anything else. Such a dreadful sound. Like the herald of doom heading straight for us . . .'

'As least we know we can hear it from here,' Nick assured his mother. 'All the way over from the church. That must be two miles as the crow flies. Anyway, it was a false alarm, so Leonard Castle said on the telephone. Just testing.'

Standing next to Nick on the hearthrug, her arm linked with his, Eliza listened contentedly to her family's small talk about Mr Castle's homing pigeons, the healthy state of the hop harvest and what war would mean for Morris's little brewery in Canterbury. Eventually, the matter in hand was got round to, bubbling glasses were raised and Martyn made a toast.

'Many congratulations to my big sister and to Nick, the man who, all of my life, I have looked up to, and who I wish, one day, will teach me everything he knows . . .'

'Not sure you'd really want to know, old boy.'

Everyone laughed. Eliza looked around to catch the smiles on their faces. Her mother's was wide and understanding; Sybil's a little guarded. Martyn's grin was of pure acceptance; Morris still looked grim; and Nick's smile rose and fell, happy and ponderous in equal measures. Eliza's face ached from smiling, so she gave up and concentrated on sipping her champagne.

Eliza heard her mother say under her breath, as if to reassure herself, 'They look right together. I always thought they did.'

There was a brief pause before Sybil observed, 'I expect the churches and the town hall will be very busy these next few weeks. I remember in '14. You couldn't move for khaki and hastily got-up brides.'

'Really, Auntie Sybil,' said Martyn. 'You make it sound like –'

'– not a hasty shotgun wedding at all,' Nick interjected. 'This is no surprise to anyone, surely?'

He looked at Eliza and she lowered her head. She felt incredibly shy, suddenly, as if Nick was a stranger rather than the boy she had known all of her life.

'Even if it is a surprise,' Eliza said, 'it is a very lovely, welcome one. And there's no need to rush things, is there, just because the war has started.'

'Exactly. I think a wedding in the New Year will brighten everyone's day,' Nick said.

'The war will be over by Christmas, anyway, won't it Uncle Morris?' Martyn piped up.

Morris stooped to knock out his pipe into the fireplace and Eliza could not see his face as he said, 'That's what they said with the last lot.'

'Well, if it's not, I know what I'll be doing,' Martyn said. 'I'll be eighteen next March. RAF for me.'

Mathilde gently reminded him that there was always university.

Nick said, 'You should speak to Audley Stratton. Pump him for advice. He's never short of something to say about the RAF.'

'Oh, yes, Martyn,' Sybil agreed. 'He's the big cheese over at Manston Airfield.' She moved closer to her husband. 'Are you all right, dear?'

'Perfectly.'

'All rather grim, isn't it?'

Nick wondered aloud if Stratton would perhaps be rather busy these days, in light of everything.

'Never too busy to crack open the port,' Sybil responded. 'As for his wife, Angela, she keeps herself busy in many ways you wouldn't imagine.'

As dusk fell on that first evening of the war, Eliza and Nick wandered out through the French windows, across the lawn and turned right, skirting the end of the Stour wing and sat down on the grassy steps of the overgrown patio that faced the little river. Ripples in the flat, slow-moving water caught the last of the light as the sky faded from pale blue to indigo to navy. Shy stars winked lazily at them from the eastern horizon. The crescent moon, a sliver of silver, emerged above the flat fields. The bees had gone home to be replaced by tiny brown moths. A breeze across the water brought with it a chill. She shivered. Nick folded his jacket around her shoulders.

'How do you like this view?'

'I've always loved it,' she said. 'This whole place has always been – oh, listen!'

An owl called aloofly from the thicket on the far bank.

'You could hear that gentleman every night if you wished. If he decided to grace us with his presence.'

'What do you mean?'

'Pa has told me we can have the Stour wing. It'll need doing up, mind. New curtains, a lick of paint and everything. Pull up a few weeds here on the patio, mow the lawn. How about it? Our own little self-contained home. But here, still, at Forstall.'

Eliza felt her fondness for Nick expand another notch. Seeing his face, so earnest in the half-light, it struck her, like it had done earlier when he had proposed, how much he needed her.

'You think of everything,' she said. 'You know how I love Forstall. I hadn't thought where we might live. I haven't had a moment since this morning, since everything changed.' She looked over her shoulder at the dark, dusty windows of the empty two-storey wing, named after the river onto which it faced. 'How lovely it will be to live right here.'

'And we will be happy. We can install our own kitchen and everything.' Nick put his arm around her shoulder and planted a kiss on her forehead. 'Whatever happens out there . . . this will be our home –'

'Hey, you two – you're not married yet, so you can stop all that malarkey!' Martyn appeared around the corner of the house, brandishing a bottle of brandy and tumblers. He bounded up the steps, plumping himself down beside Nick and making him budge up.

'I'm not going to leave you in peace, you know,' he teased. 'The old 'uns are back on to 1914, so I thought I'd make a sharp exit. Stealing some of Morris's finest while I was at it.'

'You're right to escape,' Nick said. 'That's it, pour us some hard stuff.'

Martyn handed around the drinks. 'I've already pestered Uncle Morris for Wingco Stratton's personal telephone number. I want to get the inside gen on training. That is, how long will it take and when the blazes I can start.'

'Go steady,' Eliza warned him. 'Think of Maman. She won't want you leaving home just yet, let alone flying Spitfires.'

Nick was chuckling. 'Do you know why Ma goes all prickly when Stratton's name is mentioned?' he asked. 'Because she believes Angela Stratton has set her cap at Pa. Remember sardines two Christmases ago? I caught them together in the snug upstairs and announced it to all and sundry. Didn't go down very well.'

'Why is it that grown-ups never behave like grown-ups?' asked Martyn.

'You think that because *you're* not grown up,' Eliza assured him.

'I wish you'd stop going on about that. I'm not Tintin anymore. I'm eighteen in the spring and eligible to die for my country. That's grown up enough, isn't it?'

Eliza recoiled, raw with shame. 'I'm sorry, Martyn.'

The owl across the water repeated its call. She shivered at the desolate sound.

'What might you do now?' Martyn asked her, forgiving immediately as he always did. 'Now it's war.'

'Give me a moment!' She feigned exasperation to lighten the mood. 'I've just got engaged. And I'd like to see what the uniforms look like first.' She laughed. 'But, I certainly do want to do something. Make a difference. I have my office skills. Thank goodness for Pitman's.'

Nick put his arm around her shoulder. 'There you go. They'll need some sort of support like that, in an office somewhere.'

'Something tells me you want more though,' said Martyn. 'Whatever happens, big sister, I will always look out for you.'

Eliza, seeing her brother's suddenly mature eyes shine warmly at her through the dusk, was struck by his understanding.

He cleared his throat. 'I propose a toast to the future. To all of us. Good luck to everyone.'

Three crystal glasses chinked as darkness fell, and they drank deeply.

Eliza watched the liquor stick like syrup to the inside of her glass, took a sip and made her own silent toast. This was the end of peace for their country but the beginning of her new life.

Chapter 3

The mournful voice of a long-dead chanteuse woke Eliza as it drifted up from her maman's gramophone. Her nose was chilled, the covers over her head. The quilt her mother had patched for her from French cottons was heavy and comforting but her bed socks had come off in the night and her toes ached with cold. The hot water bottle at her back was a dead, icy weight.

She retrieved her socks, hurried into her dressing gown, drew her curtains and opened the blackout onto the frosty morning. From her window, the medieval skyline was a jumble of crooked roofs, a confusing labyrinth with the cathedral pale and soaring against the grey sky. Wherever Eliza was in Canterbury, her eye was drawn to it, to its magnificence that told the tales of hundreds of years. Every morning of her life, as long as she could remember, it was there outside her window, presiding over her, a compass at the centre of everything. Sandbagged and with its treasures stripped because of the war, the cathedral remained as stately and as immovable as it ever had been. But today, in the colourless light of the winter's morning, through a haze of coal fire smoke, it looked more distant, its carvings and shadows less distinct.

She'd been spoilt by this view for far too long, but soon there would be a new one outside her window. She headed down the stairs to the warmth of the kitchen range and the crisp smell of newly made toast.

Martyn was crunching his way through a slice as he slowly turned the pages of the newspaper spread on the kitchen table. Mathilde was brewing tea.

'Good morning, dear,' she said as Eliza slipped into a chair. 'You look like you slept well. Busy day today. What time is Nicholas picking you up?'

'About ten.' Eliza reached for the teapot.

In the front parlour, the record came to a sultry end, leaving the needle to jump over the grooves.

'Better get lively then.' Martyn absent-mindedly picked crumbs off the newspaper. 'It's nearly nine o'clock now. Which reminds me. Now your record's finished, Maman, it's time for the news.'

He reached behind him to the dresser and switched on the wireless set.

'Oh, Martyn, nothing is going on,' Mathilde complained, taking the plates to the butler sink. 'Do we *have* to spoil our morning with it?'

'It's getting very interesting in Finland,' he said, persuading her.

As the broadcast issued out, Eliza settled in her chair with her back to the heat of the range, sipping her tea and listening contentedly to her mother and brother gently bicker over the fate of Poland. She looked around the kitchen and out into the hall of the little terraced house that Morris Staveley had bought for her mother. It had been their home since 1923 when her father had died, his lungs ruined by gas. But however kind and noble Morris had been by stepping in to keep a roof over the heads of the family of the man who saved his life, the loss of Richard Piper hung over them. Eliza had been so young when he passed. When they spoke of him, she shut her eyes, willed herself to remember. But he was a fragment, a myth.

Mathilde kept them closeted here: Eliza, at three, barely formed; Martyn, a scrap of a baby. Mathilde made the house, built some seventy years before on the grounds of a long-gone convent, comfortable with Flanders lace and red-checked table-cloths. The rugs had worn serenely and the wallpaper in the parlour, once a deep French blue, had faded to the colour, so Mathilde told them, of a Picardy summer sky. Eliza loved the faded café curtains, the wooden furniture and the enduring scent of lavender on the stairs.

Neighbours called Mathilde *Madame* (not unkindly) for she insisted on speaking in French only to Eliza and Martyn inside their home. The children had a rude awakening, Eliza remembered, when they started school and found they had to speak English.

Now, with the wireless news fading into a gentle swing tune and the lingering smell of toast on the air, she looked first at her brother's animated and still ridiculously young face and then at her mother's more pinched and defensive expression.

She flinched with a sudden reckoning of her own reality. She was to be married to Nick on New Year's Day. She would leave Nunnery Fields and move to Forstall Manor: her second, equally beloved, home.

She'd spent the weekends throughout the autumn with Nick painting the rooms in the Stour wing and shifting furniture. She had cleaned windows and swept floors. Sybil had run up curtains in whatever fabric she had in her rag bag, creating a delightful mismatch. Morris had carted in a new bed, her and Nick's first wedding present, and the ancient range in the Stour wing kitchen had been coaxed back into life for the first time in a decade.

And on this Saturday in early December, Nick was arriving in an hour or so to pack his car with as many of Eliza's possessions as possible, things that she would not need in the coming weeks. He was then to drive them over to the manor so she could start creating her new home.

'Pity you both can't move there with me,' she said.

Mathilde and Martyn both turned to face her, puzzled.

'I can't see myself traipsing over from Forstall to school every day,' Martyn said. 'You know how I feel about that endless bus ride – and what about my friends? Although, I must say, it *is* that bit nearer Manston.'

'Oh, you and the blessed RAF,' sighed Mathilde. 'I can't see them needing you anyway. Look at the way things are working out.' She indicated the wireless. 'It's all happening a thousand miles away in Scandinavia . . .'

'I will miss our home,' Eliza said quietly.

She would also miss *them*. Tears stung her eyes and she glanced quickly around the kitchen to distract herself, catching sight of her father's medals gleaming serenely on the high mantelpiece.

'We'll miss you, Eliza.' Her mother's voice was soft, her 's's soothing and mellifluous.

'That's as may be,' said Martyn, glancing at his watch. 'But you need to look lively if you're going to be ready on time. You know what Nick is like.'

It took a number of trips up the narrow stairs to bring Eliza's boxes and her trunk down and Nick's car was, as he said rather unsmilingly, packed to the gunwales. He had not, Eliza noticed, been impressed that she had only just got dressed when he arrived and that her boxes had not been closed and securely tied with twine, as he had expected them to be.

'Never mind that, old boy.' Martyn leant against the front wall of the house and fished in his top pocket for his cigarettes. 'Have a gasper and a cup of tea while she sorts it out.'

'I'd rather get on.' Nick was unusually serious with Martyn. 'I have to take an important telephone call at midday. The man from the Hop Exchange is ringing up with an instruction of our expected quota for next year.'

'On a Saturday?' Eliza gingerly held his hand and bounced it up and down. 'Really?'

'They're working all hours these days.'

'Don't tell me.' Martyn's grin widened as he lit his cigarette. '*There's a war on.*'

At last, Nick's face lifted with a smile. He took Eliza's hand and kissed it quickly. 'Sorry, it's just that I have a lot to do.'

'You're not wrong there,' said Martyn. 'You're marrying my sister in less than a month.'

Nick laughed. 'Yes, and among all these pressing tasks is the most important of all – to drive my bride-to-be, along with her rather extensive bottom drawer, over to her new home.'

'There's tea in the pot if you want it, Nick. But if not, then we'll say goodbye now. It's too cold to stand around on the pavement,' said Mathilde.

'I'll be back tomorrow evening, Maman.' Eliza got into the car, suddenly exhilarated. Most of her possessions were packed into Nick's back seat and boot – it was her first thrilling step towards her new life.

'Yes, I'll see her back in time for supper,' Nick said.

As he darted forward to peck Mathilde on the cheek and shake Martyn by the hand, Eliza was fleetingly irritated. He had yet to kiss her hello.

Nick drove east out of the city, along the Littlebourne Road, leaving the streets and drifts of coal fire smoke behind them. Very soon they were bowling along the straight road through the flat, hibernating fields. Eliza thought how pretty the enveloping hoar frost looked, clothing dead grasses and fences. The earlier milky haze had cleared and the sun now shone sharply, illuminating the slick of frost over the road ahead. She shielded her eyes. Drainage ditches were marked by silhouetted reed heads and the frames in hop gardens were bare and frozen, casting long shadows over the sleeping brown landscape.

'Gosh it's cold.' Eliza blew on her fingertips through her knitted mittens. 'Is the road icy?'

'Seems all right to me.' Nick peered ahead through the windscreen. 'It's just the way the sun hits it. The ice has all melted now. What you can see is water.' He reached for her hand and squeezed it, glancing briefly at her. 'Should have brought a hot water bottle for your feet.'

Eliza smiled contentedly. 'I'm so glad we chose New Year's Day to get married,' she said. 'Remember last year, how snowy it was? And the sledging? I must have come off ten times. I never did find my hat, did I?'

'Was that New Year's Day? Are you sure?'

'Why, yes,' Eliza said. 'That glorious time we had sledging. I thought that's why you chose that day for us to be married. Because of what it means . . .'

Nick glanced sideways, smiling indulgently. 'Ah . . .'

'Are you teasing me?'

'No, no.' He was still confused. 'What I do remember is later on trying to get Martyn to have a hair of the dog due to his excesses the night before. Does him good every time.'

Eliza jolted. Did he not remember what he had said to her in the snow? Didn't he remember saying that he loved her? For her, that was the start of everything.

She glanced at his profile with a tremor of doubt. But she dismissed it as quickly as the fear had manifested. She was just being silly. He probably remembered things about her that were precious to him and of which she had not the faintest idea.

They were now cruising along past orchards on such a straight length of road, Eliza thought it could be Roman. Nick accelerated.

'We don't have to rush so much, do we?' Eliza asked. 'It can only be half eleven . . .'

'I must get back quickly. This telephone call is important and I want to be sat at my desk, ready and waiting, when it comes through. You see, we want to continue to supply our own brewery, of course, but also want to make more money by selling on hops. I can't miss this opportunity to speak to this particular gentleman.' He paused, glancing her way. 'I'm sorry about earlier. I know I was rather irritable.'

'It's quite all right.'

'There's a lot of pressure at work, that's all. But they're not rationing beer, which is a blessing. Got to keep the nation's spirits up and all of that.'

'How are your parents?' she asked, relieved at his apology, his lifting of her spirits. 'What's been going on at the manor this week?'

'Let me see.' Nick shielded his eyes with one hand against the sharp sunlight. 'Ma has been busy stocking up your larder for you and has supplied your kitchen linens, so she tells me.

Pa planted bulbs in our patch of garden. It doesn't look much now but come the spring, I'm sure that . . .'

At that moment, Nick's hand slipped on the steering wheel and the car veered left sharply.

'Ice! Ice!' he cried.

Eliza had no time to react, to cry out, to even realise what had happened. The next thing she knew she was faced with a bank of grass and a hefty fence post. But this astonishing vignette altered as fast as it came to her. The car kept turning in a strange, violent and reckless motion. Thrown against her door and kept there by momentum, she was switched back to the road, then veered to the bank once more. Her ears were full of screaming and the sound of Nick swearing in terror as his side of the car smashed against the fence post with a revolting crunch of metal, wood and flesh.

Outside the car was silence, blank white silence. Inside, there was a strange clinking sound from the engine and the noise of terrified breathing. Eliza opened her eyes to a crooked world where the sky was not where she expected it to be. The frosty bank was above her face and her knees were jammed ridiculously, painfully under her chin. She tried to breathe in but her chest was restricted. A surge of panic crushed her. One of her boxes on the back seat had burst open, and the debris of her childhood, her life up to that moment – books, gramophone records, her three china deer linked by a chain and still miraculously intact – was strewn around her. In the long, empty silence, she became mesmerised by the cover of

Jane Eyre that had come to rest just in front of her nose. She'd only just started reading it; had felt that she ought to have done so by now. At her age. She wondered if she'd ever know the ending.

And then she dared to look beyond the book. Nick lay heavily, a dead weight over her twisted legs, the bottom of his body entangled with the innards of the vehicle. Just like the world outside the car, he was soundless. She realised that the terrified breathing had been her own. She reached down to place her hands on Nick's head. A fine trickle of blood was oozing from his temple. She began to speak very quickly and very loudly at him demanding that he wake up, look at her, say something.

The quiet of the road, of the countryside outside, was immense. A cold rush of panic trapped her. They were done for. Would be forgotten. But suddenly, somewhere within that silence came the small noise of an engine. It grew louder, whined and popped as it drew near, throbbing to a stop. There came a mechanical cranking sound and then footfalls over the gritty road. Eliza watched, dazed, as a shadow passed in front of the shattered windscreen. How beautiful the sun looked through the splintered glass; like pieces of jagged gold. The car door against which she lay shifted briefly and she screamed in terror, fearing that it was all going to happen again, that the movement, the turning, the smashing would begin once more. The shadow was there, a man steadfastly trying to open the door.

'Are you all right?'

Another stream of terror and pain spilled out of her in wordless cries. The shadow-man deftly smashed the window until the icy air touched her scalp and glass lay sprinkled over her shoulders, quieting her for a moment. Again she shouted, trying to turn her head to direct her curses at the man.

He took off his goggles, pulled off his gloves, reached in and pressed his cold fingers against her neck. He waited. His eyes, which were the strangest green she'd ever seen, like the bottom of a deep river bed, flicked to the horizon while he concentrated.

'You're OK. But don't move yet. Stay perfectly still. Let me reach past you to him to feel his pulse. Can you speak English?'

'Of course I can,' she uttered. 'What a bloody stupid thing to ask.'

The stranger concentrated on Nick for some moments and, as he leant over Eliza, a great reviving warmth spread from his body onto hers, the scent of leather, intoxicating and sweet. Close up, she watched his features intently, feeling a peculiar mix of loathing and wonder. His nose was incredibly straight, his eyebrows dark and quizzical, his cheeks bore the traces of him once having had bad skin.

'Are you saving us?' She was weak with shock.

'I need to get you out first, and then your husband.'

'He's not my . . .'

'Ah.' The stranger looked her in the eye for the first time. 'So you *do* speak English.'

Eliza felt him take hold of her from behind, carefully, easing her backwards out of the car.

'I'm not leaving him.'

'You have to.'

'I don't have to do what you say.'

'Oh, yes you do.'

Lifting her as if she was as light as a leaf, the stranger drew her out of the tangled car and delicately rested her on the bank. He found a blanket among her possessions and wrapped her in it. She had lost her shoes and the stranger rubbed her freezing, stockinged feet, enfolding them in the blanket.

'Such long, fine feet,' he uttered and she wondered if he thought she could not hear him. His caress stayed on her skin and warmed her through like a balm.

Nick was lying very still. 'He has not moved,' she said.

The stranger told her that he had passed an RAC telephone about half a mile back, and that he would ride there now on his motorbike, call for an ambulance and be back before she knew it. He hadn't seemed to be in any hurry as he made sure that Eliza was comfortable, but as soon as he left her he ran to his motorbike and launched himself at great speed back the way he had come. In an instant, he was gone.

It might have been ten minutes, it might have been ten hours. Eliza lay curled on the cold ground, under the blanket, listening to the tinkling sound of the car's engine as it cooled off and a faint dripping of liquid – water, oil or perhaps petrol? She felt the bloom of new pain creep around her ribs, but when the stranger had asked her to wiggle her toes and to squeeze his hand, he seemed relieved that she had managed to do both. But what about Nick? He hadn't woken up since the accident.

After some strange, hollow moments where her mind seemed to be nowhere at all, she gathered her strength to sit upright. Keeping her eyes fixed on Nick, she called out to him.

'Nick! Why did he ask me if I could speak English?' Speaking aloud reassured Eliza, proving to herself that she was still alive. 'Did you hear that, Nick? Perhaps he is a little crazy. Oh, he's coming back. I think I can hear it. Can you hear the motorbike, Nick? Tell me you can hear it . . .'

The next thing she knew, she was cradled tenderly in warm arms clad in soft leather, her head and shoulders kept clear of the ground. A deep comfort, the like of which she had never known before, clasped her and kept her safe. She squinted up into the stranger's face. He was smiling, a bright, wide smile.

'You passed out again. Ambulance is on its way. Just stay still.'

'Why did you ask if I was English?'

'Because you were screaming – and swearing actually – in French, so naturally . . .'

'And my husband?'

'You told me he wasn't your husband.'

He will be soon. She glanced over to the wreckage and saw that Nick had turned his head. His eyes, now open, were staring at her, fixed with shock.

'He's conscious,' said the man. 'And he's able to speak.'

Eliza called out to Nick. She told him not to worry, and that the ambulance was on its way. She begged him to hang on, just for a bit longer.

But Nick kept on staring without speaking, blinking occasionally and shifting his shoulders, wincing in pain. His eyes flicked to Eliza and then back to the stranger's face as Eliza lay supported in his arms. He looked bewildered, his eyes full of questions.

Chapter 4

Just before three o'clock on Christmas Eve, Eliza made her way down the cold staircase at Forstall and paused on the half landing. The sun was low, slanting through the window. In an hour it would be dark. Winter had stripped colour from the landscape to leave a sombre patchwork, and frost had made a tortured forest-in-miniature of Sybil's rose garden. The framed wedding photographs gleamed on the wall in the tired light. No doubt, thought Eliza, that her and Nicholas's would join them soon. But when? The accident had ripped their plans apart, had separated them and this was her first visit to Forstall since the crash. She had been convalescing at Nunnery Fields with the uncomfortable, creeping feeling that it wasn't just the wedding that had been postponed, but that, somehow, something else had changed too. In all of her confusion and distress in the aftermath of the accident, she had shifted from her path. But she had not the faintest idea what it was.

As she turned to make her way down the second set of stairs, pain shot down her side. Pain so piercing and so deep that she froze, breathless. Her ribs had taken the brunt of it when she slammed against the inside of the car, and the dull pain she'd first felt grew stronger with every breath. But at least she'd been able to walk away. She'd waited, dazed and delirious, in the ambulance while they extracted Nick from the wreckage, his leg a bloody mess, the bone splintered. She hadn't seen him, but she'd certainly heard him scream.

She paused on the stairs, grabbed the bannister and tried to catch her breath as it hissed through her teeth, moaning gently to herself as the pain subsided. She thought of them all downstairs, waiting for her in the drawing room. She was safe indoors, she told herself. Safe from the cold outside. Safe and warm amid another Forstall Christmas.

Nick looked up from his newspaper as she walked slowly into the room. His leg in plaster was stretched out, long and cumbersome, propped on a cushion with his toes sticking out the end. The glow of the hearth had caused his pale face to become flushed with two rings of red. Her mother was knitting, needles flashing and clicking and, because it was Christmas Eve, Morris and Sybil were sipping their customary sherry, while Martyn lounged with a bottle of Forstall beer.

'Here she is,' said Morris, gaily. 'In need of a snifter, no doubt.'

'Yes, please,' she said, forcing a polite, rigid smile as she made her painful way to the armchair next to Nick. Martyn sprang up and was at her side, holding her and helping her ease herself down gently onto the cushions. She thanked her brother. The warmth of the fire was a primitive contrast to the hard chill on the stairs. It would make her feel better.

'Settled in upstairs?' Nick looked at her sideways, almost shyly she thought, and landed an awkward kiss near her ear. 'Still hurting?'

'Only when I do certain things,' she said, trying to sound bright and brave. 'Like when I cough, sit down and walk.'

'So that's about everything, really,' said Martyn.

'But I feel so useless,' she said, her jaw clenched. 'I want to help with the dinner tomorrow. Make my special stuffing with the thyme and the sage like I do every year.'

'Oh, no, I won't allow it,' said Sybil. 'It'll be too much for you.'

'So we're to rely on Martyn to lend a hand?' Nick chipped in, dryly.

Eliza saw her brother flush with pleasure at his friend's teasing. She realised then that she enjoyed Nick's familiar humour, his banter with Martyn. She was grateful, glad of his good mood, for she hoped it would lift hers.

'Oh, dear,' said her mother. 'Will we ever get to eat our Christmas dinner?'

'That's enough, Maman,' said Martyn, retreating to his armchair. 'I'm surely not that bad.'

'But here's me having to be waited on hand and foot,' said Nick. 'I'm more useless than anyone, lying here pointing at things with my crutches.' He chuckled. '"That fire looks good, doesn't it?" *Point*. "Did you know there is a gap in the blackout?" *Point*.'

Eliza laughed, and as she did so she yelped out in pain.

'Take some more analgesic.' Martyn was at her side again, handing her the bottle of medicine that the doctor had prescribed them. 'Here, have another nip.'

He proffered a spoon but she took a swig from the bottle.

'You'd make a great nurse, Martyn,' she said, affection warming her voice despite her pain.

'Just like his mother,' Nick said. 'Oh, you poor thing. At least let me help you put on your cardigan.'

He held the sleeve for her and Eliza inched her arm into it. She noticed his sudden attention and welcomed it, as if it was a brand new thing.

'I say, Eliza.' Nick leant in close to her, conspiratorially, his hand still on her elbow. As he stroked the soft wool, his touch felt unusual and hopeful.

She looked at him expectantly. When she, Mathilde and Martyn had arrived that morning, it had been the first time she'd seen Nick since the accident. She had been unable to visit him in hospital as she herself had been too poorly. Nick had drifted from her thoughts. Her own injuries had made her selfish, made her hold herself in a different way.

Now, as she caught his eye, as he sat close by her, his hand on her elbow, she experienced a sudden and sweet sway of affection, as if she had at last broken through an unexpected barrier.

'What's that, Nick?' she asked, dipping her head towards him and reaching for his hand. She realised with a jolt how long it had been since they'd been able to hold hands.

'Would you mind awfully scratching my big toe for me?'

He laughed loudly and, stung, Eliza looked away from him. She mumbled, desperate not to sound churlish, 'Of course I will.'

'Come on, I was only teasing. I realise you can't possibly do that.' Nick quietened down. No one else was laughing. 'Ah, but look at your face. I didn't mean it.'

'You see, Eliza,' Sybil said, raising her voice in an appeasing tone. 'What did Nick say? *Hand and foot*?'

The neutral silence that followed, filled only by the crackle of the fire and the slow ticking clock, was broken by Morris.

'Well, I must tell you all, we're having some extras this evening for our little soirée.'

'Extras?' asked Mathilde. 'You mean as well as Audley and Angela Stratton?'

'May I just say that none of this is my fault, Mathilde,' he said. 'It is Sybil's. She invited Leonard Castle and Jessica.'

'It was inadvertent and unavoidable,' Sybil explained. 'I'm sorry, Mathilde. Leonard telephoned this morning. He has a goose for us, which is a lovely surprise and so very generous. It will supplement our chicken a treat. I could hardly ask him to pop it over and not let him stay for drinks.'

'Gosh, that man,' muttered Mathilde. 'And his filthy homing pigeons.'

Martyn laughed. 'Don't berate poor Leonard, Maman. This time next year, if rationing really gets going, we may be eating his pigeons for Christmas dinner instead of goose. Do you not like him, perhaps, because he always makes a play for you?'

'Really, Martyn,' protested Mathilde.

'Really, Martyn,' Eliza repeated in an effort to chide him also. But it was Jessica Castle who stopped her thoughts, made her go cold.

Leonard and his daughter lived at the neighbouring farm. He was a widower of many years and tended to play up to it with the women that he met in social situations. And Mathilde, as an equally bereaved spouse, was pretty much a sitting duck to his attention. Mathilde humoured him, tolerated him, and it was a Forstall joke that they should warn her of his impending arrival.

Jessica, curiously and as far as Eliza could remember, never mentioned her own mother. Her shell was hard, giving nothing away, her face immaculate, even as a child. She was the same age as Eliza and, for all the years that Eliza had been drawn inside the world of Forstall, Sybil had decreed that the girls must play together. Being the same age did not by any means signify that they would be friends, though. And so, while Eliza longed to follow Nick and Martyn as they raced off whooping through the orchards to spend endless sun-filled hours doing what boys do, she was stuck with Jessica who, without a doubt, always dictated what their game would be. In her company, Eliza fell mute.

When she'd heard that Jessica had been sent to a finishing school in Vienna she had felt a blissful and quite extraordinary sense of relief. She hadn't seen her for years, but the ice-blonde hair and cool, slanting eyes were as clear and as luminous in her mind as they had always been.

'Doesn't Jessica have a grand new job at the BBC? Secretarial, isn't it? World Service?' Mathilde was asking.

'Indeed, she does. Something in radio – better than secretarial,' said Sybil. 'So Leonard was at pains to tell me. God, that man can talk. But she's home for Christmas.'

And just a short walk away down the lane, thought Eliza. She'll be here this evening, dressed to the nines no doubt.

Morris said, 'Well, she's an enigmatic head-turner, that one.'

Eliza put her sherry glass down on the side table with a smart bang. Everyone looked at her in silent surprise.

Scanning their faces, she cleared her throat. 'I want to tell you all . . . that I want a small, quiet wedding. No neighbours. No strangers. Family only.'

'Meaning you don't want the Castles,' said Martyn, understanding immediately.

'I don't mind the Strattons,' she added, realising how rude she must sound.

Nick at her side said quietly, so that only she could hear, 'You can have whatever you want. When have I ever tried to dictate to you?'

She glanced at him and she saw him appraising her, hurt and bewildered. She gave him a quick smile and told him she knew. That it was all right.

Morris declared, bestowing on her his generous smile, 'Of course, my dear, whatever you want. Just family, then – and the Strattons. And speaking of family' – he cleared his throat, and stood up by the mantelpiece – 'I think it is ludicrous that you are stuck over there at Nunnery Fields. I think it will be grand and fitting if you would all come and live here. All of us under one roof. What do you say?'

'Goodness me!' cried Mathilde.

'I say, I agree,' Martyn chirped. 'This means I will be nearer Manston. Near the RAF. It's got to be a winner.'

Mathilde glared momentarily at her son.

'Oh, do agree, Mathilde.' Sybil's face was bright and welcoming. 'We could get through this madness together. And it means Nunnery Fields could be rented out to evacuees. We could pool our rations. Make do and mend and all that stuff together, like they keep telling us to. Oh, Mathilde, do.'

'God knows, you've plenty of room,' said Martyn.

Eliza, surprised and delighted, contemplated this pleasant notion – all of them here, at Forstall. She was used to the idea that the Stour wing would soon be her new home, but if she could have her family all together . . . how wonderful it would be. And yet she could see her mother's reservations flitting over her face.

'It would be lovely, Maman,' she said gently, 'if this was home to all of us.'

Mathilde gazed back at her, tears dampening her eyes. Eliza could see her pride was taking a knocking. She knew how hard it was for her to accept what she saw as charity. But, despite this, she drew a deep breath and smiled.

'*D'accord.*' Mathilde's voice was low and resigned. 'If it keeps my children happy, then I am happy, too.'

'Then, welcome home,' said Morris and raised his glass. 'Welcome home all of you.'

'I will drink to that,' Nick said, and squeezed Eliza's hand briefly.

He reached for his crutches. 'I'd like to get a bit of fresh air before the guests invade,' he said, 'for they all seem to use up a lot of oxygen. Come on, Eliza, let's take a stroll.'

'Stroll?' Morris was deadpan. 'Don't you mean a hop and a shuffle?'

Everyone was laughing as Eliza walked slowly beside Nick as he – indeed – hopped and shuffled out of the room. When they reached the garden, she breathed the crisp, cold air with relief. The sky was swiftly darkening; the lawn looked brittle. Winter birds were roosting, rooks gathering at the top of the chestnut trees over at Leonard Castle's farm. Morris had prepared the flower beds for the winter; the soil neatly turned and manured. She'd heard him digging earlier, the gentle thud of his spade resounding in the frigid afternoon. He was hell-bent on commandeering the herbaceous borders and filling them with veg for the war effort. But he would leave Sybil's rose garden at the front of the house well alone if he knew what was good for him.

'Your father seems more cheerful,' Eliza said. 'But he's still worried, isn't he? Underneath it all.'

'He's putting on a brave face. Aren't we all?' Nick said. 'I feel as damned frustrated as he does. He's too old to fight. I'm too crippled.' He rapped one of his crutches on the gravel path. 'It's all quiet at the moment – they're not calling it the Phoney War for nothing – but they're not going to want me anyway are they? And, at the end of the day, I have a brewery to run. Folks will still need their beer.'

'I did think about the WAAFs at Manston for myself,' she hazarded and, catching Nick's incredulous expression, she quickly added, 'but now I'm looking at the Women's Voluntary Service. Angela Stratton's group is based in Ramsgate. I'll probably need to have a medical,' she said, 'so in the New Year . . .'

'In the New Year,' Nick continued for her, 'when you're better and I'm better, we will be married. So you're right to go for the WVS, they take married women. Anyway, there'll be plenty to be getting on with here as well. I might need you in the brewery office as staff are leaving left, right and centre.'

They crossed the lawn and turned the corner around the end of the Stour wing. The river was slaty and sluggish, the reeds slumped. The trees on the banks were cold and stark. She felt a chill rising between them again; his preoccupation bothered her.

'Who knows what the future holds?' Nick said, his voice lower now, more gentle. 'All I do know is that in a few months' time this will be our home.' He lifted one of his crutches to indicate the newly painted front door in the centre of the Stour wing overlooking the river.

Eliza hated the uncertainty; the *who knows what might be*. She wanted to make plans, then at least she had a foundation to work from, to keep her steady and to fix her course. The WVS was her goal. All she needed now was to recover fully. To get back on the path she'd been following. And Nick . . . he'd be better, she assured herself, once he was off his crutches.

She helped him up the wide terrace steps where they'd sat – she, Nick and Martyn – and drunk brandy at the dawn of war. He opened the door and stood aside for Eliza to enter, hopping in behind her. The small, square hallway opened out to the left with the kitchen at the front with its view of the river, a sink beneath the window and newly refurbished range. Double doors led from the kitchen back to the parlour overlooking the main garden. To the right, from the hallway, was the large salon with a beautiful aspect on three sides onto the river and the gardens. She glanced through the door and saw that the shutters were open, and the last of the light revealed the oak panelling and smooth, waxed floors. She'd already made plans for this gorgeous room: for sewing and reading, for entertaining, for taking tea. And then, perhaps, one day, a child's playroom.

Nick shut the door on it and contemplated the rather steep stairs.

'I need to get myself off these crutches if I'm going to make it up to the bedroom,' he said.

Suddenly shy at the thought of *that*, Eliza dipped into the kitchen and began to inspect her rows of saucepans and linens, donated by Sybil from the manor kitchen. There was a fine old pine table and, either side of the range, high-backed Windsor chairs. Sybil had certainly been busy with remnants, fashioning them into patchwork cushions for the chairs. The mismatched curtains were a delight. The back parlour was small and pleasant enough, with two armchairs and a sideboard. It looked rather bare and unloved, but then, so many of her belongings had been lost or ruined in the crash. Morris had managed to salvage some books from the wreckage, a quilt or two and, miraculously, her three china deer. They sat, chained by their necks, on the mantelpiece.

'You need to fetch over your paintings from your room. That one of Margate harbour is my favourite,' she reminded Nick. 'It will look lovely over the mantelpiece. And your lamps and bookrack. Perhaps we should put up shelves in the alcoves. And maybe your mother can spare a rag rug or two?'

'I'm sure she can.'

Nick shuffled over to the window. The window to his father's study and the French windows of the main house lay at right angles to where he was standing, darkened already by the blackout.

'The reason I wanted us to come over here was so I could tell you something.'

Eliza stopped running her hand over the mantelpiece, inspecting for dust, and looked at him. His face was serious.

She took a step towards him, hesitated.

He said, 'Pa told me that we're to give over the salon here to be used as an office for the war effort. The ministry. Top secret and all that, so don't mention it to anyone at the moment. Least of all Leonard Castle tonight. Things will be common knowledge in due course but I wanted to tell you privately. We don't need it – the salon – anyway, do we?'

She shook her head. The thought of the room filled with desks, telephones and strangers coming in and out was not appealing but what could she do? Thoughts of a playroom faded like the sun going down.

'You don't mind, do you?' he asked and her surprise at his question made her mute. 'Been a bit of a false start for us, hasn't it?' He turned his back on the garden; his face in shadow. 'But we're going to be fine, aren't we?'

She stepped towards him, the rift between them seeming to close. 'I just want you to be better. To feel better,' she said, her voice cracking softly. 'We can get over this. We've had a terrible shock. But you were right, you know.' She moved even closer and he tentatively put his arms around her, but not before carefully propping his crutches against the wall.

'Right about what?'

She remembered his proposal behind the garden shed on that shocking day. She remembered his fear, his need for her. 'Whatever goes on out there, we have our lives here, don't we . . .' She faltered. 'We'll get through it together.'

'That we will.'

Nick leant forward and rested his face on her shoulder. She waited, expecting a wave of warmth, of certainty. When nothing happened she reached up and stroked the back of his head. He remained still, his breathing steady. Eventually he pulled away and smiled at her.

It was his old smile. She hugged him with relief. 'Soon enough . . .' she found herself giggling, 'you'll be able to carry me up those stairs to the bedroom.'

'Do be patient, Eliza.' His face was suddenly blank, as if he was wearing a mask. He did not share her humour; he did not see her yearning. 'I'm afraid that might take me a long time.'

Chapter 5

Eliza could hear Audley Stratton's voice, a rumbling boom, as she hesitated outside the drawing room door. The rich sound of it eased her dread for the briefest of moments for Audley was such good company and she was eager to join him. But she knew exactly who he might be relaying his rumbustious story to, for he sounded like he was trying unnaturally hard to entertain.

She took a bracing deep breath, ignored the sharp pain in her side and opened the door into the lamplit room. Sure enough, Audley was standing with his elbow on the mantelpiece above the crackling fire, large whiskey in hand, his purple bow tie and matching waistcoat gleaming. She wondered how many whiskeys he'd had already, for his nose was red and his forehead gleaming. Next to him, Morris with rosy cheeks, equally spruce and smart in a dinner jacket, was hanging on his every word, laughing. Their Great War medals shone along their top pockets just as brightly as her father's did on the mantel back at Nunnery Fields.

And, with her back to the door, a small step outside their circle but still revelling in both men's attention, stood Jessica. She was even taller and more white-skinned than Eliza remembered. Her silvery-blonde hair was tucked smoothly around her head in a graceful 'do', her shoulders covered with a fur stole the colour of ice, and her long, navy dress glimmered like a midnight sky.

She did not look round at the sound of the door, as everyone else did, but seemed to wait a moment or two before she was ready to turn her head to reward Eliza with a white smile outlined in Elizabeth Arden red.

'My dear Eliza!' cried Audley, leaving Jessica to advance on her. 'How are you? Now, I know we must all treat you like an injured kitten, for I understand you've had a pretty rotten time.'

Eliza laughed and assured him that she was really quite tough, actually.

'Come sit here,' Angela Stratton called out in competition for her attention, patting the sofa cushion next to her. She was dressed in cosy, but elegant, cream wool, emitting a cloud of Chat Noir perfume as she stood to guide Eliza to her seat, her hair as golden as the firelight.

Eliza sat down on the sofa and caught Jessica's eye. Jessica's smile hardened and fell away, but her narrowed eyes remained fixed on her. She stood perfectly still, waiting for Audley to return to her side, whereupon her face was transformed with a beaming smile solely for him.

Her mother, Eliza noticed, was wearing her new peacock-blue and looked beautiful. However, she had been collared by Leonard whose hair was a black, slick flash over his head. Mathilde saw her watching and gave her a brief, resigned look. Eliza worried that no one had thought to rescue her. Nick was in his usual armchair, leg propped up, so no use, and Martyn was upstairs still getting dressed.

'Are we going to open this damn champagne, Morris?' Sybil called across the room, indicating the bottle crammed into the ice bucket on the sideboard, perspiring nicely.

'Hold on, Ma, we're missing just one person,' Nick said.

'That boy,' Eliza uttered to Angela beside her. 'Not only does he hog all the hot water, so my bath was lukewarm, but he's late as well!'

'I'm sure Jessica is dying for a glass,' said Sybil. 'Come and tell Eliza all about your fabulous new job.'

Eliza watched in horror as Sybil took Jessica by the hand and led her towards her. Jessica looked equally uncomfortable but made a pleasant show of perching on the arm of the sofa and giving her a cheery greeting.

'Oh, Eliza, it has been so long. I believe last time we saw each other you were still in school uniform. Now look at us.' Her smile was twitchy and bright, and yet her eyes were chilly, like little chips of ice. 'We're all grown up now. And I tell you, I would hardly have recognised Martyn. I saw him when we arrived, as he scuttled upstairs to dress. I thought to myself, who is that young man? No longer a boy! As for you and Nick getting married! What wonderful news.'

Even as she listened to Jessica's friendly chatter, Eliza could feel the pinches and the deft punches that Jessica had inflicted on her during their endless suffocating games of childhood. From her perch, Jessica scrutinised her.

Tilting back her head, Eliza held her stare. 'Sybil tells me you have a new job.'

'Yes, do tell us,' Angela said, leaning in. 'If you can that is. We understand all about Official Secrets.'

'Radio announcer at the BBC,' said Jessica. 'On a bit of a trajectory, really. Working shifts around the clock ...' She sighed for sympathy.

'Going to parties around the clock more like,' Nick chipped in from his armchair.

'Keeping morale up for the troops, *more like*,' Jessica corrected him.

Jessica had more poise and grace than Eliza could ever dream of, but, she remembered, absolutely no sense of humour.

'What a lovely dress, Jessica,' she said to distract her from Nick's buffoonery. It was the most beautifully cut gown, and fitted her shape like an elegant slip.

'Couture from Vienna,' Jessica said. 'Dad went mad when I told him. But then he'd never understand the nuances of good taste or fashion.'

'I think you may be right, dear.' Angela laughed, and pointed over her shoulder. 'I think he is talking to Mathilde about radishes.'

Jessica frowned. 'Mrs Stratton, my father is very proud of his vegetables.'

Angela caught Eliza's eye and changed the subject, asking Jessica about life in London. As Eliza listened to Jessica relay the intricacies of her little flat in Bloomsbury, she realised that

Jessica was staring at her face in a peculiar fashion. She discreetly touched her top lip to find it laced with sweat.

'Yes, it is rather warm in here, isn't it, Eliza? Would you like a handkerchief?' said Jessica, getting to her feet with a sweep of fragrant silk. 'I'm certainly in dire need of some champagne now.'

Morris jumped to do her bidding and hurried to the ice bucket, fumbling with the cork and finally releasing it with a disappointing let-down of a pop just as the door opened.

'Well that's a damp squib if ever I heard one,' said Martyn, kicking the draught excluder back into place.

'At last,' said Nick, sounding pleased. 'He's here.'

They all gathered on the hearthrug to raise their glasses and wish each other a happy Christmas, Eliza standing close to Nick, while Mathilde drew close to her other side and linked her arm, giving her a playful, relieved squeeze. Eliza sipped contentedly, remembering the moment she and Nick became engaged, the celebration in this very room four months before. She stood on tiptoes to whisper as much in his ear, but he moved away from her suddenly, took a step with his good leg and reached his hand to Martyn's collar.

'You've shaving cream on your neck, old boy.'

'That box-room light is not so good,' Martyn confessed. 'Had rather some trouble seeing to use my razor properly.'

'You should have said. Next time, use the mirror in my room. It has a marvellous light. And I propose you have my room after I've moved into the Stour wing with Eliza. Ah, that reminds me.' Nick turned to her. 'That's one more thing that needs to be shifted over – my old wardrobe.'

Angela laughed. 'Well, that's certainly not the most romantic thing that I have ever heard a young bridegroom say to his bride!'

'Yes, Nick.' Martyn grinned reprovingly. 'You're going to have to do better than that. That's my sister, remember. I've got my eye on you.'

Nick's cheeks coloured and he glanced at his feet. Feeling sorry for him, wondering why he did not realise Martyn was teasing, Eliza took his arm. He did not respond, his arm like a dead weight.

She looked up to find Jessica watching her, giggling privately to herself.

'We should make another toast,' said Sybil, brightly. 'I propose we drink to the passing stranger. The stranger on the road. Shame you never got his name. You'll want to thank him. I do believe he saved your lives.'

'Unfortunately, I didn't even get a look at him. I was rather unconscious at the time,' said Nick. 'But, Eliza, surely, would know him.'

Everyone looked at her.

'Not really. I hardly remember a thing. The whole experience is like a foggy dream played out in dreadful slow motion.'

'More like a ruddy nightmare,' said Morris. 'You're as well not to remember. Would be too horrific. But you wouldn't recognise him if you saw him again?'

'No, no I wouldn't.' She remembered the ebb and flow of reality and oblivion, the impact of shock and its wobbling aftermath. She lifted her glass. 'But here's to the stranger.'

They all paused and sipped.

Angela, warming to the subject, piped up, 'So, Eliza, what *is* the most romantic thing Nick has ever said to you?'

Eliza paused, letting the champagne tickle her nose. 'I think he once said that I had very fine, long feet.'

Everyone laughed, except Nick, who looked puzzled and rather affronted.

'I would never comment on something so personal,' he said. 'Anything I say to you, Eliza, is private, thank you very much. Angela, if you don't mind . . .'

Suddenly, almost accidentally, Eliza remembered. Muddy green eyes and the smell of soft leather as he leant in, the weight of his arm on her body, comforting and close, a salvation amid the screaming horror of the mangled car.

'Are you quite all right, Eliza?' asked her mother. 'You look positively ghastly.'

'I think she's going to faint,' said Jessica.

'I . . . just . . . oh dear.' Eliza touched her forehead. It was damp, her hairline soggy. Her blood crashed sickeningly to her feet. She was queasy, faint, but not because she had just remembered the accident. It was the simple shock of suddenly remembering *him*.

'Poor dear, she's reliving it.' Angela's hand was on her arm and she guided her to the armchair. 'You must think lovely thoughts, beautiful thoughts and we must stop talking about it.'

Eliza sat down, placed her head in her hands. Angela stroked her back, while Mathilde offered a glass of iced water. She looked up eventually to see them gathered around her, all of them apart from Jessica, who was standing to one side appraising her with a mild shake of her head. Their concerned voices clamoured and merged into one oceanic noise, but it was Martyn who she heard, distinctly and insistently. His words reached her beneath the disjointed murmuring of the others and what he said had nothing to do with her current dismay but, uncannily, made the most sense.

'I will look out for you, Eliza.' His face was suddenly so mature, bold and earnest that it reminded her extraordinarily of someone. Her father: the shadow, the myth. 'I will always look out for you.'

Chapter 6

Her hand was lousy, so she picked up from the pack. Nick was winning anyway, like he usually did. He often told her that he preferred to play Martyn as it was more of a challenge, and he was less of a walkover. Her mind drifted as Nick reordered the cards in his hand, ruminating over his go. Mathilde and Sybil were knitting and reading, listening to the Forces Programme. Martyn was at the pub with his fellow RAF cadets. The French windows were open to the garden and the evening sun was turning the air the colour of honey, casting orbs of light across the walls. She caught the fragrance of new summer; the scent of green from the garden. The timbers of Forstall, having been baked by unexpectedly hot sun all day, gave off a nutty aroma.

Nick laid down a run of clubs with a snap and said, 'The wedding, Eliza. How about September? Early in the month. It'll still seem like summer.'

Eliza started from her daydream. 'Why should it being summer matter? We weren't worried about it being a cold January day before. The weather, good or bad, won't bother me.'

Mathilde placed her knitting in her lap. 'I can't believe the time has flown so. Where are we?' She squinted at the newspaper folded on the table. 'The twenty-sixth, already? We moved here properly in February and it only seems like yesterday.'

'It's been a busy few months,' Eliza agreed, sorting her cards and having to pick up again. 'And there have been far more pressing things to do than organising the wedding.'

Nick agreed. 'What with the brewery, the veg garden, me trying to learn to walk without this pathetic limp . . .'

Sybil piped up, 'Don't forget the billeting of evacuees. That's kept me occupied. I've never seen such a rabble.'

Eliza smiled, noticing the sun highlighting a film of dust on Sybil's sideboard and vowed to get the dusters out tomorrow. Their daily from the village had dropped away, citing war work far more pressing than Mrs Staveley's old, rambling and frankly impossible-to-clean house.

'I've found it quite a challenge, the running of this house,' Mathilde chipped in. 'What with all the rationing and shortages stretching us. I do admire you, Sybil, and appreciate what you have had to put up with.'

'I can guess it's only going to get worse.'

'Which is why, Eliza,' said Nick, presenting a prile of Jacks, 'we should really get it done before the hop harvest. Because after that, God knows I won't have the time spare.'

'Get it *done*?' Eliza sank her cards to her lap and stared at Nick. He kept his eyes on the game. 'Oh, you know what I mean, dear.'

From the corner of her eye, Eliza noticed her mother and Sybil give each other a look and tactfully return to their tasks.

Nick concentrated on sifting through his hand and plucking cards into order. Tears of frustration misted her eyes. She turned her head to look out through the French windows, determined that no one should notice.

The war constantly coloured their days like a cloud covering the sun and she felt herself coming adrift, having to keep pace with Nick and his variety of moods; moods she'd never noticed when she was just a guest at Forstall. She had to catch up with him and think ahead, just as she was doing with this game of rummy. And yet he was always streaking away from her, oblivious to her.

She gathered her spirits, sat upright, focussed back on the game. 'It's already the end of May,' she said, minding how irritated she sounded. 'We need to give the vicar notice.'

'Well, name the day, dear . . . that's all you have to do . . .'

'All I have to do –?' Eliza almost laughed.

The door opened abruptly and Morris burst in. 'Switch it over,' he said, marching towards the wireless. 'World Service. It just came on in my study. We need to listen to this.'

'But that was my programme,' said Sybil.

'What's happening, Pa?' asked Nick.

'The army are retreating,' Morris's voice lifted, incredulous. 'I can scarce believe it. Listen. Turn the switch, Sybil. Listen.'

Eliza leant forward in her chair, her scalp prickling and cold as the news broadcast invaded the room. How could this possibly be? This was their army, their own British army sent over to France to win. Surely. And now, they're telling us that they've got to fight a rearguard action. Retreat? Fight their way home?

'We've lost!' cried Mathilde, her hand over her mouth.

'Oh, no, Maman. Oh, no.' Eliza shook her head. Frightened, she looked at Nick's blanched face.

He reached out for her hand but she stood and went to her mother. She put her arm round her while Mathilde lowered her head and wept. '*Ma belle France . . . pas encore.*'

Morris did not say a word. His grim face remained so stiff with shock that he terrified Eliza. He patted Sybil on the shoulder and then walked towards the door.

'Are you all right, Pa?' asked Nick.

'Where are you going, dear?' cried his wife.

'Telephone Stratton. Got to ask him what I, what any of us, can do to help.'

Whenever she was heading east towards the coast, Eliza was never quite sure where the Isle of Thanet began. The trunk road from Canterbury at some point crossed the narrow channel that marked the boundary, but it was easily missed. The orchards and hop gardens in the dipping, rippling landscape of the west had the habit of receding without her noticing until, suddenly, the whole of the wide plain of Thanet opened out before her, stretching to the sea.

She had got up so early that morning that the vast flat fields had only just begun to shimmer under the rising sun. From the passenger seat of Morris's car, she saw the sweep of Sandwich Bay, the water muddy as it lapped the Links; she saw the ruined church towers of Reculver to her left and the smudge of Ramsgate peeling off around the headland.

The dawn was pure, faint blue; the promise of a fine day. And the sky was full of metal. Hurricanes were lifting out of Manston Airfield, heading south over the Channel. And, as Morris slowed the car to make the right turn onto the Thanet Way at St Nicholas-at-Wade, Eliza saw, in the wide stretch of grey sea, an unruly fleet sailing haphazardly into harbour.

'I will drop you off at the top of the town and you can walk down to Stratton's,' Morris said. 'It will be chaos otherwise. There are probably roadblocks and all sorts. I need to get on to Manston. Audley's expecting Martyn at zero-seven-hundred hours.'

Eliza looked behind her at her brother on the back seat, curled up into the corner to grab another half hour's sleep before he was to be on duty. His Air Force blue uniform was neat and tight around his throat, his hair newly clipped up the back of his neck. She saw nicks of blood on his chin from shaving.

Morris was stone-faced as he pulled into the side of the road. He glanced skywards. Another squadron of Hurricanes was taking off from the airfield. The sight of it, her pride at its magnificence, pinned Eliza to the car seat. She looked at her brother, asleep on the seat behind her, and flinched, suddenly afraid for him.

Morris applied the handbrake. 'Remember he's still a cadet, Eliza. Stuck on the ground, seeing to the chaps. He won't be flying one of those beauties just yet.'

Even so, Eliza swallowed, her throat thickening. Her country was in retreat against the very same enemy that Morris and her father had faced twenty years ago. They were poised on the brink of defeat. They were perched here, at the edge of England, the enemy not thirty miles away. And here in all this turmoil, she needed a jot of reassurance. She also didn't want to make a fuss, didn't want Morris to worry about *her*. She wanted to be brave, but all she felt was foolish.

'I'll say cheerio then, Morris.'

She gripped her carpet bag, opened the car door, but found she could not move. She glanced at Morris. His face was ashen, his eyes staring straight ahead. She'd never seen him look so dreadful.

A surge of soldiers appeared at the bottom of the road, marching up the hill from Ramsgate. They were grey, bedraggled, barely able to lift their feet, but their heads were up, smiles carving dirty faces. They held rank, despite their fatigue, and kept up their whistling as they made their way along the road, passing the parked car, towards the station and the first trains of the day to take them back to barracks and then home.

As the Hurricanes buzzed overhead, the soldiers sent up a raucous cheer.

'God bless them,' Eliza muttered and got out of the car.

'So we did all of *that*,' she heard Morris mutter. 'We went through the gas and the rats and the stench and the mud. We went through that *hell*, for it to simply happen all over again? The scrap heap, that's what they're headed for. Where we're all headed.'

Eliza shut the door. Morris was still speaking, but she did not wish to hear any more. Martyn awoke, noticed her through the window, gave her a grin and a lackadaisical wave. She hurried along the street, throwing Morris's words off because they stung and confused her. His hopelessness made the world shake beneath her feet. She deftly skirted the lines of cheerful soldiers. Some wore blankets as shawls, ragged knitted scarves; a couple sported stolen German helmets. Playful wolf whistles greeted her. She must look a picture in her neat WVS costume: green tweed with a matching hat. She turned her face away to conceal her smile.

The Georgian house that the Strattons were renting was in a pretty square at the top of the town, chosen so Audley could be at his post within minutes. When Eliza arrived, the door was opened by the daily. She pressed a pack of sandwiches on Eliza and told her that Mrs Stratton was already at the boys' school where she was to report for duty. Eliza asked if she could leave her overnight bag then set off down the steep hill, arriving at the school as a couple of army trucks struggled up from the harbour and turned into the playground.

Eliza stood back, breathing oily fumes as they came to a halt. Soldiers were crammed and bumping in the backs, new arrivals brought up from the boats. This time, there was no whistling, no playful tunes. Behind the canvas flaps, she saw ruined uniforms, bandaged hands and faces, blood seeping and heads held low, cigarettes drooping at the sides of mouths. A violence, a rage gripped her: an urgent need to help.

She hurried into the school, looking for where she should report. The building had been taken over by the Red Cross, with the WVS pulled in to assist. Volunteers were directing the walking wounded to the assembly hall to be accounted for. From the kitchens, the smell of bacon drifted out and tea was dispensed into enamel mugs from vast urns, bringing smiles of relief to some faces, tears to others. Men were awaiting their turn in the hall and in the corridors for their injuries to be assessed and treated. Others just needed a place to rest their heads. Eliza sensed an incredible care and patience in the air. Voices were low, commanding and tender. A man was squeezed in a corner, shuddering and weeping into his knees; his mate crouched next to him, his arm around his shoulder.

Eliza took a step towards them, but before she could offer her help, Angela Stratton called out, 'Eliza! Over here.' She was commandeering the first aid post and setting up a makeshift ward in the gym. She welcomed Eliza by thrusting a stack of blankets into her arms.

'Those men have been up to their necks in water, standing for hours. They've had hardly any food or water for days.' Angela looked so unlike herself with her ruddy face and her usually Hollywood-smooth hair in mild disarray. And yet she still smelt wonderfully of Chat Noir. Her deft busyness intoxicated Eliza. 'They've had a choppy crossing but seasickness is the least of their worries. We need to keep them warm. That's most important. Good morning, by the way.'

'You must be due a break,' Eliza said. 'You've been on duty all night?'

'Nothing compared to these chaps, but I might just snatch a cuppa and put my feet up now that you're here. Distribute those blankets to the men waiting, and *talk* to them. Some are barmy with worry and fear and God knows what else.'

Lugging the stack of blankets, Eliza immersed herself into the controlled melee. She went round to each bed, helped to remove cracked boots, sodden socks that were disintegrating. She eased tunics off and collected them. The worst ones would be burnt. A corporal, his eyes wandering with fatigue, thanked her.

'Will be nice to have somewhere to get a shave around here,' he said.

'We'll sort you out, once the doctor's been round. Please rest, keep warm.'

She could not help as much as she wanted. There were many things, not least the open wounds and the broken bones, that she would have to leave to the nurses.

'Right ruddy chaos,' the soldier muttered, stretching himself horizontal on the camp bed, a groan deep in his throat. 'Blind panic, as far as I could see. If it wasn't for those young subalterns barking orders every minute, holding men back with utter will-power, we'd all have bought it.'

How desperate it must have been. These men here had made it home, but what of the others left behind? The soldier closed his eyes, shut her out, knowing that she could never understand what he'd been through.

By mid-morning she had to move men on if they were fit and ready to go, as another swath of boats was heading into harbour, another mass disembarkation. She went around the ward and into the classrooms where the fitter soldiers were congregating and smoking, and gave each one a sealed envelope.

'Just write your mother's, your wife's, or your girlfriend's address on the front,' she said. 'Write a note to say where you are on the back. I will get them off to the postbox as soon as I can. Stamp is courtesy of Mr Churchill.'

The soldiers grasped the envelopes with grimy hands, finger-nails black. Some wrote like schoolboys, tongues at the side of their mouths, others with fine copperplate care. Their honest gratitude made her eyes sting.

Eliza took a bag of envelopes with her, left the school and headed down the high street to slip them in the postbox. Angela had suggested she take her break, so she slipped back up the lanes and found a bench on the East Cliff above the red-brick steps that swooped down to the harbour. As she sat, her eyes widened. The scene before her was incredible: dinghies, drifters, lifeboats, fishing boats, yachts, Thames barges and Dutch coasters all bouncing and clustering around the harbour mouth, waiting their turn. Their human cargo, visible on the open decks, was dark and lumpy, slumped and packed tight. Behind them streamed more of this unlikely fleet waiting to berth at Ramsgate or continue on to Margate.

How close the French coast was. On a clear day, Eliza could see Calais and, to the south east, lay Dunkirk, usually invisible, but marked now by black smoke billowing on the horizon. Above it and through it planes flew like darts, tiny flashes of metal in the sky.

Seagulls called and wheeled, worrying each other, oblivious to the mayhem on the sea. The brisk breeze buffeted her ears. She could only imagine the drone of engines and the menace of explosions on the far coast, the clamour of the men's voices on Dunkirk beach, and their stupefied silence, now, down there in the harbour. She remained still, mesmerised. How small she was. Tears of fear seeped from her eyes and she grabbed a handkerchief from her cuff to blot them away. Silly of her. She must not lose control; she must not fail them. Angela would be disappointed; Nick would not approve. She took a breath and loosened her laces, eased off her shoes and rubbed her sore feet. Her fear was a mere drop, a passing thing that must be ignored and put to one side. For she was safe on dry land, and so many out there were lost.

'I know those feet. I've definitely seen those feet before.'

Eliza glanced over her shoulder. She was alone. No one had walked up behind her. The street was empty.

'Now dry those tears,' the voice said, 'for you are stronger than that. I know you are.'

She spun back round, looked up and looked down. Between the railings of the steps to the harbour was a face peering up at her, just about level with her feet. A humorous face; a kind and peaceful face.

'We'll need you to be strong,' he said. 'It's the least you can do for us chaps.'

He walked up the last of the steps and sat beside her on the bench. He was wearing a tweed fishing cap, a wax jacket still wet from spray and heavy trousers soaked from the knees down. But his boots were good. Sailors' boots.

Eliza turned in her seat to face him, puzzled, frowning.

'Excuse me. I'm sorry. Have we –?'

'I'm hoping that your memory has wiped away the more unpleasant aspects of the last time you saw me.'

He offered his hand. It was strong, square-tipped and quite pale. Eliza looked down at it, nonplussed, and then back at his face. His cheeks were softly pock-marked. He had eyes the colour of a river bed.

'Oh, my.' She reached out in a surge of recognition to grip his hand, to shake it in welcome. 'Is it really –?'

Her voice cracked suddenly as if it had broken. The noise of the crash hit her, the abrupt, violent interruption of her world. And yet right before her eyes, his face remained steady and gentle, waiting for her to speak.

'Where have you come from?' she asked.

'Today? Just now? Is that what you mean?'

Eliza didn't know what she meant. She sat in silent confusion, simply staring.

'I made it back into harbour this morning on our lifeboat *High Hopes*,' he said. 'Got the fellas off; we're being refuelled at the moment. The crew are resting. Thought I'd come up here for a spell of peace away from all of that. And I'm awfully glad I did.' A broad smile lit his face. 'We're making ready to set sail again by teatime.'

She looked at him and saw his resolve, his spirits, his experience ingrained in his face.

'You're not going back?'

'Of course I am.'

Eliza shuddered and then righted herself, drew her shoulders back. 'Of course, you must. Those poor souls. To think they might be stranded over there.'

'We won't leave a man behind if we can help it.'

He was right, she had no business questioning him like that. And yet dread for him, for his safety, blossomed in her mind.

He turned to her. 'Let's start over. I'm Lewis Harper.'

She shook his hand again, laughing. His skin was comforting; curiously warm and dry. She introduced herself.

'And I see you are not French,' he said.

'Of course I'm not!'

Then she remembered, her mind clearing. She'd screamed at him from the wreck of the car.

'My mother is French, and I only speak the language when I'm frightened. I seem to revert to it when I am – oh, goodness, it was such a horrible . . .'

'You were saying some rather choice words that I seem to remember being whispered in French lessons. Hmmm, I will not remind you.' He grinned, the lines at the corners of his eyes elongating. He fell serious. 'But I see that you are well, and recovered. You are well, aren't you? And your husband?'

'He's not my husband. At least . . .' she snapped her eyes to the horizon. 'He will be very soon. And he is well, thank you. He will probably always have a limp as his leg was badly damaged. But he has recovered.'

'For that, I am glad. I did some good.'

'Oh, but you did, you did a whole world of good . . . but why mention my feet?' she asked. 'Just now, you mentioned my feet.'

'Your shoes came off. Do you not remember?'

She clapped her hand over her mouth to stop her laughter. 'Oh! Of course.'

Her long, fine feet.

Beside him on the bench, she suffered his glance and went on quickly, 'Come back to the school. We have tea, and stew and dumplings. And camp beds. You could rest.'

But Lewis's attention was drawn to the harbour below, the sea beyond. 'No, I must go back down. See how she's doing. Check on the crew.'

He shifted his shoulders and his attention in the direction he wished to go. Eliza quickly began to lace up her shoes amid unexpected and searing disappointment.

'Then I must go too. I mustn't keep Angela waiting. Or any of them.'

'Goodbye to you.' He was already up and walking towards the steps.

Her laces tangled, her fingers shook. Unsettling distress rose inside her. She hardly dared to look up, but when she did, she saw that Lewis had paused a few steps down, his face visible still, comical, through the railings. He said goodbye again and threw her a quick and dazzling smile.

The school clock showed that it was just after nine when Eliza left her duties and walked slowly, weary and raddled, towards the Strattons' house on Vale Square. The sun was setting on that long, long day and the red tiles on the roofs of Ramsgate reflected the last of the light, chimneys silhouetted against lilac clouds. Another Hurricane lifted into view, pointing its nose towards France. She wondered how she could simply go back to an ordinary house and do ordinary things such as prepare a supper and go to bed when all of this was still going on?

She stopped, remembering the last of the soldiers' letters in her bag, and diverted down the street to the postbox on the corner. The earlier melee of the town, the hum of purpose and solidarity, had quietened somewhat with just a handful of boats berthing. Sensible sailors were grabbing a short night's rest before the dawn would draw them back across the Channel. Wrens in uniform, nurses and volunteers like herself were making their way to their posts or back to billets, fading into the shadows with gentle *good-nights* and *good lucks*. A group of pilots from Manston slipped into the Red Lion on the corner, grateful to be in time for last orders. She hoped that Martyn was lounging in his barracks with the other cadets, his shift over for another day.

The door to the pub opened. Eliza heard voices rise and fall as a man exited, jostling a little with the blackout curtain at the door, to merge with the gloom.

She stood for a moment, rummaging in her bag for her torch. It would soon be dark and not knowing the town well and with the blackout down, she'd have some trouble finding her way. The street was suddenly, unusually quiet. High time she was somewhere safe.

She heard footsteps on the cobbles and looked with a start to see Lewis Harper walking towards her. He stopped and a smile split his face. She giggled her hello for all she could see of him were his white teeth in the dusk.

'There I was, quietly appreciating a swift half when the pub gets taken over by RAF types,' he said, laughing softly.

'My little brother will be one of those RAF types soon,' she said.

'Why are you out so late?'

'I had to post the last of the soldiers' letters and now I can't find my torch.'

'May I escort you? Where are you going?'

'It's not far.'

'It would be my pleasure to accompany you.'

As they began to walk together up the high street, a blush flowered her cheeks in the dark.

'I take it you couldn't leave for Dunkirk,' she said, and could not disguise her sigh of relief when he said that *High Hopes's* engine had failed, and they'd needed a mechanic.

'She'll be ready soon enough though. I'm going back at first light.'

'In that case, are you going to take my advice and drop in at the school? You'll probably not get the best night's sleep but at least you'll be warm and well fed.'

'I think I could sleep right here on the pavement I'm so tired,' he laughed. 'It's too far for me to go home, so I might just do that . . .'

She blurted, 'I can offer you some supper and a comfy sofa. At least Mrs Stratton – Angela – can. She's the Wingco's wife. I'm staying at their house while I'm on duty here.'

She saw his face as a pale earnest disc in the gloom.

'That's very kind,' he started, 'but really, there is no need –'

'Oh, there is every need,' Eliza said, cutting through the quiet dark. 'After everything you have done. How you helped us on that awful day when we had our accident. Angela and her husband would be thrilled to meet you. We all raised a toast to you on Christmas Eve, you know.'

Eliza lifted the flowerpot, found the key and gingerly opened the front door, not wishing to disturb the Strattons if they were already in bed.

'They're very old fashioned, they still have gas,' she whispered as Lewis quietly closed the front door behind them.

She found the box of matches by touch and struck one, holding it to the glass globe of the wall light and pulling gently on the chain. The lamp made a popping sound and the soft yellow flare pushed back the shadows, illuminating a note from Angela on the table next to the telephone.

'"Gone to bed. Five a.m. start,"' Eliza read out in a whisper. '"Soup, bread and fruit loaf in the kitchen." Oh, and wine, Angela says. Follow me.'

They went downstairs to the small yellow kitchen in the basement. She heated soup on the stove while Lewis carved slices of bread.

'Oh, lovely, it's butter from Forstall,' said Eliza.

She answered Lewis's questioning face by explaining that the manor house was her future in-laws' home, and hers and her family's now as well.

He carried the tray upstairs, following Eliza into the back parlour. She put her fingers to her lips with a smile as the door made its tender little squeak across the floorboards. She lit the lamps, lay out their small supper and poured the Macon Villages.

'Surely too good for veg soup.' She handed him a glass.

'But extremely welcome,' said Lewis, holding his glass up to the lamp and squinting at the wine. 'A good colour. Thank you, Wing Commander Stratton. Thank you, Mrs Stratton. Let's drink to France. And to England.'

They ate and sipped in silence. Over the rooftops of Ramsgate, seagulls keened in the darkness, an unruly cacophony dipping and fading, their cries eerily human. They're like sirens, Eliza thought, sounding a warning, lamenting lost armies, the men we left behind.

She shivered as she curled up in the armchair, wondering at the cold darkness, the cold sea out there. She drained her glass.

Lewis finished his soup and settled back into the cushions on the sofa.

'Will you be all right sleeping there?' she asked, momentarily elated at how easy it was to be in his company. 'I can find some of Audley's spare socks. I'm sure he won't mind you borrowing. Angela has blankets in the airing cupboard. I don't think any of the other spare rooms are made up. Of course they weren't expecting you –'

'No, and neither were you,' he said, stopping her. 'What a strange coming together this is.' He thoughtfully studied his wine and then peered at her. 'But then, let's face it, these are the strangest of times.'

Fatigue made his eyes flicker, but his smile remained bright and steady.

'Do you have to go back?'

'That I must,' Lewis said briskly, reaching for the bottle and pouring more wine for them both. 'But let's take our minds off it. Tell me about your family, your in-laws, how you met your fiancé.'

Eliza tasted her wine, longing for its mellowness to work on dissolving the fear and cold in her stomach. She thought of her father, briefly, an intangible shifting image. This critical time had brought him back to her – the memories of him like a portent for more trouble and danger to come. Lewis was poised for her response, his placid face receptive.

'Where do I start?' she said. 'My father, Richard, died when I was very young. From the effects of gas. He and Morris, Nicholas's father, met in the trenches at Ypres. Morris was his captain and Richard saved his life during a gas attack, but he did not think to save himself. He should have put his mask on first, you see. He met my mother while she nursed him at a French field hospital. She, a young nurse from Picardy, in turn saved his life, but his ruined lungs . . .' Eliza broke off, startled by the enormity of her sadness, her eyes out of focus with tears. She stared into a corner of the room until she had composed herself. 'I can barely remember this haunted, frail man. Always in bed as he couldn't stand for long. I was only three.' She forced a smile. 'Morris won't speak of it.'

No one spoke of it. Not really.

'And your mother?' Lewis asked.

'She is well. When my father died, Morris set us up in our lovely little house in Canterbury. But we spent so much of our time – Christmas and the summer, and Easter and all our half-terms – at Forstall. We're now all settled there. It is home to all of us.'

Lewis nodded. 'Ah, home. I can see you are grateful for it.'

'And where is your home?'

'Deal. My parents were both from the town. Both dead, I'm afraid. I have a house on the seafront,' he said. 'I've always sailed, which explains my contribution over the last few days. *High Hopes* is a lifeboat and I'm skipper of the volunteer crew. Of course, when the call came up the other day, there was no stopping me.'

Eliza wanted to know more. He was a few years old than her, she could guess. She wanted to place him, this stranger; pinpoint his life.

'And school?' she asked.

'Oh, London. Hampstead to be precise. I was born there. We lived in a town house overlooking the Heath. I've kept it on, even though both Ma and Pa have gone. I'm sentimental like that. It's still packed with their stuff, my old childhood things.' He smiled. 'Quite a fine spot, actually. Do you know Hampstead?'

'Not at all.' Eliza smiled, glad to be taken unexpectedly out of Ramsgate, out of Thanet and up to London. What a refreshingly frivolous idea, she thought. The city, the possibilities of it. She thought of Jessica, enjoying freedom and camaraderie in London, and felt mild envy. She was just about to tell him about Jessica, and her constant, objectionable presence in her life, but noticed the look on his face. His mind, she knew, was travelling not to London but across the Channel.

'Do you have to go back?' she asked again.

'You know I do. We have to go back for the French. The boys expect to.'

'England expects,' she said.

Lewis sipped his wine and gave her a tight smile.

She waited. Two more sips and he began. When the call came through, his lifeboat crew were issued with gas masks, steel helmets, fresh water for the troops and rope.

'We went across – what a motley flotilla,' he said. 'There were bankers, taxi drivers, fishermen, civil servants, all sorts manning boats cruising alongside us. The good people of Kent, and probably some bad ones too. *High Hopes* has a good shallow draft – perfect for taking men off beaches to the big ships waiting.'

'How was the crossing?' Eliza was not able, could not dare to imagine it.

'Like a bloody traffic jam. In the pitch dark, the air full of dangerous shapes – the other boats. Waves from larger vessels we had no hope of predicting. You should have seen the wash. We were soaked. And then there were the boats coming the other way, fully loaded, and the glow on the horizon – Dunkirk in flames. Unmissable. The bombing, the fire, planes attacking. The men on the beaches were sitting ducks. But they were there: great black columns of them, ankle deep, knee deep, shoulder deep. Those officers, how they kept control, with their heads just above the water, I have no idea. Such deathly, drawn-out patience. I've never seen anything like it. And the sky – full of noise. Shells, machine guns, falling planes. Can you tell, my voice is hoarse, my throat wrecked from shouting?' He paused for more wine. 'On the way back, Jerry dive bombers took up attacking positions over us five times. But they left us alone in the end. Christ knows why . . .'

Eliza floundered, put her hand up to stop him speaking, her flesh tight with terror.

'I'm sorry,' she whispered. 'It's just that I can't lose another ... I can't bear to. Martyn, my brother, I mean. After my father, you see.'

'You don't need to say it. You're terrified. And do you know something? We all are.' Lewis sat forward on the sofa, reached across Angela's rug, the space between them, and took Eliza's hand. He briefly ran his thumb over her palm. He fixed her with a stare that told her she must take courage. She must. But in the half light, she saw the fear on his face staring right back at her.

'But I must go back,' he said.

He closed his eyes and, without a word, pulled back and rested his head on the cushions. The clock on the mantel was ticking gently towards midnight. He curled his legs up and slept.

Weariness nagged at her, made her nauseous. It was time for her to sleep as well. She slowly unpinned her hair so that it fell thick and straight to her shoulders. She ran her fingers over her scalp. The events of the day spiralled into a swarm of voices inside her head: commands, demands and screams from injured soldiers. Her body was pummelled; deep down in her bones she was tired, so very tired. She longed for sleep, but knew that the noise inside would not let her. She closed her eyes.

Moments later, his voice made her jump.

'Your hair,' he said sleepily. 'It looks like treacle in this light. Like rich, golden, sweet treacle.'

He was half dreaming, she decided, half delirious with fatigue, to say something so charming to her.

She left the room, went upstairs and collected a blanket from the airing cupboard. He was sleeping again when she came back. Carefully she covered him, not daring to touch him. She switched out the lamp and went to leave the room, but at the door she stopped, turned round and settled herself back in the armchair, tucking her feet – her long, fine feet – beneath her. She rested her head and dozed.

Pale light showed around the shutters. The parlour door opened with a little squeak. Angela Stratton's head popped around.

'There you are. Why on earth didn't you sleep upstairs? There's tea in the pot in the kitchen. Oh.' Angela looked in surprise at the sofa. 'I see you have company.'

'I hope you don't mind,' Eliza said, unfurling herself from the armchair. 'He sailed one of the little ships.'

'I see.'

'He's going back over today.'

'Better give him a good breakfast then, and hurry.'

Lewis lifted his head and peered over the back of the sofa, squinting at Angela who met his gaze with poise. He said good morning, thanked her and then begged her pardon.

'No need to thank me, sir,' said Angela. She gave Eliza a cautious look. 'As our WVS motto says: whatever job needs doing . . .' She closed the door behind her, calling, 'Cheerio and good luck.'

Lewis sprang to his feet and began to button up his shirt, missing buttons and having to start again. He hopped into Morris's fresh clean socks. His hair, thick and dark, stood straight up from his head.

'I've slept too long,' he muttered. 'Far too long.'

'What time do you have to be on duty?'

'Round about now, dammit.'

'But you need breakfast.'

'Can I take it with me? Is there a bathroom? Where can I clean my teeth?'

'Stop a moment.'

Eliza approached him, reached out a hand and smoothed his hair down.

Lewis waited for her to finish, meeting her gaze with patient good humour, and then darted out of the room. He hurried down to the kitchen, while she raced after him.

She poured tea for him and sliced bread and butter.

'No time to drink it,' he said, putting the cup down and thrusting the bread into his pocket.

Back up at the front door they stood, out of breath.

'At least your clothes are dry now,' she said, all of a sudden bewildered and sad. Anxiety flickered in the air around her. She opened the front door on to the morning and the fresh air hit her as a cold, hard reality.

'Everything is dry and shipshape. Ready for another day,' he said.

A lament surfaced in Eliza's throat, a sickening jerky fear in her chest. 'But you haven't had your tea!' she cried out, shocking herself.

Lewis half smiled, dipped his head to peer into her face. 'One of Mrs Stratton's types will pass me a cup on the harbourside, don't you worry.'

His extraordinary eyes stared at her with unfaltering intent. She stepped forward and they embraced as if they knew each other, as if they always had done. Fear, spliced with confusion, bubbled upwards again. This is ludicrous. Absolute madness. She pulled away.

But Lewis held onto her hand, leant in and kissed her lightly and very quickly on her lips, as if he was asking her a question.

'Take care,' he said.

'You must take care of yourself as well.' Her voice faltered. 'And you must go.'

Swiftly, she stepped back inside the house, shutting the door with a bang.

Standing at the large, back-breakingly deep ceramic sink, Eliza glanced down at her hands – they looked dead and wrinkled as if she'd been in a bath all morning. After ploughing through stacks of washing up – first the troops' breakfast plates, then their morning tea and now dinner – was it any wonder?

Despite her spine burning from standing for so long, she was glad she was shut away in the school scullery with the steaming copper and the tap that squirted scalding water everywhere. She'd borrowed one of Angela's scarves to cover her hair – *rich, golden, sweet treacle* – and had borrowed one of the school matron's voluminous aprons to cover her uniform. Her legs ached, her shoulders twitched with fatigue. Sweat eased itself perpetually down her backbone. She didn't expect any wolf whistles today.

She was glad that she didn't have to see Angela who would start the conversation triggered by the look she gave her that morning. She was also glad that, working down here, she didn't see the soldiers arriving – broken, exhausted, stunted by fear – and she didn't hear the stories they were bringing back from the far side of that short stretch of grey sea. She couldn't, *wouldn't* think of it. Instead she concentrated on the bits of carrot and onion from the midday meal of Irish stew floating in the washing-up bowl.

The door opened and Eliza turned, bravely fixing a wide smile on her face to greet the next trolley-load of dirty crockery from the canteen. But it was Angela coming to see how she was getting on.

'Dry your hands and come and have a cuppa,' she said. 'We've tuned in the headmaster's wireless in the staffroom. Churchill's on in a minute.'

Eliza turned her sore, sodden hands over in the rough towel and followed Angela.

'I have just the thing back at Vale Square. A nice little pot of Pond's,' Angela said as they strode along the corridor. 'Are you coming back tonight, or will you get the bus back to Forstall? You can stay if you like. You look all in.'

But she did not care how she looked. She could only think of Lewis.

'So what if I am?' Eliza said, her voice unintentionally rising a pitch. 'At least I'm here. In England. Home. On dry land.'

'Why, yes, dear . . .' Angela gave her a worried glance as they squeezed into the staffroom. They joined nurses perched on the tables and armchairs, a couple of doctors, a whole crew of WVS gals helping themselves from the tea tray, and as many soldiers, some still in uniform, some in mufti, who could squash in behind them, spilling down the corridor, leaning and smoking, making subdued, speculative sounds.

Angela handed her a cup. 'Chin up,' she said.

Surely, thought Eliza as she sipped the welcome tea, surely there is nothing wrong in kissing a sailor farewell before he heads out to sea. A kiss for luck, that's all. It had happened hours ago and yet it kept repeating, over and over. She'd given him back some of the courage he'd given her, that was all. But she was dangerously troubled by the way he lingered in her mind. She was also ferociously tired – where was that blessed courage now?

'Quiet,' someone said. 'Let's have some hush.'

The chattering voices were cut in an instant and Eliza listened as Mr Churchill's voice rumbled from the wireless, starting low and grave, inching its way into her consciousness. His words, eloquent and savage, inspired her. She became strangely light and fearless. And yet somehow, also brimming with fear.

She glanced around her. Faces were still and poised. Everyone holding their breath as they strained to hear every word, frowning, nodding, tense and in awe.

'We shall go on to the end,' Churchill urged them. 'We shall fight on the beaches, we shall fight on the landing grounds, we shall fight in the fields and in the streets, we shall fight in the hills; we shall never surrender.'

There was no question. Eliza tightened her grip on her cup for she was convinced she would drop it. The room was full and warm, the air close. Everyone there knew that this is what they would do. *Whatever the cost may be.* The broadcast finished and the breathing began again, great sighs, cheers and a rippling applause.

Angela rested her hand on Eliza's shoulder, as she repeated, 'We shall go on to the end.'

She flinched as if Angela had thrown cold water over her. She shivered, caught her breath.

'I must get married,' she whispered urgently, hissing her words beneath the commotion around them. 'I must do it, and soon.'

'Of course you must. We're all waiting for the wedding of the year!' Angela looked at her. 'But are you frightened, Eliza? You look terrified. It's all right to say so. You need Nicholas, don't you? That's natural. Fear makes us even more determined.'

'Determined, yes,' she said, not understanding and dizzy with confusion.

Angela's eyes were misty. 'I miss Audley terribly. I know he's only over at Manston. But times like this, I wish he was here. Here protecting *me*.'

'And yet,' Eliza jumped in, 'it's Morris who makes your eyes sparkle.'

Angela gave her a quick reproving glance. 'He makes many women's eyes sparkle. You just have to look at him,' she said smartly. She lowered her voice. 'I know what people may say, but we are good friends. He is funny. I like him. I have too much respect for Sybil and Nicholas for anything to happen. When you're married, you'll know. There is always a man, or men, like Morris. They catch your eye. Make you sparkle. But you don't fall in love with them.' Her voice lifted, ringing with plain truth. 'At the end of the day, I need Audley. And you need Nicholas.'

Angela's gaze was intense. Eliza lowered her eyes, swirling the dregs of her tea in her cup.

Angela said, 'I know how you feel. At least Nick is not in direct danger. And I mean that kindly. I don't mean that you should count yourself lucky. Look around you. We're standing side by side in this, all of us.'

'Then I will go back tonight. Speak to the vicar. Set the date.' Eliza's voice broke with the realisation; the task she had set herself.

'That's the spirit.' Angela hugged her, pressing her against the shoulder of her blouse until Eliza found herself intoxicated by perfume mingled with talcum powder and fresh sweat. 'And put the man who slept on my sofa out of your mind. He has gone.'

Eliza pulled away from Angela and looked around at the faces of the soldiers crowding the room; the soldiers who had made it back over the Channel. The lucky ones.

Chapter 7

Morris drove Eliza and Martyn the three miles from Forstall to Wickhambreaux under a sky as clear as glass. The verges along the lanes were billowing with lanky, feather-headed grasses, the crumpled faces of poppies dotted among them. Fields were ripening to gold behind the hedgerows, and hops were burgeoning in the sun.

The car followed the Little Stour for a while, until Eliza spotted the white clapboard mill and the rectory, the green, with its mighty chestnuts, and the church at the centre of it all. The little houses were squat and homely and the trees threw a peaceful canopy of shade but, behind the church tower, against the blue, spun a tangle of vapour, a glint of hot metal; a dogfight in the sky. Eliza peered upwards, gripping the car seat either side of her knees, mesmerised by the brutal, silent and strangely beautiful battle.

Martyn, sitting beside her in the back, craned his neck to get a glimpse, swore gently under his breath, and rested his hand briefly on her arm. Was he trying to comfort her? Or was he the one who needed reassurance? One day very soon, he would hear the command to scramble and join his squadron in the sky. She saw anxiety flash over his young and earnest face as he glanced upwards; she watched him wrestle it.

But Eliza was calm, surprisingly so. Today was her wedding day and, having rushed to get to this moment, having hurried everyone else, she was determined that nothing would stop her marrying Nick: not the war, not an imminent invasion, not a battle in the sky, not a quick goodbye kiss from a sailor.

On this late-summer afternoon, as swarms of Hurricanes flew over Forstall from first light towards the coast to meet the incoming enemy, she welcomed the distraction. For Lewis had walked through her mind many times in the last few months and, using every drop of resolve she could muster, she had tried to dismiss him.

Her mother's nervous chatter as she helped her dress had also filled the dangerous void inside her head. Mathilde had recalled her own wedding day, her eagerness for a new start. 'I wanted to just get on with it,' she said. 'After everything we had been through. The war, the hospital, the terrible times. I just couldn't wait to see your father. See him standing there at the church waiting for me.'

Her mother's eyes had glazed with memory.

Eliza also wanted to get on with it, also wished that her father had been waiting for her, checking his watch, his medals gleaming along his top pocket, ready to take her to church. Her mother reached up with the corner of her handkerchief to brush the tear from Eliza's eye.

'You have a good day for it,' Mathilde said as Eliza stood in front of the full-length mirror.

The satin dress, made, in a sterling joint effort, by Mathilde and Sybil, fell smoothly, lightly to her ankles, the neckline both chaste and becoming. She was ready.

The sun was so warm and bright that Eliza was convinced her bouquet was wilting on her lap before her eyes. Sybil's *Boule de Neige* roses, surrounded by tight red, velvety buds, had been cut at dawn but now, at half past two in the afternoon, half an hour before the service was due to start, they were gasping. Eliza ran her fingers delicately over the limp petals. Poor things; cut off in their prime to satisfy her.

'Are you all right?' Martyn asked beside her in the back of the car. 'You're looking so very pensive. I see you chewing your lip. But then it's no surprise, is it? It's your wedding day, after all. And you're marrying that Staveley fellow.'

A smile broke out on Eliza's face, and she gazed in gratitude at her brother. He knew when and how to lighten her mood.

'I'm so glad you got this one day's leave,' she said.

'Audley was able to pull some strings.'

Morris at the wheel had clearly heard Martyn's quip about her marrying Nicholas but would not be drawn. Instead, he kept his eyes on the sky.

'This weather may be glorious,' he said, 'but it's certainly not doing us any favours up there.'

Morris was right: perfect weather for a bride, perfect weather for battle. He started singing, 'O God, our help in ages past,' the hymn that always made her cry.

'I hope that's not one you've chosen for the', service, for we can't have a weeping bride,' Martyn said in a stage-whisper, leaning over to Eliza. He called out to Morris. 'Keep quiet, driver! You're upsetting her. I really think we should have got you a cap to wear, seeing as you are chauffeur for the day.'

'Quiet back there, or I'll throw you out.'

Eliza broke out laughing and they were all chuckling as Morris pulled up outside the church. Mathilde was waiting for them, her new hat forward over her nose, buttonhole bright against her lapel.

'My God, did you see the planes?' She dipped to haul open the car door, sounding demented with worry. 'Oh, Eliza, I thought you'd never get here in one piece!'

The vicar was flapping behind her, his robes like a white sail in the breeze.

'Not sure I like the look of it. Don't like the look of it one bit,' he said. 'Let's get you inside, Miss Piper, quickly now.'

As Eliza allowed him to help her out of the car, she said, 'Please give me a few minutes. I'm a little early and I want to compose myself. Bride's privilege.'

The vicar looked momentarily outraged, and her mother seemed put out. However, Eliza insisted. She waited with Martyn in the shade of the lychgate, smoothing down the long skirt of her wedding gown, while Morris and Mathilde hurried up the church path behind the muttering vicar.

The sky was suddenly clear. The engagement of Spitfire and Messerschmitt had moved on. As Eliza listened to the peaceful settling down of the countryside, she became aware of an elongating of time, a turning point, a pause before she stepped into a new moment of her life. Birds were carolling in the trees, oblivious to the battle, oblivious to the war. A good sign, surely. A lucky sign.

Martyn lit a cigarette. 'So here you are, sister dear, waiting under the lychgate, exactly where they used to rest the bodies before burial. Does that bother you right before you are due to be married? Is it an omen?' he mused mischievously, puffing away.

'Does it *bother* me?'

'One was just wondering.' Martyn forced a smile. 'Now it's up to you to tell me. For that is why I am here. Dad can't do it, so I will. What else can a little brother do for you but be your confidant at a time of crisis? I will stand by you, whatever you choose to do. I will always look out for you, I've told you that. I will walk you up that aisle. And give you away. But if you don't want to . . . What I mean is, you don't have to do this, you know. Marry Nicholas, I mean. Not if you don't want to.'

Eliza glanced at her brother. She could tell from the look on his face that he was no longer joking.

'Why would I not want to marry Nicholas?'

Since May, since the crisis of Dunkirk, those long, gruelling days working with Angela and the rest of them at the school, since Lewis, she had wanted to race towards this day, the day she was to marry Nicholas – to put *him* from her mind. And whenever Angela's words followed her, caught up with her, she ran even faster.

There will be men who make you sparkle, she'd said. *But you will not fall in love with them.*

'Whatever your decision,' Martyn said, 'do I have time to finish this gasper, do you think?'

She burst out laughing, even as tears sprang from her eyes.

He pulled out a ridiculously large handkerchief. 'Come now, have a good blow,' he said. 'We can't have a bride with watery eyes and a bright red nose.'

She took the handkerchief and covered her face, dabbing her eyes, calming down.

'Martyn.' She took a deep, clearing breath. 'Put that cigarette out, it's time for you to give me away. And of course I want to marry Nicholas.'

As she took her brother's arm and stepped onto the church path, the bottom of her dress caught on a nail on a corner of the lychgate, tugging her back. She heard a rip.

'Oh, no, that's all you need.' Martyn was dismayed.

'Never mind, never mind.' Eliza grasped the hem and eased it free. 'A torn dress is the least of mine, and everyone else's, worries.'

The siren went up just as Eliza and Nicholas walked out of the church as man and wife. It blasted suddenly, keening through the air so that she could barely hear what the man cycling past on the road was shouting at them. He was gesticulating to the sky, wobbling as he went.

'What did he say?' she asked Nick, astounded.

'Something about Manston taking the brunt of it,' Nick said, abruptly releasing his arm from hers and looking around over his shoulder, agitated. 'I say, Audley, did you hear him?'

Audley Stratton, following with the small gathering, said, 'Yes. It was Manston. They don't sound that siren just for the odd dogfight. This is serious. I've got to get back at once.'

'Me too,' said Martyn.

'Not so hasty, young man.' Stratton stopped him with a hand on his shoulder. 'Not to Manston for you just yet. I'll drop you at Forstall, but stay put near the telephone and wait for my call. I'm sorry, Eliza, I'm sorry, Nick. Your wedding day and all.'

Audley hurried off to his car.

'I'm too green for this, evidently,' Martyn muttered. 'Must be serious as they obviously need aces today.'

Eliza watched him scramble after the Wing Commander and slip into the passenger seat. The car sped off.

Angela was silent, her face white, her eyes darting with fear beneath her red hat.

Beside her, Mathilde began to weep softly.

'Oh, Maman, please don't,' Eliza said.

'The mother of the bride is allowed to cry,' said Angela.

'Can't we have one happy day?' Mathilde sighed. 'Just one day, without it . . .'

'Come and get in the car, Mathilde,' Sybil urged her. 'We'll get us all safely back home to wait for news.'

Morris did his best to rally her. 'Looks like you're going to be jammed in with the bride and groom, Mathilde. They won't mind a bit, I'm sure.'

Mathilde nodded tearfully. Morris and Sybil took an arm each and, with Angela, ushered her away to Morris's car.

Eliza watched them go, while the siren continued to assault her ears. She pressed her bouquet under her chin to breathe in the scent of the roses, to drink them in, seeking comfort in their beauty amid desperate confusion. She heard someone speak and looked up to see Nick standing close to her, his mouth working its way around consoling words, his hand pressing her arm. Her spine turned rigid for a moment in surprise. For in the chaos of the air raid, under the blasting of the siren, she'd forgotten he was there.

His eyes were sharp with concern, peering at her. He took her hand and urged her to come with him, to join the others in the car, to Forstall, to safety.

'Shouldn't we wait for the photographer?' she asked. 'Look, is that not him parking up on the other side of the green?'

'He's too late. We've got to go,' said Nick.

'But, our photographs?'

'He'll still get paid.'

She merely nodded, unable to trust herself to speak. Something white fluttered at the corner of her eye. The jagged piece of satin torn from her dress was still there, caught on the nail in the lychgate. She stopped, bent down, plucked it off and let it blow away in the breeze.

Back at the house, Sybil and Mathilde were keeping themselves busy and distracted by arranging the table in the dining room with a buffet tea, the small wedding cake at the centre. They'd set out bottles of Forstall beer and a single bottle of champagne was resting in an ice bucket. Morris took one look at it and went straight to the cellar to fetch more.

'We might as well have a whole case of it,' he said. 'I'm not letting Jerry get at it if he makes it this far.'

Eliza flinched, but Nick let out a hard laugh and told him he ought to fetch two cases.

'Come, Eliza. *Mrs Staveley*. Where's that brother of yours?' he asked.

They found Martyn ensconced in Morris's study next to the telephone, already changed into his flight suit and boots.

'You're still here, then?' Eliza asked brightly from the doorway, trying to draw a smile.

He nodded. 'Yes, I am. *Unfortunately.*'

'Don't let me hear you say that sort of thing in front of your mother, old boy,' Nick rebuked him, his tone remarkably cross. 'Or, indeed, in front of my wife. You're upsetting everyone. It just will not do.'

Martyn shrugged at Nick and looked away to stare out of the window.

'I think we'd better leave him to it,' Eliza said.

They went through into the dining room and stood together in front of the frugal spread. He popped the caps on two bottles of beer and wordlessly led her out, across the back lawn, limping as he went. They sat down on the bench under the trees and he handed her a bottle, tipping his own to his mouth and drinking it in great gulps. Above them, the fair weather cloud was pretty and benign, but false, like painted scenery. Eliza waited, while Nick fidgeted beside her, sighing, wiping his palms with his handkerchief and draining his bottle. His silence meant something was wrong. And of course it was. Everything was wrong.

She went to take his hand, but he pulled away.

'I'm sorry,' he said. 'I'm rather damp and soggy today.'

'Well, it's very hot.'

'It's not the heat,' he said. 'Truth is, I'm terrified. This might be Martyn's first sortie. I know Stratton is stalling. Any other chap would be sent straight to Manston, told to gear up. Audley is pussyfooting. Favouritism is what it is. And I'm glad for it.'

He put his arm stiffly around her shoulders. The weight of it was uncomfortable, but she did not like to say. She was trapped suddenly, caught up in the sense of them all being on the edge of disaster. The fear began to cut through her as if she was suffering physical pain.

'How bad is it, really?' she uttered quietly.

'Pretty bloody bad, I'd say.' Nicholas let out a hard sigh. 'Dash it, Eliza, I feel so fucking useless. This stupid leg is useless. They're going to haul Martyn in, young as he is. And I'm half a man. I can't do anything, but push bits of paper around.'

'Nick, you know that is still important, vitally important,' she said, trying hard to be positive. 'You've said yourself, people still need beer.'

'I'm pathetic, that's all.'

He lifted his arms away and folded them, forming a barrier.

'I'm sorry,' he said eventually. 'Don't listen to me going on. I'm just frustrated like any man would be. I suppose I've just got to do what I can. Got to keep morale up, haven't we, Mrs Staveley?' He laughed softly, unexpectedly. 'To think I can now call you that. Eliza, who I have known my whole life. Now my Mrs Staveley.'

Beside him, she sensed him peering at her face but could not look at him. Instead, she waved as Morris and Sybil, Mathilde and Angela drifted over the lawn to join them. They spread out rugs and set up garden chairs. Plates were perched on knees, champagne topped up and sandwiches picked at. Eliza watched them as if she was watching a surreal play.

'Shouldn't we at least go into the shelter?' she asked.

'You can, dear.' Morris sipped his champagne, deep in his deckchair. 'But I shouldn't let Jerry spoil your special day, if I were you.'

'Here, here,' Nick raised his empty beer bottle and reached for another.

'Not feeling desperately hungry after all the to-do,' admitted Sybil. 'Might just save myself for some cake.'

Morris held his glass to the sunlight. 'There's nothing better than a spot of champers. For any occasion. My son's wedding. Imminent invasion. It doesn't much matter. Any excuse. Angela, a top up?'

Angela did not answer him, but glanced instead at the sky. 'I wish I'd gone with Audley. I'd rather be by his side. But anyway, cheers to the beautiful bride.'

She raised her glass to Eliza but her smile made her mouth go square. She took a huge sip.

Mathilde plucked at her handkerchief, wringing it through her fingers. 'I see the plums are coming on, Sybil,' she said. 'I noticed them the other day. We'll need all hands to bring them in come September. Even with all of us here, I don't think there'd be enough of us. The evacuees can help.'

Eliza followed her mother's gaze beyond the Stour wing, beyond the banks of the river to the plum orchard and wondered if they, the family, would all still be here, like this, come

September. Such an innocent, ordinary view. All around her, the garden burgeoning and abundant. Yet even in the shade, Eliza felt her skin loosen with sweat, her head begin to pound; a headache cracking at her skull. Fear dripped through her like the ticking of a clock. Could it be happening right now, even as they sat here talking about the plum harvest? Could the enemy be at their shore?

Nick glanced at her. 'You look so very pale, my dear. Why don't you have a lie-down indoors for a while? It's been a hell of a day.'

Eliza nodded with relief. In a daze, she got up and heard the encouraging voices of her family send her on her way as she wandered back to the house. Inside Forstall, it felt as if time had stood still. Hundreds of years' worth of benevolence from the walls, from its fabric, embraced and comforted her. Even the scent of it was like a sedative.

She crept to the study. Martyn was lounging on Morris's chair, his feet on the desk, with a bottle of Forstall beer in his hand. She went in quietly and sat down in the armchair by the fireplace.

'What a pair we make, sat here in all our finery,' she said. 'Although,' she glanced down at her torn hem, 'mine is a little bit in tatters.'

The telephone sat on the desk between them and she eyed it like she would her enemy.

'Don't look at it,' Martyn warned her. 'For then it will ring.'

She grimaced and stared resolutely out of the ancient casement, spotting the heads of her family gathered on the lawn.

'You know,' said Martyn pensively, 'the beauty of the RAF training, and it being so damned thorough, is that I don't feel frightened. Not one bit. And I'm learning at a furious rate. They work us like dogs. It's funny, I think of the Hurricane as the bulldog, the Spitfire the greyhound.'

Eliza settled back in her chair with warm tenderness for him at her throat.

'What do you mean?' she said.

'The way I see it, the Hurricane is the tough working animal, you see, and the Spit is the sleek, fast, racing dog. And you know which one I will be flying!'

'I think I do.' She smiled.

'But the Hurricane is easier to pilot,' Martyn went on. 'It's not as fast, nor can it go as high. We use the Hurricane to attack the bombers, the Spit to attack the fighters. And the Spit is such a neat, beautiful little plane. The cockpit is so tight, it becomes part of me, along with the smell of grease, oil, exhaust. The plane and I – a funny thing to say – but when I'm up there, we're one and the same.'

Eliza suddenly shook her head. 'That's enough. No more talk of fighting.'

Martyn looked terribly sorry. It seemed to Eliza that, for a moment or two, he could not speak. She put her fingertips to her forehead as her headache worsened.

Through the open window came the familiar sound of the family's murmuring voices, another champagne cork popping. Nick's voice carried the furthest: 'Put the champagne away, Dad, I want to start on the brandy.'

Eliza shared a weak smile with Martyn.

'So, at last you're married to the Staveley fellow. Are you happy, Eliza?'

Honesty struck her then, like a light switched on.

'I don't think *happy* is the word,' she said. 'Not today. I want to be happy, but there are so many feelings, so many inexplicable things . . . I was confused earlier, outside the church. Terribly confused. The siren, the chaos, everyone rushing off. It was almost as if I did not recognise Nick.'

'Well, the whole day is in disarray,' he said. 'But we are home now. I always feel better here at Forstall. Don't you?'

She nodded, feeling no need to clarify.

'You know, Eliza, up there in the cockpit, above the White Cliffs, above the fields, you can't miss the big places: Deal, Canterbury, Sandwich. But I always look out for Forstall. Just a degree or two to the east of Canters. This is my home now. I'm glad we moved here. We're part of this family, aren't we? But, really, don't you think, in a way we have always been? Look.'

Martyn pointed out the framed photographs on Morris's mantelpiece. Eliza followed his gaze. There they were as children, out in the orchard. Messing about. Posing with pitchforks. Nick was wearing a ridiculous hat – Sybil's actually. There was even one without Nick. Just little Tintin and Eliza. That said something, she decided. Morris and Sybil might well see them as *their* children.

Eliza got to her feet and, amid stifling sadness, walked over to the mantelpiece to study the photographs. There was the more recent one: Nicholas and herself on the sledge, the fields in frozen winter white. Her woolly hat had come off, lost in the snow. This was the day that Nick had told her he loved her. And yet he did not remember it like she did. Would their wedding day be the same? Would he only remember his fear for Martyn, his frustration at his injured leg? Convinced a sob would break out of her, she pressed her lips together.

'Remember, I used to moan and complain about coming here,' Martyn said cheerfully. 'The long journey. Getting the bus and all sorts. Was I a pain? Be honest.'

'Never a pain, Martyn.'

'Not even a little bit?'

She looked at her brother's eager face. 'All right, then,' she conceded. 'A little bit.'

He sighed, his face dropping, suddenly doleful. He set his empty beer bottle down.

'Funny, but this place – Forstall – it's in my bones. Do you feel that? This is the place where I always feel safe. This is home. I will always look out for it when I'm up there. And I will always look out for you.'

The telephone rang, hard and shrill, making Eliza flinch in surprise. Martyn leapt up to answer it and began to speak earnestly into the receiver. Eliza left the room – she didn't want to listen.

Later, as evening fell after the all-clear, she and Nick made their way across the lawn, around the end of the Stour wing and across the patio into their new home. Nick's cheeks were ruddy, his eyes unfocussed. He held heavily on to Eliza's arm.

The danger had passed, the air raid was over, invasion thwarted and Martyn was back safely in his barracks at Manston.

'Would you like a milky drink?'

She stepped into the kitchen. She felt curiously light of foot, a little excited. She was now mistress of her new home. And this was *her* kitchen with its patchwork curtains and mismatch of hand-me-down crockery. 'Horlicks? Some digestives? Are you feeling all right?'

'No, I'm not. My blessed leg is playing up again,' mumbled Nick, rubbing a hand over his ashen face. 'I'm struggling to get up these bloody stairs.'

Not wishing to mention that the brandy might have something to do with it, Eliza helped him and, together, they inched their way up the narrow staircase and into the bedroom.

He sat heavily on the edge of the bed and grumbled a little bit more. She left him to it and went back downstairs to switch off the lights and retrieve her bouquet which was, as predicted, pretty much finished, dropping petals onto the kitchen table. She put it into a vase of water, not expecting it to last the night, went back upstairs and straight into the bathroom.

She pulled on her nightie and began to brush her hair in front of the mirror. Her cheeks were pale and her eyes dull with fatigue. She studied her reflection, but was unable to read the expression staring back at her. The night was still warm, and yet inside she was shivering as she crossed the tiny landing, barefoot. Her fingers trembled on the handle of the bedroom door.

Nick was sitting on the bed, smiling at her sleepily as he unbuttoned his shirt, pulling clumsily at his tie. He motioned for her to close the door and beckoned her over, drawing her down to sit beside him.

'Martyn's back at his mess, landed safely,' Eliza said conversationally while tugging her nightie down over her knees. It was brand new, a present from Angela, and she did not realise how short it was. 'He called earlier, did you not hear?'

'Of course I heard.' Nick was momentarily irritated. He sighed. 'Sorry, yes, it's wonderful news. Martyn is safe. We can thank God for that.' He began to struggle with his cufflinks.

'Are you tired?' she asked, almost hopefully, as she helped him remove them. They rattled as she dropped them into the dish on the bedside table.

'Just a little.' He rested his head on her shoulder, leaning on her like a dead weight.

Tentatively, she put her hand on his shoulder. She remembered how she had stared at him from the cold, frosty bank in the aftermath of the accident and had thought that he was dead. It had been just for a moment, but ever since then she had been fighting to get back to him, to reach across the gulf that the crash had forced between them.

He put his arm around her, laying it heavily over her shoulders, breathing deeply as if he was half asleep. He leant towards her face and, smelling the alcohol fumes, Eliza closed her eyes as he began to kiss her. The moment was here. He had never kissed her like this before. This was her wedding night. The man she had loved for most of her life was about to take her to bed as his wife.

Nick's hand grappled with the yoke of her nightie, the other was heavy on the back of her neck, his fingers in her hair.

Rich, golden, sweet treacle.

Eliza froze, fighting off the vision of Lewis. Her husband was here, preparing to take her. And so she should stop thinking of Lewis. She must. For if she didn't, she'd be lost.

Nick embraced her and her stomach stiffened, her limbs becoming rigid and useless. Her breath stopped in her chest. Knotted misery lumped in her midriff. She turned her face away in confusion.

He pulled back, sensing her retreat, uncertainty flitting momentarily over his face as he groped blindly for her, hitting only the air. He touched her, patting her clumsily on the head, before collapsing backwards onto the bed and beginning to snore.

In the small hours, Eliza lay in bed nursing the dismal realisation that she'd never be able to sleep. The warm darkness of the Stour wing bedroom crackled excruciatingly around her. Her mother had not warned her what sharing a bed would be like. How unfamiliar and invasive it would feel. She shifted on the sheet, unable to stop herself rolling inwards towards the sleeping bulk of Nick.

Gingerly, she slipped from the bed and stood barefoot by the opened window, relishing the cooler air around her ankles. Here was the view Nick had promised her. The terrace below, the little river, the plum orchard beyond, glowing under an inky sky, made piebald in the darkness by ragged silver clouds. Beyond the curve of the sky, just a handful of miles to the south, across the water, squatted their enemy, poised to send in the bombers. And yet Forstall Manor slept on as it had done for hundreds of years; the countryside slumbered, vulnerable and trusting. It was not dark enough for stars. The owl was quiet tonight, or had he gone away? Behind her, Nick let out a low groan and turned over, the brandy working like anaesthesia.

She stood alone by the window in the darkness on her wedding night and her mind switched to Lewis. Always, Lewis.

Chapter 8

Eliza heard the planes around the same time every day. She could set her clocks by them. In the early evening, as the sun slanted golden to the west, gilding the leaves in the orchard, they flew overhead, a great black tide of bombers droning in over the sea. They skimmed over Kent and left them alone at Forstall, at Canterbury, at Manston, diverting their fury onto London and thousands of other unknown souls.

Forstall had a good plum crop, just as Mathilde had predicted. And, encouraged by Sybil, the village evacuees had indeed helped bring in the harvest. Morris had been far too busy as captain of the Wickhambreaux Home Guard to get involved and Nick was spending longer hours at the brewery now that the hops were in. He had been defiant about joining the 'Dad's Army', saying that his working day would leave him no time for parade. But he relented, on one condition: that he was made sergeant because that was Leonard Castle's rank, although of a different section. He must, without fail, be equivalent to him. Eliza, meanwhile, kept herself busy making plum jam.

As she stood at her kitchen table that tranquil autumn afternoon, finishing the last of the day's batch, she caught the scent of wood smoke and sensed, almost unconsciously, a change in the season. And then, earlier than usual, the distant approaching roar, a broad vibration across the sky, creeping towards her like a great storm. She raised her shoulders, dipped her head and carried on, pinning her concentration on the jam.

She heard the volume of the wireless in the salon next door increase suddenly against the noise of the approaching planes and immediately her shoulders fell, her spine softened. The War Office men next door, with their covert, intense industry, their discreet comings and goings, were a comforting distraction.

As she cocked her ear to the fury of the planes, the front door opened and she heard a step in the vestibule.

'Tea in the pot?' asked Nick, coming into the kitchen.

She turned wordlessly to the kettle and set it back on the range where it began to hum and fizz.

'Sounds like they're sending everything they've got tonight,' he said, taking his evening paper through to the parlour, expecting her to follow with the tea. As Eliza watched him go, she heard Sybil saying again: '*There you go, hand and foot.*' If only they knew now that it was no longer such a joke. She picked up the tea tray and bumped her way through to the parlour.

Nick looked up at her over the top of his paper and, misreading her expression of disappointment for fear, said, 'There's no siren, Eliza, so we've nothing to worry about. They're flying far too high to be bombing us. Crikey.' He stretched out the broadsheet. 'Have you seen this? The docks have been taking a right ruddy pasting. In my opinion, I don't think they give the full picture. If they did, we'd all give up right now.'

'I'll look at it later,' she said, not wishing to be sullied with bad news. She was becoming rather like her mother in that way: unable to face the full horror of what was happening in London and letting it wash over her.

The sight of Fisher wheeling his bicycle past the window distracted her from thoughts of the Blitz. He was due to start the late shift in the salon and had just cycled in from The Gables Guest House in the village where he and Bingley, his colleague, were billeted. She gave him a cheery wave. He would not make a very good spy as he looked far too much like a civil servant – all sleek hair and spectacles, trilby and mackintosh. He and Bingley seemed to have been cut from the same cloth, although with Fisher being stocky and heavy around the chops and Bingley lanky and tall, they had been rather different amounts of cloth.

Nick also noticed Fisher's arrival.

'So, have the fellas needed you much today?' he asked her.

'No, it has all been rather quiet. That's why I've been able to get on with my jam.'

Nick went back to his newspaper without continuing the conversation he'd started. Eliza sipped her tea, imagining how they must look to Fisher, Bingley or indeed anyone else glancing in their window: a contented married couple, seeing through the war together and going about their daily lives.

She heard a rap on the kitchen door and peered through from her armchair in the parlour. Bingley popped his head around.

'Excuse me, Mrs Staveley, Mr Staveley. I'm so sorry to disturb you.'

His eyes darted to the neat regiment of plum jam pots on the kitchen table and Eliza saw that he was salivating. Bingley was clean-cut, blandly handsome and a stickler for protocol. She was sure that whenever he greeted her, he clicked his heels.

'What's that, old boy?' Nick asked.

'Just that we need a message collected urgently from Castle's. Thing is, Fisher's only just got here and something is kicking off on Morse. We can't leave our posts. I know this is not usually your remit, Mrs Staveley, but –'

'Nonsense.' Eliza was on her feet, delighted, and already tying on her headscarf.

'Castle just called it through, but he is regretfully tied up –'

'Leave it with me.'

She called a cheerio to Nick and Bingley and was soon strolling quickly in the evening sunlight, hurrying along the short cut to Castle's farm. The footpath meandered between rolling orchards that had given up their fruits and were now shedding crisp leaves. The hawthorn hedgerows were black with berries and the long hair-like grass of the verges resembled golden silk. A quick breeze batted at her scarf. She breathed deeply on the crisp, turning air and relished it. She wasn't often alone, but now, away from Forstall and doing something useful, she felt clear-headed, strong, herself again.

The first wave of bombers had disappeared, the danger passed over. They hadn't even bothered with the siren. The sky was tranquil again. She left the footpath and turned onto the lane.

'Just look at those clouds,' she whispered, as she gazed at the transient beauty of the banks of white, tinged pink by the lowering sun. And then, just for a moment, one sweet, passing moment, she thought of Lewis.

A car tooted and she quickly stepped up onto the verge, knee-deep in grass, to allow a taxi to squeeze past. The driver lifted his hand in thanks. To him, to anyone, she was an ordinary Kentish country housewife, in her jacket, headscarf and corduroy trousers, but, in reality, she was a small link in an enormous, complicated and vital chain. She was needed by the War Office boys in the salon; her services were very much required. Her step was light, her mind alert as she hurried on.

The red-tiled oasts of Castle's farm topped by the sprinting fox weather vane appeared between the hawthorn thickets. She opened the wide gate, then shut it firmly behind her and crossed the cobbled yard, parting a drove of white geese who honked and glared at her. The grand red-brick farmhouse with Dutch gables and a Georgian porch was perched on a little rise above the melee of the farmyard. Beneath the curving walls of the oast sat the pigeon loft containing its roosting, fluttering inmates.

Leonard Castle often boasted that his were the finest birds in the county and Eliza decided that, on this occasion, he could be forgiven. Because, for that very reason, the War Office had commandeered his loft at the same time they moved into the Stour wing, instilling in him, as Mathilde observed, even more of a sense of his own importance. And all this on top of being sergeant in the Home Guard.

Eliza hesitated in the yard, not sure whether to report to the house, or go over to the coop. The best of Leonard's pigeons had been taken to Manston to be taken as passengers on sorties out of the airfield. If the crew went down – and survived – they could send the pigeon back with a message detailing their coordinates.

The birds also brought messages back from the Resistance. Now that he was a pilot officer, Martyn's missions consisted of dropping the 'little feathered blighters' into France. They were packed safely in boxes, the boxes fitted with a miniature parachute, to land somewhere in Normandy and be collected by the fighters. And the intelligence came back, sporadically, but vitally, all the way to the loft at Castle's farm.

There was no sign of anyone. A suitcase lay abandoned on the house step – the passing taxi must have just dropped someone off. Sure enough, Leonard came through the front door to retrieve the suitcase. He caught sight of her. Beaming broadly, he called out his hello.

'Eliza! I expect you're wondering who's just come home?' Without waiting for a reply, he called back over his shoulder, 'Jessica! Jessica!'

She stood perfectly still for a moment and then began to walk slowly towards the house, fixing a welcoming smile to her lips.

'Yoo hoo! Hello!' Jessica appeared on the threshold in her travelling clothes of a blue cape with a neat fur collar, her red-lipped smile, no doubt, still as bright as when she'd applied it that morning. She was waving quite unnecessarily wildly, as if Eliza might miss her.

'Look at you, Eliza Piper. Sorry Staveley. Mrs Staveley now.'

Jessica gripped Eliza by the shoulders and gave her a kiss in the air by her ear, issuing a waft of perfume. She flicked her eyes up and down, sending a line of discomfort through Eliza's body.

'So, you are an old married woman now. My, my. Sorry I missed the wedding. I've been awfully busy.'

Eliza looked at her askance. She hadn't been invited.

'Won't you come inside for a bit? We're going to have tea.'

'I can't. I really can't,' Eliza said. 'I've come to collect something from your father for the War Office. I must get it and dash back.'

'Then I'm coming with you,' Jessica said. 'I could do with a nice stroll. London is so chock-full of dust and dirt and *people*. It's so good to be home again.'

Leonard slipped past them to hurry across the yard to the loft. He returned promptly and handed Eliza a slim, bright red Bakelite phial.

'Monty brought this one in,' he said. 'He's a fine, brave gentleman.'

Eliza pushed the phial deep into her pocket, noting first, as was procedure, that it was still sealed.

'Come on, agent Staveley.' Jessica giggled, linking her arm. 'Dad, I'll have my tea with Eliza and Nicholas, if you don't mind.'

Eliza was conscious of the urgent need to hurry, felt she had been dawdling far too long. Bingley was expecting this message, was waiting for her. Jessica would have to trot quickly in her little boots if she was to keep up with her.

'What a lark this is,' Jessica said, a little out of breath as they hurried along the lane. 'Both of us doing our little bit for the effort. Coo, you're a fast walker.'

'I'm not surprised you've come home,' Eliza said, making an effort. 'What with all the raids. We see them going over all the time. It must be so very frightening.'

'Oh, yes.' Jessica glanced sideways at her. 'Only the very wicked are staying in London.'

Eliza opened her mouth to wonder why but stopped when she saw the glint in Jessica's eye.

Jessica laughed. 'There's passion there for the taking, if you want it, Eliza. The fear brings it out. The constant danger, it heightens everything. Oh, don't look so shocked. You are a married woman!'

They'd reached the footpath. The chill of the evening was deepening, the warmth of the sun disappearing into the west. Eliza increased her pace; she mustn't keep Bingley waiting.

'I was having the time of my life,' said Jessica, 'until Dad insisted I came home for a bit.'

'How long are you staying?'

'Oh, this is just some annual leave. I'll flit back up there soon enough. My job at Broadcasting House – I can't tell you how important it is. They really can't do without me. And I'm used to being away, remember. I was at school in Austria for three years.'

Jessica was keeping up with her, matching her strides. It was dark now, in the gaps between the trees in the orchards, even though the sky was still pearly.

'It's really quite extraordinary, this war, in London,' Jessica said. 'Each morning I wake up, glad to be alive. Sometimes alone, but not always. During the day, you could easily think that we were at peace, walking through Regent's Park, across Bloomsbury Square. It all looks the same as it has always done. But at sunset, the sirens start. And at any moment, it could all end.'

Eliza glanced at Jessica and saw that her perfect face was sincere and solemn. And, hearing her speak, she felt sympathy. It made her see Jessica anew suddenly. Perhaps she could, after all, be her friend. She seemed to have changed. Perhaps Vienna and the BBC had done her good.

Forstall came into view and Bingley would be tutting, looking at his watch. At the front door to the Stour wing Jessica paused.

'It is so lovely to see you again, Eliza, this is such a treat. We must have fun together, like we used to.'

In the full beam of Jessica's smile, Eliza was struck by her unconscious sense of entitlement. In essence, she had not changed one jot since they were children. Eliza wanted to laugh at the thought of her demanding that they have fun. Instead, she suggested Jessica go through and see Nick while she delivered her message.

'Ah, I see what Dad was saying. The War Office certainly have taken over, haven't they?' said Jessica, turning into the kitchen. 'Oh, what a charming little home you have. Nicholas, dear Nicholas! Guess who?'

At the salon door, Eliza handed the phial to an exasperated Bingley who tore off the seal and began to pluck the rolled-up paper from the inside, ordering Fisher to make ready at the Morse machine. He thanked her and shut the door.

Eliza went back through to her parlour to find Jessica sitting daintily in an armchair, lifting her chin and widening her eyes expectantly while Nick poured out tea and handed her a plate of biscuits. She'd removed her cloak and it lay in a sweeping wave of blue over the back of her chair. Her Jaeger suit was couture, the plaid skirt had a perfect kick pleat. Eliza was amused that little dollops of mud had adhered to the toes of Jessica's boots. The biscuits Nick was dishing out were her mother's last precious batch before the next butter ration. And there it was: a sour memory, a knock and the pain from one of Jessica's pale, delicate but sharp knuckles.

They only had two armchairs, so Eliza stood by the door, an interloper in her own parlour.

'How is your leg these days, Nick?' Jessica was asking.

'I still have a limp.' He sounded proud as he handed her a brimming cup.

'Which leg was it?' she asked, and, as Nick indicated his right knee, she reached down and brushed his trouser leg with the ends of her fingernails. Two rings of red blazed on his cheeks.

'You must have been brave to stay so long in London,' he said. 'Have you seen the latest headline? Poplar nowhere near you is it?'

Bingley knocked on the door. 'Sorry to bother you, Mrs Staveley, but I need you for the message you just brought in.'

Jessica looked up in curiosity at Bingley and said expectantly, 'Good evening.'

When he did not acknowledge her, Jessica countered with, 'Well, I'm sure an introduction will be forthcoming in good time . . .'

Eliza, relieved and supressing a giggle, followed Bingley quickly from the room. As she closed the door behind her, she heard Jessica continue, 'Dad insisted I came home this leave, Nicholas, or he would stop my allowance. He doesn't want me dead under the rubble.'

Nick said, 'None of us do, Jessica. None of us do.'

Eliza threw Bingley a look as she entered the salon and closed the door. Bingley locked it behind her. The blackout was down and pools of lamplight were trained over the bank of four desks in the centre of the gleaming floorboards, each with a telephone, a typewriter and pots of pencils and stacks of papers sitting on the top in regimented rows. Filing cabinets, broad plan chests and shelves of directories stood in the shadows, along with a solid, cast-iron safe that was chained to the wall. Fisher was poised over the Morse code machine, a shaft of light dazzling his Brylcreemed hair, glinting off his spectacles. The room had a sense of purpose and Eliza thrived on it.

She slipped into her chair and carefully unrolled the flimsy slip of paper that Bingley had handed her. She read the scrawled words carefully, meticulously, and set to work.

Stumbling just once on the dialect, she translated the Breton-French quickly: *Maquis cell, codename:* Homard, *Saint Malo. Intelligence: enemy troops railway operations incoming, north west, two days hence.*

She spun a sheet of paper into her typewriter and touch-typed the message in seconds, and handed it to Bingley. 'Germans are moving troops into Brittany,' she said. 'Two days from when this message was sent. It's dated two days ago.'

He swore and handed the paper to Fisher who had already started sending his code. Bingley sat down on the chair beside Eliza and stuck his pipe between his teeth.

He waited for Fisher to finish and in the calm moment that followed, he said, 'It really is against protocol that Miss Castle walked over with you while you were delivering this message. The messages are to be brought to us by a member of the Home Guard – her father is one, for God's sake – or yourself. *By* yourself. Castle – and you, Mrs Staveley – should have insisted on this.'

'The phial was sealed,' Eliza assured him, but her eyes widened in self-reproach, her scalp prickling uncomfortably.

Bingley struck a match and stoked his pipe. Thick, oily smoke puffed to the ceiling, making her eyes smart.

'Yes, the phial was sealed,' he said, 'but even so, I will be having words. I know she's Official Secrets and all, with her job at the BBC, but these people on the ground . . .' He nodded to the slip of paper written in haste by a Normandy villager possibly crouched in the dark of a cellar or attic. 'They risk their lives. The bloody bird made it all the way back over the drink. I don't like the idea of us not following correct procedure. Think on.' Bingley got up, yawned ferociously and put on his mackintosh. 'Could have been a prize cock-up. God knows what Major Arlington would have to say about this.'

'It's too late anyway,' Fisher said, as the signal faded down the wire. 'Useless now. There is no hope of acting on it.'

Eliza swallowed hard, relief washing over her. She didn't want to put a foot wrong with these two, let alone Major Arlington. He had not been able to believe his luck when he had found a French translator right on his doorstep at the Forstall office and he had recruited her with a snap of his fingers.

She asked, 'And where is the major?'

'The rum old buffer has moved on to pastures new,' Fisher told her. 'We won't miss him. No one stays very long anywhere, anyway. We're getting a new chief. But don't ask who or when for we've not been told, as per.'

'I thought I had not seen the major in a while. One doesn't like to ask these days.'

She thought of Arlington's brutish and masterly control of the two civil servant boys. His sheer size was intimidating in itself and his thickset bulk was topped off with a completely bald, rather fat head.

Fisher lit a cigarette and put his feet on the desk. 'Farewell, Arlington,' he said.

Bingley unlocked the door and waved at them both with his pipe, making Eliza wonder why a man not out of his twenties should start such a habit. Why didn't he stick to cigarettes like everyone else? Perhaps to give himself a greater sense of intellect or maturity? He looked old before his time.

'Toodle-oo.' Bingley was despondent as usual. 'Have a good night, Fisher. Good evening, Mrs Staveley. And, thank you.'

They said goodnight.

Fisher, once the door was shut and they could hear Bingley wheeling his bicycle over the patio, mused, 'That's why he is so tetchy at the mo. He thinks he's in charge until the major's replacement arrives, so takes it all on himself. But, really, we both know it's me who runs the show.'

'In that case, Fisher, should I be fetching you a cup of tea?'

'How about a brandy?' He grinned. 'Oh, no, don't look like that. I did not mean Mr Staveley's. War Office issue – in the safe. Medicinal, of course. Join me if you like.'

'Best not. I need to get on and cook Mr Staveley's dinner. Oh, God, just remembered, we may have a guest.' She opened the door. Jessica's voice in the parlour rose and fell, with Nick's laugh chuckling underneath.

'Miss Castle certainly looks the part, doesn't she?' said Fisher, stubbing out his cigarette. 'I bet she can't cook to save her life. But she could certainly snare a husband. Possibly someone else's.'

'That's your opinion.' Eliza gave him a quick smile to shut him up. 'And I think you can pour your own brandy tonight. Call me if you need me.'

'I'll use the broom to bang on the ceiling, shall I?' Fisher began to laugh.

'Do that again and Mr Staveley will have you court-martialled. He's a sergeant in the Home Guard, you know.'

Eliza could hear the faint tapping of Fisher working the Morse code machine in the salon below as Nick started to initiate sex in their darkened bedroom. But instead of the noise annoying her, she was glad of its distraction. She could place her mind elsewhere while Nick fumbled with her.

Since the disastrous wedding night, Eliza resolved to be compliant and patient. But she wondered if the joy that she'd imagined, ever since that snowbound sledging day, would ever happen for her. Whatever he did or did not do under the covers left her dry and cold. She wondered about the passion that Jessica enjoyed up in London, the lovers who aroused her, teetering on the edge of danger, of death. Wondered if it would ever be hers.

As another wave of bombers tailed off towards the dawn, she woke, lonely and wilting in confusion, her mind fixed on Lewis, wondering if he was alive or dead, her pillow wet with tears.

Chapter 9

1941

'So pleased it's just the three of us this afternoon,' said Mathilde, slicing into her freshly baked sponge and laying a slab onto Martyn's eagerly held-out plate.

The cake was an experiment. Mathilde wanted to see how well it would turn out made with wholemeal flour – white being so very scarce – just an ounce of sugar, and preserved plums mixed in for sweetness.

'Just the three of us, Maman?' Eliza asked. 'What do you mean?'

'Don't look like that, Eliza.' Mathilde looked peeved. 'As grateful as I have always been to Morris and Sybil and how they have always looked after us, I sometimes like to remember that we were our own little family once.'

Eliza poured the tea and gave her mother a smile of agreement. She, too, had been relishing this stolen afternoon spent alone with her mother and brother. What better thing to do on a cold, dark January day?

Nick and Morris were at the brewery office. Fisher and Bingley were keeping themselves to themselves in the salon next door. Sybil was busy with the WI in Canterbury. So with the manor empty and chilly, Mathilde had come over to the Stour wing and they had spent the morning baking.

'That big old house has that certain echo when nobody else is home,' she had said. 'It makes me shiver somewhat.'

'Do you miss Nunnery Fields?' Eliza had asked, taking the cake from the oven and piercing its centre with a skewer.

'A little.'

Eliza smiled at her mother's accent: *lee-tal.*

'I love Forstall. Always have. But it's the silly things I miss: the smallness of it,' Mathilde had said. 'The neatness. Feeling cloistered, enclosed. Not so much to clean!'

They called Martyn over to have his tea when he arrived home, and they had sat during the fading, frosty afternoon, a little like renegades, drawn close to the fire in Eliza's parlour, gently nattering, blankets pulled over Mathilde's and Eliza's knees. Martyn, home for a couple of days' leave, rejected the offer of a blanket.

'Because I'm not fifty yet,' he uttered, his face beaming cheerfully in the gloom.

Eliza suggested that he better not let Sybil hear him say that.

'How are the staff doing next door, anyway?' he asked. 'Behaving themselves? Keeping mum like we're all urged to?'

'Who knows what goes on behind that closed door,' Mathilde mused.

'As long as they keep as quiet as mices,' said Martyn, thoughtfully, 'then we'll all be fine.'

Eliza laughed. She loved it when he said *mices*. When he was a boy, and they called him Tintin, he could not fathom what the plural for mouse was.

But would they be fine? The delicate hope that she often felt at the start of a new year was absent this year, despite the newspapers being fairly quiet and nothing much happening as all sides pondered their next move. Even Morris's statement that only a fool moves his army in the winter did not relieve the weary, nagging dread. For, if that was the case, then what would happen in the spring?

But when Eliza looked at Martyn taking an enormous, enthusiastic bite of cake – his eyes wide with wonder at its taste – her spirits rose. He was dressed in warm flannel trousers, the jersey that Mathilde had knitted him for Christmas and his woolly scarf. A pleasant change, Eliza decided, from his flying suit or uniform.

'I think the cake is a success, Maman,' she said, 'for Martyn can hardly speak.'

Mathilde took the compliment. 'I'm just wondering how our little house might be faring in this cold snap. Morris was going to see if he could pop over today, to check. Would be awful if the pipes froze.'

'Do we not have evacuees there?'

'No, those ones went home to London,' Mathilde said. 'They couldn't bear not being with their own. Mad fools.'

Eliza thought of her home, snug within its terrace, with the view out the back to the cathedral. She imagined briefly that the rooms were preserved as if she'd just left them, quiet and ordered and waiting for her return. But then, she reminded herself, another family had been living there, and Forstall was now her home.

She'd learnt very quickly how everything can change. On that cold December day more than a year ago, she'd left her childhood home, and in the space of half an hour, her life had turned around just like the car sliding on that icy road, her world spinning off its axis. She'd lost so many of her possessions, the objects that she had attached her life, her happiness to. Objects that, in the absence of her father, had given her stability, were scattered and broken.

Chilled by a rush of cold sweat, she took a ragged breath to calm herself, hoping that her mother and Martyn had not noticed her discomfiture. She glanced up at the mantel. Nick had moved her three china deer, shoving them along carelessly so that he could display the new carriage clock his parents had given him for Christmas. They were not arranged as they should be; the large one had tipped over. A wave of rage rose hot into her throat, the depth of her anger pinning her to the chair.

When she felt she could move, she got up and went quickly to the window and took out her handkerchief to wipe off the condensation, hiding her face from her family. The air was cooler here and she breathed it greedily. The tenuous daylight was disappearing swiftly; the blackout would have to come down. Through the criss-cross of tape across the panes, she saw that the lawn was cold and saturated, the flower beds brown and broken down. She concentrated on the window of Morris's study, which was at right angles to her parlour window. All was as it should be: desk neat, papers aligned, his pot of pens glinting in the faint sunlight. Some mornings, Morris would catch a glimpse of her in her parlour and wave her over, so that she could share some of his precious coffee. The room was empty now, of course, for he was busy at the brewery, but she stayed where she was, gazing across the little corner of the garden, letting the supreme orderliness of Morris's study calm her down.

Presently, she turned back to the room with a smile. 'The cake really is delicious, Maman.'

'It is that,' Martyn chipped in, evidently not noticing the way she had absented herself from the conversation. 'But I could murder for some cheese toasties.'

'You're wanting your sweet and savoury the wrong way round as usual.' Eliza laughed easily now, delighting in her brother's company. 'It'll be a week, remember, until you can have one of Maman's cheese toasties again. There's no getting around the ration.'

'Not even for an officer pilot like me.' He licked cake crumbs off his fingers.

'They feed you well at barracks. But not as well as I try to feed you here,' Mathilde said, then paused, glancing at the window. 'Oh, heavens, is that who I think it is?'

Leonard Castle bustled past, his small steps making his short, uniformed frame waddle somewhat. His forage cap was pulled down over his oiled hair and his sharp black moustache twitched when he saw that they had spotted him. Soon enough, they heard him knock at the door.

'God, he does fancy himself, doesn't he?' said Martyn, helping himself to another slice. 'Worse thing Morris did was promote him in the Home Guard. I should remind him, he's just a *brown job*. For goodness' sake, Eliza, don't invite him in. He'll eat all our cake.'

'I have no intention of inviting him in. He most probably has a message for the boys, anyway. But that may mean that, for me, tea is over.'

She went to the front door and found Mr Castle in full flow with Bingley, who was leaning against the door to the salon, arms folding, nodding blandly as he listened.

'. . . damn fool. Made me look a right Charlie. Deal, they said. Pick him up from Beach Street, the seafront. Must have missed him. Gone in the wrong direction; I don't know the town very well. I went round the block umpteen times. Saw that castle from all angles, I tell you. Suffice to say, your new commander is not with me and cannot be found. Won't be joining you today.'

Bingley muttered blithely, 'I'll make a few telephone calls. See if I cannot get this sorted.' He called over his shoulder, 'Fisher, telephone HQ, will you.'

Leonard, his cheeks blazing, muttered, 'It's a right ruddy mess.'

'Not for us, Mr Castle. Er, sorry, *Sergeant*,' Bingley added, with a nod to Leonard's uniform. He gave Eliza a whisper of a smile. 'You can stand down, Mrs Staveley. There's no carrier message. And this muck-up is not your problem.'

Leonard looked at her, his puffed-up frame softening as he removed his hat. His crooked teeth showed in a broad smile.

'Ah, Eliza.'

She endeavoured to be amiable. 'How is Jessica?' she asked.

'Oh, she's forgotten about her old dad. Having a roaring time, last I heard from her, which was just after Christmas. Got to accept it, I suppose. Flown the nest well and truly. Never know what's going on with her. That girl is so secretive. Always has been. Inscrutable, don't they say?'

Bingley nodded vaguely, looking bored.

'Well, good to hear she is enjoying herself,' said Eliza unconvincingly.

'Is Madame Piper with you?' asked Leonard. 'I'd like to pay my regards. Might as well, now I've trotted over here.'

'She's resting,' she said, straightening her shoulders.

Leonard Castle certainly didn't believe her because they could all hear Mathilde's soft laugh drifting through from the parlour.

'Give her my best anyway, won't you?'

He flashed a look of barely suppressed outrage, turned on his heel and left.

The garden was coal-black, the dark pressing on Eliza's eyes as she inched her way along the path that skirted the lawn. She'd put on her hat, coat and scarf for her expedition to return her mother's cake plate to the manor kitchen but, in doing all of that, had forgotten her torch. On this, the darkest of January nights, the soupy blackout was at its most intense. Cold crackled through the air, frost thickening on window panes. Her footsteps were crisp and clipped. She sensed rather than saw the manor house, the gables looming as a deep shadow, blacker than the sky. The stars arched over, frozen, their light faint, far away and of absolutely no use to her. Arms outstretched she felt for the bench, a landmark at the bottom of the steps that would lead her up to the terrace and the door to Sybil's kitchen.

Nick had gone to bed early, complaining of tiredness and headache, so returning her mother's plate was the perfect excuse for a breath of fresh air, some company, perhaps to be asked to stay for cocoa and a bit of supper with the Staveleys, instead of sitting in her parlour on her own. If Fisher needed her, he'd have to shout loudly.

She stopped. In the sheer darkness, she heard the chink of a heel against a stone and blindly turned towards the sound. Someone was there, on the terrace. Whoever it was seemed to be floating, unearthly, a dark mass that flickered and moved as her eyes struggled to adapt. Appalled suddenly by her fear, she lifted her hands involuntarily. The plate slipped from her fingers and splintered on the path.

'Who is it? Who's there?' she called.

'Eliza, Mrs Staveley. It's you, isn't it?'

'Who?' She was almost shouting now. 'Who is it?'

'It's Lewis, Commander Harper. Remember me?'

Eliza let out a breathless cry of disbelief.

'Goodness . . . *remember* you? Of course I –' Her words were round, like bubbles of joy.

He stepped towards her and in the darkness she distinguished his height, felt him standing close. She could not see his face, but inside her head, he was there: the man who she had wondered about, hoped had made it back across the Channel to the safety of dry land.

'Of course I do,' she finished evenly, careful not to give away the enormous effort it took her to keep herself steady, her voice neutral. 'But what in the name of . . .?'

'I wondered if I might run into you tonight,' he said. 'I've got a torch in here. Look, sorry you broke your – whatever it was. Hope it wasn't expensive.' His foot crunched on a piece of china.

'Well, really.' She attempted to sound cross but failed. 'You know you could give someone a terrible fright, creeping round here in the dark.'

He took a step closer. 'I told you, I'm a sailor. I can see by the light of stars. Navigate by them. That's what sailors do.'

'I know, but what did you tell me? What is it sailors do? Why are you here?'

Lewis's laugh reached her softly through the darkness. His voice made her remember his kiss all over again. She felt a warm shield draw around her heart, protecting her. She wanted to step away from him, but at the same time had a wild urge to move closer. Her eyes were adjusting steadily and she began to see his face.

'I've just met your mother and brother, and your parents-in-law,' he said. 'Delightful. What a splendid house. You mentioned how old it was. Oh, be careful. Where's that damn torch. Blast it, perhaps I should just strike a match.'

She heard a rasp and the flare lit up his face. Out of the darkness sprang the familiar jaw, the line of his chin. His eyes were quite black, searching for her.

'Don't tell me you're to be the new chief here.' She felt the momentary heat of the flame on her cheek.

'Well, I've had better welcomes than that.' He sounded affronted until, just as the burst of light faded, she saw his face soften and curve into a smile, his teeth bright.

'I really should clear up this mess,' she said.

'Nonsense, I'll get one of the boys to sort it out in the morning.'

The match went out and complete darkness pressed in again as he disappeared. She began to shiver.

She felt his hand on her arm, felt his finger move over the sleeve of her coat.

'Get yourself indoors, for goodness' sake, Eliza. It's too cold.' His voice then, in the dark, was low and protective.

She put out her hand and touched the leather of his jacket, the smell of it registering in her memory. This man had saved her life.

'So you've come on your motorbike?' she said. 'I didn't hear it. You've ridden over from Deal? I understand that Mr Castle mucked up. He couldn't find your house. I wonder, would you like some tea?' Her voice lilted with childish wonder. She sounded small and young.

'Yes to a lot of your questions, but no, thank you, to the tea. I must get to work. Just starting the night shift. Must relieve Bingley or he'll think I've been shot. Or deserted. Take care, now. Will you be all right?'

'Perfectly.'

'Perfect, you are.' He was gone.

She paused a moment in astonishment, hearing his steady footsteps retreat along the path and around the corner of the wing. The animal in her urged her to be reckless, to follow him. She made herself cross the dark patio, arms outstretched, to feel her way through the door and dive into the warm and cavernous manor kitchen. The range was glowing, the oil lamp stupendously bright. She shut the door and leant back against it.

He was always coming out of the dark at her. The place on her arm where he'd rested his hand was hot, alive and real. Her heart beat violently and she felt a soaring crack of joy. She covered the spot he had touched with her own hand, thinking, he is alive, he is safe and he is here. But her shooting delight suddenly plunged like a stone and into its place crept cold, brutal shame.

Lewis was wrong about her, so utterly wrong. For she had wanted to follow him. And, because of that, she was far from perfect.

Chapter 10

The radio was playing softly with the evening programme; the lamp was on and the room mellow with Bud Flanagan's sing-song, humorous voice. Eliza sat by the fire with *Jane Eyre* on her lap, trying to remember where she had got up to. She had not picked up the book since she'd packed it away at Nunnery Fields, before she left home. Before everything had changed. It had been a comfort to her, amid the terror of the crash – it had landed so close to her nose and she'd fixed her eyes on it while she lay trapped in the cold and silence inside the car. One corner of the hardback cover, she noted, was alarmingly crushed.

She tried to read, but the same sentence ran over and over before her eyes. The coals hissed and gave off their pure mineral scent. She started again, three times more, then stared, instead, at the wall. How very odd this was. For just the other side of her own parlour wall, under the very same roof, was Lewis.

She hadn't seen him since the night before when she'd encountered him in the dark. Her mother had assured her that even though the new chief had arrived so late, it had been no trouble at all. And he was really quite charming.

'So far,' Sybil had suggested. 'Remember it is early days.'

'The War Office fellows like to stay on our good side,' Mathilde had reminded her.

'Or what?' Sybil had countered. 'We can't put up much of a fight if they don't. I really hope they will remember to take off their boots if they come indoors. I specifically told Commander Harper to do so. And I'm sure we had a bottle of brandy in the sideboard, which seems to be missing now.'

Eliza had smiled. 'I think Morris may have donated it,' she told her mother-in-law. 'He said he was feeling sorry for Fisher the other day. They'd run out of the War Office issue stuff. And Morris knows he has a penchant for it.'

'More likely he should be keeping a clear head, then,' Sybil had snapped but then she had softened. 'Anyway, our new commander is easy on the eye, isn't he, Mathilde? Quite the gentleman. I might well forgive him if he comes in with his boots on.'

Eliza put her book face-down on the coffee table, got up and walked towards the wall, gripped by a peculiar desire to press her ear to the plaster.

She stopped just in time.

'Oh, for goodness' sake,' she said out loud, admonishing herself, and went quickly through to the kitchen to put the kettle on the range. She put her hand into her pocket and nervously tugged at a loose thread, wondering briefly if she should do some sewing; she had to while away another hour on her own. Nick was on parade at Wickhambreaux Parish Hall with the Home Guard. He would not be home until ten.

She glanced at the clock, took the kettle off the heat and opened the larder door for some milk instead. Cocoa would be more the ticket, she decided, and then an early night.

She heard the front door open and someone knock on the salon door.

'Message for you, lads.' It was Nick.

Eliza turned automatically to the kettle and set it back on the range. Her husband would want tea. She wondered why he was home early, but equally was showered with relief that he was. His presence would stop her restlessness, stop her pacing, stop her wanting to listen at the wall.

She waited, lifting the kettle again for it was making far too much noise.

She heard Lewis's voice and Nick's response, all pally and cheerful, telling him he was most welcome. The door to the kitchen opened and she turned swiftly. But it was Bingley, asking her to come through and translate something.

'Right now?'

'If you wouldn't mind.'

Fisher was working furiously at the Morse code machine and the tapping filled Eliza's ears as she walked in and sat at her usual desk, holding out her hand towards Bingley for the chit of paper.

She was aware of Lewis, aware that he had stood up, as any gentleman would do, when she came in, but she ignored him, dipped her head to the message, focussing only on her task. She worked with her pencil on a clean sheet of paper, the French words forming, translating and tripping through her mind.

From near the door, she heard Nick say with pride, 'I don't know how she does it.'

She did not catch Lewis's response and yet perhaps, somehow, she had done, for she felt her body relax, a smile form on her lips as she swiftly typed out the message.

'*C'est tous*,' she announced without looking towards Lewis. She sensed his eyes on her, watching her, his face still and solemn.

Bingley thanked her and Nick followed her out of the salon, extending his bonhomie to all the men and saying cheerio.

'Are you tired, dear?' Nick asked when she'd made him a cup of tea. He sat in his armchair in his khaki uniform and began to unlace his boots. 'You look rather pale and pinched.'

'All I need is a bit of fresh air.'

'It's rather chilly outside. Is that a wise idea? I'm going to go straight up after this.'

'I will just take a little turn on the patio. The cold won't bother me,' she assured him. 'It'll do me some good. The fresh air will get some colour in my cheeks. Help me sleep.'

Nick shrugged and reached for the evening paper.

She walked quickly out of the door and down the steps into the darkness. The river was bubbling invisibly, swollen by winter rains, the stars a fantastic sweep across the sky, a waxing moon luminous, large and high. The silence was immense. Eliza felt it like a physical thing that she could step into and lose herself.

'The blackout makes them brighter.'

His voice made her jump. She turned to see Lewis standing beside her and involuntarily began to giggle, relief spinning through her blood. She was quite giddy.

'Not you again,' she said, softly.

He stood by her side, at a polite and decorous distance from her.

'The stars,' he said. 'They're brighter.'

They both looked up into the heavens, their eyes wide. Eliza was struck by the deepness of the sky but distracted by Lewis's proximity. She was aware of the gradual, gentle tenderness linking them. And it needed no mention. The bond had been forged all those months before in the wreck of the car. And it was theirs. Treachery rose like a warning siren.

Lewis broke the silence. 'When we *last* met, I think I omitted to tell you that I am in the navy. The lifeboat *High Hopes* is just for when I am on leave. And when Dunkirk kicked off, I happened to be off duty. I organised my crew myself. Couldn't be bothered to wait for orders.'

'I've heard you referred to as commander,' she said. 'That's pretty good going.'

'Well, I won't be seeing much of boats for a while. They want me here.'

'So I gather. In plainclothes. Are you undercover?'

She turned her head to see him smiling as he continued to survey the sky, studiously ignoring her question.

'See that star there,' he said. 'The brightest star?'

'Indeed, yes.'

'That's Polaris, the pole star. When I'm at sea, all I need is a sexton, a good eye and that star. I can go anywhere.'

'I know about the stars, Lewis,' she said.

This was the first time she had addressed him by his name. And with it, she'd crossed over, felt closer still.

'Well, tell me this . . .' he began.

In the darkness she turned to him. Her eyes were adjusting to the night; his face appeared as a shimmering pale oval. He looked serious, rather cross.

'Why did you not tell your husband that we had met before? Just now, we had a little chat in the salon before Bingley called you in. I mentioned Mrs Stratton, the house in Ramsgate, the night I spent there on the sofa. He knew nothing of it. I felt a right fool. He was a gentleman, however, and reckoned that the whole episode, dealing with the evacuated soldiers, had been so traumatic for you that you had wanted to forget the whole thing.'

'I could not forget that night,' she began quickly, desperate to explain. 'And before that, the crash . . .'

A cold breeze picked up, coming in across the fields. It ruffled her hair, chilled the back of her neck. She felt she was hurtling towards an inevitability. A hard and serious certainty that was difficult to explain, even to Lewis. She took a deep breath to steady herself, wringing her hands together, trying to warm them. Her heart beat hard in confusion.

It was some while before Lewis spoke again. 'He is proud of you, I could tell.'

'He is my husband, so I suppose he is.'

'He doesn't know, does he?'

'Know what?'

'You haven't told him that it was me.'

'You?'

'That I helped you both after your car crashed.'

'It slipped my mind, it – I didn't know what to tell people, because I didn't know where to start.'

Lewis made a noise that told her he didn't believe her. 'I find that rather hard to –'

She interrupted him. 'Please listen to me. It's far too . . . too important to share. If I share it, I no longer have it. Do you understand? The memory of it . . .' Her voice broke. She didn't trust herself to say another word.

When Lewis spoke, his voice changed. It seemed to Eliza that he was refusing to understand her. 'It's too late to tell him now. It would sound really very odd.'

'I've done nothing wrong,' said Eliza, believing it.

Silence settled between them. She was aware of his breathing, steady and strong as he gazed out into the night. She felt astonished then that they'd had an argument – a short, sharp altercation which would have been perfectly normal if they had been lovers.

'That is a bomber's moon,' he said eventually. 'It would make the Thames look like a ruddy landing strip. But it is quiet tonight. Unusually so. Almost as if there is no war going on.' He looked at her through the darkness.

'That's what I keep telling myself,' she said, her voice unnecessarily high-pitched. 'That it isn't going on.'

'But it is going on, Eliza, isn't it?'

She did not answer him. Instead, she turned on her heel and went back indoors.

The next morning, she woke to a delicate pink sunrise and a hoar frost thickening on the naked branches, transforming even the most torturous stalks, the soggiest piles of brown leaves, into beautiful sculptures. The clear, cold, starry night had left its calling card.

Shivering, she got the fire in the kitchen going after a fashion and began to make Nick's breakfast to set him up for his day. Once he was gone, she thought, she'd have her own breakfast, read a few more pages of *Jane Eyre* by the fire before she tackled the laundry. If she kept busy this way, then Lewis would surely drift from her mind. But she didn't have a lot of hope, for he'd be arriving any moment to begin his shift next door. She could not escape.

She followed Nick to the front door to say goodbye.

'It's been rather quiet recently,' said Nick, putting on his coat in the vestibule, indicating the salon with a dip of his head. 'Wonder if you might spare some time for the brewery. There is a stack of paperwork. Tax accounts need going through.'

Eliza could hear the soft hum of the wireless, tuned into the World Service, through the closed office door.

'I can't possibly leave them. What if they need me?'

Nick flinched at her reaction. 'I meant, bring the paperwork home here,' he said slowly, as if she might be incapable of understanding. 'You can sit at the kitchen table with it. You'll still be in earshot.'

She felt the fire of her blush sweep her face. 'Of course. Silly me.' She tried to laugh.

Nick looked puzzled, hesitated, then leant in to kiss her modestly on the cheek, barely touching her.

'Cheerio, then.'

Her relief, as she closed the door on him, was tangible, its intensity frightening. She'd left her book in the parlour. The blackout was still down and the room in darkness. Crossing to the window, she tripped on Nick's boots that he'd dropped there the night before. She uttered a mild curse and kicked them into the corner, then opened the blackout and pulled the curtains, revealing the sunny, frost-speckled garden.

Glancing across the garden, her view obscured by the crisscross of tape, she noticed that Morris had also removed his blackout and was already sitting at his desk, bright and early. Perhaps he was not going in to the brewery with Nick today, she thought, and straightaway began to look forward to a mid-morning cup of coffee with him. Another distraction, she thought, another means of avoiding Lewis.

Through the clear, cold air, she heard the muffled ringing of Morris's telephone and idly watched him as he answered it, his pen poised over his notepad. His hair, she noticed, was glossy and wavy in the sunlight. He didn't appear to speak to whoever was on the line, but merely listened. After some moments, he threw his pen down, slowly placed the receiver back in its cradle, stared at the telephone, and left the room.

Eliza saw a robin scuttle from beneath her window and over the gravel path to dance across the sparkling lawn, making the tiniest of tracks in the frosty white. She watched, amused, hoping the bird was not too cold and wondering if she could spare some breadcrumbs. A terrible waste, she knew, to feed the birds, but as long as Sybil didn't notice . . .

Out of the corner of her eye she saw Morris come back into his study, bringing her mother with him. She watched through the windows, vaguely amused that it was like viewing a silent film, trying to gauge what they were saying.

Morris gestured that Mathilde should sit down. And when she didn't move, he *made* her sit down. He knelt before her.

Mystified, Eliza craned her neck as far as she could to peer through two distorted window panes, squinting as the sun on glass dazzled her. What on earth was going on? She concentrated on the back of Morris's neat head, watching for clues. He appeared to be relaying something to her mother; something of earnest and slow-forming delicacy.

Suddenly, Mathilde recoiled. Her mouth widened into an ugly hole. She tilted her head back and raised her fists to her face.

Eliza froze in shock for half a moment, before turning and running across the room, out of her house and around the end of the wing. It wasn't until she reached the lawn that she realised that she was in stockinged feet and the icy ground was tearing at the fabric, burning her soles. But she ran on. The robin scattered, raising the alarm. She could hear her mother screaming.

She reached the patio and burst through the back door, thumping across the kitchen, across the hall. Only then she realised that her mother was calling for her brother. Screaming for her brother. But Martyn was on duty. He had left at lunchtime yesterday. He wasn't at home.

Eliza opened the door to the study and burst into Morris's book-dark, sequestered room. They both turned sharply and in horror to face her.

Morris spoke quickly, his eyes wide and bright. 'Eliza, Audley Stratton has just telephoned.'

Mathilde, her mouth moving with silent unformed words, reached both arms out to Eliza, imploring her, begging her. And as she walked towards her mother, reality smacked her with an almighty blow.

Audley Stratton has just telephoned.

She saw the sudden truth in her mother's eyes, the bloody, deranged truth. Her knees buckled and blood drained from her veins. She sank down, trembling, and crouched on the floor at her mother's feet.

Part II

Evening Star
'herald of darkness'

Chapter 11

There was no funeral, for there was no body.

A month after it happened, Morris arranged a memorial service at the church. Mathilde would not agree to it any sooner. 'Just in case they find him. He's out there somewhere. He must be.'

Eliza pressed Bingley, until he reluctantly told her that some wreckage and a slick of oil had been spotted a few miles off the coast. No sign of the crew, just a couple of life jackets and a tail fin.

It was best she knew, she convinced herself, as this unspeakable picture projected itself onto her mind. She needed to place him somewhere.

The church was busy, murmuring with low voices. Eliza walked in under the cold, stone arch and helped her mother find a seat in the front pew. She was confronted by the mass of concerned faces: villagers, neighbours, all saying the usual thing, then looking quickly the other way. Half of Manston was there, the other half on duty. She spotted a gaggle of tearful WAAF girls, dabbing delicately. Lewis sat in one of the back pews next to Fisher and Bingley, but she refused to look at him. She did not want to see what he had for her in his eyes. Instead, she linked Nick's arm and walked stiffly beside him to her own seat.

The dusty organ cranked wheezily. A boy from the village sat on the stone flags pumping madly at the handle as they sang three laborious hymns. Eliza scanned the service sheet and froze when she saw her mother had chosen 'O God, Our Help in Ages Past'. But when it struck up, and the hollow singing started, she was perplexed and then relieved that her eyes remained dry. She did not, could not, cry.

As the congregation exited, it made an awkward little gathering outside. And before Eliza could slip past him and escape, the vicar ambushed her, clasped both her hands in his and made comforting noises. She opened her mouth to thank him but could not speak. She quickly pulled her hands away, darted from his ministrations and walked alone across the churchyard.

Snowdrops were scattered like a sprinkling of little white beacons around the lychgate and Eliza was drawn towards them, their innocence and vulnerability shivering in the cold. She remembered Martyn telling her, as they waited here on her wedding day, that he would always look out for her. She remembered his macabre comment about the way bodies were rested under the gate before burial. She could hear his voice, chattering and cheeky.

Morris will buy you a headstone, Martyn, she told him inside her head. So me and Maman will know where you are, where to come.

She looked up just as the sun came out to sparkle across the grass, expecting some sign to brighten her spirits. But all she felt was a realigning of her numbness, the bleak, grey cloud expanding further inside her, blotting her out.

Two elderly men from the village had drifted from the scattering crowd, making their way to the lychgate, and had nearly caught her up. They were old coves with their Sudan medals gleaming on their top pockets and, in the quiet chilled air, their voices, high-pitched and geriatric, carried.

'Too right, Jim. We've been giving it good and proper to the Eyeties in North Africa. Blasted them out.'

'Yes, we got the blighters. But it will be Rommel next.'

Eliza didn't catch the conclusion of their commentary on the theatre of war in the desert, but she knew that, for them, Martyn had simply become one of so many. People unconnected to him, she realised, had already ceased to care. As the old men shuffled past her, doffing their hats in courtesy, trembling panic drew like mercury into the void inside her. The mystery of death was inevitable, unavoidable. And Martyn, in his innocence and in his wisdom, had known.

Eliza stood alone in her parlour a few hours later, staring from the window. The sunny spell from earlier had faded. The garden was grey and drab. She closed her eyes, placed her hands on the sill and leant her forehead against the glass. The coldness of the pane seeped into her skin, and she allowed it in. She wanted to feel it, feel something.

Her mother had been given a tablet by the doctor and gone to bed. Sybil had insisted that Eliza stay with her and Morris in the drawing room in the manor, to keep warm by the fire. But

Eliza told her she wanted, also, to sleep. Nick, barely speaking to her, his shoulders hunched, his chin down, had left the Stour wing half an hour earlier, saying he was going for a walk. It was quiet in the salon next door. Bingley had the day off and Fisher had taken Jessica to the pub after the memorial service.

Eliza peeled herself away from the window and walked unsteadily back through her kitchen. She knocked on the door to the salon.

Lewis answered it. He stepped back for her to enter and closed the door behind her. He stood apart from Eliza with delicate courtesy, waiting for her to speak. He tilted his chin in question, his eyes searching her face.

'Don't ask me how I am,' she said, not looking at him. 'Just fix me a drink.'

Lewis took Morris's brandy from the tray and poured two fingers into a tumbler.

'The service was beautiful,' he said, handing it to her. 'Traumatic, but beautiful.'

She sipped, wincing at the strength of the spirit. People drank brandy when they were shocked, didn't they? The vapours ballooned up her nostrils, burnt her throat and made her temporarily giddy.

'Please give me some work to do.'

He suggested she take a seat at one of the desks and then turned to the safe. She automatically stared at the opposite wall to give him privacy while he dialled the lock and shuffled around with some papers.

'I've been working on this,' he said. 'Perhaps you will help me.'

He laid a large sheet of paper before her, holding it down at opposite corners with a stapler and a paperweight. On it was marked a single point on the far left. And this was joined with straight lines to a series of other points, which fanned out across the page, creating an irregular trapezium-shaped pattern and resembling an exercise from a long-forgotten geometry lesson. Next to each point was written a codename. Lewis had drawn a compass point in the corner complete with a little flourish, pointing North. Eliza had never seen Lewis's handwriting before. It was neat and curvaceous and pleased her momentarily.

Eliza stared at the document, baffled briefly, but her numbness and her fatigue made her too resigned to ask what it was, exactly.

'What would you like me to do with this?'

'I need you to make a copy of this diagram,' said Lewis. 'But onto this much smaller piece of paper.' He pushed a lettersized sheet of tracing paper towards her across the desk. It was covered with a faint grid, like graph paper from a mathematics exercise book.

'Of course.' She reached for the pot of pencils.

'Accuracy is paramount,' he said. 'The scale, you see. Can you do this?'

'Why can't you?'

She looked up at him. His eyes narrowed, turning opaque as he was thinking.

'I can, but I think it will take your mind off . . . If I tell you how gravely important this is, perhaps you will focus. For a while, an hour or more, you may be able to stop thinking about Martyn and –'

She interrupted him. 'I see. I will do that, so . . .'

'You don't want to know what it is?'

'I've no need to know,' she said, straightening the sheet before her, rearranging the paperweight a little. 'Will you pour me another brandy?'

He picked up her empty tumbler. She took up the ruler and sharpened a fine, hard 2H pencil, testing the point by pricking her finger with it, momentarily savouring the sensation.

When he placed her refreshed drink at her elbow, she said, 'I'm sure this is a job Bingley would enjoy. But I think Fisher will not have the patience. And his eyes are not so good. We might have to have the lamp on soon, Lewis. It's getting dark.'

'Bingley and Fisher know nothing about this.'

She looked at him, surprised. 'Then I am honoured that you trust me.'

'Of that there is no doubt.'

Eliza heard a catch in his voice, but did not see the expression on his face because he had turned to the windows.

'Have you noticed,' he said, drawing the first of the many blinds around the triple-aspect room, 'that it is not dark so early in the afternoon these days, and the birds are beginning to build their nests.'

Eliza had recognised the subtle shift in time. The season had moved on but that meant, she realised, that she had also moved further away from Martyn. She'd left him behind in the winter and soon it would be spring. She gripped her pencil, swallowing hard to compose herself. Peering past Lewis at the window she noticed a luminous, lonely point burnt steadily in the indigo sky, just above the darkening western horizon.

'Is that the evening star?' she asked.

'Indeed, yes,' said Lewis, and his voice took on a playful edge. 'But I dare not mention to you that the evening star and the morning star are one and the same – the planet Venus. As you, of course, know all about the stars.'

'No, you dare not mention that.'

But she had not realised. And his smile told her that he knew this. Of course he did.

With the evening sky shut away, the blackout down, Lewis switched on the lamp, and in the soft yellow glow, Eliza bent to her task and concentrated. Her mind began to clear, miraculously, as she focussed in on the work. The brandy worked its magic. She felt the flesh on her face relax, the knots in her neck ease a little. The smaller map began to take shape at the tips of her fingers, a carbon copy of the original.

Lewis sat at his own desk and began to type a report. Eliza worked steadily, checking the scale of the larger diagram to transfer it to the smaller sheet of gridded paper. Her handwriting was not as neat as Lewis's but the code names she annotated onto the drawing began to amuse her: Mustard, Haricot, Onion, Stoat . . .

'Very inventive, these code words are – very *rustic*,' she said as she broke off to sip her brandy.

Lewis looked up and beamed at her, delighted. 'Glad you think so.'

She felt as if she was plotting a course, starting with Swede at the far left, moving on a fraction to Mint, and then branching out to Haricot to the west, Mustard a little to the north west.

She put her pencil down. 'Hold on a moment. When I've taken his morning coffee into the study, I have heard Morris on the phone to Leonard Castle mention 'mustard' quite distinctly, and quite often.'

'What did you think it was?' asked Lewis.

'Not sure,' she said. 'Any communication with Mr Castle is either a little bit bizarre or a little bit uncomfortable for us ladies of the house, so I just accepted it as the former, I suppose. Didn't think much of it, until now. Is it to do with the Home Guard? The pigeon loft? Oh, are they pigeon names? Oh, no, sorry, don't tell me.'

Lewis was amused. 'You'd not make a good spy, Eliza Staveley, that much I can tell you.'

Footsteps approached the Stour wing across the patio and the front door opened.

'Ah, that must be Nick,' said Eliza, and suddenly the reality of the world outside moved in to menace her again. She sighed in resignation. 'I must go up and see him. I must go to him.'

Without a word, Lewis gathered up her paperwork and was securing it in the safe as she left the salon, closed the door and followed Nick up the stairs.

Her husband sat on the end of the bed still in his coat, hands deep in pockets. His pale face was down, his cap shielding his eyes. The end of his nose was red-raw from the cold.

'Did you go far? It looks as though you did. Would you like some tea?'

Nick looked up at her, his grey eyes vacant and bewildered.

'Bingley didn't want to go far,' he said. His voice was flat and neutral.

'Bingley?' Eliza asked.

The explanation struggled out of him. 'I went for a walk with Bingley.'

She sat beside him and tried to hold his hand. His fingertips were stiff, unyielding, not returning her touch. He did not look at her.

'Would you like to come downstairs to the fire?'

He shifted bodily and turned away. All Eliza could see of him was his back, stiff and cold.

'Stop with your questions!' He grunted hard, disguising a sob, covering his face with his hands.

She recoiled. 'But we've hardly spoken. Hardly had two words since it happened. I want to know how you feel. For you to know how I feel. I need to tell you. Talk to you.'

'Not at the moment, no. I don't want to talk about it.'

Panic assailed her, as if she'd been cut loose and had left her moorings. As if Nick had severed the ropes. Fear burnt and chattered inside her.

Fighting it with all her might, she blurted, 'He was so looking forward to his next ration of cheese. He loved Maman's cheese toasties.'

Nick turned his head slowly to look at her, his eyes sharp with desperation. 'What *are* you talking about?' he said.

A snap of anger propelled her to her feet. 'I'm talking about my *brother*,' she cried and ran out of the door, slamming it behind her.

On the stairs, she paused. She heard voices below in the salon. It sounded like Jessica had returned with Fisher. Eliza walked slowly down the stairs, her spirits drowning.

'Shan't I have any peace?' she uttered to herself. She could not face seeing anyone, particularly Jessica.

Voices could be heard coming from the salon.

'. . . simply dreadful isn't it?' This from Jessica. 'Poor Martyn. That poor boy.'

Jessica had known Martyn since he was a child, but her words, it seemed to Eliza, were insincere. She was speaking as if she, herself, should be comforted.

Eliza made to hurry past the door and dive into her kitchen when she stopped in the vestibule, confounded, as Jessica rattled on.

'My friend, you know Susan in the WAAF, works at Manston. Well, let me tell you, the stuff she hears through her headphones. It doesn't bear thinking about. So awful. Sometimes, she hears the pilots screaming.'

Eliza clenched her fists, grief shifting to rage. She pushed the door to the salon open. Jessica and Fisher turned in surprise to look at her.

Lewis saw the look on her face and stood up abruptly.

'You silly cow,' he threw at Jessica. 'Why can't you shut up!'

Eliza did not utter a word but turned and ran out of the house into the darkness, across the patio and around the corner of the wing. She stopped abruptly, aghast and sickened. Cold sweat drenched her collar. The violence of her despair made her double over, terrified that she was going to vomit. She panted against the agony that cut through her mind like flares flashing, blinding her. Inside her head, she heard Martyn screaming. She pressed her hand over her mouth to stop her own cry.

Lewis came up behind her and instinctively, without hesitation, she turned to enter his embrace. His arms held her, swaying them gently. His cheek resting against hers. His hand smoothing her back. He whispered over and over that he was sorry. An extravagant sob broke from her, at last, and she pressed her face into his neck as her tears spurted.

'There it is,' said Lewis. 'There it is.'

She was crying, at last. For the first time since Martyn's death. He continued to hold her until the weeping dwindled.

'Take me to Canterbury, Lewis,' she whispered into the wool of his jacket, which was wet from her tears, hiccupping back a sob. 'I want to go home. Martyn's not here. He is simply not here. I want to go home.'

The road was so dark and the night so black that she missed the spot where they'd crashed, where Lewis had found them. Every time she'd travelled on this road, in the past year or so, she'd looked out for it. But now it barely mattered.

'You'll have to give me directions,' Lewis said as they neared the outskirts.

It was gone teatime; the city was quiet, the streets empty, the people of Canterbury keeping to their hearths. Eventually, he turned into Nunnery Fields and pulled the car up. Eliza's childhood home was in darkness; the windows blank, shuttered.

She got out of the car and stood on the freezing pavement, trembling.

'What did you tell Morris?' she asked him.

'That I needed his car on War Office business. As you could expect, he didn't ask any more. I could hardly have put you on the back of my motorbike.'

'I would not have cared.'

She opened the front door, stepped into the cold, dark house and took a tentative breath. She smelt dried lavender.

'The blackout's down, which is a blessing. Is the electricity on, I wonder?' Lewis asked, shutting the door behind him.

Hearing his voice, here in her childhood home, seemed normal and comforting. Suddenly, she was safe.

'I don't care about the electricity,' she said. 'For I am home.'

Tears began to fall again, blinding her and scorching her cheeks. And with them, a sense of relief, of a passing.

She felt her way into the front parlour, her eyes adjusting gradually to the darkness. Her mother's old furniture emerged out of the shadows. She hoped that the evacuees had cared for it and polished it like she would have done. Lewis found a stock of candles and began to light them, setting out the candlesticks on mantelpiece and windowsill in front of the blackout, illuminating the scrolls on the wallpaper that was as blue as a Picardy sky. She stood in the centre of the room and tried to breath normally, to think normally, and allow the relief of her tears to give her strength. But it was no use. A wail of grief shattered her and her strength failed. Lewis knew this, walked swiftly to her and held her tightly to his body. He cupped the back of her head with his hand.

'I'm alone,' she said. 'And I can't do this alone.'

'You don't have to. Oh, God, you don't have to.'

His lips touched hers with a kiss, hesitant, stolen and light – the twin of the one he'd given her at Angela Stratton's front door. He drew away and peered at her with eyes at their deepest green.

Eliza reached for him, wrapping her arms around his neck. She didn't want him to release her; she didn't want him to stop. She needed him to remove the shroud of grief that bound her. She told him with her kisses how much she needed him.

'Eliza,' he whispered, kissing her back. 'You are married.'

'It never feels like it,' she said.

It never feels like this.

Lewis reached down and tucked his arm under her knees, lifting her. She was flying, then, as light as down. He rested her on the sofa and tucked a cushion behind her head. The candles flickered in a draught, sending enormous shadows over the walls.

'Are you cold?' He began to unbutton her coat.

She shook her head, fascinated by him. She reached for his hands, touching his fingers one by one, wanting him to touch her in return.

'If you are cold, you must tell me. I will keep you warm.' Lewis knelt on the carpet, leant over her and cradled the back of her head gently in both hands, burying his fingers into her hair.

'Do you remember that I told you that your hair is the colour of treacle; rich, golden, sweet treacle?'

Eliza gazed up at him. She nodded, unable to speak.

'All those months ago,' he whispered. 'I thought this could never happen.' He gently kissed her throat.

Serene and liberated, Eliza lay on her mother's sofa in the candle-light, encircled by Lewis's arms, her blood soaring, her tears soft and quiet. At last, at long last, her breathing settled. She stretched and relaxed herself against him. His body, long and slender beside her, shielding her. Her mind blissfully adrift of thoughts. She was aware only of the sensations of her heartbeat, the sound of Lewis breathing.

'Eliza, my love . . .' His voice beside her was deep and lazy. He tightened his grip, held her closer. 'What are we going to do?'

She opened her eyes to look up at his earnest, querying face. He was obscured, in shadow. The candles around her mother's old parlour had burnt very low. One spluttered at that moment and went out. An hour or more, a whole evening had passed and she was lying naked in a house empty of her family, previously empty of life. Hard reality suddenly ran her through like a cold, steel sword and a great panic overwhelmed her. She sat upright and reached for her clothes.

'*Do*? What are we going to *do*? We must get back to Forstall, we mustn't be late. They'll be wondering. Oh, God –' She struggled with her brassiere, reached for her blouse, which was inside out, crumpled on the floor.

'Wait, Eliza, wait a moment, please, calm down.' Lewis moved slowly, reluctantly.

'We should not have done this. What was I doing? We should never have. Why did we come here –?'

She slumped back against the sofa in cold misery. She had been beside herself with grief; she'd needed her home. She'd needed her brother to be still alive.

In utter misery, she whispered, 'What will they think of me?'

Lewis reached for her foot, still encased in its stocking, and stroked the arch tenderly, separating her toes.

She watched him stroke her, remembering how, outside the wreckage of the car, he had commented on her feet, her long, fine feet.

'They will think what they always have thought,' he said, gently coaxing her. 'They don't have to know.'

In sharp anger, she pushed his hand away and fumbled for her shoes.

'Lewis, I can't do this.'

'Eliza . . .?' He reached for her, trying to pull her back beside him. 'We'll find a way through this, to work this out.'

She glared down at him. 'You feel invincible don't you, Lewis, after all the things you've done? Rescued men from beaches, sailed under fire. Yes, you're very brave, aren't you? Well, I'm not!'

He stood up, caught hold of her. He pressed his chin into her shoulder.

'Brave, am I?' His voice was muffled against her skin. 'I'm not such a hero. Look at me now. I'm in love with you. Have been since the day I pulled you from the car. I see you nearly every day. And yet I can't have you.'

'Don't touch me, Lewis,' she snapped at him, extricating herself.

She turned her back on him, dressed quickly.

'Take me back home, will you,' she said.

Lewis began to dress. He walked slowly around the room, snuffing out the remaining candles.

'This could be better than you think,' he offered her, as candle smoke began to fog the air. He was standing close to her as the shadows of the room pressed in.

'Better than this?' she said, her voice clear as a bell. 'How can it ever be anything other than just *this*? Lewis, this can never happen again. I will not be your mistress.'

Chapter 12

Hurrying along the footpath away from Leonard Castle's farm, message phial tucked deep in her pocket, Eliza felt a surprising caress of softening air on her face. Raw, wet earth glimmered under new, fresh sunlight and buds dotted the trees with precise and luminous green. Birds were rustling and nesting, singing a different tune. Around poles in the hop gardens, young tender vines began to curl skywards. The morning chill had lifted and promised a fair and sunny day; the season had turned a corner. But in her bones lay the miserable chill of winter. Despair trailed after her, caught up with her, however fast she walked, however hard she tried to shake it off. The breeze across Leonard's fields quickened and Eliza, too weary to fumble for her handkerchief, let it attempt to dry the tears running down to her chin.

She met Fisher on the lane outside Forstall wobbling on his bicycle homeward to his digs in the village, his shift finished.

'Chief is in a foul mood,' he told her, stopping himself with a heel in the dirt. 'Nearly ripped my head off earlier and all I'd done is dropped a bleeding file on the floor. Thought I better warn you. Not sure what the answer is: a great interception of intelligence or a good night's sleep.'

'Possibly that's something we all need,' she said.

Fisher glanced at her and immediately averted his eyes. She self-consciously brushed the back of her hand over her tear-stained face.

'Indeed.' He nodded to the phial that she was now turning over and over in her hand. 'I hope this new message will be fruitful, for all of our sakes. It is hard work for all of us, I know. But you particularly look like you need a rest, Eliza.'

His wide-eyed bespectacled sympathy caused a new bubble of despair to erupt in her. She knew that he wanted to talk about Martyn.

'Yes I do, Fisher, so very much,' she uttered briskly, fixing on a wide bright smile. She turned to go, bidding him goodbye before he saw her face dissolve.

Lewis was on his own in the salon. She faltered in the doorway as he stepped back to let her in.

'Bingley is sick,' he said, with a weary blankness around his eyes. 'What have you got for me?'

She handed him the phial and watched as he broke the seal, easing out the message chit.

'It's *Homard* again. Will you?'

Evading his eye, she slipped into her chair, held out her hand for the paper. His fingertips touched her palm and she flinched.

'Sorry . . .' he uttered.

A confusion of desire and misery burst through her body, and all of her strength was concentrated on keeping calm, remaining at her post, ignoring the sickening fluttering in her stomach and the spinning compass in her head. She did not trust herself to speak. Instead, she forced her mind to clear, to focus on the scribbled French sentences on the crumpled piece of paper and bend to her task.

A month had passed since the night at Nunnery Fields; a month in which she had tried to gather together and parcel up her reeling spirits as best she could, and yet they still littered the ground around her. But so far she had been able to avoid being alone with Lewis. Either Bingley or Fisher were usually at their desks in the salon, sometimes both of them. Eliza had kept her head down, remained engrossed in her translation tasks, barely speaking to anyone. Words exchanged with Lewis were polite – mainly *please* and *thank you*. Her face remained stiff and blank on the outside, while her pain and guilt continued to boil inside. Exhausted by her efforts, her strength draining from her flesh like melt-water, she left promptly at the end of her duties, slipped next door to her parlour and wept in private.

Wading through misery, she had not seen how Lewis might be faring. But now, as the clock struck five and she began to tidy her paperwork, she stole a glance. He was reading a file, hand pressed to forehead and a deep line between his brows. He was skimming the words, turning pages, some two at a time. His expression was lost and bewildered. His eyes flickering aimlessly. She recognised the barely concealed fury.

'Lewis, go easy on Fisher,' she said, her voice breaking the cloistered silence of the room. 'He is still so young, remember. Finding his feet.'

Lewis looked up at her, startled. He let out a short burst of shaking laughter.

'I don't care about Fisher. I don't care much about anything else at the moment. Apart from one thing.' He shut the file and walked to the filing cabinet. Stuffing it in, he closed the drawer smartly. 'I'm thinking about asking for a transfer.'

Eliza jolted in her seat. She kept her eyes pinned to her desk, terrified that he would read her expression and see her turmoil.

'They won't let me, of course, but one can still ask . . .' He slumped into the armchair. 'Eliza . . .' His sigh petered out into a groan. 'You make this so very hard for me.'

She looked up at him, squinting. 'Hard for you?'

'Don't you realise?' Lewis was aghast, his eyes darkening.

'No, *you* don't realise.' She cut him off. She could not bear to hear him speak of his anguish. If she witnessed it and acknowledged it, she would crumble. 'You don't realise that I have never – not *ever* – felt anything like I did that night with you. And it wasn't just that night. Before and since . . .' She struggled, her eyes stinging. Her words tumbled out in a dry whisper, 'I have not *done* that, like that. I didn't know that it could be so very –'

Lewis watched her. A spark of joy crossed his face. 'Eliza, you see, I want us –' he started.

She snapped him shut. 'Lewis, I am married to Nick. And so this can never happen. I don't want to talk about it anymore.'

She did not want to feel anything, not a jot. So much safer that way.

'I want to work,' she announced, her voice lifting. 'I'm going to finish copying this damn map of yours if it takes me all night.'

His voice broke with weariness. 'If that's what you want?'

'It's not what I *want* . . .'

Eliza picked up her pencil and sharpened it furiously, feeling the burden of Lewis's stare. She shuffled papers unnecessarily, feigning interest in them. Eventually, he stood up, unlocked the safe and drew out the sheet of paper along with the smaller copy, pushing the paperwork towards her across the desk.

She had quite a way to go but it was still reasonably early, and Nicholas was on parade with the Home Guard for the evening. Lewis went through to her kitchen to make a pot of tea. He retreated to the armchair while she continued her work, carefully duplicating the details of the diagram onto the reduced version.

When the clock on the shelf chimed eight thirty, she rubbed the back of her neck and flexed her fingers. She double-checked her last, carefully drawn line.

'It looks to me, this map of yours,' she observed, 'just like a constellation. But instead of the names or numbers for the stars, we have our own codes: jolly old Mustard, Haricot, Onion, Stoat.'

Lewis roused himself, stretched, and came over to the desk to look over her shoulder.

'A constellation, you say. And you are absolutely correct.' He smiled down at her, admiring her. The tautness of his face had faded into a delicate veil of acceptance. 'To the untrained eye, anyway. In fact, the diagram represents the constellation of Andromeda. Not particularly accurate, and before you say anything, that is not a criticism of you, but simply how it is, for our purposes. An astronomer would realise that it is entirely unscientific.'

He went to the filing cabinet, rummaged around in one of the drawers and took out a map of the county of Kent, the same size as Eliza's smaller diagram. He placed this over the top of the map, lifting it up and setting it back down a few times so that she could see what he was showing: that the constellation points were represented on the map by various features – farmhouses, hamlets, river banks and woods.

'What does this mean?' She looked up at him. 'No. Don't tell me. You really shouldn't.'

He was standing close to her, as close to her as he had been in her mother's parlour. Madly, wildly, her heart thumped at the base of her throat. He considered her for some moments.

'I'm going to tell you because I trust you absolutely. And because I love you.'

She gave him a quick shake of her head. 'Just tell me.'

Lewis walked to the salon door and locked it. He sat down beside her, his mouth close to her ear. The heat of his breath coursed over her skin, making her resolve break into fragments. She closed her eyes and listened as, in a whisper, he began to impart to her classified information. He told her that the points on the map, on the 'constellation' that she had so painstakingly recreated, indicated the foxholes of secret auxiliary units. These were the men, mostly from reserved occupations, enlisted all over the county of Kent under the auspices of the Home Guard.

'But, unlike our blessed old Dad's Army, they are young, fit men. Guerrilla fighters,' Lewis whispered. 'They're your dairy men, farmhands, the men you see now setting the frames in the hop gardens. They're your railway men, teachers, factory workers. They've been trained in covert operations and sabotage and cold-blooded killing. If the Germans invade, they are tasked with rising up out of nowhere to scupper any advance. They will do anything to hinder the enemy. Blow up railways and telephone lines, ambush German platoons. Murder. And no one outside the circle knows they exist. No one knows of these hideouts – their operational bases. Their wives don't know; their friends don't know. This is top secret. You must tell no one.'

Eliza drew back. She stared at Lewis, at the map she had created over many long days of painstaking work.

'Our very own Resistance?' she whispered. Then she was appalled. 'I wish you had not told me.'

'I trust you. Absolutely.'

'Morris? Leonard Castle?'

'They know only so much. They don't know of the existence of your map. Quite clever of me, I think, to ask you to draw it. For you are the least likely person in this whole set up to be suspected.'

Eliza smiled. 'Not sure if that is a compliment or not . . .'

He grabbed her hands, folded his own around them. Their warmth was a sudden comfort. She wanted to collapse into his arms. She sensed his body tense up, his muscles flex as if he was fighting himself.

'Please don't ever accuse me of treating you badly.' His eyes were wet, appealing to her. 'What you said to me, at Nunnery Fields. That terrible, nasty thing about me expecting you to be my mistress. That isn't how I feel, or want it to be.'

Eliza heard her front door open, a footstep in the vestibule. She rose to her feet, shook her hands free.

'Well, how is it, Lewis?' she whispered. 'I have my husband and my family. Everyone at Forstall. And since Martyn . . . They need me. I can't do this.'

'I understand, and I am so sorry. I just can't help myself.'

Eliza stared at his face, remembering the first time she'd seen him: the shadowy figure through the shattered windscreen, the peculiar warmth of his leather jacket, his body as he leant in over her, rescuing her. She loved him. But the meaning and the consequences of that were unthinkable.

'I love you completely,' he said.

She gently pushed at him, entreating him to move away from her. 'I wasn't myself,' she said, 'when Martyn died. Who would be? I let myself be comforted by you. That's all that happened. We had both better try to forget it.'

She watched the sting of her words twist his features. As he turned from her and went to the safe, locking the map – their map of stars – away, his shoulders slumped, his head drooped. He looked like a different man.

Lewis said, 'Whatever you think of me, Eliza, this is your work. This map is of supreme importance. I don't think you realise the magnitude of it.'

As she reached for the door handle, her hunger for him tore at her. Fresh sorrow wormed its way through her. She did not dare to look over her shoulder to wish him goodnight. She kept her eyes down and her back to him.

'I have to go now, Lewis,' she said. 'I have to cook my husband's supper.'

Chapter 13

Angela Stratton insisted on buying the tickets for everyone, counting out her pound notes onto the copper tray at the ticket office window. 'If our little trip is not a morale booster in the eyes of old Winnie, and therefore absolutely permitted, then I'll eat my hat.'

She nodded towards the poster on the waiting room wall, which warned: *Is your journey really necessary?*

Mathilde started to fish in her purse. 'You are far too generous, Angela. Now, if you'll just let me . . .'

But Angela wouldn't hear of it. 'You'd need to thank Audley, anyway,' she said, insisting that Mathilde put her money away. 'He's a very benevolent husband. Lets me get up to all sorts of mischief.'

'We know about your mischief, Angela,' Sybil said pointedly.

Angela let out a peeling laugh and Eliza smiled, remembering Nicholas telling them about the infamous sardines incident, when Angela had been caught in the snug with Morris. The three of them sitting on the patio steps, drinking brandy, with the new and unknown war prowling around them. Martyn had still been a boy, a brave and trusting boy.

Sybil's voice rose competitively. 'Morris might well have also treated us but, as you know, he was very reluctant for us to go to London in the first place.'

He had certainly expressed his concerns. Even though the air raids had eased off, planes still flew over Forstall and the siren went off every other day. But they were getting complacent. The siren in Canterbury had even been changed so that people would take more notice of it.

But Sybil had insisted. 'We have to have our yearly shopping trip, Morris my dear. It's our ritual. And we can't live half-lives. Then he really will have won, won't he?'

Morris couldn't argue with that and so their little party of four, all in best costumes and hats, clutching their tickets, were being ushered by Angela through to the platform.

Eliza wandered along with Mathilde to the end of the platform so that her mother could admire the displays of daffodils shivering brightly in the breeze. As she bent to catch the delicate fragrance, Eliza studied her: best hat and shoes – her feet would be killing her before lunch – and proud tilt of her chin; her fragile, carefully-placed smiles. And every moment, thinking of Martyn. The trip was for Mathilde, really; paid for out of misplaced guilt by Wing Commander Stratton.

She heard vibrations on the tracks and the level crossing cranked into life. Engine smoke peeled upwards and the train pulled into the station. There was the usual bustle of finding first class – Audley's treat again – the opening and shutting of doors, until, sitting in their own carriage, Angela breathed a sigh of relief. She looked across at Eliza and Mathilde.

'My, my,' she said, 'you two could be sisters, sat there side by side.'

'Oh, you do flatter so, Angela,' said Mathilde.

'It's your hair,' insisted Angela.

Mathilde patted the new roll that Eliza had pinned for her that morning, copying a photograph in *Home Notes*. She'd done the same for herself.

'Same colour, same style. You both look quite the thing. Don't look so horrified, Eliza.' Angela laughed and pulled out a paperback, while Sybil settled back for a snooze. Mathilde was watchful, scanning the countryside through the train windows either side, her eyes wide as if she was frightened of what she might see. Angela was wrong: Eliza hadn't been horrified. She rested her head against the seat and gazed out of the window, remembering Lewis in her mother's parlour plunging his fingers into her hair.

She would walk forward with Lewis into anything. He knew her, had been the only one able to soothe her when Martyn died. Nick had refused to speak of it, confusing her further with his dismissal.

How could she ever have thought that Nick's familiarity was love? That pleasing others was love? That growing up with Nick meant that they were in love? It was love, she supposed, in a mild, comforting way. Nick was long-standing. And yet he made her feel entirely alone.

She shut her eyes and pretended to be asleep for some moments. When she opened them, satisfied that she was no longer going to cry, she noticed that her mother had got up to go to the ladies. Sybil was still napping. Angela put down her paperback.

'Are you all right, Eliza, dear? You're looking very pale.'

'Just a bit of motion sickness, I think. I'll open the window.'

'Yes, that'll help,' Angela smiled. 'Let's take your mind off it. Tell me how you all are at Forstall. How Nicholas is. I haven't seen him much, not since . . .' Angela's eyes moistened. 'Oh, God, how could I be so tactless?'

Eliza glanced fearfully out to the corridor for her mother's return.

'Don't worry, Angela,' she said. 'None of us have seen much of Nick. He and Morris work so hard at the brewery. And Nick has, how would you say it, withdrawn since . . .' She nodded towards the sleeping Sybil. 'I think it's the same with all of us.'

Angela opened her mouth to speak, her face heavy with concern, but Mathilde pulled the sliding door open and slipped back into her seat.

'Ah, so tell me, Eliza.' Angela brightened. 'How are things next door in the salon? A hive of activity, no less?'

Eliza flushed. 'I don't really know – how should I –'

Mathilde interjected. 'Eliza has no idea what is going on in there, and so she should not either. None of us do. All classified information. We let them get on with it.'

Angela assented to Mathilde's reasoning, giving Eliza a sharp, puzzled look.

Continually skirting around the subject of Lewis was so very hard. She turned her face to the window, aware of Angela's stare, and distracted herself by looking out for the auxiliary foxholes from her map, seeing the countryside in an entirely different way. And the guard who clipped their ticket? The signal man in his box? Could they be the everyday men that Lewis told her of, doing such extraordinary things?

As the train pulled into Victoria Station they stood, stretched, and collected hats and coats. They gathered beyond the ticket barrier with the station announcements echoing around them and passengers dashing for trains.

'I'm heading straight for Selfridges beauty counter,' said Sybil, checking her handbag once again for her coupons. 'Mathilde, is that where you want to go as well?'

'Yes, it is,' said Mathilde. 'But you wanted Simpson's, didn't you, Eliza?'

'So do I,' said Angela. 'So we can go our separate ways here and rendezvous later. We're agreed we'll meet at the restaurant on Lexington Street for early supper. The train home is at eight o'clock.'

Eliza turned to look as a familiar coil of blonde hair under a green hat caught her eye. A slender back and long, stockinged legs. Jessica Castle was standing on the far side of the concourse speaking earnestly to a tall broad-beamed gentleman in a trilby and overcoat, her chin tilted upwards, her gloved hands animatedly patting the air. Hurrying people blocked Eliza's line of sight for a moment and she moved her head a fraction.

The man laid a hand heavily on Jessica's shoulder and leant into her as if he was going to kiss her. In a flurry of confusion, she recognised the unmistakable bulky frame of Major

Arlington, his hefty size dwarfing Jessica, whose eyes, glaring up at him, were sharp with anxiety. She saw the deep folds of his thick neck beneath the back of his hat, his large fingers gripping Jessica's arm.

Eliza's bewilderment escalated. The major was far too old and ugly for Jessica, but perhaps she found his eminence and power attractive. Eliza baulked at spying on this unlikely lovers' tryst but saw, instead of a smooth, loving caress, the major's fierce eyes and flabby features stretched with anger. She realised it was not a kiss he was going to give her but a barely controlled teeth-baring tirade.

And Jessica burst out laughing.

In surprise, Eliza moved her hand nervously to her hat and, in that instant, Jessica noticed her. Her eyes widened in recognition. Eliza remained still, hoping that she wouldn't have to engage with her. But Jessica disregarded her. She dashed Arlington's hand from her arm, shook him off, turned on her heel and hurried away, melding with the crowd, her hat bobbing into the distance.

The major remained where he was, frozen with suppressed rage. If he were her lover, surely, he would have given chase, scooped her up to vanquish their tiff. But he looked like he wanted to kill her.

Eliza glanced at her companions, imagining the fuss and the unnecessary to-do if anyone else had caught sight of Jessica here on the concourse at Victoria. But no one had noticed. She peered once more to see Arlington, a good head and shoulders above most people, turn and walk the other way. She wondered what he had said, what he had done to make Jessica bright with momentary fear; a fear she broke by simply laughing in his face.

In the cab to Piccadilly, they passed bombed houses that were now tombs of rubble. The gaps in the rows resembled rotten teeth, and the dirty-white façades of Grosvenor Place looked brittle, ready to subside, just like the people on the pavements going about their business with uncertainty on their faces.

Eliza browsed, rather uninspired, the rails of clothes in Simpson's ladies' wear while Angela was assisted at some length in the lingerie department. The store was hushed, the staff miserable. London was grey and tired. Even the buses and taxis rumbled past the store with a drear, cheerless sound.

'This trip is supposed to cheer you up,' said Angela, who was at last content and laden with bags. She linked Eliza's arm, leading her towards the staircase. 'Look, let's go for some tea. Fortnum's surely will do us proud.'

As they sipped some astonishingly good Earl Grey in the sumptuous confines of the tea room, Angela grew serious.

'I'm very sorry I was so chatty about everything earlier. About the situation at Forstall. You must all be in such misery. It was unthinkable of me. I'm glad Mathilde did not hear me. But to you, Eliza, I apologise. You seem . . .'

'I'm fine, Angela,' said Eliza, measuredly sipping her tea.

'In that case,' Angela said, cheered, 'may I mention something altogether different? This has been bothering me for a while. I speak as a friend, you understand. A very discreet friend.'

'Whatever do you mean?' Eliza set her cup down, immediately seeing an old-fashioned look on Angela's face.

'Commander Harper is quite charismatic, isn't he? Such a startling coincidence that he has been stationed at Forstall! Now, tell me to mind my own business because this was before you were married, but that night at my house, the night of the evacuation from Dunkirk . . .?'

'Angela, nothing happened. Not like that. Oh, Angela . . .'

'I see,' she said guardedly. 'Again, I must apologise . . .'

A silence stretched between them. Eliza felt compelled to break it, to explain. 'We spent the night in the same room, yes, but nothing like what you are hinting at happened. We'd only just met – he needed a roof over his head – it was an unusual situation –'

'But he has a quality, does he not?' pressed Angela. 'He is so very handsome and charming. I've met him just twice. The first time being that morning in my own home. But why would he stay the night with you at my house, a total stranger, when there was a perfectly good barracks at the school for him to sleep at. A proper bed for starters.'

'Nothing happened,' Eliza insisted. '*Really.*'

Angela summoned the waiter, ordered another pot of tea. When it arrived, she lifted the lid and stirred the leaves. She milked the cups and set her teaspoon down. She sat back, quite still, and the scent of her Chat Noir perfume settled with her.

'And so why, my dear, and I mean this most sincerely, why did it look as though you were totally lost when I mentioned him just now? You look like you're in pain.'

'Do I?' Eliza blurted and tears fell out of her eyes before she realised she was crying. Angela waited patiently for her to compose herself.

'The reason I . . .' she began, realising in a rush that she had to explain. 'You see, I felt able to spend a night with him in your front parlour for I trusted him. I had met him before.' Eliza paused, teetering on the edge of truth. 'He's the *stranger*.'

'The *what*?' Angela leant forward.

'*Our* stranger.' Eliza faltered and fresh tears coursed down her face. She fumbled for a handkerchief.

'The man on the motorbike?' Angela sat upright.

Eliza mumbled through her handkerchief. 'He's the man who saved my life. Saved Nick's life.'

'Well, no wonder . . .' Angela looked relieved. 'Of course you must think highly of him. You must –'

Eliza interrupted. 'But no one at Forstall knows that he is the stranger. He is my secret. I've kept him a secret.'

'But why on earth . . .?'

Eliza looked at the older lady, at her perfect hair, her alabaster skin – lined a little, pinched in places, perhaps a bit too much rouge – her sharp, knowing eyes.

'Nothing happened in your parlour, Angela. But, this will sound all rather strange . . . I don't want to share him. He saved my life, you see, and he is . . .'

'You love him.'

Under the full beam of Angela's stare, Eliza lowered her head. She could not look up, and even if she could, she would have not been able to see her through her tears.

'My dear, this is not uncommon,' sighed Angela, ever prag-matic. 'Someone does something like that, something so heroic, and wonderful, you're bound to –'

'If you say it's normal *because there is a war on*,' Eliza mut-tered through her teeth, 'I will walk out that door.'

'No need for that,' said Angela. 'I'm telling you now. Look at me, Eliza Staveley. *At* me, Eliza. Whatever has or has not happened, you must think of your family, think of your husband. You care for him, I know you do. You've known him all your life.'

'Perhaps that is the problem,' said Eliza.

'You must forget Harper.'

'And you're qualified to lecture me?' asked Eliza, bolder than she expected.

'Do you want to survive this war?'

'Of course I do.'

'You won't survive if you don't have your home, your husband, your family. Do you remember I said to you once that even when you're married, a man or two may turn your head? You'll be attracted to him. So be it, but don't follow him. Do you understand what I mean? You can admire, but don't *follow*.'

Eliza looked at her.

'Am I to think that it is too late?'

Eliza remained perfectly still.

Angela sat back, stirring her tea, sipping and stirring again. The look of surprise on her face was replaced by pity.

Eliza lifted her cup. Her tea was stone cold.

'What now, Angela?' she asked eventually. 'What am I to do now?'

Angela motioned to the waiter, indicated that she desired the bill.

'Go home tonight and set yourself straight. Tell Harper you've made the mistake of your life and that there is no future with him. Make peace with your unsuspecting husband.' The pity on Angela's face did not falter. 'And, above all, my dear, make peace with yourself.'

As Eliza took her cinnamon cake from the oven, she heard Lewis's motorbike roar along the lane, peeling away from the manor, back to his house in Deal. It was Saturday; he had a few days leave and, fleetingly, she tried to imagine his seafront home, wondering if she'd ever see it.

Angered by the stupid futility of her thoughts, she plunged the skewer into the centre of her cake. She wanted to stop feeling this; to put an end to the tearing duplicity. She wanted to be brave.

Seeing how well her cake had turned out, a determination settled inside her. She felt suddenly, peculiarly at ease, confidence bubbling lightly. She switched off the oven and put the kettle on.

Nick called from the parlour, 'Cake smells good.' He sounded on the verge of cheerfulness. 'Are you making tea? Come and read the newspapers.'

'Ah, but let's not read about the war,' she called back. 'Can we not do that this morning? Let's read the funnies.'

She carried the tray through and he reluctantly folded away the paper. Immediately she knew he'd been forcing jollity.

Without his broadsheet as a shield he was uncomfortable. He sat quietly while she cut the cake, his pale face highlighted by two rings of red on his cheeks. She passed him a plate and he took it without looking at her. He could do with a haircut.

'Shall I get the shears out after lunch?' she asked.

'Good idea . . .' His words trailed off with ill-disguised boredom, his eyes flickering around the room.

Eliza remembered Angela and her cool advice.

'Nick,' she said weightily.

The change in her tone made him glance at her.

'I know it has been so very dreadful for all of us. And I, myself, I . . .' she hesitated, aghast that she found it incredibly difficult to speak. 'I realise that I have not been able to talk to you properly about Martyn.'

He flinched, crossing his long legs and hunching his shoulders.

'And I so want to talk to you,' she hurried on, generously, 'because I can see that you are terribly distressed too. Since it happened, you have withdrawn. It seems you have disappeared. That's how it feels to me.'

Nick's eyes were like shards of glass. He began to talk slowly, thoughtfully, 'You know, I don't think I've ever really been . . .'

Frightened suddenly by the hollow timbre of his words, Eliza whispered, 'What on earth do you mean?'

'. . . ever been here. With you, Eliza. Here with you.'

Nick's words cut her with a strange and illuminating truth. She swallowed hard and waited.

'You're right,' he said, matter-of-factly. 'What you just said. I think I disappeared a long time ago.'

She leant forward in her chair. 'Oh, Nick, no. But we are together. Remember what you said, that we'd get through this madness.' Confusion rose, sweating through her skin. She spoke quickly. 'Think back over all the years we've had, those wonderful summers when we were children. Such times! Remember the sledging? That was such fun. I've never laughed so much.'

Nick stared at her, his face as placid as a newborn's.

'You know, all I ever wanted was to be here with you and your family,' Eliza continued, hearing the shake in her voice. 'The war changed so much but we made the best of it. We belong here. I know I belong here. This is our home.' She stopped, remembering her return to Nunnery Fields with Lewis.

'Forstall is my home,' she declared bravely. 'We all grew up here together.'

'Yes, the three of us,' Nick uttered bitterly. 'You, me, Martyn. Wonderful, wasn't it? And yes, the war did change so much. It changed everything.'

She paused, trying to catch up.

'We got married because of the war,' she reasoned.

Nick pulled back, recognising something. 'Yes, I suppose you are right. If war had not been declared, I'm not sure I would have asked you.'

She recoiled. His words peppered her with sharp little stings. She got up, went to the mantelpiece and stood quietly with her back to him, reeling at his admission, trying to take a breath. With nudges of her finger, she rearranged her china deer so that they faced forward.

'Nick, I really think we must try together. Let's start again and try . . .'

An enormous sob split the air. She turned to see him bowed over in his chair, his hands covering his face. His back jerked violently; she saw tears falling through his fingers.

He tried to speak, but his voice cracked, and, gulping, he tried again.

'I loved him!' he bellowed.

Eliza gripped the mantelpiece. The huge hole Martyn left in her world, the grief he left her with, rose suddenly like a black wall.

'Yes, Nick,' she said, 'we all loved him so very much.'

Her husband lifted his face. His skin was streaked with tears, his mouth hanging slack. His eyes were screwed into slits of agony. 'You don't understand. None of you do. You don't understand this.'

'But I do, Nick. We are all suffering. That's why we should rally round. Help each other.' She thought of Angela saying: *Do you want to survive this war?*

'But I am queer. A fruit. Do you understand *that*?'

'Nick, what are you –?' Her bones turned cold. A sluice of nausea rose up her throat. She stared at her husband; saw a well of sorrow in his eyes.

'I loved Martyn. And he loved me. I believe he did. He did.'

'Martyn?'

'Yes, *Martyn*.'

Eliza tried to swallow. 'My *brother*?'

Nick said nothing. His eyes were opaque, pleading.

'So our marriage . . .?' She choked. 'Our *marriage* . . .?'

Nick dipped his head, cowering. 'I wanted to make it all right. Everything, all right. You were – are – so dear to me. I'm not proud of this.'

'But my . . . my brother . . .?'

She did not want to say his name, for he was her darling one, the boy she loved, put first before everyone. Her little brother. Her Tintin.

'He knew? Knew about you?'

'He loved me. He wasn't happy about it.'

'He knew our marriage was a sham?'

'He wanted you to be happy.'

'Call this happiness?' she declared. 'I am ashamed.'

There were no tears. She was dry, sore, her head pounded as if her skull was crushing inward.

'You must tell no one.' Nick rose to his feet. His tall frame stooped; he looked haggard. 'This is my shame, not yours. Eliza, can you give me that? Give that to me? Tell no one. Do you understand? Can you understand *me*?'

She looked at him. His hands were shaking, his pale face cracking. This was the man she had admired all of her life; who her mother revered, and who Martyn, of course . . .

Nick was wrecked; he was broken. 'I will be jailed,' he whispered.

She fumbled her way to her armchair, her arms reaching out in case she stumbled; her knees were straw, ready to collapse.

'I won't do that to you,' she said blandly. She sat down carefully, speaking precisely. 'I won't do that to our family.'

He uttered a cry and fell to his knees in front of her. 'Eliza I do love you, but not how you deserve. I'm so sorry. So very very sorry.'

He was close to her, at her feet on the floor. She leant backwards against the cushions. She couldn't bear him near her. She looked over the top of his head, staring through the window, seeing the lawn bright green in the spring sunshine, tender new buds on Morris's vines, the sublime yellow of the forsythia which was churning in the breeze. The day looked warm but she was cold, colder than she'd ever been her whole life.

'Get up, Nick.' Her nausea vanished, in its place an unspeakable void.

She stood and returned to the mantelpiece, her trembling fingertips patting at her china deer. Like a recurring nightmare, the crash happened again, flickering before her eyes, but this time slowly and with complete clarity. It ended finally, the noise and the terror vanished, leaving Lewis reaching for her through the shattered car window and setting her back on her feet.

She turned to face the room. 'Get up, Nick,' she said, measuredly. 'Why don't you make us a cup of tea? No, forget that. I think you better pour me a brandy. And make it a double.'

Chapter 14

1942

Clutching a blanket, flask of tea and torch, Eliza followed Nick, her mother and Sybil as they hurried across the lawn into the wilder part of the garden behind the shed and dipped into the low hole of the shelter. Fisher tucked in behind her, drawing the blanket over the door. The mournful, terrifying siren broke the scented, velvet air of the summer night. And they came droning in, hard and steady, the enemy breaking the bounds of their county, locating the ancient city, dropping incendiaries to shatter the dark and light the way.

Eliza huddled with Mathilde on the bench, which was topped with cushions and blankets. She flinched as the deep boom of the Canterbury ack-ack resounded in defiance.

'This is close. This is very close.' Fisher's face was indiscernible at the other end of the shelter. 'They're saying this is for Cologne.'

'Is that helping? Really?' Sybil said, her voice a tremor. 'God, I wish Morris would get down here. He says he can't. He simply can't sit here underground.'

'Where is he?' asked Mathilde.

'Sitting it out in his study,' Nick replied.

He squeezed in beside his mother, their matching fair, sandy hair visible in the gloom. He began to check if all the torches worked.

Sybil said, 'I told your father he was a fool. This isn't the trenches. It's our back garden. But he simply won't listen.'

'Well, we can only leave him be, Ma,' Nick said, harshly. 'What more can we do?'

Eliza peered at her husband. Just as she'd done many times in the last twelve months since his astonishing confession, she saw him anew, glanced at him like she would a stranger. He was supremely attentive towards her, unnervingly so. Excruciatingly polite, nothing was too much trouble. He skirted around her. Whatever he did, like now as he unnecessarily switched torches on and off, he seemed preoccupied, with a bland veneer over his features.

How far they had come from the moment Nick asked her to marry him. She remembered the dreadful news on the wireless, how he'd pulled her across the lawn away from their families gathered on the terrace. The crescendo of fear and misguided joy as he knelt to propose. The blackbird peeling away in the tree above her.

Sitting in the cold, damp shelter, she realised they were huddled on the very spot where he had knelt down and promised to care for her, to change her life.

The world was different now. She had resigned herself to duplicity and tore herself in two, between Forstall and Deal, and sometimes a hotel in Canterbury. Nick knew nothing of Lewis, and she wanted it to stay that way. For what would it do to the family? She was duping everyone, not just Nick, when, a year ago, she changed her moral compass and gave in to loving Lewis. Shivering – with fear or shame, she was not sure – she shuffled closer to her mother.

'Is it too early for tea, do you think, Maman?' she asked, pulling the blanket closer over their knees.

Fisher piped up, 'Never too early in my book. I need to keep myself awake, at any rate. Harper messaged through from London just before the raid started. He says I'm to check in once an hour at least. As soon as these fireworks are over, I'll probably go back inside anyway –'

He stopped, cut dead by a rumbling squadron passing low overhead. The noise was blanketing and thunderous. Deafened, Eliza felt it deep in her bones and dangerous panic crept through her. She was used to the others mentioning Lewis in an off-hand manner, and used to fixing her face into neutral while she listened. He had travelled up to the War Office in London a few days ago, had hoped to get back to Deal tomorrow. She wanted him here with her through these unending, mortifying hours. But if he was in this shelter, how could he possibly sit next to her and take her in his arms?

Her mouth suddenly went dry and nausea oozed up hot from her stomach. She managed to get up quickly and creep out of the shelter in time. Kneeling on the damp grass, she brought up her supper.

'Eliza!' called her mother. 'Are you all right?'

'I just need the lavatory, I'm fine.'

She rushed back across the lawn under the throbbing weight of the bombers in the sky. The midsummer night was a mere twilight, parts of the sky were as luminous as day. A false dawn glowed eerily red on the western horizon. Canterbury was burning. The silhouette of the manor loomed precariously out of the half-light at her. The bombers would see her there; they'd spot her so easily: a slight figure hurtling across the lawn. Fear – cold and primal – made her scuttle into the house.

She blundered into the lavatory, took deep, ragged breaths and bent once more to vomit. Bathing her face with cold water, her raw terror began to fade.

She found Morris in his study. He had not put down the blackout and was sitting in the gloomy light of the unearthly dawn. He'd been snoozing and when he heard her close the door gently, he started and sat up.

'Are you all right, Eliza?' He rubbed at his shoulder, his old war wound. 'Is the show over?'

'We haven't had the all-clear yet. I had to come indoors. Not feeling very well.'

'You look white as a ghost. You're shaking, girl. Don't let the buggers scare you.'

'But they do.'

'Come on, you need tea.'

He made them a pot in the warm kitchen, letting it brew on the top of the range before Eliza carried the tray back through.

'I'm having something a little medicinal in mine. Care to join me?'

She nodded.

In the quiet of the clock-ticking room, with the spines of hundreds of books emerging from the shadows, she sipped her tea and brandy. It was surprisingly good and her nausea gradually eased. She found her courage returning, little by little, breath by breath.

'You couldn't bear it out there, could you, Morris?' She tilted her head towards the window to indicate the garden, the shelter.

He shook his head. 'It's always with me. It's hard to forget,' he said. 'I wonder, sometimes . . . Ah, seems odd to harp on about it, when all this is going on. But I see other men the same age as me, in Canterbury, around the lanes, who must have been over there, too. And I wonder, how do you sleep? How do you manage to do this? Your everyday life? With all of *that* on your mind? For I know in hell, I sometimes cannot.'

'Do you want to tell me?'

Morris looked at her, his eyes bright in the gloom. 'There are some things that should not be told. Should not be known. By Sybil, Mathilde. By you. For they will spoil you.'

Eliza half smiled. How could she tell him that she was already so very sullied?

'And Ypres . . . That is one of those things. They say memory comes in senses. And it's the smell, you see. The mud. I *taste* it. And the noise, the filth, the cries of the men caught on the wire.

And the thought of being below ground, even in our own shelter out there . . . it's impossible.'

Morris took a large sip of tea, draining his cup. 'Oh, yes,' he mused, 'I garden all the time and I love the fresh, crumbling Forstall soil, the chunks of flint and chalk against my spade. Clean and healthy, it is. And I have the breeze around me, the trees above me. Trees, ha! What trees? They were all blown to hell along with us. Bones in the mud. But, you know, Eliza, the mud over there was not of this earth. It was putrid. It was, I would say, as death might be.'

He leant forward and poured more tea, adding another tot to his cup, inquiring if she required one. She shook her head.

'Your Papa was a reckless man, my dear. But also very brave,' Morris said. He stopped, swallowed hard. Eliza watched his bristled Adam's apple move up and down. 'And that courage is the reason why you are with us now. Here at Forstall. You, your mother and, of course, dear Martyn. I always hoped you all felt welcome and always secure . . .?' His voice trailed off with question.

'Are we safe now?' she asked, glancing out of the window at the lightening sky.

'This is Forstall,' he said. 'It will protect you. And, in return, we defend Forstall, we defend our land as we have always, always done. The enemy come and go, the years pass, and yet . . .' He lifted his finger to make her listen. The raid had subsided, and silence blanketed the air. Below the ticking of the clock was the gentle clamouring of the house: a scratching in the wainscot, a creak on the stairs, a drip of a tap.

'Forstall is alive and breathing. Can you not hear it?'

Despite her father-in-law's company and his comforting words, and the tenuous peace around her, Eliza felt as if fear had entered the room like a person. She needed Lewis, for he would make her fear go away. But she looked at Morris, and smiled and nodded.

'I hear it.'

'And can you hear our blackbird out there?' Morris asked. 'It must be nearly morning.'

Eliza listened hard and heard the song lazily and incongruously bringing in the dawn.

'And there,' Morris said, satisfied, cocking his head to the siren blasting over from the village. 'That's the all-clear. I'm going to go and see what those bastards have done to us.'

'The cathedral stands, which is a bloody miracle,' said Nick, coming back to Forstall with Morris at midday. Their faces were ashen, their clothes grey with dust. 'As does the brewery, and Nunnery Fields. But as for St George's, it's simply no longer there. It is as if they've changed the map of the city.'

Sybil made her husband and son sit down, brought them soup, tea and stacks of toast.

'You must be all in, my dears,' she said.

But Morris was looking at Eliza. 'Where are you going dressed like that? You were up all night, too. You need to rest.'

Eliza was tucked into her WVS uniform, her hat perched just-so, and was making ready to leave the house.

'Deal also took quite a hit last night,' she said. 'I told my chief I'd head over. I need to relieve the girl on the tea van.'

'I didn't hear the telephone?' Sybil said.

'She came through to the salon. Fisher took the call.'

Eliza believed her own wild lie. Fisher, indeed, had taken a call, but it was from Lewis. And he was home.

'Take care of yourself,' her mother said, walking out with her to the car, hovering around her protectively.

'I will, Maman.' Eliza got behind the wheel and pressed the starter button.

She glanced through the window. Mathilde's earnest face was long and drawn, her downturned mouth drooping with fatigue. Her gaze looked fractured. She was tired to distraction.

'And you need to do that, too, Maman. Please do.'

Her mother's stricken look stayed with her as she eased her little Ford along the narrow Forstall lane, brushing hedgerows, the tyres clunking over flints. And her guilt followed her as she turned onto the main road.

In the aftermath of Nick's revelation last year, she'd asked him to teach her to drive. He was compliant and courteous, of course, and hosted her jerking hesitant lessons along the lanes with good grace and humour. When he suggested he buy her a car, she'd replied with equal humour, 'But of course you will.' The car was the start of her freedom.

Last summer, when the buses to Angela's headquarters in Ramsgate became unreliable, Lewis signed off a petrol ration for her 'in lieu of War Office work'. She'd mentioned in passing to Nick, Morris, Mathilde and Sybil that she'd heard that the Deal WVS needed new members. As it was closer to home, she wanted to hand in her notice to Angela. After all, she could drive to Deal in twenty minutes. But she didn't do as many shifts in Deal as everyone thought she did and her duplicity deepened.

But the dangers of the night before started to blow away as she motored due east along the lanes on her way to the sea. They'd survived the raid; the relief was tangible and the exquisite day lifted her as she wound through villages of sleepy cottages and red-brick oasts. Through her open window she caught the scent of the hedgerows, the candy perfume of cow parsley and the earthy green of hawthorn. She glanced in her rear-view mirror, certain that she'd just passed Haricot, one of the foxholes hiding amid a lonely copse of willow. Two days before, she'd updated the map for Lewis, adding two more secret hideouts. And, on the top sheet, two more fictitious stars.

At last, Deal. She slowed down as she spotted the castle turrets standing out silvery grey against the haze of the sea and wondered how on earth it could protect them. Centuries ago, perhaps from the French or Spanish. Now, it was down to the undercover auxiliaries crouching in tunnels in the ground. But even then, they could only protect them from invasion across the sea, not from death raining out of the sky.

She stopped the car on Beach Street in the shadow of the tall, white terraces facing the sea. The deserted shingle was split in two by reams of barbed wire. Beyond it, little waves clattered onto the shore. The cordoned-off pier was silhouetted against the blue; the sun was in her eyes, seagulls cried with mournful voices, declaring the innocent beauty of the day. But the glorious summer's day she'd driven through was a mirage, existing to remind her of the life she had once had, that she could have had. It was the stuff of dreams, of childhood fantasies, for two streets up, houses lay as smouldering rubble. A gang of volunteers were bent to their dreadful task and the hoses of the fire services snaked across the road. The sight of it tired her to her core.

As she walked up the steps to Lewis's front door, a realisation suddenly flared in her mind. She noticed that her blouse buttons were straining and remembered that her skirt button had popped off last week. And as for last night's sickness. Could it possibly be?

She glanced again at the busy activity around the fire engine, and saw that there were plenty of WVS girls handing out tea. She whispered to them, to herself, 'I'm so sorry. I know I should be there, too. But this morning, today, I have to look after myself.'

She lifted the mat and fumbled for the key.

Lewis was waiting for her, sitting out in his little white-painted yard bright with sunlight. She could see the top of his head through the open back door, his dark hair lifting cheekily in the sea breeze. In the parquet-floored, white-washed passage that ran the length of the house, she paused. The glass fronts of the barometer and the clocks – tide and conventional – shone at her like familiar faces. He had not heard the door, did not know she was there.

She felt an unbearable movement inside her chest. Her life at Deal seemed to exist outside of her present, outside of the grinding sadness that had filled Forstall since Martyn's death. Nick had moved into the spare room in the Stour wing. No one knew or, if they had noticed, no one mentioned it. Lewis was there in the salon almost every day and life at Forstall was like bumbling through a stifling and unpleasant dream. But here, in Lewis's house, she was removed from the hard, headache-inducing work of the salon, and the lies she told Nick and her family. This was her refuge.

She stepped out into the sunlight and gently placed her hands on his shoulders, the warmth of his skin immediately present through the cloth of his shirt. He turned with a sigh of pleasure, stood up and embraced her.

'You're safe, thank God. You are safe.'

They kissed with hunger, with longing that brought tears to Eliza's eyes. Lewis tipped her hat off the back of her head and pushed his fingers into her hair. His hands went to the collar of her jacket, fingering the stuff of her uniform and began to feel for the buttons, quickly releasing them. He forced her jacket over her shoulders, discarding it on the ground.

Without a word, she pulled him back into the house. The spiral staircase twisted upwards, over three floors. They did not speak, saving their breath for the climb. At the final flight, the banister was replaced by a ship's rope by which they pulled themselves up. They landed, laughing and panting, sideways on his wide bed in front of the enormous window that looked out to sea.

'Been waiting long?' she asked him, kissing his mouth.

'Always too long.'

He took her quickly, not waiting to ask. She wanted to erase the horror of bombs, fire and death that had travelled far too close the night before. His face was serious, concentrated, almost in pain. She held him tightly in her arms.

They lay resting, Eliza with her head in the crook of his arm, sinking into the depths of the feather mattress, thinking of the life that may be sleeping now inside her. A cocktail of fear and excitement bubbled through her mind. Lewis lazily ran a finger over her collarbone and asked her if she was hungry.

'Terribly.' She sat up to tease him. 'Frightfully! I hope you have something in your larder.'

He looked at her, laughing. 'I'll see what I can rustle up.'

He made to go downstairs but, changing her mind, she pulled him back.

'Stay a while. Later maybe. Let's just be together . . . let's just *be*.'

She lay with him, gazing at the squares of sunlight over the low ceiling, listening to the shrieking of the gulls so loud, so close from the chimney pots just above her head. She loved this room, the freedom it gave her. But only once had she ever spent the night here.

Last December, when she'd slipped away from Forstall to steal an afternoon, a winter storm had swept in with the tide, rain battering the window, wind sucking at the rafters. She'd welcomed it, was exhilarated by it. The storm became her excuse. The rain was horizontal; it was far too dangerous on the roads to try to drive back. She'd telephoned home, telling Nick she was staying with the WVS chief and then curled up with Lewis, deep in the centre of his bed as night came down abruptly. She imagined she was cradled on a ship pitching through the waves, cast adrift but perfectly secure.

Later, he'd switched on the wireless and they heard the bulletin: Pearl Harbour bombed; the Americans were in the war.

'I think we both need a drink.' He'd gone to his cabinet where he kept the whiskey. Eliza teased him about stowing alcohol in the bedroom but as he explained, he didn't want to climb up and down three flights of rickety stairs every time he wanted a snifter. They'd solemnly chinked glasses and watched, felt, the ferocity of the storm as it rattled over the tiles.

'Let's hope it will soon be over,' Eliza had said. She meant the war, for she did not want the storm to die. She wanted it to keep her there.

The summer afternoon stretched on luxuriously. Eventually, Lewis went downstairs to cut some bread and butter. He had some cheese and shouted up that he could warm some soup. She didn't fancy that so he brought the cheese and a slice of apple pie that Sybil had pressed on him before his trip to London.

'It might be a bit stale,' he said.

She didn't care.

As he set the tray on the bed, she picked up his shirt to use as a dressing gown and rested against the pillows. Lewis sat at the end of the bed and thoughtfully cut into the cheese. She remembered the broadcast last December and how she had foolishly imagined it would all be over in a trice. From the look on Lewis's face some days in the salon, she knew how treacherous, how deadly, how difficult the state of everything was. And that pondering look was there now, as he took a bite of bread and cheese.

'I wonder,' he said. 'Have you seen Jessica Castle recently?'

'Goodness,' said Eliza. 'Why do you ask?'

Lewis gave her a look that told her she should not ask *that* question.

'Well, no, I haven't. She hasn't visited in a while. She is still in London I think. At the World Service as far as I know. So, no, I've not seen her in over a year. Not since . . .'

An image of Jessica spun into her head. Her pale hair under her green hat disappearing into the crowds. Her eyes bright with momentary fear and, despite this, laughing in Arlington's face.

'I saw her, actually, in London.'

Lewis looked up sharply. 'You did? When?'

'Last year. Gosh, I'd forgotten about it. When we all went on our day trip last spring. She was at Victoria. She saw me, but decided to ignore me. I was pleased she did. Her companion didn't look very happy.'

'Who was she with?'

'Major Arlington of all people.'

Lewis's face turned white. 'You're sure?'

'He is pretty unmistakable, isn't he? Although I only ever saw him a few times in the salon office, I wouldn't forget him. You know him, don't you?'

'That I do.'

'Major Arlington seemed particularly angry with her. I thought at first . . . this sounds strange, that they might be lovers. She seemed scared, but also in control, oddly. I'm sorry. I can't remember any more.'

Lewis raised his chin in acceptance. 'There's no need to worry,' he said, and yet his eyes betrayed him, for they were glazed with unease.

'Is it important?'

'Not particularly.'

She knew not to ask him anymore. She also did not believe him but forced herself not to try and work out the puzzles he must encounter, the secrets he must keep. Perhaps this was to do with Jessica's work at the BBC? Perhaps her skills were needed by the War Office? Perhaps she'd been approached but refused to work for them? After all, as Leonard Castle told anyone who'd listen, his daughter, with her linguistic abilities, was very much in demand.

Lewis continued to chew his bread and cheese, but his mind was not with her in the room. Eliza rallied herself, scrapping thoughts of Jessica Castle. She considered her own body's promise; their future.

'Have you not noticed something about me?' she asked, tearing at a piece of bread.

Lewis glanced at her, his smile weak and a little forced. 'Don't tell me you've been to the hairdresser's.'

'I did actually, yesterday. Well, she came to me. The lady from the village.'

'Very nice,' he said, concentrating on licking his fingers.

'Lewis, look at me.'

He glanced up from his plate, his eyes flickering over her hair. 'Like I said, very nice. I love your hair. You know I do.'

'Lewis, I think I am expecting your child.'

The knife fell with a clatter to the plate. His face changed colour: a quick blanch followed by a deep flush of red.

'Holy God.' He ran a hand over his hair. 'I've been so careful.'

He stared at her, examining her. His eyes dropped down the line of her body. She waited.

'But you . . . you don't look . . . When? Oh, God, when?'

'I'm guessing, but perhaps the beginning of November. I still need to see a doctor, but the signs are there.'

'But how are we going to . . .? Heaven and hell, what are we going to do?'

She stared at him and saw raw emotion littering his face. This was Lewis: the brave naval officer who rescued men from the burning beaches, who battled the waves, who navigated by the stars, could *see* by the damned stars. And yet he was floored by a tiny human no bigger than his thumbnail.

She stood up and went round the bed to him. He appeared to her little more than a boy. His questions were still falling from his mouth when she kissed him. She pressed his face to her chest and spoke without thinking. 'But I will not leave Nick.' She dipped her lips to his hair.

'What? You won't? What does he know?' Lewis's voice rose in panic. 'I can't look that man in the eye at the best of times.'

'Then you must.'

'But you will not leave him?'

'Our marriage is over. Was over before it began.'

Lewis did not understand. 'And still, you will not leave him?'

She took a shuddering breath, but would not allow Lewis to make her break her promise to Nick and reveal the world he lived in.

'How can I leave him? It's not what people do. It's not what I'm going to do!' She swallowed hard, thinking of Morris and Sybil, of her mother. 'The Staveleys have been so good to me. It would be unspeakable.' She stopped on the brink of a sob. She whispered, 'Lewis, please don't ask me.'

'Ask you what? To be with me. Live your life with me. Surely that's what you want?'

'You know that can never happen! I can never have *that* life!' she cried out.

She pulled away from him and went to the window, trying to overcome the frustrated beating of her heart by watching the waves on the sea, the benign protecting sea. She was with Lewis in his home by the water and yet the manor house tugged at her; everything inside it – its permanence, its protection – pulled her home.

'I cannot leave Forstall.' She jerked her chin in defiance. 'What would it do to everyone? To Nick?'

Lewis watched her with raw questions in his eyes. He enunciated carefully, 'So, Mrs Staveley, what will you tell him?'

His use of her married name stung her but she turned her face to him, to show him how brave she was trying to be. 'I will tell him that I had a fling with a pilot, who died. He would understand.'

'That's ridiculous. What self-respecting man would understand. I know I wouldn't!' Lewis shouted. He exhaled with anger. 'You've certainly thought this through.'

But she hadn't. The idea had come to her in a flash, and she surprised herself.

'Well, I can't leave Forstall,' he said. 'It is imperative I remain at my post and continue to take these messages from the French. I can't tell you how . . .'

Eliza whispered, bitterly, 'Of course you can't.'

Lewis looked dismayed by her sarcasm. 'Something is in the offing, Eliza. Something quite audacious is planned. I cannot leave.'

Staring out at the sea, Eliza placed her hand on her gently protruding stomach, ran her hands over the cloth of Lewis's shirt. She had always thought a baby would make her happy. And now she realised how fleeting any joy was going to be.

She turned to Lewis, opened her arms to him. 'Lewis, I'm not asking you to leave Forstall. That's ridiculous. I would not expect you to. We go on as we are.'

'Except come November there will be a child. And I will be the most rotten cad to walk this earth. Under the man's roof, for God's sake.' He shook his head, bewildered. 'And you expect that Nick will bring it up as his own? How on earth will he be inclined to do that?'

Eliza walked back to the bed, reached for him and cradled his face with her palms. She gazed down at him. 'Believe me, I can handle Nick. It's you I am worried about.'

She watched his anger erased by a tentative smile. 'You're worried about *me*?' His voice was softer now. She saw devotion deep in his eyes. 'I'm petrified for you,' he said.

He thoughtfully placed his palm on her tummy, carefully swept it upwards. He reached for her buttons. Eliza hesitated, pulled back for a moment, waiting to experience happiness again. It arrived momentarily, like a shadow.

Lewis pulled her down onto him, onto the bed, sending the tray and plates crashing to the floor.

Chapter 15

'That's settled, then,' said Sybil. 'A dinner party. Last weekend in August. We have to bring up our morale one way or another.'

Unusually, everyone was gathered for supper in the manor drawing room, seeking comfort from each other's company and eating buttered toast.

'A dinner party?' Eliza asked. 'Goodness. What a novelty.'

'We need smiles on faces,' Sybil said, pouring tea. 'Frankly, I'm not afraid to admit that I'm beginning not to be able to stand much more of this.'

The night before, Eliza and Nick had been called over to sit in Morris's study in the summer twilight as reports of the Dieppe raid came over the wireless. They'd all stood listening as the extent of the disaster unravelled. Morris had wrung his hands, muttering about them never being able to turn the tide and, with Canterbury all but flattened, what was the point of carrying on? Nick had been boisterous in his opinion that his father should pipe down and be stronger, have more guts.

Sybil had cried, berating her son for his attitude, vehemently disappointed in him, and Mathilde had put her hand on her son-in-law's arm and cautiously pointed out that after what his father had seen at Ypres, his nerves probably could not hold out as long as Nick's could. As Nick dipped his head and apologised, Eliza wondered if Dieppe had been the audacious plan that Lewis had mentioned. He'd only just got back from London and so she hadn't had a chance to ask him.

'We'll invite friends, neighbours, colleagues.' Sybil set down her teapot decisively. 'Fill that old mahogany table like we used to in the old days, when we were first married, Morris. I'm even going to bring out the silver candelabra. Nick, do you know where they are? I might need you on polishing duty.'

'Possibly in the attic, along with so many of the other things you have misplaced, Ma.' He went back to toasting slices of stale bread.

'Even Leonard Castle?' Mathilde asked. 'Will he be on your guest list, Sybil?'

'Yes, indeed, and Jessica if she is down from London.'

'Ah, Ma,' said Nick, amused, 'perhaps you are thinking of Jessica for Bingley, or maybe Fisher? I take it you are inviting all of the War Office fellows, Harper included.'

Eliza jerked her head up and caught Sybil's attention.

'I think Jessica has already been through Fisher,' observed Morris.

'Really, Morris, if you wouldn't mind,' Sybil scolded him, but kept her eyes on Eliza. 'And, Nick, I'm not sure of her taste in gentlemen, but think of the society she has in London. She'll probably have already set her cap elsewhere.'

'She probably won't come,' Eliza said, hopefully. 'She hasn't been home in ages. Why would she bother to traipse all the way down here for one dinner party?'

'I heard,' said Nick, 'that she quite fancies Harper, so there you are. She probably *will* traipse all the way from London.'

'Where did you hear that, Nick?' asked Sybil.

'Fisher, I think.'

'Ah,' said Mathilde, 'don't listen to him. He's the biggest gossip. But I can see it, actually. They'd make a handsome couple.'

As Eliza walked back to the Stour wing with Nick through the warm, dark garden, her mother's observation rang in her ears and she wondered about the strangeness of her life: hearing silly gossip about the man she loved, while carrying his child and yet keeping up the pretence to her family that she was happily married to her husband. And all this only made bearable by the fact that everyone else's world was in disarray. Nick was becoming more cynical and withdrawn. Her mother and his parents losing faith. The war had blighted them all, turned everything upside down.

She fixed her eyes on the bank of jasmine glowing white in the darkness like unseasonal drifts of snow. As they turned the corner, she could hear the buzz of the wireless in the salon; Lewis was in for the night. Eliza paused on the patio. The little river bubbled below them, innocently in the darkness, the scent of the jasmine reaching her even here. The surreal beauty of the night caused a sweetness to stir inside her, alongside her sleeping child.

'Nick, wait a moment,' she said. She was grateful that dark had fallen to hide her expression. 'I want to thank you for the way you have been these last few months. None of this is easy. The child . . . everything.'

'And I want to thank you in return, for understanding me.' In the darkness, Nick sounded humble. 'I will welcome the child. I have told you that and I assure you I will care for our son, our daughter. We've been through such sad times. I want you to be happy. If I can make our lives seem reasonable and acceptable, then I will do that.'

Overwhelmed suddenly and unable to speak, Eliza put her hand on his arm to thank him.

Nick said, 'I'll always remember that night war was declared. The three of us here.' His voice lifted with courage then broke. 'I asked you to marry me for a reason. There was a *reason* . . .'

'You don't need to say any more,' Eliza said, sensing their acceptance of each other.

'I just wanted us to be like we always were when we were children. To stay close, to stay together,' he sighed bitterly. 'We both loved him.'

'And we will make the best of our family,' Eliza said, conscious of Lewis working a mere few feet away from where she was standing. 'For everyone.'

Nick opened the front door, walked through the tiny hall and into the kitchen, checking for the blackout.

'Ah, but what of *his* family?' he asked abruptly.

Eliza looked at him, puzzled.

'Surely, your pilot had a family?' Nick went on. 'I expect they will want to know.'

Eliza's mind cascaded dangerously. 'But . . . but if we tell them, then they may take our child from us.'

'Really?' he asked. 'Do you think so?' He tilted his head back to look down, appraising her.

She took a breath, frantically straightening her thoughts. Lewis would be disappointed with her: she had not thought this through.

'Is it so bad that they don't know?' she said carefully. 'Surely they would hate to think of their poor dead son having a fling with a married woman. Surely we cannot leave them with that awful thought? That shame?'

'If you say so,' Nick said cautiously.

'Anyway,' Eliza lied, and lied so easily she terrified herself, 'I do not even know his last name.'

She sat at the manor kitchen table, preparing the elderberries for the roly-poly, straining at arm's length as her belly formed a barrier between her and the table, uncomfortable whichever way she turned. Her mother was busy chopping chuck for the ragout, for which she had queued an hour in the village.

'Any queue, I will join it,' she said.

Sybil got to work on the vegetables. The air was muggy, the sun a demon across the lawn, glaring through the windows. The smell of the fatty beef warming in the room sent queasy waves through Eliza. Her ankles were swollen and tendrils of hair were stuck to her neck; she was bushed already, and still had the long evening to get through.

Sybil had indeed invited Mr Castle and his daughter, plus the 'boys from the War Office'. Of course, not all of them could attend, as the post needed manning constantly and Bingley was outstandingly courteous in the decline of his invitation. Lewis told Eliza that his manner was edging him into the realms of martyrdom.

When Angela and Audley sent their apologies, Sybil found it hard to disguise her relief.

'Eleven for dinner would stretch even Marguerite Patten,' she declared. 'With these rations, I'm having to bulk out the chuck with potatoes anyway. So nine it is. Is it lucky or unlucky to have an odd number?'

Eliza, too, was relieved. She would avoid Angela's clever way of observing her, of knowing her; the silent question in the raised eyebrow. She had not seen her since she'd announced her pregnancy and for Angela to be presented with Lewis and herself in the same room would be intolerable. Lewis would ignore Eliza, perhaps too much, and Angela would notice. Then Nick might notice, see through her lie, and the whole family would be torn apart. A faint panic began to escalate inside her. The air in the kitchen grew closer, hotter; sweat pooled on her top lip. She must keep going, keep pretending.

She forced herself to listen to Sybil, who continued to fuss intractably about the meal.

'Shame we can't have plum pudding, as that would have been absolutely glorious.' She inspected Eliza's colander full of washed glistening elderberries. 'But we're not as flush with them as we were a few years ago. Remember that fabulous harvest of 1940, Mathilde? How we picked those plums furiously while the battle raged in the sky. But good thinking, Eliza. The hedges are packed with elderberries. And they cost nothing.'

'I'm glad these pass muster,' said Eliza, wiping the back of her hand across her forehead. 'How about I get on with the pastry?'

'No, ma chère,' Mathilde said, peering at her. 'You need to lie down. Look at you. Come upstairs with me to my bedroom. It is quieter than in the Stour wing, with all that wretched tapping and wireless noise. And cooler. My room is in the shade. Come, come with me.'

In her room, which was indeed a scented, quiet haven from the heat of the day, Mathilde told Eliza to take off her shoes, lie down.

'Now I will bring you some lemonade, how's that? And you shall have a tepid bath later. Can't have you going all peculiar on me. But first, look at this.'

Mathilde drew Eliza's cocktail dress out of her wardrobe. It was her favourite: black lace, sleeves and skirt, with a ruched silk bodice and a sweetheart neckline.

'I was wondering where that was. Oh, what's happened?'

Mathilde giggled. 'Look what I have done.'

She turned it round to reveal the front where she'd added a beautifully draped pleat of sapphire blue silk to accommodate Eliza's pregnant tummy.

'Maman, it is beautiful. You are so clever to do this for me.'

'Don't thank me, thank the sewing column of *Home Notes*. Make do and mend indeed. Couldn't do without it.'

Eliza hugged Mathilde and agreed that she should have a little snooze. She gazed around her at the comforts of her mother's bedroom, brought with her from Nunnery Fields: her gramophone, her perfume bottles, the Normandy lace cloths on the dressing table. But as her mother hung the dress up and left the room, panic, like a slow turning screw, returned.

The pretence was intolerable and Lewis was right. How would they cope when the baby came? How could they even imagine living here at Forstall under the same roof?

As she drifted into restless sleep, she entered the map of Kent. She was inside it, walking through the ordnance of the chart, through the city and past ancient tumuli and settlements, creeks and harbours. As she walked, the map of stars and its constellation laid itself over her in a sheet of silvery gossamer, trapping her in its net. She was in the salon plotting the points meticulously, over and over with her pencil and ruler. Accuracy was paramount. Sybil was watching her; she must not make a single mistake. The foxholes were secret, sacred: a hidden world beneath the veneer of ordinariness, of simply carrying on. She mustn't breathe a word. But she did, and to punish her, Lewis transformed her into the constellation on her map of stars. She was Andromeda, the girl chained to the rock awaiting her fate. The monster approached, vile and enormous, ready to rip her apart. But where was Perseus to rescue her? She looked for him, frantically. He was not there. She looked for Lewis and he was not there.

Eliza cried out, surfacing swiftly from her sleep, waking with a burst of unexpected laughter. She heard footsteps and her mother rushed in to the bedroom.

'What is it? Are you all right?' she cried in French. 'Are you unwell? Were you *laughing*?'

Eliza hauled herself up, her baby protesting inside her swollen stomach. She had, indeed, laughed. But her laugh was crooked with irony, made from despair. And the enormous and sickening sense of foreboding did not fade like her dream.

It was a choice between enjoying the lingering twilight or shutting down the blackout and lighting Sybil's many candelabra, which Nick had polished so meticulously. Eliza was glad that everyone elected to keep the French windows open to appreciate the birdsong and deepening shadows of the garden for, this way, she had more space to move around, avoiding proximity with Lewis and so easing their need to engage with each other.

'There won't be many of these evenings left this year,' sighed Jessica, accepting her flute of champagne from Morris. 'So we're right to leave the blackout until we absolutely have to. Thank you so much for inviting me, Morris. You too, Sybil. I must say, I have certainly missed the country. London is becoming dangerously drab. Either that, or I am becoming dangerously bored.'

From her spot by the French windows, Eliza watched Lewis, so attractive in his dinner jacket, start an animated and charming conversation with Sybil. Outside, the scent of the roses intensified with the dusk but she could smell the thick, powdery sweetness of Jessica's Chanel No. 5 across the room. Jessica was wearing another piece of couture, in complete contrast to Eliza's pretty but makeshift cocktail dress, and seemed to glow in the cream floor-length gown, the colour of which highlighted her hair. She'd replaced Elizabeth Arden with a lipstick shade that was even more outrageous.

As Jessica regaled an attentive Nick with tales from bombed-out London, Eliza decided to tolerate the cloying perfume and stepped forward to join the conversation. She listened while Jessica said that, certainly, the raids were less frequent now, but a night in a shelter, whether that be someone's wine cellar or the basement of the BBC, were the norm. And really quite a hoot.

'We make the best of it,' she confided, with the ghost of a wink. 'We're happy to be alive.'

Eliza secretly wondered if one of these wine cellars might have belonged to Major Arlington.

'I do worry for my girl,' Leonard said, overhearing and breaking away from his conversation with Mathilde who looked spectacularly relieved.

'Oh, such nonsense,' Jessica snapped at her father. 'I'm right as rain, as you can see.'

Leonard shrank back, rebuked, and went off in search of Mathilde, who had scooted off outside to the terrace.

'I saw you, Jessica,' said Eliza. 'At Victoria Station, ages ago. Wished I'd said hello.'

'Did you . . .?' She stared hard at her, obviously remembering.

Her face was calm and passionless, her confidence disarming. Eliza saw Fisher hovering at the corner of her eye. He was hooked by Jessica, staring at her quite openly, and falling for her once again.

'You must be mistaken, my dear –' Jessica turned sharply as Lewis walked past them, and tapped him smartly on the shoulder. 'But, I have certainly seen *you* in London, Commander.'

Her ringing voice had an accusatory edge.

Lewis stopped and gave her his bright smile with a mild shake of the head.

'It is probably best not to chat about such things, Miss Castle,' he said. 'Don't you think? Even in such treasured and trusted company as this.'

He walked off abruptly to chat to Mathilde and his snub turned Jessica's alabaster cheeks an unbecoming shade of red. She looked momentarily furious with him. Jessica was speechless.

Sybil, observing her favourite guest's discomfort, broke into the group to suggest that Eliza hand around a plate of hors d'oeuvres, leaving Nick with the valiant task of cheering Jessica up. And from across the room, Lewis caught Eliza's eyes and he risked a subtle nod towards her, a reassuring twinkle in his eye.

Snatches of conversation rose and fell as she offered the platter of starters.

'... called the vet in for Monty...'

'... so the little blighter's not so good?'

'... have you tried hay box cooking?'

'... takes absolute *hours*...'

'WI want me to make more jam. But we've no plums...'

'We're like squirrels, hoarding food...'

'... fabulous silks in at Selfridges from America...'

'... bit of a scrum, was it? Fight your way through?...'

Fisher was alone and dejected in the corner. He gave his hunger away by taking three of the triangles of toast spread with fish paste and eating them like a sandwich, draining his glass of champagne.

Eliza asked, 'How is Bingley? Sore that he is missing out?'

'He is the world's social pariah,' Fisher said. 'By choice. He'd rather be stuck out there, monitoring reports from the listening stations. Call of duty. Above and beyond, and all that. I sincerely think he needs to get out more, get laid – oh, God, sorry, Mrs Staveley. That was very rude. I mean, meet a nice young girl who he can take to the pub or the cinema.'

She laughed. 'You know you must call me Eliza. And I understand. The strain you boys must go through. It's nice to have the company of ladies from time to time.'

'Him especially. The strain, I mean.' Fisher nodded towards Lewis who was now in conversation with Morris. 'Big chief over there. His nerves are shredded most days, but somehow he keeps it together. Seems to have that extra ounce of vim inside him. Goes that extra mile.'

Eliza's pride for him swelled her blood. 'I've noticed . . . since he's been here. He really is . . .'

Fisher glanced in question at her.

'Goodness,' she said. 'I must keep moving with these hors d'oeuvres or Sybil will kill me.'

They were seated by seven thirty so, at Sybil's insistence, they could continue to enjoy the view of the garden while it was still light. Morris and Sybil were naturally at the head and foot of the large spread of crisp linen, with Mathilde and Jessica facing each other at Morris's elbows. Jessica looked rather miffed at being seated away from Lewis and did not hide her disappointment at being lumbered with Fisher who sat, smiling appreciatively, between her and Eliza.

As the starter of oysters and bread was served, Eliza found herself absorbed by whatever Leonard had to say across the table from her, deliberately tilting her head away from Lewis who was seated close by at Sybil's left hand. Jessica, in turn, kept flashing smiles at Lewis down the table, but he was, in any case, commandeered by Sybil who was pronouncing on the debacle of Dieppe.

'It was, if you would pardon this expression,' Lewis said, his face shadowed with sorrow, 'a diabolical cock-up. They relied on holiday photographs to deduce the gradient of the beach, for goodness' sake. The Canadians were sitting ducks.'

Fisher piped up, 'I can only deduce, sir, that the Germans had been forewarned.'

'Double agents?' asked Sybil.

'No, Fisher.' Lewis threw his anger at him, his face quite firm. 'We were incompetent.'

'Did anyone hear that funny story,' chimed in Jessica, 'that apparently, in the *Daily Telegraph* crossword on the seventeenth – which, remember, was two days before – there was a clue: *French port, six letters*. The answer the next day was *Dieppe*. And the day after that . . .'

She was trying to impress Lewis. Eliza gripped her knife and fork in a flash of jealous irritation.

'Miss Castle,' Lewis said, looking down the table, pointedly past Eliza and snuffing Jessica out in mid-flow. 'Yes indeed, and the day after that the raid took place. A coincidence. That's all.'

Eliza tried to hide her smile of admiration.

'Do you read the *Telegraph*?' Fisher asked Jessica. 'I must say it's by far my favourite paper . . .'

Jessica shook her head in annoyance at Fisher who shrank back and toyed with his shellfish. In the silence that followed, Leonard Castle struck up conversation with Nick, booming about his impending fatherhood. Mathilde was able to turn from Leonard and engage in conversation with Morris, wondering how the repair to the bomb damage at the brewery was progressing.

Eliza allowed herself to glance at Lewis and gave him a quick rationed smile.

'Time to pull down the blackout,' she announced, folding her napkin and rising from her seat as elegantly as her pregnant tummy would allow. 'No, no, Mr Castle, I can manage a few blinds. I'm not an invalid.'

As she shut out the summer evening, struck matches and lit the candles one by one, she was aware of Lewis taking this chance to watch her. The silver candelabra glimmered in the light and faces all along the table became radiant.

'How are you tonight, dear?' Sybil asked her when she sat back down. 'After your nap. Looks like it did you the world of good. And your lovely dress that Mathilde ran up for you. Simply divine.'

'Thank you, yes, I am feeling much better,' Eliza said, and caught an unguarded look of concern from Lewis.

The ragout was surprisingly delicious, so agreed everyone and as the roly-poly was being served, Jessica leant forward.

'I say, Eliza, it's astonishing good news, you being in the family way. My, you do look fit to burst. Have you thought of any names yet? Monty if it's a boy, surely? What would you like, Nicholas?'

Eliza saw Lewis wince and make a grab for his wine glass.

'Not sure we want to name him after one of your father's pigeons,' she said.

'A healthy, happy child, Jessica,' Nick said. 'It's all a man can wish for in these times.'

A little flushed by the wine, Morris raised his glass of Baron de Rothschild. 'I drink to that, Nicholas. Put all our hopes into the next generation. Got to shake off this damn war curse one way or another. Thought I'd seen the last of it, with what happened to poor Richard. You'd think we'd learn the first time round, wouldn't you?'

Mathilde's head dropped and Leonard reached for her hand, which she batted away. Sybil admonished her husband, told him to shush for such words were frightening folks.

'I say we fix up the card tables for tonight,' said Leonard. 'Nothing like a bit of friendly gambling to take your mind off things.'

'Well, I say I must go back on duty.' Lewis rose to his feet, bundling his napkin onto the table. 'Sorry to spoil the party, Mrs Staveley, but I need to relieve poor old Bingley.'

Noises of empathy, with a slight groan of dismay from Jessica, reverberated around the table.

'Surely just a hand or two, old fella,' Leonard pressed him.

'Yes, Commander,' Jessica urged, her smile a sweet, red bud in the candlelight. 'It seems such a terrible shame. Is there anything I can do to persuade you?'

'Well, Miss Castle,' he said, and his tone drew everyone's attention, 'you may need to give me a little more time to think about that.'

At that, Eliza stood up abruptly and picked up a tray of pudding dishes. She hurried outside, across the hall and into the kitchen. She slammed the dishes down on the table, gasping with rage at Jessica, at Lewis, at herself. She knew that tiny flirtation was to create a smokescreen, but she saw the light go on in Jessica's eyes, saw the brief dazzle there, like the noonday sun, and hated it. Hated Jessica.

She ran the tap at the sink, filled a glass and drank her fill to flush the anger away. She waited, longing for the fury and frustration to dissolve. She pressed a fist to her forehead. Her baby struggled within her, protesting. From the drawing room came the sound of chatter, a tinkle of laughter and a pleasant variety of *goodnight*s. She had to leave the kitchen. She could not hide there forever.

Lewis was tarrying near the front door.

'You're beautiful,' he said to her, as if it was the simplest thing in the world. 'Goodnight.'

His words were pure and loving; exactly what she wanted to hear. Her rage vanished instantly, but she was assailed suddenly by a terrible emptying loneliness, as if her insides had simply poured away. As if his words meant nothing.

She walked towards him, wanting to hold him, for him to take her and keep her close. But this could never happen. Desperate, feeling faint, she reached for the banister.

She whispered, 'Lewis, I really can't take much more of this.'

'Oh, my love . . .' He put his hand to her waist just as a footstep rang on the hallway flags. Sybil appeared behind them.

'Not feeling well again, Eliza?' She looked puzzled.

'No, I was just saying . . . That's right. I will take myself off, over to bed, if that's all right, Sybil.'

'Of course, dear.' She was not looking at her but staring hard at Lewis. 'And goodnight again, Commander Harper.' Her smile was broad, not reaching her eyes.

Chapter 16

The bus took a different route into Canterbury, pedantically skirting the ruins of St George's. Straining her neck, Eliza caught a glimpse of the wasteland through the back window: splintered beams, rubble and the dust of Elizabethan bricks. Venerable timbered houses that had survived for centuries had been vanquished during one solitary, fire-filled night; that night in June on which the map of the city had been redrawn.

She looked away. The faces on the bus were mute, grey with fatigue: housewives in head scarves, old gentlemen in tweeds, a man in pinstripe. She watched their expressions, trying to glean a suggestion of how she, herself, should feel, for lately she had no idea. For this was wartime. She was in exile from the life she had once expected.

The gentleman was reading his newspaper. Eliza read over his shoulder, the hierarchy of headlines, the importance of the news already decided for them by the size of the print. Her own war-world at the manor was tiny, where normal life was submerged amid the daily tasks of just getting by. There was no sugar, they were running out of soap and there was simply none to be had in the shops. Should she avert her eyes from the bus window, from the devastation of her beloved city to remind herself that Singapore had fallen and the British Army had waved the white flag; that Stalingrad was surrounded and winter was coming; that the Duke of Kent, bless him, Maman had said, such a jolly good chap, had been killed? And Martyn was dead and would be gone forever.

As the bus turned into Burgate, Eliza silently asked inside her head: was it *really* a pain to leave Nunnery Fields and visit Forstall like we did, all those times? Did you really think it took aeons on this bus to get there and back again? Or were you joking, Tintin, making a meal of it in your forgivable, boyish, attention-seeking way?

She could ask him as much as she liked, she realised, but could not expect him to answer.

She alighted at Burgate and hurried along the pavement as well as she could with her baby sleeping blind and heavy inside her. The medieval city was her protectorate, the pinnacled cathedral towers her focus. She wondered how so much of it could possibly remain standing, while people simply carried on, bustling with shopping trolleys, trailing children. Office secretaries were catching a breath of fresh air over lunchtime, a delivery man was unloading boxes onto the pavement; the postman hurried past her, wheeling his bicycle.

She zig-zagged her way through all this busyness, past the War Memorial and across the cobbles of the Buttermarket Square.

And before she entered the door to the right of the mighty cathedral gate she threw a guilty glance at the lanky statue of Christ presiding at its top. She was, after all, making her way to a hotel room for an afternoon rendezvous with her lover.

The rambling, discreet hotel was part of – and absorbed by – the walls of the cathedral precinct and her room looked out the back over the green towards the buttressed cathedral façade. She waited in the armchair by the window, watching the pure, silvery stonework become inflamed by autumn sunlight. Russet leaves drifted from the trees, filling the sheltered air with gold, to submit themselves gently over the lawns.

She stroked her tummy, sensing her baby shuffle.

'We're getting near the time,' she told her child. 'But what a world to be bringing you into.'

She heard his rap on the door and a smile lifted her face as Lewis came in, his eyes clear and keen.

'Sorry to be a little late,' he said.

'You are perfectly on time.'

He kissed her forehead, pressing her into him. He had ordered luncheon to be brought up to the room, he said, and then glanced wryly at the twin beds covered with lilac candlewick bedspreads.

'This won't do at all.'

'Commander Harper,' Eliza chided playfully, even though she sensed the dirt in her soul. 'Whatever are you thinking?'

They ate their sandwich lunch, drank their tea.

'It's not half bad,' said Lewis optimistically.

Eliza smilingly agreed, although really she wanted to complain about having to put up with meeting in a hotel room and eating tasteless sandwiches.

'Maman and Sybil are kicking themselves,' she told him, trying to be cheerful and gossipy. 'Yesterday it seems that Mrs Churchill and the First Lady were in Canterbury. An unexpected visit.'

'Seems they missed out on some flag waving,' mused Lewis. 'But I can't quite see Mathilde and Sybil shuffling with the crowds.'

'My mother is excellent at queuing, you know. But more likely, they would have wanted to see what hats the ladies were wearing.'

'How is Sybil?' he asked pointedly.

'Her watchful looks seem to have petered out. She appears to be a bit more relaxed. Nick and I get on so well these days, I think her suspicions have stopped. If indeed she ever actually did. Suspect us, I mean.'

'You and Nick?'

'Oh, Lewis. He is in the spare bedroom. Has been for a long while. He seems quite content. He is looking forward to the baby.'

'*Our* baby,' he corrected her.

He took one look at her and set the tray aside, reached for her hand and led her to one of the narrow beds. They lay down, facing each other, the baby between them. He held onto her, cradled her, but she did not want to yield to him.

'You are quite cross today, aren't you?' He ran his fingers through the hair at her temples. 'Is it with me or just in general?'

'I'm no more cross than I should be.' She forced a smile. 'I should be thankful for many things. We are alive, are we not?'

She watched him agree with her, his face opening with concern, with love. But then his features clouded over. His eyes darkened. He frowned and looked away.

'You're thinking of Dieppe?'

'Our intelligence simply wasn't good enough,' he said. 'We created a right bloody disaster.'

She sat up; it was her turn to comfort him.

She pressed his face to her shoulder and whispered, 'My love, you're not the only one fighting this war.'

And she felt it again, the cord that was strung between them, tugging at her. The cord that kept them together.

'Things are changing. I have to up my game,' he said, suddenly, his voice muffled against her collar.

Eliza drew back. 'What did you say?'

He shuffled to face her. She stared at him, close enough to kiss him.

'It seems that I am being sent away from Forstall,' he paused. 'For good.'

She jerked, suddenly desperately afraid. The shaky world around her vanishing.

'Will you be far? Where will you be? Will you miss the baby? The birth?' She was nearly shouting, her voice shaking.

He ran his fingertip down her cheek and up again to smooth her brow.

'Can't you see that it will be best that I am not here. At Forstall,' he said. 'What would I do with myself while you are up there in your bedroom giving birth? As brave as I might sometimes appear, I think that might very well defeat me. So the timing is good. Don't you see?'

Crushed and bewildered, Eliza tried her hardest to nod agreement. 'I'm not going to ask where, or why,' she said. 'But is it . . . *abroad*?'

He looked away from her. 'Not abroad, no.'

'You're not lying, I can tell, even though you won't look me in the eye,' she said. 'You just don't want me to see the truth. Your fear.'

'Keep our baby safe,' he said.

'I will,' she said. 'As safe as this world will allow me to.'

'It might be that you wake up one morning very soon and I will be gone. But you are becoming upset, Eliza.'

'Is it any wonder?'

'We should not talk about this now.'

He began to kiss her neck but Eliza pulled away from him. 'There'll be none of that today,' she said, trying for humour. 'You didn't see the look the Christ statue outside gave me.'

Lewis said, 'You should have shouted up, "Don't you know there's a war on?"'

He chuckled but she was a long way from laughter. 'Do you mean that, really?' she asked. 'That because of the war we're allowed to do whatever we like?'

'Yes.'

He reached for her buttons but she patted his hand away, her thoughts moving beyond the sleaziness of the drab hotel room to the life ahead of her without him.

'If we should not talk about this now,' she said, 'then I expect we never will.'

Lewis, reading her face, whispered, 'I'm sorry, Eliza.'

Eliza took a shuddering breath. 'All we do is say sorry to each other.' Her voice was small and hard. 'I'm not sure that I can . . .'

'What?' he urged her gently, fear drifting over his face. 'What are you not sure of?'

She could not tell him that she was not sure that she could continue loving him, for that would be a lie. She would always love him, but this was becoming too hard.

He waited.

She said, 'In the wreckage of the car, you frightened me at first. You were like a shadow, a terrible angel. But your eyes . . .' she halted, wondering if she'd be able to continue. 'And you smelt beautiful. You looked beautiful. Then the oddest thing happened.' She broke off and he held her hand, encouraging her. 'The oddest thing,' she whispered, 'is that I *recognised* you.'

He pulled back from her, watching her. Gently, he cradled the back of her head in his hands and tilted her face towards him.

'I recognised you before we'd even met. Does that make sense?' she asked. 'I'm not sure it does to me.'

'It makes perfect sense,' he whispered. He wrapped his arms around her, held her fast and tight. 'I cannot let go,' he said. 'I cannot let you go.'

She could not see his face, but she sensed the liquidity of sadness, love and hopelessness in his voice.

'And, Eliza,' he whispered, 'you will recognise me again.'

*

While Lewis checked out at reception, Eliza waited under the porch of the hotel. She sniffed the air, unmistakably autumnal with a smoky freshness. It was teatime and the cobbles were still busy with people. She idly watched the comings and goings of the Buttermarket Square, with its crooked buildings and rippling-tiled roofs. But even as she breathed the refreshing air, she sensed a change, a rush of static, the stopping of a heartbeat, the silence just before the siren blared hard and sharp like a ship's horn.

On impulse, she looked up and saw a plane, a German plane, swooping into her own precious patch of sky. And then another. And another. The noise was ferocious. She was spellbound by their audacity; hardly having time to feel fear at all such was their speed. She sensed Lewis behind her, his arms around her waist, pulling her backwards under the porch. He was shouting in her ear to come under cover, shouting about fighter planes and bombers and that she must duck down. But the flash of riveted metal, the spectacle of the tips of the wings turning in the sky, fixed her to the spot. The plane was so low, she could see the pilot's helmet. She flinched backwards as a deafening stick of bombs exploded on Burgate. A rattle of bullets strafed the market square cobbles like a metallic hail, chipping dust and stone, which rose in a dirty cloud. People were moving like darting, ducking shadows – a surreal mayhem.

Lewis covered her body with his own, turning his back on the square, pushing her back into the doorway, shielding her. And at that moment, over his shoulder, Eliza saw Sybil standing alone, quite still by the Memorial in the centre of the Buttermarket. She was oblivious to the flak, the rain of fire from the sky, her shopping bags tipped over at her feet, her face pale under her hat, her mouth open as she stared at Eliza, stared at Lewis.

A scream of engines ripped over the rooftops, over Eliza's head, and the shock of an explosion altered the air, changed the direction of her blood. A terrible repetitive noise, a mechanical pecking, obliterated all that was normal and she saw Sybil, in eerie slow-motion, tear her eyes away from hers, turn and run into a hail of bullets.

Chapter 17

In the drawing room at Forstall Manor, as Mathilde served tea on a tray, the china chinking unsteadily, the funeral director let slip how extraordinarily busy he was. Eliza watched Nick's face twist sideways in pain. He returned his bewildered gaze to the man in his shiny, black suit who was sitting in the best armchair turning his bowler hat over and over in his hands.

'I heard a bus was targeted on the road near Sturry.' Nick made unnecessary conversation; a ghost of himself. 'I heard fighters were brought down by our boys over Pegwell Bay and Sandwich.'

Morris leant forward in his chair, resting his arms on his knees, his face a map of astonished lines as he addressed the undertaker.

'My wife was very particular about roses,' he declared. 'It has to be the right rose. You've seen the garden. You can see her work out there. It's splendid.'

'But it is autumn, Morris. The roses are over,' Mathilde spoke as gently as breathing, cradling Sybil's teapot as she rested it back down on the table.

'We must have roses,' Morris insisted. 'Boule de Neige, is that right, Mathilde? They're white, white I tell you.'

The pinch-faced funeral director opened his mouth, but Morris raised his hand like a signal, slamming him down. 'If you are going to say, sir, that in the circumstances there are no white roses to be had, you can get out now.'

Eliza glanced fearfully at Nick and then at the visitor, whose face pulsated with outrage.

'The gentleman will do his best, won't he?' she asserted, nodding at the undertaker, encouraging him to agree. 'He will try his very best.'

'I will, madam.' The funeral director stood, smoothed down his wrinkled jacket. In any event, it appeared, he actually had no time for tea. He was, after all, so very busy, but he would thank them and leave right away.

'You are on the telephone?' he asked Eliza as she crossed the hallway with him, showing him out. 'Any further requests can be placed over the telephone. And we will do our utmost. Unfortunately, roses . . .'

She put her hand up to indicate that he needn't explain further and followed him outside. He hurriedly dipped into his car and drove away with undisguised relief.

Alone on the lane in the cold sunshine, gazing at the bare orchards and the neatly-clipped hedgerows, the silence mesmerised her. The familiar order and peace of her countryside, her world, had once comforted her but now began to gnaw at her, hollowing her out until she was a void. She was giddy and lost. There was nothing left of her. Except her baby. And a soul black with guilt.

Eliza held her breath, closed her eyes and waited. Birds continued to chatter, to have their lilting wintry conversation. She wanted to be alone, like this. She wanted to have no idea where she was, or who she was. The sense of being nowhere and no one curiously soothed her until reality seeped back in all too easily, like the breath back in to her body.

She wasn't brave enough to go back into the drawing room. Instead, she walked the path around to the back of the manor house, towards the Stour wing. She crossed her own threshold and turned right to tap on the closed door to the salon. Lewis opened it. He'd been on duty for twenty-four hours. His eyes were tired and glazed. His dark hair ruffled where he had run his hands through it, lifting a little at the front. She remembered smoothing down his hair in Angela's parlour. That first touch was branded on her memory, its intensity and significance shocking her even now.

Neither of them spoke as she stood in the doorway to the salon. She turned and walked back out to the patio, to the steps that led down to the lawn, the river beyond. Here, the reeds were broken, bullrushes rising like velvety brown flares. Beech nuts and husks crunched under her shoes and the low, lazy sun flicked light at her through the hop gardens on the other side.

She knew he would follow.

'We need to be careful.'

He stood at her side, facing the same direction as her, the sleeve of his jacket a hair's breadth from her arm. If she could turn and hold him, just once more, she knew he would give her the strength to carry on. But she must not touch him. Her guilt kept her rooted and condemned her to loneliness.

'They're all too stunned to notice us,' said Eliza, feeling her resolve stiffen inside her. 'But even so ...' Her voice trailed, strangled in her throat. 'You know this is over, Lewis. I can't do this. *This*. I simply can't do it any longer.'

'What?' Lewis's surprise was like a bark. 'You mean that?' He turned his face away from her, to gaze at the rattling, naked tree tops, the cold sky above.

'She saw us,' Eliza said.

'And yet ...?'

'If you say that it is all right because she is dead, then you don't know me at all. Can't possibly love me as you say you do.'

'You're wrong.'

'This is wrong. So very wrong. It always has been.' Eliza's words left her lips with shivering realisation. 'Anyway, you are leaving Forstall, so what does it matter? What does any of it matter -?' She pressed her hand over her mouth, unable to form the words that raged in her head. Words that told her it was over. Their love could not survive *this*.

He whispered her name, and that single word perforated her heart.

'Don't speak to me, Lewis.' She struggled. Her body was splitting in half. 'You are leaving Forstall. Tomorrow, the next day ... who knows? You're leaving. And I don't want you to come back.'

She saw him turn to her, motion his pain, reach for her. She darted away from him, did not look back. She walked back up the steps, across the patio, her mind suddenly clean and open, filling with an incredibly soft and righteous wave. It was false, of course. It would not last long. But if this feeling could just stay with her, give her the strength she needed, she would be able to get inside her house and shut the door.

As Eliza placed her hand on the handle, she felt a warm rush of liquid gush down. It soaked her underwear, splashed her legs and shoes. She paused for a second and looked down at herself. Her hand went to her stomach. She let herself into her home and closed the door.

Lying on her side on her bed, she could see that the weak sun was sinking, gleaming through the taped bedroom windows, mapping a pattern on the floorboards and across her threadbare rug. She lay motionless, breathing deeply, her mind still empty, still calm. Seconds, minutes, hours later, she was not sure, the first pain found her, gripped her, cleansed her.

She panted, waiting. Time moved on, immeasurable. A fresh agony crunched around her middle. The violence of it left her breathless and unable to scream. She coiled up on the bed.

A motorbike started up, revving, manoeuvring onto the lane at the front of the house. Lewis was leaving her. This was her new beginning. She was truly alone.

She saw him from the tangled wreck of the car while he went to get help. She saw his extraordinary eyes, the colour of a river bed. She remembered the smell of him and how she had known, then, that he would surely come back.

But his motorbike faded and left behind the empty afternoon.

Doubled over in agony, she eased herself over the side of the bed and fell to the floor. She began to crawl on all fours across to the window that overlooked the lawn and the manor, the pain of her contractions taking her breath away. She reached up to push the casement open and sat beneath it. She cried out: '*Aide-moi! Aide-moi!*' Her mother tongue returning.

Part III

Polaris
'a fixed, motionless point'

Chapter 18

1943

Eliza switched off the wireless and sat in the armchair by the fire. Flames guttered low in the grate, red fire around caverns of black coals. The lamplit mirror above the mantel reflected the manor's drawing room back to her, a misted extension of the space; another, parallel dimension potently different to her own. Restless, she got up and stood in front of the looking glass. Yes, she was still there: a ghost of a face, hair russet brown – '*rich, golden, sweet treacle,*' he had always said – and at the front, now, a lock of white, the colour of the snow outside. It was the talk of the manor, Eliza's streak, appearing suddenly soon after the birth a year before. And, Eliza pondered, soon after Sybil turned from her in the Buttermarket square, her eyes bright with realisation, and ran to her death.

Recklessly, Eliza pulled the blackout aside a chink to stare out at the night. Snowflakes had been falling all day, as surreptitious as spies, and now the garden was covered, the lane a blur of white. Beyond, in the darkness, fields were frozen and silent. There was no moon tonight. No stars either and yet, below the darkness, the wide, rolling landscape was luminous with snow light. She stared, waiting in suspended mourning, like the wife of a sailor lost at sea; waiting in futility for the return that would never happen.

But she was safe, she was home, she told herself fiercely. She was aware of the smells of plaster, wax and smoke, a whiff of the oil in the locks – cared for so tenderly by Morris – and sought their comfort. The familiar creak of the floorboard as she heard her mother walk down the stairs, the winding of the clock in the hallway; a regular lullaby.

The wireless still hummed, bringing her back to reality. The evening news had been of the bombing of Berlin and she wondered what sort of world had she brought her baby into? What kind of horror might yet be heading their way? She glanced suddenly around the room. Had it crept in again, behind her: that vibration of fear? But all was soft with lamplight, no need to feel afraid. Again, that presence. Not just the house, which comforted her in its constant immortal way, but *someone*. A sense of someone always in the room, always there.

Mathilde opened the door and came in, bouncing a year-old Stella in her arms. The child was sleepy, ready for bed, red-cheeked, her eyes luminous and green, clutching with pudgy fingers on to her grand-mère's sleeves. Instinctively, Eliza reached her arms out to her but her daughter shifted and hid her face in Mathilde's neck.

'Ah, come on, say goodnight to Maman.' Mathilde strolled around the room, jigging the child up and down. 'Come on, little Ess, Ess, Ess.'

Stella looked in surprise at her grandmother's mouth, putting her forefinger on Mathilde's lip, then copied her, repeating the sounds.

'That's it, good girl. She nearly said it just now, upstairs.' Mathilde planted a loud kiss on her granddaughter's round cheek. 'Stella Sybil Staveley. Ess, Ess, Ess.'

Eliza dragged her eyes from Stella's for the colour of them always reminded her.

She stood up, brushing her hands briskly down her skirt. 'Has Nick been over yet to say goodnight?'

'Oh, no,' said Mathilde. 'Usually, he would never miss this little one's bedtime. But he has gone to the pub with Bingley. Probably back at closing time.'

Eliza glanced at her mother, wondering if she ever questioned it. This winter, Eliza had moved back across to the main part of the manor with Stella, claiming that the Stour wing was draughty and uncomfortable and not suitable for a child. Nick, of course, elected to stay there. He'd explained that someone needed to be on hand for the War Office lads in the salon. He liked to spend time with Bingley and Fisher, particularly Bingley, who had become, he said, a proper pal.

For Eliza, there was another reason. Shortly after Sybil's death, Nick had propped his favourite photograph of his mother on their mantelpiece next to her three china deer. It was a lovely photograph, they both agreed, but her eyes followed Eliza, intruding every day, reminding her and compounding her guilt. And she couldn't bear to remember the look in Sybil's eyes.

'Ah, but earlier Nicholas had a little bit of news,' Mathilde said, smoothing Stella's wispy dark hair across her forehead. 'He said Bingley was talking about the erstwhile boss making an honest man of himself, and guess what? He has gone and got married.'

'The *boss*?' Eliza asked but, even as she said this, she knew. Lewis. She winced as she said the word, '*Married*?'

'Something about it seems odd, though. I don't know,' her mother said. 'What's the point of third-hand gossip, I say? We need it from the horse's mouth. Usually Fisher is my best source.'

Mathilde carried on speaking, but Eliza did not hear. She turned her face to the fire. She'd told him to go; what did she expect?

Stella screwed up her face and began to bawl. And with that, Mathilde tipped her in to Eliza's arms.

'I'm making Morris a milky drink,' she said. 'Do you want one?'

'Not for me, thank you.' Eliza lifted the struggling weight of Stella. 'I'll get this one straight to bed and I might turn in myself. I've had quite enough for today.'

She said goodnight to Mathilde and climbed the stairs with Stella heavy in her arms. The child protested, wanting grand-mère. She elongated her body, refusing to be held. Eliza tapped her leg to chide her and Stella gave in to tiredness, snuffling against her shoulder.

She paused to rest on the chilly half landing, and let out her breath in a cloud; the cold, it seemed, came from deep inside her. She glanced down, relieved that her daughter was now snoozing, slumped over her shoulder and that her eyes, a projection of her father's, were closed.

'Hello! Yoo hoo! Anyone home?' came Leonard Castle's unmistakable call of greeting below the bedroom window.

It sent a mild echo into the empty, snowy landscape, the sound of his boots squeaking over the snowy path. Mathilde's forced, cheery reply came from within the house and Eliza, standing by Stella's cot, trying to entice her into her afternoon sleep, experienced mild irritation. She shrugged it off. Annoying man that he is, she thought, at least he'll be bringing us the now traditional Christmas goose. She went to the window and twitched her curtain to one side. She stepped back with a jolt of surprise.

Jessica was striding purposefully beside her father, brushing against the twigs of Sybil's dormant rose bushes. Her long legs were clad in jodhpurs and boots, a good wool coat tightly belted. Her self-assured smile beamed forward, a flash of red amid the heaps of white around her.

Eliza dipped back behind the window frame, hoping not to be spotted. Behind her, Stella's sudden keening cry made her jump. Her daughter stood up in her cot and held her chubby arms out. Eliza shushed her, told her she should be having her nap.

'I'm staying here with you,' she whispered. 'Stay out of their way.'

But her mother's rather plaintive call resounded up the stairs. 'Eliza, dear. Leonard's here . . . with Jessica. Do come and say hello.'

Hell, thought Eliza. I can't possibly leave Maman alone with them both.

'Be a good girl and go to sleep.' Eliza leant into the cot, laid a light finger on Stella's cheek and reluctantly left her daughter.

Downstairs, she paused in the kitchen doorway for a moment to arrange her thoughts. The goose lay with its severed neck hanging rudely over the end of the kitchen table; its body long and full. Leonard sat beside it, chatting away, telling Mathilde how he'd reared this one especially for her, had fed it the best scraps and wrung its neck himself. Beside him perched Jessica with her placid face perfect, her chin tilted for admiration.

Eliza took in a jagged breath and entered the room.

Jessica was twitching her left hand in Mathilde's direction.

'Never mind that silly goose, Dad,' she said. 'Take a look at this Mathilde. Just a simple plain band. But it's all I wanted, really. Can't be too extravagant these days, can we? Lewis wanted something a little more special, of course he did, but I told him – ah, Eliza, hello.'

Eliza stopped dead and fixed her eyes on the goose's ragged feathers, its severed neck, the bag of giblets that Leonard had kindly brought along with it. Blood seeped through the paper, staining it in the shape of a flower. She tried to smile at Jessica but failed. Jessica had just said Lewis's name and it bloated her heart with pain. She garnered all her strength to walk, dazed, to the far end of the table, reaching blindly to pull out a chair. Her blood drained from her heart, like the poor dead goose's on the table.

'Brought over my waif and stray to see you, Eliza,' Leonard said brightly. 'So nice to have her safely back from London, settled in Deal now. An old married woman. What a turn-up that proved to be. I'd say that fellow was a dark horse. I didn't have a single inkling that he liked my Jess. Still, she's back in Kent and I hardly see her now anyway. Typical, isn't it?'

'What a surprise for all of us,' Mathilde said as she took the kettle from the range to top up the teapot. 'Our very own Commander Harper marrying Jessica. You must tell us all about it.'

Eliza was rooted to her chair, icy shock raking her body. She fixed her eyes on the decapitated goose, the drops of blood on the kitchen floor. Any moment now, she would be sick.

Jessica did not hesitate. 'We bumped into each other in Bloomsbury, near my flat,' she gushed. 'Oh, only this summer, Mathilde. We'd seen each other occasionally in London in the past. But this time ... As you know, he'd been moved on from Forstall ages ago. To the Ministry. I shouldn't be saying, really. We met in a dark little drinking den I know. A wonderful surprise to see a familiar face from home. I felt he had sought me out, but then I suppose I am flattering myself.' Jessica's lips twitched with satisfaction. 'That night seemed to change everything.'

'We're so very pleased for you, Jessica,' said Mathilde, setting the cups and pouring the tea.

Eliza looked wildly around the kitchen, anywhere but at Jessica. She regaled the facts of the wedding: whirlwind and romantic, with no guests and bringing two witnesses off the street just like they do in the films. She glanced at Jessica's left hand and saw the wedding band, no engagement ring. It was expensive, a glimmering rose gold. Whirlwind, indeed.

What a betrayal. Utter betrayal. She was exhausted, and hounded. And still, Jessica rattled on.

'We've set up home in his house in Deal. Going to do it up once the war is over. New kitchen I think and a bathroom on the top floor. Anyway, I was bored there today, so I cycled over to see my old dad. Bit of a trek really, but it'll do me good. Lewis is always away. Days on end. Some war crisis or other. Getting a bit lonely out there by the sea.'

Eliza looked away from Jessica's luminous, deadly beauty while her memory turned a sharp corner: the winding staircase, pulling herself up by the rope, sheltering from the storm, lying in Lewis's arms. His face, intense and as if in pain, his eyes both dark and bright as he made love to her.

'Perhaps you should go and visit Jessica in Deal, Eliza?' said Mathilde. 'A nice day out? Eliza has her car, still, you know.'

Eliza jerked, found her voice. 'I'm too busy these days,' she said, as evenly and precisely as she could manage. Her fingertips pressed a hard line along the grain of the table. 'My work here in the salon takes up a lot of my time, plus there's Stella.'

'Oh, yes,' said Jessica, 'your dear little one. I still haven't seen her. She must be growing up now. Is she over a year? And Nicholas? How is he? So sorry to hear about Sybil, by the way.'

Stella's cry reached them down the staircase, falling and pitching with outrage.

Mathilde, eager and proud, said, 'Oh, listen to her. I'll go and fetch her, bring her down.'

Eliza's skin tightened as her mother bore her daughter, who was evidently delighted at being brought downstairs, to be admired. She flinched when Jessica stood up and held out her arms to her little girl. She didn't want her anywhere near her.

'What an angel,' said Jessica, without conviction and promptly handed Stella back to Mathilde. 'I must say, a baby is certainly not on my mind at the moment. Wartime brides have other priorities. Ah, but look at her eyes. Extraordinary.'

'I must get on,' Eliza muttered, making a move towards the door. 'Back to work.'

'I love your new look, by the way.' Jessica stopped her, staring at the lock of white over her forehead. 'So you're keeping busy in the Stour wing? Dad, you don't mind waiting if I pop over with Eliza to see the boys? Lewis certainly misses his old chums. I can tell him how they are doing.'

Eliza knocked on the salon door; Bingley opened it.

'Afternoon, Mrs Staveley and – oh.' He peered over her shoulder. 'Miss Castle.'

'Mrs Harper now, Roger.' Jessica giggled and reached through to shake a reluctant Bingley's hand. 'How do you do? It's lovely to see you again.'

Eliza slipped past Bingley into the salon and sat down at her desk. She saw immediately that he had left her a little stack of chits, of messages brought in by pigeon that morning. He had already prioritised them for her, and they were not marked urgent. She sifted through them, noting the names of the French cells and their various locations in Normandy and Brittany. Wondered how they were faring; this was to be their fourth Christmas under occupation.

Jessica's voice pitched with mild grievance. 'Well, Roger, aren't you going to ask me in?'

'Really, Mrs Harper. You know as well as any of us that that is totally against protocol. Mrs Staveley will be busy here all afternoon, and I must press on.'

Eliza sharpened her pencil and bent to the first slip of paper.

'Aw, Roger,' came Jessica's voice from around the door. 'You know I have Official Secrets clearance from my time at the BBC. Wouldn't hurt to sit a while in the old leather chair over in the corner. It's nice and warm there by the stove. I'll keep very quiet. Don't you want me to tell my husband how well you are all doing?'

Eliza looked up to see Bingley physically blocking the entrance.

'I'm going to say no.'

'I am disappointed. If Lewis – Commander Harper – was here, he would possibly tell you straight.'

'Well, I wouldn't have to act on his order, as he is no longer our chief. If you wouldn't mind, Mrs Harper, I will say good afternoon.'

He shut the door.

Jessica called from the hallway, her sing-song voice even higher, 'Lovely to see you, by the way, Eliza. Hope to see you soon. Do come and visit me in Deal.'

Eliza saw her slip past the window and hurry away, seemingly unmoved and still beaming her bright red smile.

Bingley sat down opposite Eliza, rolled up his shirtsleeves, took off his tie and rested his arms on the desk.

'Wonder what Arlington would have to say about that,' she said, whirling a sheet of paper into her typewriter and beginning to type.

'For all his strictness, he was a soft touch in her hands.'

'Really, I do wonder –' Eliza began.

'Why on earth,' Bingley interrupted, 'does she think she can call me *Roger*?'

'Words fail me,' Eliza replied lightly. 'What's that you have there?'

'Ah, yes, something her husband delegated to me before he left last year. I need you to update it. I wanted to make sure Tinker Bell had definitely left the premises before I showed you. Forget those messages, they're past it, irrelevant now. Take a look at this but don't ask me what it means.'

Eliza cocked her head at him in question.

'Don't ask me because I haven't a clue.' Bingley passed the two sections of the map of stars over the desk to her. 'Just update it where indicated. Here, see, and here? The top sheet must be kept separate from the bottom. One goes in the safe, one in the strongbox here in my drawer. Bit of a sod, really, working on paperwork that has no meaning. Kept in the dark as usual, like sodding mushrooms. But that's our lot, isn't it, Mrs Staveley?'

She looked at the notes he handed her. The patrols were expanding in number, recruiting new members. There was a new one at Ash, and one at Sturry, and their foxholes needed to be marked. Her work was of the utmost secrecy. Even the units hardly ever visited their hides, Lewis had explained once, in case they were spotted by passers-by. 'You know how nosey people are in general,' he'd said. 'Just look at Leonard. He's the worst. He knows nothing.'

The farmers, postmasters, schoolteachers, coastguards and fishermen were in constant training, learning how to blow up convoys, practising covert warfare in woodland. They did not tell their wives, their families. For, if you stumbled across a hideout, you would probably be shot. She folded the top sheet down over the map and stared at the constellation, at Andromeda, then glanced up at Bingley, who was eyes-down, studying a report. He pretended not to know anything about the map of stars but, she decided, he probably knew more than she did.

She smoothed out the map and carefully annotated it. She took her time, understanding its importance, taking immense pride in it. It was for her country, for their struggle, for their own resistance if the worst thing should happen. And it was also for Lewis, still always for Lewis. She could hear his voice, catch the scent of him. See him inside her map. She had seen her future in him. And now, she was alone and utterly beaten.

By marrying Jessica, he had finally left her.

Chapter 19

1944

The morning sky through the window was unseasonably grey for early June. Daylight, muddy and dull, found her curled, half dreaming and half awake, into her pillow. Raindrops pattered on the pane and squally breezes worried the tops of the trees. She'd slept in. It was past eight o'clock. She sat up and yawned. Stella was snuffling, still closed in sleep inside her cot, curled just like Eliza had been, her little body mirroring hers.

Mathilde knocked on the bedroom door.

'Eliza, ma chère, Fisher needs you urgently in the salon. Poor devil looked like he was about to tear his hair out. Could you come now?'

She quickly washed her face, hurried into her clothes and ran a comb through her hair.

'But, Maman, how did he *sound*?' she asked as she ran down the stairs.

'Harassed,' Mathilde called after her. 'At the end of his tether. He had to shout for you out of the salon window.'

Eliza raced across the lawn, through the bothersome, wind-blown rain, around the end of the Stour wing, opened the salon door and stopped.

Jessica was lazing in the leather armchair in the corner, sipping a cup of coffee, while Fisher was bent to his Morse machine tapping furiously.

'Mrs Staveley, if you wouldn't mind . . .' he said, not looking up but pointing to a stack of chits waiting for her on her desk. 'Mrs Harper kindly brought them over from the coop first thing. We are up to our necks. I needed you here at dawn, really.'

'I had no idea, I'm sorry. Bingley did not brief me last night.'

'Seems Roger is all at sixes and sevens, these days,' Jessica offered. 'And seeing as I am visiting Dad, at a loose end, I thought I'd help out. It's the least I can do.'

Eliza ignored her, sat down and sifted quickly through the messages, prioritising them in an instant. So Lewis must be away again. She shook her head. She must not think of him, of *them*. She looked up to see Jessica staring at her in pointed concentration.

'Don't mind me, Eliza,' she said and bared her teeth in a brief smile. 'I'll be gone in a jiffy. Just wanted to keep Ernie here company. Brewed him a coffee, see?'

Fisher raised an eyebrow as he continued with his cyphering. Eliza hadn't known Fisher's first name and she contemplated Jessica's knack of wheedling them out of the boys, like she'd done with Bingley.

Jessica, at last realising it was her cue to go, stood up and stretched luxuriously, catching Fisher's attention. She put on her raincoat, turned up the collar, placed her hands in her pockets and said lingering goodbyes.

Fisher waited until she had shut the door and her footsteps receded over the patio. 'I really should never have dabbled *there*.'

'What on earth do you mean?'

'It's just so awkward now,' he said, looking disgusted with himself. 'Fair enough,' he went on sheepishly. 'I took her out once or twice to the pub, but that's as far as it went. She let me kiss her once. And it was a long while ago. But it is just the fact she is now our old boss's wife, and is a link to Castle's pigeon coop. I simply find it hard to say no to her. She knows it, too.'

'She should not have been in here,' Eliza said. 'Ex-boss's wife or not.'

'Don't tell Bingley, please, Mrs Staveley. We're in the proverbial here. These dreadfully urgent radio messages have come through from HQ, evidently from the US Army. Strict instructions to send them out as code into a particular frequency. They don't make a heap of sense to me. But that is probably just as well. And what you have there,' he nodded at the paperwork Eliza had to translate, 'appears to be the French Resistance screaming for help, wanting instructions, begging for orders. This is all too much. Something is afoot. Something really is.'

'Well, stop talking about it and crack on.' Bingley appeared in the doorway, dishevelled and grey from lack of sleep. 'I've been ordered out of bed to come and help you. Show me your brief, Fisher. Good morning, Mrs Staveley. How is La France this morning?'

'Frantic, I'd say.'

Bingley sat down and began to sort through the messages that Fisher had to send out, while Eliza bent to her task. She heard them mention General Patten and the 21st Army, but closed her ears to it. She did not want to know.

Long ago she had realised how critical her work here was but did not like to dwell on it, absorb it or let it affect her. When her day was done, when she left the salon, she left it behind. All apart from the map of stars, for she often dreamt of that. That was Lewis's creation, and she had completed it for him. It bound them together. How clever he was, how vital he had been. The safety of her and her country lay in his hands. The safety of the men who would populate the foxholes lay in his hands and would continue to do so as long as his work was kept secret. Her pride in him was something separate from her love for him. It was a distinct and powerful thing, and it made her catch her breath.

She turned back to the task in hand. The messages from the Resistance were poignant, uplifting and desperate. They, like Fisher, had been briefed and seemed to be at the end of their tether. They, too, were awaiting instruction.

The following morning, the sound of the wireless, the reports, the sombre voice of the newscasters conveying the enormity of what was taking place, urged Eliza to get away, get outside, far from Forstall. Angela, on the other hand, arrived first thing, craving company.

'We are witnessing something simply momentous,' she said, joining Morris, Nick and Mathilde in the study. 'Audley went to ground at Manston days ago. I guessed something was happening, but put on my brave face. Ask no questions, you know how it is. But when I switched on the news this morning, my so-called resolve failed me. The king was on but my stiff upper lip has gone for a Burton. I'm terrified and I have to be at Forstall with my friends. I cannot listen to this on my own.'

As Eliza started to make her excuses, desperate to leave, Angela stopped her with a manicured hand on her arm.

'How are you keeping, my dear? And how is the little angel?' Angela picked up Stella and plopped her on her lap. Stella pushed her fingertips into the hair at the base of Angela's neck. 'Ouch. I haven't seen her in months. Goodness what a beauty. She's toddling well, I see.'

Eliza watched as Angela did what most people did: look at her daughter, look at her again, then look away, seeking the answer to the puzzle in their head. Stella's eyes were not of Staveley stock, or, indeed, Piper.

'So how are you, dear?' she asked again.

'We are well, thank you.' Eliza's politely dubious reply caused Angela to peer at her.

'That's good to hear. Chin up.' Angela caught her eye. 'You're a survivor, remember.'

Eliza eased Stella off Angela's lap and took her outside to the hallway to pack her into her pushchair. 'I won't be long!' she called, and shut the front door without waiting for a response.

She had not gone ten yards down the lane before the tolling of the newscaster's words caught up with her, staying with her like the portentous ringing of a bell.

'*All still goes well on the coast of Normandy . . .*'

As she walked in the dappled shelter of the hedgerows, the orchards billowed around her and, over her head, planes soared, their engines a crescendo through the sky. Lancasters and Halifaxes – the 'heavies' as Martyn would have called them – all with their noses pointed one way: across the water to France.

The bulletin resounded in her head: '*Ships and still more ships . . . an immense Armada of four thousand ships . . . Thirty-one thousand Allied airmen over France . . .*'

She reached Wickhambreaux. What a near-perfect summer's day it was, in deep contrast to yesterday's cloud and gloom. The green was peaceful, the houses sleeping around it, oblivious to the mayhem. Stella was chirping, laughing at the birds, at the nodding ox-eye daisies filling the verge, trailing her hand to pluck at the petals. Eliza followed the pavement, jolting the pushchair over chunks of flint, making her way to the church. The trees were in their full summer leaf, casting shadows over the headstones. There was a bench near Martyn's spot, his memorial cross over an empty grave.

She headed for it, pushing Stella through the lychgate and along the narrow path through the luxuriously long church-yard grass. Sitting down, she parked the pushchair so that Stella could see.

'This is Uncle Martyn's grave.' Eliza paused and was going to correct herself. But how could she begin to explain that his body was not there. 'See the wooden cross, there? That marks his life. This is how we commemorate him.'

Stella laughed brightly and pointed at it.

'Thing is, Stella, I so want to ask him a question,' Eliza confided, knowing she would not be judged. The little girl looked at her with solemn green eyes, rubbing her chin with the back of her hand. 'I want to ask him so many things.'

What does he think about this, what is happening here today . . .?

Her daughter wriggled, reaching forward to tug at her own toes.

Eliza gazed over at the Great War Memorial wondering, too, if the old soldiers in their graves, wherever they may be, on this land or abroad, would turn their faces to the skies and to the water, towards the enemy? Would Joan of Kent's Black Prince rise again with his sword? Would Arthur, the once and future king, ride out to meet them, a guiding spirit to the soldiers today, and tomorrow? Eliza shivered. What was going on across the narrow channel of sea?

For a moment, there was a gap in the distant roar of the planes, a respite from the noise. Eliza forced herself to relax, settling back on the bench to relish the gentle sounds of the countryside,

Stella's soft chatter. But the quietness lasted just a moment for it was filled suddenly with the popping sound of an engine.

'Will there ever be any peace, Stella?'

The little girl giggled as her attention was caught by something. Eliza followed her gaze, turning to peer over her shoulder.

It was Lewis. He had parked his motorbike by the kerb, and was easing off his helmet, smoothing down the ruffled-up portion of his hair. He turned and began to walk purposefully towards the churchyard, his boots ringing on the path.

In a cold flash of instinct, Eliza picked Stella up out of the pushchair and pressed her to her body. She watched, as protective as a she-wolf, as Lewis continued his approach. He appeared thinner, taller and more tanned, his face wary and questioning. He did not take his eyes off her.

Chilling shock crept into Eliza's bones, pinning her so that she could not move. Her arms were so tight around Stella that the child sensed her discomfort and began to wriggle.

Lewis stopped when he was halfway up the church path, his gaze dropping from Eliza's to Stella's face. He was close enough for Eliza to see an instant of agony in his eyes.

'May I?' he asked and extended a hand. 'May I join you?'

Eliza shifted to the far end of the bench. The long line of months that stretched out since they'd last been together, standing on the Stour wing patio, snapped into the present. Little jolts of confusion pierced her, and made it impossible for her to speak. A bolt of pain fixed her to the spot.

Lewis removed his leather jacket and sat down, leaving a courteous distance between them.

'I was greeted by your family like a returning hero just now at Forstall,' he said. 'Like the prodigal son. I didn't ask, but Angela made a point of telling me where you'd gone. Thing is, Eliza, I desperately need to speak to you.'

She dared herself to look at him. Her attraction to him felt like a smack on her cheek, physically hurting her.

'Why now?' she asked. 'Why now when I have begun to manage, to be able to live without you?' Her voice faltered, betraying her.

'Have you?' he asked.

Eliza squared her shoulders, holding Stella even tighter. The little girl whimpered.

'Have you come all this way, Lewis, to tell me all about your wedded bliss?'

He ignored her. 'May I?' he asked, gesturing to Stella.

Eliza assented, her still-present love for him making her momentarily soften. He lifted Stella from her lap and settled her gently on his knee, his face torn with pain.

'Look at her, just look at her,' he whispered, motioning gently around Stella's face.

Released from her mother's grip, Stella seemed delighted at his attention, and reached a chubby finger to press Lewis's cheek.

'Eliza, how can this be wrong?' he asked and dipped his head to smell the child's hair.

Eliza watched, startled by love for a moment until her core stiffened in defiance.

'It is wrong. And it is even more wrong now that you are married.'

'I'm so sorry.'

His apology was weak and of no use to her.

'Why *her*?' she asked. 'Of all the people . . . Did you do it to punish me? I know I hurt you, Lewis. We hurt each other. It was unbearable. You must know me so very well. For you certainly knew what to do to destroy me.'

'I could try to explain why I married her, but it is impossible –'

'Don't bother, for I don't want to hear your pitiful justification. Your excuses. Are you the same as all the rest of them? The others who seem to turn to putty in her hands? Fisher, Bingley, Arlington for goodness' sake. Even Sybil somehow could never stop singing her praises. And Nick . . .' She exhaled a hard bubble of laughter. 'Even Nick!'

She looked at him tentatively, like she might look at the sun.

'You look so sad,' he said, 'even when you are trying to smile.'

'I wasn't smiling.'

He touched her cheek. 'Yes you were. You were trying.'

'I feel like screaming, hitting you.' She flinched away from him, crushing her hands together to keep them still, to stop them trembling. Her fingers hardly felt like her own.

'But I am too much of a lady for that. Perhaps that's something *she* would do. I expect she is all passion, isn't she? You just have to look at her. To see why men love her –' Eliza stopped herself, took a deep breath. 'Kindly hand me back my daughter. I'm going home,' she said calmly.

'Eliza, please . . .'

She felt a terrible muddle, a white-out of her thoughts.

Lewis waited.

When at last he spoke, he said measuredly, 'Eliza, if I was able to explain why I did it, why I married her, then I would. But it is not possible.'

'Is her charm so potent that it is inexplicable?'

'I'm not here to talk about Jessica.'

'But she is your wife, remember?'

Eliza picked Stella up and set her back in her pushchair. The child began to protest, stiffening her little body and refusing to sit down. Lewis reached over to her, gently soothing, lifted her out and set her on the grass. She toddled over to the cross at Martyn's grave and began to trace her finger over his carved name.

Too weary to feel affronted, to demand that he stop interfering, Eliza asked, 'Why did you come here to find me? Why did you follow me here? I don't want to talk to you. I want you to go away.' She took a shuddering breath, knowing she was lying. 'I have managed, I have tried so hard in the last year and a half to forget you.'

'Eliza, I can see that. I can see how much this is hurting you. It is killing me.' Lewis drew closer, his eyes intense and flickering with regret. 'I haven't come here to hurt you. That is the last thing I want to do.'

He fished in his pocket and drew out a set of keys. Another volley of planes rumbled over the southern horizon. Lewis gazed at them, mesmerised, until they were out of sight.

'These keys are for my house in Hampstead. I want you to have it. Look.' He showed her the label tied to them with string. On it was written a London address.

'I do not want them. Why should I want it?'

Was he *leaving* her his house? Did this mean he thought he might die?

'It is somewhere you can go. Somewhere for you and Stella. Away from all of this. When the war is over . . .'

'But remember, Lewis, that your wife has a right to your property. This house will be hers, if . . . if . . . Don't tell me you have forgotten about her.'

Lewis lowered his eyes. 'She knows nothing about my house in Hampstead.'

'But that is ridiculous!' Eliza looked at him, and her courage failed, her trust in him fading again. 'But, anyway, even if I take these keys, go to your house, what do I tell Nick?'

'You can make things up, can't you? What about your fictitious pilot officer?' He grinned at her suddenly and Eliza felt a treacherous smile play over her mouth.

'That's better.' Lewis leant forward and placed a tender, questioning kiss on her lips. 'Will you stop being cantankerous now and kiss me?'

'How dare you,' she uttered, but despite her anger, despite her pain, she was instantly inside his arms, held fast in his embrace. Here was the moment she'd longed for since she'd sent him away. This was everything she'd craved and hadn't allowed herself to believe would ever happen.

He kissed her, soothed her, cradled her gently until weeping broke over her in a tremendous, shattering wave.

'Lewis, is there any point to us? Should I continue to care? To hope? Is there a future?'

He drew back and tilted his head, to get a good view of her face. He was enthralled by her, and she, in turn, captivated by him.

'You know what I want, what I have always wanted . . .' he began, and his tone made her want to struggle, to leave his grasp, her fury returning. 'But no, listen, Eliza. Please hear me out. The way I have behaved has been audacious. And, yes, ridiculous. I am not proud of myself. Please, listen to me.' He took a swift intake of breath, steeling himself. 'I am leaving this evening on my deadliest mission.' He peered at her, waiting for a response.

Despair crippled Eliza. She opened her mouth to cry out, but there was no sound.

Lewis looked up at the sky across which a new formation of bombers was moving with menacing drowsiness. 'I am following that lot,' he said. 'I am on my way to Manston now to fly into Normandy. I am parachuting in. We're tasked with following the advance, assisting the Resistance. This is just the start. There is a long battle ahead. There is a high chance that –'

'That's it!' she wailed. 'You think you might die!'

'It is a possibility. It has always been a possibility.' His face stiffened with tremendous pain. 'And the most terrible thing, and also the most astonishingly beautiful thing, is that I still love you. I always have.'

Eliza shook her head. She saw the look on his face and never wanted to see such torment again. She knew that she loved him completely but she scarcely heard what he was saying. Instead, her anger rose like fire.

'But, Lewis, you married another woman. You married *Jessica*!'

'I can't talk to you – you do not understand.' He stood up abruptly, gesturing with his hands as if to block her out. 'Care for our daughter, Eliza. Care for that little one. The house is hers.'

He walked away from her and picked up his crash helmet, which had been lying on the grass. He strode away, disappearing momentarily under the lychgate. He started up his motorbike, the engine popping and rumbling.

Eliza watched him as if he was the stranger again, leaving her in the wreckage. The noise of the engine grew louder and louder. She cried out, left her daughter on the grass and ran out of the churchyard. He was astride the bike, revving the engine. He'd strapped on his helmet but she could still see his mouth, his eyes. They were greener, brighter than ever before, and soaked with tears.

She touched the sleeve of his leather jacket, but it was thick and impenetrable. He would not have felt her touch.

'I can't have you leave me again,' she said, her voice tight with anger.

'I have no choice.'

'In that case,' she said in despair, 'there's just one thing I need you to do before you go. Can you kindly inform your wife, when you have your long goodbye with her, that she really shouldn't be sitting in on Fisher while he is sending Morse, and while I'm translating messages from the Resistance. As the wife of an intelligence commander, she should know better than that.'

His eyes widened smartly in alarm. He nodded.

'Thank you. I love you,' he mouthed.

He pulled down his goggles, turned his face from her, pushed in the throttle and roared away.

Eliza watched until he was out of sight and listened until she could hear no more of him, straining for every last throb of sound. Anguish raking through her, she finally turned and walked back into the churchyard, feeling the ground shaking beneath the soles of her feet. She found Stella sitting by Martyn's cross, merrily picking bright daisies from the grass.

Chapter 20

'I don't like the sound of these Boche flying bombs,' Morris said, turning back to the front page of his newspaper. 'Don't like the sound of them one jot. This is his counter-attack for the invasion. And we're right in the firing line. Deal was hit, for God's sake. Too close for comfort.'

'And Leonard said he heard that Maidstone was hit. It'll be in tomorrow's evening paper,' Mathilde said. 'Makes you not want to go out.'

'Or stay indoors,' said Eliza, under her breath. 'Or be anywhere at all.'

She glanced out of the French windows. The beauty of the garden, ablaze in the late afternoon sun, stung her with its contrast to her grinding despair.

The battle had been raging for a month, the names of French towns scattered through the news bulletins as the Germans resisted: Bayeux, Saint-Lô, Caen. And each day that dragged on, she sank lower, trapped in a loneliness of her own making. She could tell no one.

The air inside the house was warm and close. Stella, her face rosy from the heat and playing on the rug around her feet, was in danger of laddering her stockings with her little nails. Suddenly a breath of air reached Eliza in an intoxicating wave carrying the green scent of the little river. She turned her face to it, longing to drink it in.

'Well, what a turn-up,' said Morris, folding his newspaper to read a story in small print. 'Remember Arlington, Mathilde? The fella who was here at the start? He's in prison.'

'Good lord,' said Mathilde. 'Whatever for?'

'Spying. He's double crossed us all!'

Eliza was captured by the conversation. Suddenly she was back on the concourse at Victoria, spotting Jessica through the crowds, standing there with the major; his seething rage and her dangerous, dismissive laughter. But she did not want to think of Jessica. She wanted her gone from her mind and she felt she'd suffocate if she stayed indoors a moment longer.

'Come, Stella,' she said, gripping her daughter's chubby hand. 'Let's walk by the river for a while, where it should be cooler. Then I'll take you in to see Daddy. Early bed for you tonight.'

She left her mother and Morris discussing the news and whether or not sherry was appropriate on such a warm day, and took Stella's hand, leading her slowly, zig-zaggedly across the lawn.

At the bottom of the garden, beyond the air-raid shelter, the little path opened onto the river bank. Eliza picked Stella up for their way was hampered by sultry beds of forget-me-nots and the blades of tall rushes. Deep in the water trailed streams of cress, the surface bubbling and sparkling. Beyond the river, the orchards of ripening plums surrendered to the last heat of the day.

'There, see that!' cried Eliza, suddenly excited by the flash of a dragonfly captured in the sunlight low over the water.

'What, Mama, what?' Stella demanded.

But of course it was gone before she could even point to where she thought she had seen it.

The Stour ran languidly on. They left it under the shelter of the trees and headed towards the wing. Stella climbed unsteadily up the steps beside Eliza, insisting on not holding her hand. The door was open, Eliza assumed to let in a draft of cool air from the river, and so she pushed it wide and ushered Stella to the left and into the kitchen. Nick was snoozing in his armchair in the parlour, his feet on a stool, the radio softly playing Glenn Miller.

Stella woke him with an enthusiastic 'Dada!' and patted him hard on the legs.

'Goodness, you little horror!' He scooped her up as she giggled and wriggled.

'She's in a bit of a hot bother,' said Eliza, 'so perhaps you could calm her down a bit?'

Nick glanced up. 'Of course I will. Whatever you say. I'll read to her. How's that, Smidgen? Shall I read to you?'

Stella laughed and tugged at his sandy hair.

'Yes, please do,' Eliza told him. 'But not Dickens like you did the other evening. I think it gave her nightmares. Why not try some Peter Rabbit?'

'Would you like that, Smidgen?' Nick asked Stella. 'That naughty little rabbit?'

Eliza left her husband and daughter browsing the shelf for the book and wandered back out to the kitchen to see if there was any milk for Stella. She heard the Morse machine tapping next door in the salon and decided to pop her head round the door. Fisher or Bingley might need something. Since the Normandy landings their workload had become intolerable and euphoria at the invasion had given way to the reality of a long hard slog ahead. It was the least she could do, when not required to translate, to provide cups of tea, or sometimes something stronger.

She knocked on the salon door, called out hello and pushed it open. Jessica was at Bingley's desk, hunched over the Morse code machine, her lacquered fingernails poised. She looked up in a flash, her startled eyes widening. There was no one else in the room. Where on earth were Fisher and Bingley?

'Jessica?' Eliza said, low and evenly, closing the door behind her. 'What is it you think you are doing?'

'I *think* I am sending a Morse code message. What is it *you* think I am doing?'

'On whose authority?'

'My husband's authority.'

Eliza flinched. Jessica noticed and narrowed her stare, firing a cold, hard smile at her.

'Yes, Eliza, dear,' she said, running the tips of her fingers over the edge of the papers in front of her. '*My* husband.'

Eliza squared her shoulders. 'Commander Harper is no longer part of this unit, as you know, and has not been for some time,' she said. 'This office is out of bounds to anyone other than the people stationed here. This is completely irregular. I need to call HQ.'

'I wouldn't do that. Why should they listen to you?'

'Where's Fisher?'

Jessica said lightly, 'He popped out to the village. He wanted some cigarettes.'

'I'm calling Bingley.' Eliza sat down at her desk and lifted the receiver, reaching for the address book that listed The Gables telephone number.

'Do you realise . . . ?' Jessica said, amused, her confidence startling as she leant back in Bingley's chair. 'Do you realise, Eliza, that you are interrupting the reporting of critical information?'

'Critical to whom?' Eliza retorted, her fingers trembling as she began to dial. She made a mistake, had to start again. She tapped the buttons on the telephone, urging a dialling tone. She *had* to get hold of Bingley; he would tell her what to do.

Jessica stood up abruptly, came around the bank of desks and perched herself in front of Eliza, crossing her legs, long and shapely in their jodhpurs. Her crisp white blouse flattered her figure, a figure that Lewis had admired. A flash of pain temporarily blinded her. She stared at the dial as the exchange clicked and clacked in her ear.

'Come on, Eliza, let's talk this through,' Jessica implored her, her face lifting with a crookedly sweet smile.

Her powdery perfume and the proximity of her body were formidable, but Eliza spotted a glare of desperation in her eyes, a crack in the veneer that she wore to deal with brutish men like Arlington. And who else? The person who had tasked her to rummage through the files in the salon at Forstall. Send Morse code to God knows where. *Arlington?*

The telephone at last rang out to The Gables. With the receiver pressed to her ear, her palm wet with sweat, Eliza imagined it peeling through the little hallway, up the stairs, waking Bingley from his night-shift-induced sleep.

'We've had our ups and downs, but I always thought that we were friends,' Jessica said, raising her voice to grip Eliza's attention. 'We go back such a long way and I know I was a bit of a cow to you, but, goodness, we were only children! You can't blame me anymore. It was all so long ago.' Her words were now fluid and low. She put her hand to her throat as if to express vulnerability. As Jessica smiled down at her, sweat drenched Eliza's collar. She silently urged Bingley, the landlady, anyone to pick up the telephone.

'I used to think of you and Nicholas and dear Martyn when I was in Vienna,' said Jessica. 'I remembered all our summers together here in Kent. Can you guess how lonely I was? You were my only friends. And I always wanted what you had. All those people around you. So much attention.'

The ringing of the telephone was insistent in her ear.

Baffled, she glanced up at Jessica. 'You *had* attention.'

'Not the right sort. Father was a nonsense to me. Mother was dead and he sent me away to that damned finishing school. Shut away in the middle of nowhere.' She smiled in memory. 'You know, I think they all wore jackboots even then.'

The telephone continued to ring out, blaring in Eliza's ear.

'And I would like to think that you would understand my situation. Lewis is on one of his missions. I want to do all I can to help. With him gone, you of all people must know how terribly worrying this is for me?'

She placed her hand on Eliza's shoulder just as the landlady answered the telephone with an insistent, 'Hello? Hello?'

Eliza cringed under Jessica's touch and replaced the receiver without a word.

'Terrible for *you*, Jessica?' she whispered, as the weight of the hand on her shoulder made her feel dirty and rotten. 'It's not just *you*.'

'I always wanted what you had when we were children.' Jessica's face brightened with triumph. 'And now it seems I have what you want. And don't say you don't know what I'm talking about. I saw the look on your face just now, as soon as I mentioned him. It's written all over you. Christ!' She let out a brief, wild laugh. 'I guessed ages ago, Eliza. Aren't you ashamed?'

'Yes, I suppose I am. But I'm not a traitor.'

Jessica stood up, grabbed the satchel that was hooked over the chair and marched towards the door. With her fingers on the handle, she paused. 'Different levels of treachery,' she said. 'And you won't, of course, be mentioning finding me here, will you? Right decision about cutting off Mrs What's-her-name, by the way.'

'I can ring her right back.'

'I wouldn't, dear. Because I do wonder what Nick would have to say about you and Lewis. We can soon find out, can't we? He's just in there, next door with your daughter, isn't he? *Your* daughter, of course. I assume she's not his. Ho, let me guess. Your child is two and half, so if you give me a moment to work that out . . .' She pretended to count on her fingers and broke out into laughter. 'It won't take me a moment to tell him, will it?' She glanced at her watch with relish. 'I think I have some time.'

Eliza stared at her beautifully cruel face. Nick was fully aware that Stella was not his daughter, she wanted to snap back at her. But if her lies were going to unravel, if the whole family was going to know the truth, she wanted it to happen when she was ready. Not like this. But she wouldn't plead with Jessica – that would only goad her.

'Nothing to say, Eliza? Dad's pigeons have come home to roost.' Jessica's mocking laugh rang out. She flung open the door. 'And so will your sins.'

Eliza waited, her hand still on the telephone. Her pulse soared in her throat, her hairline was cold with sweat. Fragments of anxiety fired at her like bullets: the explanations and accusations. The stark reality of her life, all of her lies laid bare. Her family knowing how black her soul had become.

But she didn't hear the door to the kitchen open. Moments later, there came the distinctive rattle of Jessica's bicycle as she wheeled it across the patio. Surely, she hadn't had time to tell Nick. Eliza rushed to the window and watched her go. But, instead of heading around to the front of the manor as she expected her to, Jessica hurried to the bridleway along the river.

Eliza frowned, briefly confused, but then slumped back onto her chair, weakened by a wave of relief.

'Oh, where the hell is Fisher?' she muttered.

She went to the desk where Jessica had been sitting. Something was wrong. She'd been rifling through lists of code words for auxiliary foxholes. They should have been in the safe. Eliza rushed over to it and knelt down. The door was shut but not locked. She wrenched it open, and desperately turned over piles of charts, sheaves of buff files stamped *Top Secret* and pushed aside a bottle of brandy. The top section of the map of stars, the 'constellation', was gone.

Eliza dived to Bingley's drawer and hauled out the strong-box. It was unlocked, its contents spilled. She sifted through the documents. The map of Kent, the bottom part, wasn't there either. She rummaged again, and again, and again. Each part of the map was useless and meaningless without the other; but both were gone, simply gone.

She gave a muffled cry of despair and slammed the drawer shut. Jessica had helped herself to the map of stars, and walked out of the salon with it secreted in her satchel. Eliza's anxiety blossomed into fury. She could not sit there and let this happen. Whatever would Lewis think?

She raced out of the salon, but stopped abruptly at the kitchen door when she heard Nick reading a story to Stella in the parlour, his voice lifting and falling below the little girl's laughter. She whispered a relieved thank you, her gratitude enormous, and hurried around to the front of the manor where her car was parked. Breathless, she fired the engine and turned the car around, jerking the gears in her haste. Almost delirious with anger, she spun off down the lane, meeting the main road, heading east.

She pulled up in a tiny lane some four miles away from Forstall and parked the car close to the verge. The bridleway that Jessica had taken veered away from the Stour a few fields away, meeting the lane around about here. She killed the engine and kept hold of the steering wheel, her palms slick on its surface. There were hints of an evening sky over in the west and the green countryside, rolling down to meet the old kingdom of Thanet, looked innocent enough. But, Eliza knew, it held surprises for the enemy. Not a hundred yards to her left, if she remembered rightly, was the foxhole codenamed Haricot, tunnelled deep into the ground within a small copse of willow.

She had never seen a foxhole before, for it was too dangerous for her to know much more about them, but Lewis had explained how the hideouts were built: underground chambers with two camouflaged entrance shafts sunk into the earth at either end, with iron bars for steps. There was a ventilation pipe, supplies, tools and guns and bullets; and space inside for five men.

If the tide turned, these men would be poised for the most murderous type of warfare. The first and most precious line of defence of English soil: guerrillas who were trained to kill, silently and swiftly. But the map showing their secret positions was missing. It was in the hands of her enemy.

Eliza got out of the car and waited in the still evening air. She glanced down the lane, her heart racing with primal, animal fear, her stomach vibrating like a nest of wasps. The grasses at her feet curved and nodded, heavy with pollen. Hedges grew high on either side, tangled with honeysuckle and dog roses, still busy with the last of the bees as the sun sank. And in to all this peaceful beauty, Jessica appeared, pedalling her bicycle, looking as serene and glorious as she always did. She began to laugh as soon as she spotted Eliza.

'You don't give up, do you?' she called out. 'You've been rather clever coming this way to head me off. Good work. I know who

I should recommend you to, but it might prove difficult as he is in the clink.'

She hopped off her bike and held onto the handlebars, standing upright, commanding, her smile remaining as cold as steel.

'Turn out your bag, Jessica.' Eliza was dangerously, chillingly, calm.

Jessica shrugged, did not move.

'I know that Lewis would not allow you to do what you were doing,' Eliza said. 'Sending Morse code like that from the salon. He certainly would never have allowed me to perform any such task.' Eliza felt her voice break. 'You should never have been left alone there.'

'Ah, you see, I cannot mistake it.' Jessica's voice was rising and sing-song. 'You are so transparent, Eliza. How long have you been in love with my husband?'

Eliza watched Jessica warily. Despite the cruel twist of her features, a film of sweat had appeared along her top lip. The red lipstick was smudged and broken.

'Never mind that, Jessica. Hand me the map.'

'What map?'

'I'm not going to stand here and argue with you. Hand over the map – both parts of it – and I won't mention any of this to anyone.'

'You're so loyal to the salon. So loyal to him, aren't you? It's quite heartbreaking and pathetic really. Still in love with him even when he's gone and married me. What a big fool you are.' She glanced down, distracted by the ring on her finger. She began to fiddle with it. 'I tell you what, Eliza, let's broker a deal.

I won't tell your stupid husband that his child is not his, and you can have this as a memento, if you like. I don't want it any more. I'm probably a widow by now anyway.'

'*What*?'

'I don't love Lewis, you fool. I never did. But there's a war on and a girl like me needs stability. Needs a foot in the door. He has so many connections in the places I need them. What with them all dropping like flies. He's a man in the know. And quite a catch. Or maybe *was* . . .'

Jessica tugged off her wedding ring and held it up so it glinted rosy-gold in the light, then slung it at Eliza's feet.

'There, take it if you want it.'

The ring hit Eliza's shoe and bounced into the dust.

Eliza ignored it. 'The map, Jessica. Hand me the map.'

'You can say it as many times as you like but I still don't know what you are talking about. Look, this is getting tiresome –' Jessica glanced up towards a noise in the sky.

Eliza heard it too, but was loath to take her eyes off Jessica. There was a low vibration, a buzzing sound swooping in from the south, or was it from the east?

'Just go back to your husband,' Jessica said, 'and leave me alone. You're in this way over your head.'

She picked up her bicycle and began to wheel it away down the lane, her satchel banging against her hip. As she turned the corner, she peered upwards, shielding her eyes. Eliza kept her eyes on the satchel: the map of stars was in there. She wanted to run after her, force her, grab the bag but something made her hesitate. The peculiar droning in the sky grew closer, heavier and lower like a swarm of angry flies. At her feet lay Jessica's ring. She bent down to pick it up. The noise escalated. It was nothing like flies; it was an engine, a rocket. She saw it briefly as it plunged out of the sky arching over the little copse of willow: a flying bomb with fire at its tale.

Suddenly, there was no noise, just a normal silence. Eliza cried out, shouted a warning. She crouched, leaning sideways into the verge, crushing herself against the hedge. The rocket exploded, ripping the air, tearing it apart. The force of it flattened her into the brambles. A fireball, brief and startlingly beautiful, red and orange, blew skywards above the willows, above the Haricot foxhole. She pressed her hands over her ears, over her head, terrified, unable to scream.

Then a ghastly, empty silence.

Eliza got up from her knees and crept along the hedge, to peer into the field. A mangled heap of shrapnel had torn a crater in the earth. The grass and the willows were scorched, fire flickering around the jagged shell, burning out. Jessica lay face-down on the ground, her limbs at unnatural angles. Her head was lacerated, her blonde hair a bloody mess. The bicycle lay on its side next to her, the wheels still spinning.

Eliza went towards her, cautiously stepping over tufts of grass, pieces of shrapnel. Jessica lifted her head, digging her elbows in to the ground to haul her shoulders up. She looked at Eliza, her face wide with pain. Her eyes were flashing with terror.

'Keep away,' she cried weakly. 'It might explode again. The fire. There's fire.'

Eliza froze. She spotted that Jessica's satchel had been flung to one side. She walked towards it, quite calmly, and picked it up. It was empty.

'There's no map.' Eliza threw it down. She looked back at Jessica and jolted with shock as she noticed that her leg was crushed under a lump of violently twisted metal. Eliza saw the lacerated flesh and bone and felt cold sickness break over her.

'I told you,' Jessica muttered, her brow punctured with pain. 'I told you I didn't have the stupid map. Didn't stop me sending out the messages containing the secret codes though, did it. Good job I picked up Morse so quickly from the major. Fisher is so stupid –'

She grunted, tried to turn over, to sit up. She glanced down at her leg and began to sob, blurting little screams of agony. She looked up at Eliza, craning her neck. Blood trickled down from her head, staining the snowy whiteness of her blouse.

'Eliza . . .' She began to plead.

Eliza unfurled her fist to see Jessica's wedding band lying in the palm of her hand. She had been holding it so tight that it had imprinted itself into her flesh.

'Someone will find you,' she said. 'Someone from Ash, or the farm over there will come for you. They would have seen the explosion. Heard it at least. Someone will find you.'

'Are you *leaving*?' Jessica sounded incredulous. Her voice was rusty, a film of sweat glistening on her pale forehead. She was staring with ice-cold eyes, but Eliza could already see that they were turning opaque, the light was going out. Jessica lowered her head as if longing for sleep.

Eliza turned and ran back down the lane. She got back into her car and sat quite still, her hands on the steering wheel, her forehead resting between them.

'What do I do? What do I do?' she whispered to herself. 'Someone will find her. Help her. Surely, someone will.'

The screaming of the bomb and Jessica's soft sobbing did not disappear, even as she fired the engine and pulled off down the lane. The noise stayed with her, the flash of the explosion and the way Jessica taunted her, even as she negotiated the tight bends, the forks in the road and the bumpy flints of Forstall's drive. By the time she reached home, the sun was setting. The day was over, but Eliza knew that it would never leave her.

Chapter 21

1945

Eliza stood next to Nick on the Hampstead street with Stella in her arms. Behind her the Heath flowed and undulated, long, streaming grass punctuated with trees, secret hollows, hidden dells. Children played, their voices carrying in the breeze. Families strolled by, complete because the soldiers had come home, or incomplete because they had not. Further down the view into the great valley of London, the city was grey, curving along the river.

'Looks like it has survived the Blitz,' Nick said, looking up at the house, which stood towering upwards in the centre of the terrace. The large sash windows were homely, the front door painted an oily green. 'There are a few slipped tiles and the windowsills could do with a lick of paint. But apart from that, seems Angela has a good investment here –'

'Let's see what it's like inside,' said Eliza. She glanced over her shoulder at the Heath, aware of its unfamiliarity, its wide open space looming at her back. 'Hurry, I want to be inside.'

Nick gave her a worried glance, picked up her suitcase and ushered her and Stella in.

Ranged over four floors, with a fine staircase, a long hallway and stained glass in its windows, the house epitomised Victorian suburban grandeur. Nick checked the water and the boiler in the little scullery at the back – 'Goodness, there's an old tin bath in here!' – while Eliza climbed up the stairs with Stella and walked along the landing. She watched her daughter trot along the long, shining parquet floor, her russet curls bouncing from under her little felt hat.

'Another stairs?' Stella asked. 'More stairs? Can we climb up?'

'Yes, but be careful.'

Stella darted up the next set of stairs and peered at her through the banisters, laughing. Eliza saw Lewis smiling at her through the railings above Ramsgate harbour.

'Go and find Daddy,' she said.

Alone on the first floor, Eliza decided that the bedroom at the front overlooking the Heath would be hers. From the window, she could make out St Paul's, another survivor of the war, its dome gleaming like pewter in the midday light. There was a scrolled wallpaper, fading from purple to pink, and heavy damask curtains. The furniture was oak, turn-of-the-century, the framed mirror nicely foxed. She ran a finger along the polished surface of the dressing table. The char had done a good job of airing and preparing the principal rooms. She guessed that this had once been Mr and Mrs Harper's bedroom.

She found Nick and Stella in the basement kitchen, opening their sandwiches on the table beneath the wide window.

Looking up, Eliza glimpsed the street through the railings and the wild Heath beyond. They'd bought a flask of tea, but Eliza insisted on boiling a kettle on the gas cooker to make a fresh pot.

'I want to make sure this oven works before you leave,' she said.

The water looked rather brown when she first turned on the tap, but she let it run.

'Are you sure you will be all right on your own?' Nick looked at her with a worried frown. 'Sorry, I'm going on. You need the time, I know. Time to be alone. It's just that Smidgeon, here, might not understand. Well, I, for one, know she will not.'

Eliza smiled briefly at her husband and absent-mindedly reached over to wipe Stella's mouth. Her daughter was chewing her sandwich, oblivious, transfixed by the high ceiling of the kitchen – used as she was to Forstall's low, dark beams – the parquet floor and the huge, cream-painted mantelpiece. A car tooted as it went past and caused Stella to break into giggles. The sound of neighbours chatting in the street, the anonymous noise of the city was unfamiliar but soothing to Eliza; a distraction.

'Stella will be fine,' she said. 'She has you, she has Morris, she has Maman.'

Nick got up to stretch his legs and wandered out into the passageway and up the stairs. Eliza heard him opening doors above to peer into rooms.

'Have you seen the back parlour yet?' he called down. 'Beautiful window onto the garden, with steps down. Come and have a look!'

But Eliza decided to stay put. She did not have enough energy to explore the entire house in one go. She would have plenty of opportunity in the next weeks, and months, if necessary. Lewis's old family home would reveal itself to her all in good time.

Nick came back. 'It's not as fine as our own garden, I might add. I think Ma might have had something to say about those scrubby old roses out there, but . . . So good of Angela, wasn't it? A year's lease on a London bolthole. Adequately furnished, to boot. And in rather good condition. She has this knack of coming up trumps, doesn't she? I expect she would rather this house was being lived in, and not become another thing to worry about now that Audley's passed away. I must say, I didn't know they owned so much property. A town house in Hampstead. Fancy.'

'Nick,' said Eliza, dipping in quickly. 'You do understand why I must do this, don't you? Why I must get away.'

He looked at her, his face confident. 'Yes, I totally understand.'

Eliza, returning his gaze, believed him; her gratitude was humbling.

'And Angela has been doubly marvellous, hasn't she?' Nick went on. 'Recommending the psychiatrist.'

Indeed, Angela had thrown her such an unexpected lifeline.

Audley's passing, dying of a stroke at his desk at Manston before peace was declared, was a terrible blow. Soon after the funeral, Eliza had visited Angela in Ramsgate to find her a spectre of her vital self; pale, uncertain and stiff with grief, her tall frame stooping. But she had spoken eloquently about loving her husband, and the chances of happiness that were, in her experience, so fleeting. Death was always, she had warned Eliza, just in the next room.

And then, in her old way, she had peered at Eliza, and asked how she was. Sitting in the parlour where she and Lewis had spent the night together, he on the sofa, she on the armchair, Eliza had broken down. But when Angela pressed her, words failed Eliza.

Angela had persisted. She'd said, pointedly, 'I sent Lewis Harper after you, on that terrible day of the Normandy landings. And he found you, I take it?'

Eliza had pulled out the key he'd given her, the key to his Hampstead house.

'He knew he would not be coming back,' she'd said. 'He left me this. I want to go there, I need to. I need to see that house. I want to hide in it. He was born there, you see. I might feel closer to him. But how can I explain this to Nick, to anyone . . .?'

'I can see what love has done to you,' Angela had said, gravely. 'This is my mistake, making you feel so guilty right at the start, insisting you stay with Nick. Was that wrong?'

'No, of course it wasn't. How can I blame you?' said Eliza.

'Say the house is mine. That I'm letting you stay there.'

Eliza gaped at her in surprise.

'And here, there's something else.' Angela stood up and went to her bureau, dipping into little drawers until she found what she was looking for. She handed Eliza a dog-eared card.

'I can see how much you've been struggling with everything.'

Eliza stared at the psychiatrist's card, registering the London address, then back at Angela.

'Do you think he can help me?' Eliza asked, surprised at how faint her voice had become.

'This is your chance to pull yourself out of it,' Angela said. 'By God, I can't bear to see you like this. When I think of you as a bright young girl . . . I want to see you bloom again.'

In the Hampstead kitchen, Nick was worrying about there not being a telephone. 'Just make sure one is installed as soon as possible,' he said.

'You have Dr Weinstein's number?' she asked him. 'Just in case?'

Nick assured her that he did.

Stella slipped down from the table and began opening drawers on the large dresser.

'Perhaps you shouldn't do that,' Eliza warned her. 'This is someone else's house, after all.'

'What is *all*?' Stella asked, touching in wonder an old-fashioned rolling pin lying on a veined marble slab.

All is *everything*, thought Eliza. Being here in Lewis's family home is everything.

She looked at her watch. 'Don't you think you'd better make tracks if you want to catch the train from Victoria? You know they're only once an hour.'

'Mama, aren't you coming with us?' Stella asked.

Eliza picked her up and sat her on her lap but she wriggled, determined to be set free.

'Want to go up more stairs again.'

'There isn't time. Oh, this child never stays still. Never wants me to hold her.'

Nick said, 'She's just a livewire, our little Smidgeon.'

'But she doesn't want *me*.'

Eliza watched, shattered by a torrent of despair, as Nick coaxed her daughter and scooped her up.

'We've had a nice trip, haven't we, Smidgeon? But we don't want to spoil it by missing our train home. And being stuck in the rush hour like sardines in a tin. Now, give Mama one of your lovely cuddles.'

'What's sardines?'

'I'll tell you when we get on the Underground. That'll help you understand what I mean.'

She sat perfectly still, perfectly obedient for him, while he eased her miniature white gloves on to her hands.

'Ah, Eliza, I just remembered,' he said conversationally. 'Morris told me just before we left this morning. They definitely think Jessica Castle – sorry, Harper – was working as a spy for the Germans. Mixed up with that Arlington bloke, it seems, which is a double blow. She's officially on the wanted list. Been missing just over a year now.'

Eliza busied herself tidying their sandwich papers away, crushing them tightly in her fist.

'It's over now, all over,' she said, concentrating on collecting the crumbs on the table.

'Over in Europe only, my dear.'

'But they can't just leave it?'

'Never. They'll want to arrest her. Try her. It's treason, you know. It perplexes me, it really does. How she could do such a thing. Right under our noses. Don't understand why Bingley and Fisher, and that Harper fellow – her own husband for goodness' sake! – didn't rumble her. It's beyond me. Perhaps he was in on it too.' Nick eased the screwed-up papers out of her tightly squeezed fist and asked Stella to find the bin. 'Although, I think the Vienna finishing school had a lot to do with it. Look what happened to that Mitford girl. What must Leonard be going through now?'

Eliza thought of Leonard Castle doggedly tending his pigeons, talking to them like he had always done, answering endless questions from the authorities. She thought of the salon in the Stour wing, now empty; Bingley and Fisher gone back to Whitehall, their machines and filing cabinets taken away. It was over now, all over in France. And still, Lewis had not come home.

Stella refused to kiss her, refused to look at her and Eliza had to let her go without a goodbye. She gave Nick a brief hug at the door to say thank you.

'It's all right,' he said, somewhat shyly. 'You don't need to thank me. You understand me, and I will always try to understand you.'

Eliza looked at him, believing that he would. He had encouraged her to make an appointment with Dr Weinstein. He even, after a fashion, agreed to her staying at the Hampstead house alone, if that's what she wanted. If that would help her get better. And still, she wove her lies, even as he supported her, willed her to rest and recuperate, unknowingly, in Lewis's house.

When they were finally out of sight – tall man in raincoat and trilby, little girl holding his hand, dancing along beside him and around the corner – Eliza shut the front door, turned her back on it, leant on it and faced the silent, empty house. Alone, she heard

Jessica sobbing; saw her eyes fade, drift into unconsciousness. Heard herself saying: '*Someone will find you.*'

But evidently, they hadn't. Had Jessica crawled away? Found help and got herself patched up? Gone to ground? Left the country? Was she, right now, laughing about it?

She walked slowly up the stairs, with every step hoping to shed the memories, like peeling off a layer of skin. But they crowded back in on her, chattering at her, seeking her attention. She opened the door to the back bedroom. Deep green, William Morris pattern wallpaper made it feel like she was stepping into a cocoon. She lay on her side on the single bed with its thin, navy candlewick covering and stared at the gallery of paintings on the walls: yachts, ships in full sail, Ramsgate harbour with fishing boats, seagulls and fluttering flags; a Margate sunset; Deal seafront. She wept quietly, privately. This, she knew in the darkest part of her soul, had been Lewis's room.

Chapter 22

Leaving the Heath behind her and walking down the long hill into the leafy avenues of Golders Green, the grand Victorian houses gave way to semi-detached villas. Dr Weinstein's home was typical: bay windows, a gabled roof and a stained glass windmill set in the window of his front door. She sat in the waiting room on a modern Scandinavian armchair perched in the bay and gazed at a cheap print of Montmartre on the wall, and then, in turn, at one of the Lake District. There was a small fireplace tiled in pink and a well-thumbed stack of *Reader's Digest* on a coffee table.

She was early and had to wait until she heard a door open and someone leave. Dr Weinstein himself popped his head around the door and told her to come through. The pale peach walls of his room were lined with framed certificates. Blinds filtered sunlight, the slats sending beams dancing on the fireplace, bookshelves and curvaceous ceramics. An ashtray on his desk held a lit cigarette which sent a straight plume of silvery smoke to the ceiling. He indicated that she sit in a high-backed leather chair which squeaked when she sat down. By her side was a small, low table with a glass of water, a pot plant and a box of tissues. She had to ram her heels into the carpet to stop herself slipping off the leather cushion.

Picking up the cigarette, he took a drag then sat down opposite her, looking across at her, cocking his head. His clothes were brown, nondescript; his shoes expensive. He said not a word to her. He had neither notebook or pen. He simply waited for Eliza to speak.

Angela had warned her that Dr Weinstein never asked questions, that this was his method to encourage his patients, to prompt them to start at the beginning.

Eliza put her shaking hand to her forehead and ran her fingers through her lock of stark white hair, searching for the reason she was there, desperate to pinpoint why, finding it so very difficult to know what to say first.

After a several long minutes, during which the clock on the mantel ticked despondently, Dr Weinstein sighed, leant forward to offer her a handkerchief and broke his professional habit.

'Mrs Staveley,' he said. 'Where shall we begin?'

Walking back up to Hampstead, the breeze dried the tears streaming down Eliza's face. Pedestrians side-stepped her, motor cars passed her, buses rumbled by, all continuing in everyday ordinariness while she walked in a daze, through waves of mild euphoria. The appointment with the psychiatrist had momentarily quenched her pain and her hot, startling tears washed it away. It would be three days before her next session. Would this false elation last until then?

She had her answer as she approached Lewis's house, as she opened the oily-green door and went in. Darkness fell in a black wind of terror. She was again alone; once more bereft.

She wandered up the stairs, along the landing and up again, feeling in the pocket of her coat as she did so.

During Nick and Stella's brief visit, Stella had only ventured a few steps up the second staircase and it was later that evening that Eliza had explored the top floor and found a maid's room next to a bathroom and a laundry cupboard at the far end. She went there now, to the furthest corner, to the deepest part of this house that she could possibly go.

She drew out Jessica's ring from her pocket. It lay on her palm, the rose-gold shining. She had fumbled with it throughout the session with Dr Weinstein and as she stared at it, she remembered his words as he rounded off her session that afternoon: that this journey might take a very long time indeed.

Eliza opened the laundry cupboard and leant in, reaching as far into the back as she could. She tucked the ring in behind a pile of old towels, heard it settle on the wooden slat, and closed the door.

Chapter 23

1946

Eliza stood on the path, her hand resting on the gate. Sybil's roses were thriving, glorious. Through their melting colours of pink and scarlet she saw her daughter sitting on the gravel in front of the doorstep. Stella was trailing her fingers through the ragged thyme that grew there, humming to herself as she pinched off leaves to extract the scent, cradling them in the palm of her hand. She whispered, sang and conversed with herself, oblivious to the world beyond her own, or to her mother, watching.

Eliza found herself smiling, while, at the same time, tears pricked in her eyes. The journey that Dr Weinstein had talked of on her very first appointment had taken the best part of a year. And a year was an age in childhood, an absolute age. How Stella had bloomed. And how she had drawn even further away from her.

Eliza took a tentative step forward, wondering if her footfall would alert the child. But Stella was unaware of her, continuing with her chatter. Eliza recoiled. Stella was also unaware of the boy standing quite still behind her, watching patiently over her.

Scarcely breathing, Eliza moved gingerly up the path through the roses. The humid, scented air shimmered and parted, made way for her. She flinched with blunt recognition. The boy was Martyn. And he was not more than ten years old. He shadowed Stella, watching her and protecting her. And the shock of seeing him, his apparition, scalded Eliza. She opened her mouth to call out – a greeting or a warning, she was not sure – just as the sun appeared from behind a cloud, suddenly sharp over the eaves of the house. Eliza shut her eyes, blinded for a moment. Just a moment. But within that indiscernible instant of time, when she looked again, he had gone.

Stella glanced up, sensing movement among the roses and cringed in brief terror when she saw her. Eliza spoke her name, cautiously, gently. But the little girl didn't respond. Instead, she looked behind her, looked to where Tintin had been standing.

Eliza saw loss flickering in her daughter's wary eyes. And by the time she reached the step, Stella began to cry.

Eliza picked her up but Stella wriggled. Now nearly five with grubby knees and scabbed shins, she was heavier, sturdier, so much more of a little girl than she'd been when Eliza had last seen her.

Eliza pressed her lips to her hair and breathed in.

'It's Mama, come home,' she whispered, and the child looked at her solemnly as if she didn't believe her.

Eliza glanced down at the front step and read the motto. Her journey was over.

She pushed open the front door and walked in carrying Stella. As she called out, her voice cracked and shattered with joy.

'Hello, Nick, Morris, Maman. I am home!'

Part IV

Morning Star
'the bringer of light'

Chapter 24

Stella, 1953

Kneeling down, Stella peered into the water. The bank was a soft, grassy cushion beneath her scuffed knees, the river bubbling and giggling, trailing weeds like green hair: her own little river running through her garden.

Mesmerised, she watched its resolute, unceasing course as it sparkled over pebbles and around kinks in the low banks. Grasping squeaking reeds to hold on to, she leant over until she could see her face in the stream. She should not go so close, should not lean so far; the grown-ups always told her. But she wanted to see if Tintin's face was there too, just like hers: smiling and watchful, sunlight reflecting off cheeks and forehead. But beside her, in the water, he was not there. It looked like she was alone. She reached forward with one hand, dipped her fingers in. The water was silky, malleable and, despite the balmy afternoon sun, an icy-cold surprise.

The van honked outside on the lane. She jumped up and scooted across the lawn, holding out her hand so that it dried as she ran, droplets flying. Around the end of the Stour wing, across the lawn, crashing through the house. She made it to the rose garden and out to the front in time to see the vehicle ease its rocking way along the uneven road surface towards the house, squeezing through hedgerows, raking off twigs, leaves, whole branches at a time.

'Dad! Mum! It's here!' she whooped and scuttled back inside, racing up the stairs to her habitual perch on the half landing. She sat, panting, in her vantage point. Tintin, as usual, had caught up with her, and was waiting for her there and watching her in solemn appraisal. She never saw how he did it, but he was often behind her, at the corner of her eye. But now they were huddled at their usual spot, out of the way of the grown-ups.

The back doors of the vans crashed open, followed by cheery cries of 'hello' and 'right-oh, guv'nor'.

Two men in caps and long fawn coats steadily carried the television set through the door, concentrating and joking. Stella was surprised. It was just a large, quite ugly, cumbersome box, brown and shiny, with twiddly knobs and a golden mesh at the front. And evidently very heavy, for Dad felt the need to step forward to help and join in with the grunting and groaning until he knocked his knuckles on the door jamb, and swore quietly. She pressed her hand over her mouth to stop her giggles. She'd not heard that word before. But Tintin, ever wise, looked like he had.

Mum, her arms folded over her apron, winced as a corner scraped the panelling on its way into the drawing room. Gramps thrust a generous five pound note into each man's hand: they'd realised they were going to have to reverse the van all the way out.

'It's magic, Tintin,' she whispered, leaning forward to peer through the banisters and down the stairs. 'It's a sort of magic box. We're going to watch a princess become a queen.'

The bubbling joy that escalated while she perched on the landing with Tintin had all begun much earlier in the year. She could pin it to the day when she hurried to Wickhambreaux with Mum, who was reciting the list of requirements, and Grannie, who could not keep up. It was not a particularly special-looking day: the sky was low and grey, cold wind rattled the naked orchards and ice puddles broke under her boots. But inside, it was special, her excitement expanding with her lungs as she ran ahead, sucking in cold air with giggles bursting from her mouth under the wrap of scarf that left woolly bits in her mouth.

She always sprinted as fast as she could along the lane past Castle's farm. It had a peculiar, neglected and dismantled look. The house was empty, windows curtainless and haunted. The door was hanging off the pigeon coop, which was void of inhabitants and the straw long since blown away. Behind it, in the dark, musty, cold oast, was where they had found Leonard Castle.

'Hung himself,' Dad had said once, when he thought her out of earshot. But she had been old enough to know the expression relayed a particular richness of horror. 'Soon after the war.'

The war and that unknown man's demise conjured for Stella the darkness of the mysterious past. The time before she was Stella. She imagined a body, somehow suspended, turning. No one explained anything; no one found him for weeks.

They reached the village, cheeks pink and noses moist from the cold.

'Acid drops, glacé fruits for Gramps,' Mum ticked them off on her gloved fingers. 'Not forgetting a slab of Cadbury's for Nick. Gosh, I didn't think there'd be this much of a queue!'

'First day of sweets off the ration, Eliza,' puffed Grannie, wearing her ruby red woollen hat. 'What did you expect?'

'I can't face it, Maman. You were always better at queuing than me. Let's send Stella in,' said Mum. 'Shall we go and sit with Martyn for a while, while we're here?'

Stella watched Mum and Grannie walk sedately over to the church, talking quietly in their Mum-and-Grannie way. Let them go and be mournful, for good things were to be had right here, she decided. The shop window was stacked with jars, a rainbow of sparkling morsels in wondrous shapes: spirals, lozenges, perfect spheres dusted in sugar. She squeezed her way through jostling elbows, saying hello to school chums and villagers she knew, finding a spot where she felt comfortably alert and poised. The shillings Mum had given her were clutched ready in her mittened hand, her nose pressed to the window. Acid drops, glacé fruits, chocolate: she would not let them down.

And for the Coronation that summer, Grannie treated them all to an enormous tin of toffees to share. Dad and Gramps fiddled with the spiky aerial on top of the television set, fussing about the test card.

'Got to get the signal right,' Dad muttered.

'Ease it that way, Nicholas,' said Gramps. 'Christ, this is tricky.'

Mum said, 'Martyn was always good with electronics. He could sort out things like this.'

Grannie wondered, 'Where are my new spectacles? I bought them especially. Stella, could you pop upstairs and have a look for them?'

Stella pointed at the television set and said, 'Is that where the voices come from? It looks like someone could crouch inside it.'

Grannie made melon balls and ham for starters, and a curried chicken concoction the colour of mustard, with glistening raisins which looked like trapped flies. She found the recipe in *Woman's Own*. And Auntie Angela arrived in a waft of perfume, brandishing bottles of champagne.

Stella sat on a pouffe, sipping lemonade, with everyone huddled behind her, gaping at the set. She watched the small, bulbous screen wide-eyed as sound came in whispers and the pictures faded in and out, revealing and concealing the dark-haired princess shimmering in white with a glorious crown upon her head.

'Just like a fairy tale in our own drawing room, Tintin,' Stella said later as she settled to sleep. She addressed the boy in his usual spot, watching her from the Lloyd Loom chair by her bed. 'And you missed it all.'

He followed her, always one step behind. She knew when he was there, because he answered when she spoke. But sometimes, when she was busy, her head filled with homework, reading or sleeping, or when her family came into the room, he knew to withdraw, and was silent.

He looked over her shoulder as she set to work folding sheets of paper, stapling them together to make little books to fill with the stories blossoming in her head. She wondered if he had any stories he wanted to share. For he must have been to other places, or did he only live at Forstall, waiting to play with her?

He told her, without speaking, that he'd seen Forstall from the air. She laughed, disbelieving at first, but stopped smartly when she saw a new and gravely sad look in his eyes.

'We'll do better than these,' she said, squirrelling away her library of homemade books into a shoebox. 'We'll do it like proper writers do.'

Stella left him behind and ran downstairs, past the doorway to the kitchen, through which issued pleasing wafts of Grannie's French chicken in cider, and tapped on Gramps's study door.

'Will you show me your typewriter? Can I have a go, please?'

Gramps set his pipe down and flexed his fingers. 'Haven't used it for ages. I'm a bit rusty,' he said.

He lifted the stack of dusty books from on top of it, pulled off the cover and tentatively wound the platen. 'There were once lots of typewriters over in the salon, clacking away. Very important war work. Wonder what they did with them all.'

Watching him feeding in a sheet of paper, lining it up and tapping out an experimental *the quick brown fox*, she said, 'I'm going to write stories on it. Lots of them.'

'I have no doubt you are.'

'Tell me the tales about Forstall, Gramps.'

He laughed. 'Is that in the meantime, Smidgeon?'

Gramps settled into his armchair and reminisced about the Fair Maid of Kent, the most beautiful lady in the land, in the time of chivalry and knights.

'She lived in a manor just down the road,' he reminded her. 'She was the bride of the Black Prince, the greatest king we never had, I'd say.'

'And Elizabeth the First?' begged Stella, enjoying it. She'd heard it all before. 'Which room did she sleep in?'

'Which one do you think?' he teased. 'Yours of course.'

The rain had not stopped all day, stripping golden leaves off the trees so that they turned brown on the sodden lawn. Grannie said she could not go to the river for it was full, fit to burst its banks. Or go anywhere outside, for that matter, for she would be soaked. Never mind; it would soon be her birthday. The shift of season, the closeting of her indoors suggested other pleasures: blackberry crumble, the warm and fragrant fireside and hot chocolate before bed.

She raced around the salon on her scooter, punting off with her slippered foot to skim across the large expanse of floorboard and whacking into the wainscot to stop herself. She loved being in this room; imagining the clacking of the typewriters. She loved to open the shutters all around the room, one by one, revealing rain-splattered windows and a little more of the pale daylight. She played with her skipping rope, trying to get up to a hundred, and bounced her rubber ball against the wall, until Dad, reading in his parlour next door, told her to stop making *such* a racket. After that, she quietly skirted the walls, looking for long-forgotten detritus stuck in gaps in the boards: disintegrating rubber bands, a nib of a pen and rusty paper clips.

'It's like we have our own little run of houses, here, Dad,' she said as, tired of her games, she ventured into his parlour. She liked that she sounded grown up and observational.

'How do you mean, Smidgeon?'

'I can visit you here, in your house.'

'It's a *wing*, Stella. It is connected.'

'Hmm. And then I can go and see Gramps in his study, Grannie in the kitchen. Mum upstairs.'

Inside Forstall, her family was departmentalised. All in their own little sections. And living with them too was Tintin, who was her own secret, and who was everywhere.

'We each have our own domain here, if you like,' Dad said. 'But all of Forstall is your home.'

Domain. She liked that word. She surprised herself, understanding him. She felt a scattering of love, different kinds of love for her, in any room she should choose to go, all over the rambling, creaking, mysterious house.

'What about that other home, Dad? The street we visited in London?'

'I'm surprised you remember.'

'We went on a train. A big train and funny little underground trains. There was a wild park, a row of houses, all in a line. And two sets of staircases. And a basement. We had sandwiches. But we didn't stay. Only Mum stayed. Why?'

'She had to go away for a while.'

Stella recalled the severing, the exquisite departure. A sourness in her mind, pulling her down. Not understanding.

Sitting there with Dad, remembering, her sadness returned, aching in her stomach. She shifted in her chair, trying to get comfortable as the pain in her tummy subsided, then flared again.

'But Mum was up there alone? In the city?'

'It's OK. *We* looked after you.'

'But who looked after Mum?'

Stella sought her out, heard her running a bath, and tapped on the door.

'Can I get in after you, please?'

A muffled affirmative from inside and presently, the sound of a body emerging from water. The click of the lock.

The room was steamy, the mirror misted up, the lino holding little puddles. Mum had tucked a towel under her armpits, one wrapped like a turban around her head. She stood in front of the mirror, wiping wide sections so she could see.

'Hop in then.'

Stella stripped off her clothes, leaving them in a little pile, knickers inside out, balled up socks and all, as if she had just become invisible. She dipped her toe in first. The water was grey, soap scum on the surface but deep, oh, so beautifully deep and still warm, warmer than she was ever allowed to have her own bath. As she sank in, everything disappeared: knees and shoulders. Just her toes poked out, prodding at the dripping taps.

She lazily sponged herself and watched Mum, who stood with her back to her, slowly drying herself, drawing the towel over her shoulders, down her back, under the curve of her bottom.

Reaching for her dressing gown from the back of the door, she said, 'If I'm destined to be a housewife all of my life, I might as well be elegant.'

The housecoat was brand new: full-skirted, three-quarter sleeves and sprigged with yellow and pink roses. Mum tied the belt and unwrapped her hair. The white lock fell into her eyes and Stella watched her stick her comb in it, untangling and smoothing it back.

It had happened when Stella was born. The shock was her fault. All her fault.

Watching her mother looking at herself in the mirror with a critical depth in her eyes, Stella was aware of more unaccountable wretchedness.

'I remember you leaving, Mum,' she said from the bath.

Mum turned sharply, as if she'd forgotten she was there.

'That time you went to London.'

She continued to comb her hair, settling it over her shoulders so that it dampened the dressing gown. Her face was blank, her eyes suddenly empty.

'I didn't mean to leave you.'

'But you did. And it was horrible.'

'I thought you wouldn't remember.'

Stella was aware of the pain returning, dragging through her stomach. Tears soaked her eyes.

Mum did not notice. She was patting on face cream.

'Hurry up, Stella, you will become like a wrinkled prune. It must be lukewarm now.'

Stella stood up out of the bath, feeling a heavy tightening of her belly, as if the water would drag her back down. She yelped. A thin trickle of red ran down her thigh. The water around her knees was turning pink.

At last, Mum looked around.

'My, you're early. I would have thought it would have been at least another two years.'

Mum made her wash herself again, then gave her a pad that was about the size of a loaf of bread that she had to wear suspended from a girdle, and a couple of aspirin.

'You're a young lady now,' said Mum.

Lying in bed, curled on her side with the awful invasive thing between her legs, Stella's stomach throbbed. She was horrified. Nothing would ever be the same again. Her landscape had changed. Even though the shapes of her dressing table, curtains, mirror in the dark looked the same, when she glanced at the Lloyd Loom chair it was empty; Tintin was no longer there.

And, in time, as her body blossomed and stretched and changed itself, in the weeks, months, years that followed, she forgot all about him.

Chapter 25

Stella, 1967

She switched on her transistor radio and the languid notes of 'California Dreaming' coloured the air, while the scent of the roses that Mum had placed on her dressing table breathed out a steady sweetness. They were her favourite: petals of the palest pink, open faces honest and bright, basking in the sun through her window.

Taking her transistor with her, she went downstairs and out into the garden, crossing the sun-dappled lawn barefoot to where Grannie was settled on a lounger in the shade of the tree. A book lay face down on her lap, her softly wrinkled face shielded by large sunglasses.

Sitting on the rug beside her, Stella looked back to the house, relishing its unfluctuating beauty. She breathed deeply on the air, intoxicated by the snowy-white jasmine scrambling along the brick wall. Over on the river, water fowl were piping and splashing in the drifting afternoon.

'Are you sleeping, Grannie? Sorry, is this too loud?'

'No ma chère, it's wonderful,' she said. 'I love this new music. Goes so well with the sunshine, doesn't it? What are we listening to?'

'Pirate radio. Bit naughty but . . .'

Like Stella's, Mathilde's feet were bare, her painted toes poking out from the bottom of her kaftan: an item of clothing, she'd confided, that was intensely comfy in all this warm weather. Something an elderly lady like her appreciated.

'Did you sleep all right last night?'

'Eventually,' said Stella. 'It was difficult seeing Mum so upset like that. Worse thing was, I couldn't do anything for her. She just wouldn't let me. I heard her crying in the night.'

Mathilde looked at her. 'So did I.' She sat up and removed her sunglasses with a large sigh. 'It has been a bit of a to-do, hasn't it? I'm afraid this is the past catching up with us. Tell the truth, I came into the garden to get out of her way. Give her some peace. Your father is doing the same. Shut himself in the Stour wing. Gramps, as always, is being splendid. Taking cups of tea up to her bedroom every now and then.'

Stella turned the volume down, so that 'Waterloo Sunset' became almost inaudible.

She asked cautiously, 'So Mum knew this man during the war?'

'Yes, we all did.' Mathilde paused, remembering. 'He was quite a chap.'

'Go on.'

'He worked here in the Stour wing. Ministry of War. Nice man, he was. Always disappearing off on missions. Never knew when he'd reappear. We didn't ask, of course. None of us knew what happened to him, and so I suppose this unfortunately confirms the worst. Looks like he was shot down over France after D-Day and sent that last message via carrier pigeon.' Mathilde's voice lifted with pride. 'Did you know your uncle Martyn used to take the pigeons in his plane, drop them for the Resistance?'

Stella jolted. She'd been dreaming of the uncle she never knew just as Mum came in with the roses, waking her. Just before this whole thing started. 'Clever little blighters,' Grannie was saying. 'How they find their way home across so many miles, across the sea. Although, pigeons . . .' She quivered with mild disgust. 'I do hate the look of their feet.'

But Stella was fascinated. Last night, Dad had wrapped the pigeon carcass in newspaper and put it in the dustbin. The creature had missed its coop at Castle's farm by a matter of a mile and had been stuck, mouldering in her bedroom chimney, for over twenty years.

'But why do you think Mum is so devastated about hearing from this man?' Stella wondered. 'I know she'd been hit hard by Uncle Martyn's death so young. Perhaps this brings it all back?'

'We all were devastated, ma chère, when Martyn . . .' Mathilde caught her breath. Her eyes sharpened. 'But your poor mother yesterday. She doesn't, at the best of times, let on how she is feeling. Shuts herself off. But, I must say, I have never seen anyone look quite so unravelled. I wonder if this has triggered a return of her trouble.'

They both glanced up. Eliza was walking across the lawn to join them. She looked shattered, walking as if she could not hold a straight line and wearing her old-fashioned dressing gown with pink and yellow roses, her relic from the 1950s; the one that made her feel glamorous.

Stella imagined that she'd dug it out to pep herself up, to put on some sort of elegant shield. But, watching Mum find, almost feel, her way to the lounger next to Grannie's and ease herself down onto it as if her body were injured, she wondered how well it was working. Eliza's eyes were bloodshot and puffy, her flecked hair tousled, the imprint of her pillow still on the side of her pale cheek. The lock of white was startling in the sunlight.

'Tea?' asked Mathilde.

Eliza blurted out a surprising, sarcastic laugh. 'If I drink another cup my insides will go brown.'

'Perhaps something a little stronger?'

She glanced at her watch but appeared not to see the dial.

'What time is it?' she asked, confused.

'Blow what time it is,' said Mathilde. 'Stella, will you go and fetch a bottle of wine? And bring three glasses.'

Stella dashed off to extract a dusty bottle of Beaujolais from Gramps's cellar and brought it back on a tray. She poured out three hefty draughts and, as she sipped, kept an eye on Eliza, questions about the message, the man, pulsating in her mind. She wanted to ask, but Mum looked so fragile, the skin across her cheeks so tight, almost transparent, that she might break.

Lifting the glass to her lips, Eliza's fine hands trembled as if it was far too heavy. She squeezed her eyes tight shut against the vapours, sipping tentatively.

'Is there anything else you need, ma chère?' asked Mathilde.

Eliza opened her eyes and looked straight at Stella, glanced away as if she'd seen something fearful, and then looked back at her. She drew a shuddering breath.

'Did you not know the extent, Stella –' her voice broke and fell into a hard whisper, '– the importance of what went on in the Stour wing during the war?'

'Of course there were the stories Gramps told me when I was a little girl,' she began cautiously. 'Stories I thought I should take with a pinch of salt; particularly the one about Queen Elizabeth the First.'

From her lounger, Mathilde laughed mildly.

'So I expect I haven't appreciated the real stuff, like the salon office business,' Stella went on. 'I knew something had gone on in there. But *all* of the tales of Forstall sounded so far-out and amazing . . .'

'Amazing is one way of describing it,' said Eliza, her voice fatigued.

Grannie chipped in, 'If you want to be a writer, Stella, write about that. Sometimes fact is stranger than fiction.'

Stella flushed with shame. Dropping out of college had been a terrible blow for them and her truncated writing career in Hampstead fruitless and lonely. She should make up for not meeting everyone's expectations, for wasting time.

'There are many things I want to do, to write about,' she said, her confidence draining. 'But it's not exactly a steady job, is it?'

'Just get on with it,' said Mathilde. 'This is what the summer is for, Stella. Forget college, forget all of that. If you have something to say, sit down and write it.'

'Yes, yes, Grannie.'

But she was looking at Mum, longing for her to say something, for her approval, her understanding, her encouragement. What story did Mum have to tell? What secrets did she shut away? What depth did the unearthing of this crumbling old message reach inside her?

She waited. Something was shifting and surfacing behind her mother's face.

Eliza drained her glass and set it down on the lawn. It tipped over and the dregs of the ruby liquid began to drip into the grass. She noticed; decided to leave it.

She mumbled as if her mouth was full, 'Maman is right, Stella, about truth and fiction . . .'

Stella sat up. 'Yes, Mum?'

'Perhaps, one day . . .' A brief flare of anger burnt in Eliza's eyes, fading to despair, 'you'll want to write about this . . .?'

She reached into the pocket of her dressing gown and drew out a crumpled paper: the map they'd pulled out of the phial. As her mother carefully unfolded it, Stella noticed the whiff of mildew, a scent of age exhaled as if from an old hymn book. Eliza smoothed it tenderly and delicately across her lap, as if she was touching silk.

'I drew this,' said Eliza with the wonder of someone suddenly remembering. 'Took me months; it was so difficult. I was so careful. So very careful.'

She traced her finger over the faded handwriting that snaked across the map as if trying to communicate through the looping words.

Rubbing her face to expunge a memory, she said, 'This map was more than *far-out*, as you say, Stella. See this? It's a fake constellation, showing positions of foxholes belonging to our auxiliaries. If the Germans had got hold of this, and invaded, we'd not have had a chance. Kent would have been overrun, obliterated. On course for London.' She spoke neutrally as if repeating orders. 'They were our last line of defence. Just ordinary men . . . doing an extraordinary job.'

Stella gazed at the fragment of paper, the web of secrets held shakily in her mother's hands.

'And this man used the map to write you a message? From France . . .?'

'Stella, I want you to read it.'

'But it's yours, Mum. Are you *sure*?'

'I'm not sure,' said Eliza. She reluctantly raised her eyes from the map to look at her. 'Just desperate to understand.'

As Stella took the document, she brushed Mum's fingers. They were trembling and cold. She felt the weight of her watchful gaze as she glanced down at the words scrawled across the graph paper, dotted with the fake constellation. Flickering shadows under the canopy of trees made it difficult to read. Stella hesitated, feeling an odd sense of responsibility and curiosity. She looked up at her mother in question.

Eliza nodded.

21 June '44

Dearest Eliza,

I hope to God this message finds you. Came down near Falaise behind G lines. Allies nowhere near. You have to know: J was G spy. My duty was to marry her, keep her close to ops. Orders from the top. Can you understand, forgive me? I had no choice. At the church – that last afternoon – you told me she'd been snooping. I guessed she was about to give away our secrets. I took the map with me for safekeeping, but it is the only thing now that I have to write on. I write to you with great love. Please don't forget me. Please forgive me. Forgive me and come to Deal. If I make it home, I will be waiting for you.

Lewis.

Stella, lifted the top sheet where the message was written and gazed at the map of Kent beneath. The paper was threatening to dissolve into dust. It was all her mother had left.

'Oh, Mum.'

She breathed out, blinded momentarily by tears. Where had Lewis been when he wrote this message? Crouched in a field, mortally injured, ducking from the enemy, desperate not to be found?

'Lewis . . . He loved you, didn't he?'

'It sounds like it, doesn't it,' said Eliza, her voice suddenly brighter.

Stella looked at her mother in shock. 'What about Dad? Does he know?'

'Dad?' Eliza said and a crooked whisper of a smile broke over her pale, shattered face. 'He will surprise us. He will understand.'

'But did you love *him*?' Stella asked.

Eliza took a shuddering breath. 'Of course I did.'

Chapter 26

Stella

Stella stopped typing, and gazed at the posters on the wall above her desk, mesmerised as always by their pensive beauty. They had been a steady, familiar light since the pigeon landed rudely in the fireplace and disturbed the peace of Forstall. In the past few days, trauma seemed to seep slowly from the walls around her, exchanging the serenely aged air inside the rooms for something far more brittle.

But the posters sought to comfort her. How they inspired her: the four women full of potency, depicting the moon and the three stars, and created by Mucha not many years before her grandfathers met with hell on the Western Front. This, the moment that was the start of their family, the beginning of her story.

Stark realisation ricocheted around her mind, for her story was sullied: Mum loved a man other than Dad, had been loved by this man in return. Had lost him to another, more recent war. And yet, somehow, her mother had picked herself up and stumbled on.

She left her typewriter, went to her bedside table and rummaged in the drawer to pluck out the wedding ring she'd hidden there for safekeeping. Turning it over and over in her hand, she went along the landing to Mum's bedroom and gently pushed the door open.

Three days had passed since the message from Lewis Harper had emerged from the dust and rubble of years, and Mum had spent most of the time sleeping. Just as Stella expected, here she was, curled up under the sheet in her bedroom made warm by the balmy, airless afternoon. The map, with its scrawled message, lay on the bedside table close by. Stella crept over and picked it up. *If I make it home, I will be waiting for you.*

She put down the ring carefully and glanced briefly at her mother, feeling shy and intrusive. Eliza's face was wide and peaceful in sleep, with just one frown line etched into the space between her eyebrows, her hand clutching a bunched-up corner of the sheet. The ring must have meant something to Mum; perhaps Lewis had given it to her as a token of love and she'd hidden it at the house in Hampstead; denied that she'd ever seen it before.

But Stella wanted to return the ring. Tell her not to worry for it was safe, and she should keep it. Surely, she'd want to keep it. Stella also wanted to ask if she could borrow the map, study it in more detail but she dared not wake her. For it seemed, in sleep, she'd found a snippet of peace.

As Stella unhooked the keys to the Mini Cooper from their spot on the kitchen wall, Dad came through on his way to the fridge.

'Off out, are you?' Nicholas asked. 'Going into Canterbury?'

'Oh, no, no I'm not. The opposite direction I think.'

'You *think*?' he looked at her, amused.

'It's too hot to be cooped up here. I want to get out of the house and I thought I'd see if I can find one or two of these mysterious foxholes on this map of Mum's. I'm sure she won't mind if I borrow it for the afternoon. Oh, and her car.'

Her father laughed. 'What a splendid idea. I'm coming with you.'

Stella looked at him, surprised.

He said, 'I know as little about what went on in the salon in wartime as you do. I'm as intrigued as you are.'

'Really? But this map, Dad. It's a love letter from another man.'

He ushered her out of the house, speaking quietly. 'I will stand by her, any way I can.'

'But, Dad –'

He got into the driver's seat of the old Mini. 'I know it's rather odd, our lives here at Forstall. But believe me, I owe your mother a lot. More than anyone realises.'

His determination was not new to Stella. She'd always been aware of his struggle to hide his injured leg and the perpetual limp, to not complain. His cool, grey eyes were steely in acceptance. But beneath their serious depths and a drifting sadness, there was a humour that always drew her to seek him out.

Nicholas drove along the twisting lanes, winding down the window, complaining about the muggy air, that the car sounded as though the exhaust was about to fall off and that his knees nearly touched the steering wheel. Stella smiled to herself, letting him talk on as she studied the map.

'How are we doing, Smidgeon?'

'Keep going for a bit,' she said. 'I'll tell you when.'

The map was old; not very clear. But, surely, the bridleways, footpaths and boundaries were indelible in the ancient, unchanging landscape. The little car eased down the route towards the sea, Stella navigating the unclassified roads.

Dad said, 'Gosh, it's so close this afternoon and this thing's like driving a tin can. It reminds me of driving with Mum. The crash. We had a bit of a clapped-out motor then, too. And I often wonder if it was my fault and not the car's that we skidded.'

'It was an accident, Dad,' said Stella. 'Don't let it bother you now. It was a bit of everything, surely. You, the car. And didn't you say it was icy that day?'

'Icy, yes.'

Stella indicated a narrow lane. Nicholas slowed down to turn.

'You know, something about it has always bothered me,' he said. 'That chap who came to help us. I was never able to thank him. But I did see something of him, just before I passed out. I was pretty badly concussed and in terrible agony. But things like that stay with you.'

Stella nodded, distracted by the lane curving ahead.

'The crash changed your mother,' said Nicholas. 'It was pretty dreadful at the time. Changed me, certainly. Let alone leaving me with a gammy leg.'

'Oh, hang on. See this fork coming up, you need to take the right-hand turn,' Stella said. 'And if we pull up fairly soon, we can use the bridleway to cross that field over there. This one, according to Mum's map, is Onion. Fancy that!'

'Ho, I love all those charming names. Typically understated, I'd say. Good old War Office lingo. Where are we then? Oh, I see. Sorry, just got to –'

He abruptly stopped the car, slipping it into a passing place on the narrow lane. He pressed his fingertips to his forehead, screwed up his eyes.

'Whatever's the matter?' cried Stella.

'Sorry, Smidgeon, I just had to stop. All that talk of that chap,' he said, squeezing his eyes tighter, shaking his head. 'His face just came to me again after all these years. As if this windscreen shattered and I saw him. I saw him and . . . somehow, I'm remembering it differently. He is familiar to me *now*. Does that make sense?'

'Oh, Dad. Are you all right?'

'I don't know, Smidgeon. Rather bewildered, if you ask me.' He rubbed his hands brusquely over his face. He took a series of deep breaths. 'It's OK. I'm OK now. Let's get some fresh air. Let's get out and walk.'

They left the car and went down the lane for a hundred yards or more, then hopped over a stile and strode together along the grassy pathway, Nicholas's limp a little more pronounced than usual. The rolling land was punctuated by copses of silvery willow and low, marshy stretches sparkling like emeralds in the sunlight.

In the distance, beyond the dazzling green Thanet plain, a section of pale blue sea. There was not a breath of breeze, the air was clotted and muggy; the heavens looked thunderous far away to the south.

Nicholas glanced at the sky. 'I'm worried we might get rained on within the hour. Would be a blessed relief if we were. It's so blooming hot.'

He seemed recovered, his eyes brighter and not haunted by a half-remembered picture in his head.

'You OK, Dad?'

'Fine. Fine. Now, Stella, what exactly are we looking for here?'

'Right, well, an entrance in the ground? Ventilation holes, perhaps? Look, I'm guessing. I suppose most of the people who knew about these things are dead now. I wonder how accurate this map is,' she said. 'But if I know Mum, then very.'

Nicholas stopped and turned in surprise. '*Mum*?'

'She drew this.'

'She didn't tell me that.' He breathed out with wonder, running his hand over his balding head. 'I knew that she translated the French Resistance's messages. Working with Roger and Ernie. Oh, the fellows in the office. But I didn't know that she'd had anything to do with the map, let alone drawing it. When we found the map, that blessed pigeon . . . I thought it was Harper's because he used it to write his message. But oh, my goodness. I've just realised. He's the one who . . . '

His face frightened her.

'Dad, what?'

Nicholas sat down with a thud onto a tree stump, put his head in his hands.

Stella stood still, a pace away, and watched him nervously. She reached a hand out. Unseen, she let it drop back by her side.

'Dad, I'm so sorry. You know this man loved Mum?' she ventured.

'Yes, yes, I do *now*.' He exhaled hard. 'That's difficult enough to take in. For any of us. But also . . .' Nicholas fumbled for his handkerchief and wiped it over his face. 'I see him now. He was the one who rescued us from the car wreckage. Saved my life, in all honesty. It was *him*. The chap who worked in the salon all those years. *Lewis* saved us.' He began to twist the handkerchief into a tight knot. 'It doesn't make sense. She knew him, right back then, at the beginning of everything. But she never said a word.' Nicholas blew out a long hard sigh, his eyes quite wet. 'She loved him, but married me.'

He lifted his face slowly and stared quite piercingly at Stella. She looked away but he continued to gaze, examining her face as if seeing her for the first time. He shut his eyes and abruptly shook his head.

'Dad?'

He glanced at her again, a revelation washing over his face.

She sat tentatively down next to him and waited, looking out over the fields.

'Excuse me for asking, Dad. You seem very shocked,' she said. 'But you don't seem *upset*? Not angry. I don't understand . . .?'

He took a long, purging breath. 'During wartime, all sorts of things happen. Some things you wouldn't believe. And I will forgive that woman anything. I will stand by her, for she certainly stood by me.'

Puzzled, Stella watched a little gang of sparrows dive back and forth into a hedge of hawthorn. 'So it wasn't just a fling, then.'

'You saw the way she reacted when she read his message.' Nicholas reached over and tapped the map clutched in Stella's hand. 'So, yes. But she never told me. Never let on . . .' His voice drifted in wonder, in disbelief. 'She never told me about *him*.'

Stella glanced at her father, expecting sadness and anger. Expecting misery. But he looked extraordinarily content.

She accepted that her parents' relationship was rather unconventional. But it was all she had ever known. Ever since she had been grown up enough to understand, their sleeping in separate parts of the house was a clear enough clue. But they'd always had a good relationship. They liked each other, of that she was certain. This was her touchstone; what made her life at Forstall secure and content. Even when she was bound to leave, she knew she would always return.

Stella looked down at the faded handwriting and wondered what extremity Lewis Harper had been in when he'd scribbled it, rolled up the map and put it in the phial, hooked it on to the pigeon's leg and sent it up to the sky. What an incredible life. What an incredible end. The desperation of his words, their knowing sadness echoed inside her.

'I have to tell you, Dad, I feel so very sorry for Mum. How awful this is for her.'

Her father clasped her hand gently and briefly in his. 'She needs us more than ever now. I think that in the past I may have failed her. Remember when she went away to the house in Hampstead? You might not, you were very young.'

Stella looked down, running her fingers along the seams of her jeans. 'I do. I thought she'd abandoned me.' She flushed. 'It was always a thing for me. I hated it.'

'She was seeing a psychiatrist.'

Stella turned in speechless dismay to look at him. So she hadn't picked herself up and stumbled on, after all.

'By the end of the war, she was beaten. She – we – had lost Martyn.' Nicholas put his hand over his eyes as if he was blotting out her uncle's likeness. 'That was a very bad time. And now I am beginning to understand even more why she needed help. And how . . .'

'But I had you and Gramps and Grannie. I didn't need to be so awful to her.' Tears filled Stella's eyes. 'So dreadfully unforgiving.'

'You were very young. You didn't understand. But I think we both need to help her through this. We'll do that together, won't we, Smidgeon?'

Of course they would, she agreed. 'But who is 'J', Dad? A German spy? Isn't that incredible.'

'Jessica Castle. She lived at the farm. Her father bred the pigeons.'

A dark memory; the suspended body. A figment of horror, of imagination.

'We grew up together: Mum, Uncle Martyn, Jessica and me. Always above our station, she was. I knew that, even as a boy. There was a quality about her. Men loved her. Fell like flies. Lewis

Harper married her. And now, it seems . . .' Nicholas glanced at the map, '. . . we know why. Under orders to. Looks like he'd realised what she was up to. Or what she was about to do.'

Can you understand, forgive me? I had no choice.

'But what happened to her?'

'Disappeared. Like I said, during the war all sorts of things you can't imagine go on. She just disappeared one day. Not long after D-Day. They're probably still looking for her now.' He gave a wry laugh and stood up, stretching and casting around. He nudged the silky grasses along the edge of the path with the toe of his shoe. 'I think Onion's a dud, don't you?'

'Perhaps it was a decoy,' Stella agreed. 'Perhaps Mum added a pretend one on her map to put the enemy off the scent. God, Dad, what a time you and Mum lived through.'

'Just thinking. All a bit of a rush of mixed memories, you know . . .' Nicholas sounded breathless as they walked back down the bridleway. 'But it was a stroke of luck at the end of the war that Angela Stratton could lend us the house in London for however long your mother needed it. And then actually passing it over to us as a gift. She's a good sort. Extraordinarily kind. I think we need to commandeer her for this crisis, don't you?'

'I haven't seen her in a long time,' said Stella. 'I must say, I barely remember her. Does she still live in Ramsgate?'

'She does indeed. I can't remember the last time we talked. But she is the sort of person, I know, who would drop everything to help us.' Nicholas laughed. 'Gramps always made out that she had a thing for him. Even when Audley, her husband, was alive. I've never been convinced. I'm sure it was the other way round.'

Nicholas stopped by the car and leant on the bonnet, looking weary. Behind him, above him, a thick, grey quilt of cloud drew in from across the Channel: a storm approaching, heralded by puffs of warm saturated air. Stella placed the map on the bonnet and spread it out carefully. It was a delicate thing, a precious document, a thing of history. And her mother had drawn it. Stella sighed with pride.

'Now, what part of this wild goose chase fiasco are you going to make me go to next?' Dad said, peering over her shoulder. 'Oh, I see, near Ash? Come on then. Let's get there and back before we get soaked through and struck by lightning.' He got in the car and fired the engine. 'Which one is this, then? Baked bean?'

Stella got into the car, laughing. 'No, Dad, Haricot bean.'

They pulled up on the tight little lane close to the hedge and left the car with its back end sticking out a bit too much for Nicholas's liking.

'It's a Mini, Dad,' said Stella. 'People can squeeze round her. Also, looks like no one ever comes along here. We haven't seen a soul since we left Forstall.'

She climbed the stile and headed towards a little copse of willow, wishing she'd worn shorts instead of jeans. Sweat beaded her forehead, trickled down her back.

'If Mum's work is accurate, and I'm pretty confident it is, Haricot should be somewhere around here.'

Haricot was a lonely spot, a soft hollow guarded by willows and their shelter of slender, silvery leaves. Stella walked forward, feeling a pulse of excitement that they could be at last upon a secret foxhole. The grass was long and luxuriant, each blade bowing the same way, sculpted under indigenous breezes from across the flat plain. But today those breezes were elusive. The air was still, thick and scented. Stella counted the stars of wild flowers that nestled in the grasses: ox-eye daisies, poppies and cornflower, lady's bedstraw and cow parsley, sparkling with hover flies and bees.

She laughed. 'I feel I should be prodding and probing with a walking stick like a detective.'

'We're looking for a trap door in the ground, I take it,' Dad said, following behind her. 'Whether it survived or rotted away, we don't know.'

Stella gazed around the little sheltered copse. There was no sign that anyone had ever been here; that the auxiliaries had ever built their hideaway beneath it over twenty-five years ago. There were no clues, no crumbling brickwork or curl of jagged barbed wire. All she could see, and sense, were the aloof, bowing willows and thistle seeds drifting gently through the still air.

Quite mesmerised, she stepped forward and stubbed the toe of her sandal against something hard. Swearing under her breath, she bent down, parting the grasses and clusters of buttercups to reveal a small dark hole not more than a foot square. Around it was a concrete edge, rising two inches from the ground.

'Bloomin' thing,' she muttered, 'that just hurt my toe.'

'Ventilation shaft!' Nicholas cried in a surge of excitement. 'We've found it! Ha! Your mother is a clever woman. You wait till we tell her. She should be so proud of herself.' He stooped to get a closer look. 'It's pretty dangerous, really, that slab of concrete. Could break someone's ankle.'

'Imagine what's down there,' said Stella, peering at the hole. It was black, revealing nothing. 'There might be equipment, guns, and all sorts.'

'Museum pieces now,' said Dad. 'Worth quite a bit, I bet, for those cranky collectors.'

Stella looked beyond the hole to the deeper grey shadows under the willows.

'And that?' she asked, pointing. 'What on earth is that?'

'Damn, I didn't bring my glasses,' Nicholas said.

Stella squinted. Something lay on the ground. It was made from leather, with a long curling strap, flattened and rotting gently among the wild flowers. Buckles gleamed dully. An old satchel? It was as if it had been flung there casually and was waiting to be found.

'Someone's lost a bag,' Nicholas said.

'No, not that, Dad.'

She was distracted by something else beyond the old leather bag, deeper still under the trees: a peculiar scattering of white sticks, strangely regular, all streaked with the colour of string, the colour of sand, the colour of teeth, the colour of bone. They were as stark and as naked as cuttings from a winter thicket but, oddly, scattered with rags. Had Boy Scouts been camping here, collecting wood, collecting scraps? Had a tramp made this copse his home and hoarded some strange booty?

As Stella stepped forward, the queer arrangement drew into sharper focus. The tatters and rags shrouding the sticks merged to become recognisable as clothing, a belt, shoes. Shock flashed through her head and revulsion rose with the saliva at the back of her throat. For the arrangement of sticks was a body, curled up with its long back curved towards her. It was a body, skeletal and rotting. Flesh melted away. A body here at Haricot, lying alone in this solitary spot, sleeping in its own flowery bed.

Chapter 27

Stella

She stood beside her father in her grandfather's study and watched him as he dialled the number. The excruciating trickling down the exchange between each snap of the dial made Nicholas's cheeks flicker and tremble, and yet his eyes stayed fixed in disbelief. Stella heard the vibrant ringing down the line, the operator answering. 'Fire, police, ambulance?' She listened as he spoke urgently into the receiver, his voice pitching higher as he said the unbelievable words.

The window was open but the air was breathless and woolly, making its presence known. Mathilde came in, her eyes wide and inquiring.

'It's a body,' Nicholas told her. 'We've found a body.'

Mathilde said nothing but fumbled for a chair.

'What's this, old boy?' Morris followed Mathilde in, wiping his glasses on the corner of his shirt. 'What have you found?'

'A body,' Nicholas repeated, loudly, incredulously. 'A body. Well, a skeleton. Half clothed. Half –'

'Goodness gracious, *where*?' Morris cried.

Stella's scalp contracted. Through the doorway, she saw Mum wander drowsily down the stairs, her shoulders hunched and defeated. Her deep, afternoon sleep still clinging to her, slowing her down so that her head dipped like a sleepwalker. She crossed the hallway, drawn by the congregation of voices.

Eliza stopped in the doorway, silent and dazed, her eyes wandering until they fixed on the map that Stella was still clutching.

'So that's where it is.' She leant forward to pluck it from Stella's hand. 'Oh, you've made it even more creased!'

'But *where* did you find it?' Morris pressed.

'Find what?' Mum asked, glancing from one face to another.

'Eliza, dear, it's the most awful thing.' Dad lowered his voice, softening his words. 'We've found a dead body.' He took a tentative step towards her, a light gesture of affection radiating from his hands.

'But *where*?' insisted Morris.

'At Haricot,' Stella said. 'I mean, at this copse, which we found on the map. It's called Haricot on here but, I don't know, it's on a tiny lane near Ash.'

She wished that she hadn't picked up the map, taken it from Mum's bedside, out of her safekeeping.

Eliza kept absolutely still, the flesh on her pale face stiffening, growing whiter, glowing like a skull.

'*Haricot*?' she whispered.

The map fluttered from her hand, falling side to side, drifting to the floor like a crisp autumn leaf. Her eyes were unfocussed as if she was watching a film play out inside her head. She turned and walked out of the study, back across the hall, and began to climb the stairs, measuredly, her body stiff, as if pulled up by a winding cord.

Stella, taking a slow, cold dive into reality, watched her mother's unnatural progress. Something was seriously wrong. There seemed to be no life left in her, no breath, no blood; she was an exoskeleton of skin and clothes. A phantom, no longer alive. And yet Eliza kept going, looking neither left nor right and when she reached the half landing, Stella felt her heart stop. For there, in the shadow of the tapestry curtains, stood the boy, Tintin. And there was Mum walking straight past him as if he did not exist.

Stella took an impulsive step across the hall and lifted her hand in greeting, opening her mouth to say hello to him. She had not seen him for years. She was back in the bubble of childhood again, a world of sweetness and ignorance, where Tintin was her companion, sitting on the chair in her bedroom at bedtime. The receiver of her secrets, the instigator of giggles. Always behind her, watching over her.

Stella stood open-mouthed, staring up the stairs. How could she have forgotten him? And why, after all this time, had he come back?

She felt Dad, Gramps and Grannie move in behind her, gathering close in concern, watching Eliza.

And in a moment, Stella recognised her absurdity, the fool in her. How could she think she was able to call out to Tintin and say hello? On the half landing, Mum continued her trance-like progression up the stairs. *She* was the sane one, for she had not seen him. He did not exist. Not anymore.

Stella stared. He was still there in the corner where they'd hidden together, sniggered together, huddled in close and listened to the adults downstairs. She remembered the idiotic things they had said to each other. But she had grown into a woman and he was still a boy.

'Is your mother all right?' Morris's voice boomed behind her, startling her.

But Stella had no way of answering. The spot where Tintin had been was now empty, a luminous darkness, as if a light had just gone out.

'She's worse than ever.' Mathilde shook her head in distress.

In the study, Nick lifted the telephone receiver and tapped on the buttons. 'I'm calling Angela. She'll know what to do.'

Stella could not remember the last time she'd seen Angela Stratton. A family tea in the Forstall parlour when she'd been in her last year at school? A Christmas Eve sherry by the fire? A chance meeting in the Buttermarket square when she was with Grannie, shopping for a new dress? She recalled a willowy, tall lady with glorious hair, lingering perfume and a large laugh. But as Angela walked hurriedly across the hall that evening, ushered by Gramps, she was so much smaller, frailer and her laugh had vanished. Her once legendary hair was now forced into a helmet-like do and her A-line suit was stiff and unfashionable. It would have been unflattering on so many but, on her, was simply formidable. But as Stella said a brief hello to Angela before she went upstairs to Eliza, she saw that her eyes still held their fire.

'I think we should sit outside. It's stifling in here,' Mathilde suggested.

Stella followed them out to the chairs on the terrace.

The evening had come early, clotted by thick, grey cloud. Eddies of hot air worried the treetops. Roses and orange blossom glowed white like stars in the gloom, picked on occasionally by the breeze. All was strangely quiet up in Mum's bedroom. Stella saw that her lamp was on, behind drawn curtains. And still, the storm did not break.

'Are the police coming?' Gramps asked Dad.

'They are going to pick me up, take me over there,' he said. 'God knows how long they'll be. You don't have to come, Stella.'

She sagged back into her seat with relief. 'You're right. I'm not going anywhere until I know Mum is OK.'

Angela appeared at the French windows, her anxiety fizzing around her. 'Can I trouble you for some brandy, Morris?'

'Of course, my dear. Anything.' He hurried inside to pour it, offering it all round. Dad refused, saying that he'd better be sober for the coppers. Stella took her glass gratefully while Angela took two glasses upstairs.

Stella heard a car draw up on the lane and someone ring the front doorbell. In a matter of moments, Dad was gone, with Gramps for support, amid the rumble of efficient, officious voices.

A little while later, Angela came back down onto the terrace. All of the brandy glasses were now empty. Mathilde muttered to herself tentatively in the dusk, glancing up at the bedroom window. The light in Eliza's room had been switched off.

'My, my.' Angela eased herself into the garden chair, reaching a hand blindly for the brandy bottle that Gramps had left out. 'How quiet it is here. At home, I hear the seagulls, the constant mournful crying. You'd think I'd get used to it – but I never have. They make me feel lonely, now, without Audley. But it's so peaceful here.'

Stella was impatient. 'How is Mum?'

Angela turned bright eyes on her. 'This has brought it all back for her. This has very much done her in.'

'Shall I go to her?' Stella made to rise from her chair.

Angela stopped her. 'Wait. It's perhaps better that I can talk to you both now that Nicholas and Morris have gone off with the police.'

'Does she think the body is Lewis Harper?' Stella blurted.

Angela's eyes widened in surprise. Mathilde leant forward in her chair, cocking her ear as if she had not heard right.

'Because I can tell her straight,' Stella blundered on. 'There was blonde hair, scraggy tufts of it. I think it was a woman. And anyway, Dad knows about that man now. He knows . . .'

Great sparse drops of rain hit Stella on the head. Their coolness coaxed goosebumps up her spine and down her arms.

They hit the dry surface of the terrace and her bare feet with little hot hisses.

'No, Stella, there's no need for that. She doesn't think that it is Lewis.' Angela's fingers were like hot embers as she touched her gently on the back of her hand. 'But I've got a feeling we need to get your mother to a doctor. She's worrying me.'

'I must go to her!' Mathilde cried.

'Please wait,' Angela appealed, raising her hand to stop her. 'I'm sorry, Mathilde, please.' She paused and took a long sip of brandy. 'When Nicholas phoned me, he told me about the carrier pigeon message from Harper and that it had devastated her and now, for whatever reason, finding this body has made her even worse. Who knows who it is, or how long it has lain out there but just from talking to her now, it's not only bringing back the death of Martyn, but also the death of Sybil. Her dreadful, most terrible guilt . . .'

'What can you mean?' asked Mathilde. 'It was truly horrifying: Sybil's death, the raid on Canterbury, we know. But surely Eliza can't feel *guilty*. Well, I know you can go through that, guilt, when someone dies but . . .'

Angela looked at Stella. 'Your mother has that lock of white hair.'

'Yes,' Stella said. 'She told me it happened when I was born. Quite suddenly, just appeared. And *I've* always felt guilty about that.'

'It happened – her hair turned white – because she saw your grandmother, Sybil, being gunned down.'

Mathilde gasped, put both hands over her mouth. 'Did she?'

'She was with Lewis Harper – her lover – coming out of the hotel on the Buttermarket square. She told me, just now. She's not raving, you know. She's completely and peculiarly calm. She said that Sybil did not take cover when the planes came over, because she saw her with Harper. Sybil froze, apparently, in the middle of the square. And that was the end of her. Morris and Nicholas do not know this.' Angela stared with meaning first at Stella and then at Mathilde.

The drops of rain became persistent, faster, louder. The smell of earth rose to meet them; white petals breaking under them, falling to the ground. Stella breathed deep on the spicy, fresh, clearing air. Thunder rumbled menacingly, far away. She thought of the body lying out there in the willow copse, the police stepping round it with torches, rain pattering on cagoules. Dad and Gramps standing to one side, quizzical and concerned.

She tried to picture Mum with this strange man, this Lewis. And her grandmother Sybil seeing them together. She could visualise Mum's face, but could only guess at Lewis Harper's. She had no way of imagining the horror of what happened in the Buttermarket square.

'But why is she telling you this now, Angela?' she asked.

'It's called a breakdown, Stella. And it's not her first.'

The rain was now a deluge. They hurried indoors, rescuing the brandy and the glasses, and sat in damp clothes in the drawing room with the lamps low. Outside the French windows, the rain fell in grey sheets streaked with silver.

Stella thought of Mum, curled up in bed upstairs, and longed to see her, to speak to her. To tell her she would help her. She thought of Lewis Harper, and how now she must do her very best to find him. Or find out what happened to him.

Forgive me and come to Deal.

Someone, somewhere would know.

Chapter 28

Stella

The roses on her dressing table had wilted, their golden hearts shrivelling, petals wrinkling and yellow, fallen and scattered over the glass top. When Mum had brought in the vase, their perfume had filtered into her dream of Uncle Martyn, sweetening it and drawing her awake. She'd been on the verge of telling her about it – the strange way the dream had taken her flying with him over Forstall – but the pigeon falling into her fireplace, and the melee that followed, had thwarted her and snuffed it out.

The scent of the flowers had faded now but it lingered in her memory, like the dream, unable to grasp but calling her from the depths of years, suspended behind the closed doors that shut away her childhood. The dream remained intangible and secret, the scent, buttery and honeyed; unforgettable and indefinable.

The letter flap rattled. Stella leapt up from her desk, scooped the petals up into her palm and dropped them in the bin.

She flitted down the stairs, across the hall flags, and plucked the *Kentish Gazette* from the mat. As she hurried back, the clock struck the quarter, making a little announcement to the quiet house. She almost had the place to herself. Dad had left earlier for the brewery; Gramps and Grannie were pottering in the garden. Mum's bedroom door was closed.

Back in her own room, she sat on the bed to get her breath back and unfolded the newspaper over the candlewick. The headline screamed at her in twenty-four point from the front page: 'Body found near Wick'breaux is suspected WW2 spy.'

Breathless, she skimmed the typeset paragraphs below, her eyes leaping over words as they blurred into one: *hunted, local girl, agent, espionage, Mrs Jessica Harper née Castle.*

The corpse of her Mum and Dad's childhood friend, the girl from the farm over the way, had been lying in the undergrowth at Haricot, not four miles from Forstall, slowly rotting for over twenty years.

'Goodness, but what *happened* to her?'

Stella gasped and glanced towards the door, hoping that no one had heard her outburst, hoping that she hadn't disturbed Mum.

She glanced at the bedroom chair expecting, wishing, to see Tintin. He would smile and tell her not to worry. Tell her that everything would be fine as long as they were quiet as mices. The chair was empty.

She read the story again, slowly this time. Was it murder? Suicide? Lewis Harper, in his message to Mum, had written that he knew Jessica was up to something. He knew Jessica was a spy. Stella shivered as the secrets of Haricot crept back to her one by one: the rags, the bones, the tufts of hair.

She folded the newspaper into a tight roll, as if to prevent any more horror spilling from its pages, and sat back at her desk. She pulled out the sheet of paper from the typewriter and added it to the pile growing beside it, her slowly-building body of work. That would have to wait. Selecting a fresh sheet, she winched it in, adjusted the paper guide so that it sat perfectly. She poised her fingertips over the home keys and, seeking guidance, her eyes flicked up. She gazed from tranquil-faced *Moon*, to drowsy *Evening Star*, to unmoving *Polaris* and finally to dazzled *Morning Star*.

'Tintin,' she said and looked over her shoulder. He was not there, just as she expected. 'The thing is . . .' Her exuberance bubbled and spilt out of her, an idea moving like mercury through her mind. 'I need to draw Lewis Harper out. People do not talk about the war: like Mum, like Dad, my grand-parents. Dad said that all sorts of things I could never imagine happened. And they hide from it. Never speak of it. Surely they cannot be ashamed?'

There was no answer but she knew that Forstall, at least, was listening.

'If he made it out of France, if he made it home . . . Surely this will help.' She was determined. 'Surely this will do the trick. For I think that Lewis is the only person who can truly help her.'

She picked up the *Gazette* and turned to the masthead. Grabbing a buff envelope from her drawer, she carefully copied onto it the name of the news editor and the address.

On the blank sheet of paper she typed the headline: 'Map found in Forstall chimney reveals wartime secrets'.

She winched the paper up and added the byline: *Stella S. Staveley.*

Chapter 29

Eliza

The tap-tapping of Stella's typewriter stopped suddenly and the silence was far worse. The pauses and clacking when the carriage return cranked and the vague thumping of the back-space was something to pin her mind on. The noise blocked thoughts seeping in like a spreading, dark stain. But in the abrupt quiet, Jessica's voice, the taunting and the laughter, filtered in through the fibres of her memory like interference on the radio waves, as if she was still hearing a fly buzzing long after she'd swatted it.

Eliza pressed her face to the pillow. The sound of Stella working so determinedly, so admirably, brought back the Stour wing days and the industrious racket that resonated there. She smiled with fondness as she remembered Bingley and Fisher and their heroic work ethic, spurred on, as always, by Lewis.

She sat up abruptly in bed and clamped her hands to her temples. The insides of her head were moving like the liquid in a spirit level. She must not, could not, think of him. The tablets the doctor had prescribed filled her skull with cotton wool and gave her a raging thirst. She reached for her glass of water and fumbled with the lid of the bottle. It was time for another tablet, surely. Getting over the first side effects would take a week, the doctor had said. A week? Surely, the more she took now the quicker she'd get used to them.

'Mother's little helpers,' Nicholas had quipped as he drove her back home from the doctor's in Canterbury. He'd glanced sideways at her and Eliza had watched his features fall with shame when he saw the look on her face. They passed the spot where they'd crashed all those years before and she felt her heart slide hopelessly in her chest.

Sitting up in bed, Eliza knocked a pill to the back of her throat, gulped water and lay against her pillow. The tapping along the landing recommenced but did not block out Jessica rising in her mind like a blonde Lucifer, the fallen angel: poised and cool. Eliza pressed her fingertips onto her screwed-up eyelids to try to block the woman's own blank, dying eyes.

Someone will find her. And yes, so they did; far too late.

Mathilde knocked on her bedroom door, calling out that she had soup, and Eliza stumbled out of bed to undo the latch.

'You really shouldn't lock the door,' her mother chastised her as she set the tray down.

What was Maman worried about? That she might do something stupid?

Mathilde looked around the room, finishing with her soft gaze on her.

'Do you think you might have a bath today?'

'I might.' Eliza swallowed hard. The smell of the soup was making her queasy.

'I could change your bed while you do so.'

'No need to worry –' Eliza stopped.

The ring on the bedside table tucked behind the alarm clock caught her eye. The rose-gold glimmered.

'How on earth –?'

'What's that?'

Eliza tapped the ring across the bedside table with her nail, and gingerly picked it up.

'Stella brought it back with her,' she said. 'Found it at the Hampstead house. She must have decided that it needed a home. That I wanted it, after all.'

Mathilde stepped to her, placed a hand on her arm. 'Are you all right?'

Stella stared at the ring. The connection from Lewis to Jessica and to herself radiated from it, mocking her. Jessica had thrust it at her, to ridicule her with a sadistic memento. She'd tried to lose it, let it sink into the detritus of the house in London. It lay undisturbed, just like Jessica, for years, until Lewis's daughter brought it back to her.

Mathilde said, 'Are you worried about it? One of your London tenants must have lost it. Probably not worth much.'

'It needs to go in the bin,' Eliza said, viciously.

'Really, Eliza.' Her mother looked shocked. 'I wouldn't do that. You might be able to get something for it –'

She cut in, 'Is the newspaper here?'

Mathilde glanced at her. 'It is but I don't think you should look . . . anyway, it's in Stella's room.'

'Is it her?'

Her mother released a pained sigh. 'So, it says, apparently. Thank God Leonard isn't around to find this out. His precious Jessica. What a thing to happen.'

'But he must have realised then. That's why he . . .'

'There was talk, of course, about her. I think the gossip hounded him. The shame. Drove him to it. But he didn't know she'd died. I simply can't accept that we had such a traitor in our midst.'

Eliza looked sharply at her mother and saw rage move swiftly over her wrinkled face. Her eyes moistened.

'And to think of her wretched husband,' said Mathilde. 'The wonderful man, the hero we had here at Forstall all along, and we didn't even know it. Poor man.'

Maman, Eliza realised, was prompting her, wanting her to talk about it. Instead, she bent double and regurgitated a slop of water and a half-digested pill into her hand. She slumped back down on to the bed and Mathilde sat beside her, placed her hand on her back, soothed her gently with the soft French phrases of her childhood.

'What *is* it, Eliza?' the older woman asked, her voice nearly breaking.

'Please don't ask me.'

She looked up and felt her mother's eyes appraising her, seeing right through her.

'You loved him so very much, didn't you?'

*

The bath water was murky and lukewarm; a soupy, opaque grey. Her mother's Yardley bubble bath had long burst and faded, along with its scent and all of its promises. Lying in the water, Eliza heard the pipes tink and sigh, the tank finally refilled. Stella stopped typing. Was it teatime already? Eliza could hear a tune from the pirate radio station drifting from Stella's bedroom. *San Francisco* and *flowers in your hair*. Such a new world. A fantasy world of hedonism and superficial love. What did they know of real love? Eliza suffered a flash of anger as she eased herself out of the bath, splashing water onto the lino and reaching for the towel. She wondered if they would ever sing about the kind of love that made her do such a terrible and unforgivable thing.

She stood in front of the mirror and ran a comb through her hair. Her face in the reflection looked ragged and pinched, as if her features were melting. The expression in her eyes was flat and guarded. She tugged her old dressing gown tightly around her still-damp skin.

'If he was alive . . .' she whispered to herself, shivering. 'If he'd made it home, *surely* . . . he would have come here. He would not have waited for me to go to Deal.' She pleated the edge of the dressing gown and thought of Hampstead and the house he'd given her. And of Stella, unsuspecting, not realising that she'd been holed up for six months in her father's house. The tangled enormity of her own spectacular lies and her ugly half-truths made Eliza catch her breath.

'And *I* was in Hampstead for a year,' she said to her reflection as hot tears ran past her nose, pooled over her lips. '*Surely*, he would have gone there, too, to find me. The war was over – it was *over*.'

Finally: the proof lay wide open before her. Plain, agonising evidence that he had not survived the war. He had not come home.

She unlocked the bathroom door and hurried barefoot along the landing to her bedroom. The cold reality of what she had always, always known followed her, chased her, thumped her. She made it to her bedroom and lay down, wounded and more weary than she'd been when she woke that morning. More weary than she'd ever been in her life before. Her bones ached with despair.

Lewis's face materialised. Whichever way she turned, he was there, and so was the memory of how he'd made her feel, how she'd screamed her love for him: on the sofa at Nunnery Fields, in the Buttermarket hotel, in the top bedroom at his house in Deal. But that's where he'd lived with *her* in *their* marital home.

Her mind cleared suddenly, straightening with awful clarity. She believed now that he was dead. He was gone. And she was strangely relieved. She gave up. Her journey was over.

She could hear Stella typing again against the sound of the Beatles oompahing through their latest hit. Stella will be fine. She will go on to be a writer, a journalist, perhaps move back to London to Lewis's house. She heard her mother's light laugh from downstairs and Morris's response. They'd be fine, the pair of them. Nicholas was at the brewery; he'd be fine, as long as he was busy.

They all had each other. They had Forstall. She had nothing. She sat up and counted her pills.

The nights were drawing in, so Morris always quipped the day after midsummer's night. And everyone always groaned and told him to be quiet. But he was right, for the light, on this last day of July, was already fading as the hall clock chimed eight. Eliza came downstairs wearing a clean, sprigged maxi dress. Her hair was now dry and tidied back with one of Stella's old hairbands.

She let herself out of the back door and across the patio, past the spot where she'd smashed her mother's dish in surprise at hearing Lewis's voice, seeing his shape in the dark. The pain, this time, did not seem so severe and she was grateful for the double dose of tranquillisers she'd taken. She walked across the shadowy, emerald lawn, beyond Morris's prized borders and reached the coolness of the bank. The river was languid and full, rampant reeds thickening the water with green; the creatures of the water making ready for the night.

The sleepy mutterings of the birds in the trees seemed to coax the evening down. Faint, solo stars blinked their welcome: some glowing yellow, some white, some almost pink. She heard an owl and, suddenly, her mind brightened for a second beyond the hazy curtains that were drawing slowly either side of her eyes. But, she told herself, it wouldn't be the same owl as before. That gentleman was probably long dead.

She tapped on the front door of the Stour wing and responded to Nick's cheery call of welcome. He was in the kitchen, dipping to the fridge for a bottle of beer.

'I'm just having a Forstall. Would you like one?'

Eliza thanked him but refused. She walked through to her old parlour and sat down facing the windows overlooking the lawn and the darkening garden. Her eyes fell out of focus. She stared blindly as her mind wandered. Nick followed her in, clipped the bottle top off and took a sip.

'Always good, this one,' he said, raising the bottle and settling into his usual armchair. He looked at her. 'Are you OK? You look rather bushed.'

'Just very sleepy,' she said. 'I'm OK though . . .'

He picked up his folded broadsheet on the coffee table and let it fall back down, attracting her attention. 'Seems like it was definitely Jessica. See, it's now made it to *The Times*. Small story on page two, but even so. They're sounding a bit cagey but I guess they're still investigating. That's the Secret Service for you.'

'So they say.' Eliza averted her eyes from the newspaper and swallowed a tiny drop of nausea.

'It's her. It has to be. It all adds up. You do look worried, Eliza. But don't be. Let's face it, we grew up with her. We knew her, or thought we did. But for some bizarre reason this does not surprise me at all. They say she was hooked in with the Nazis from an impressionable age, while she was in Vienna. God knows what they promised her to betray her country like that. I hope she thought it was worth it. My guess is that Arlington was in on it. Remember him?' Nicholas took a long sip of beer. 'I'm guessing she realised the game was up. Probably took cyanide. Roger said they used to keep capsules in the safe.'

'Roger . . .?'

Eliza saw red rings instantly burst over Nick's pale cheeks.

'Roger Bingley,' he said.

His blush reached his hairline, sweeping backwards over his high, receding forehead. He took a long, distracting draft of beer and, when he'd finished, suppressed a mild burp.

'Roger, of course,' said Eliza, sleepily, an affectionate memory of Bingley filtering through the vapour in her mind. 'You like him?'

'Indeed I do. We keep in touch,' said Nick. He ran his fingers over the drips of condensation on the bottle. 'There's something I want to ask you, Eliza.'

He waited. Eliza forced herself to concentrate, to pin her eyes on her husband.

'When are we going to tell Stella?'

Eliza jolted. He'd made her think of something beyond tonight, beyond this darkness.

'Tell her what?' Her thirst returned. A cold bottle of beer seemed like a good idea. She got up and walked carefully through to the kitchen, to the fridge to collect it.

Nick waited for her to sit back down. 'Tell her? That Harper was her father, of course.'

Eliza sat upright. 'You know that Lewis . . .?'

'Really, Eliza,' Nicholas was almost laughing. 'I've guessed. It struck me when I was with Stella the other day when we were on our wild goose chase, and I remembered Harper. Realised he was the one who saved us from the crash. It started then, between you, didn't it? It's OK, Eliza. Really, I understand . . .'

She looked at him with fondness, knew he forgave her now, just as she had forgiven him so long ago.

'It hardly matters now, but yes,' she said tenderly, her giddiness returning. 'Lewis was her father. Not that poor, dead, fictional pilot. We should tell her, sometime . . .'

'I think she has the right to know.'

'The right?' Eliza said. 'You're talking about rights? Have you suddenly become a hippy? Started going on marches? Waving placards? Yes, I suppose she does. But do I?'

She saw his face drop in confusion. Did she have a right to happiness?

'And also . . .' Nicholas cleared his throat. 'Things might well change for me in the near future.'

She wanted to say: yes, Nick, after tonight, I'm afraid they will. Instead, she sipped her beer, realising she'd never drunk it straight from the bottle before; the first and last time. The hoppy flavour quelled her nausea, tasted fresh and sweet.

Nick picked up *The Times* and turned to a story. 'Have you seen this? This is what I mean about changes.' He folded a section, tapped the newsprint with his fingertip and passed it over to her. She could barely focus, her mind hazarding dangerously from memory to the present and back again.

'Homosexuality is no longer seen as an illness that can be cured,' he declared, sounding triumphant. 'The coppers can no longer round-up us poor fellows and slam us in the cells to bump up their arrest rates. I am no longer a criminal. Fancy that. Although they are saying they'd like us to show our thanks by comporting ourselves quietly and with dignity. It's all I've ever been, don't you think, Eliza? Quiet and dignified. Don't you think?'

'And this is why we should tell Stella?'

Nick's blush returned, burning the top of his ears. 'Roger is coming down from London next week. He's dropping by. We're going to go away for a few days. We're going to go somewhere, a quiet seaside town.'

When he did not elaborate, Eliza felt a lazy smile draw across her face.

'I hope you have a splendid time. But don't tell her just yet. I think she may one day be able to work it out for herself. I'm proud of her. She's going to do great things.'

Nick seemed puzzled equally by her lethargy and her sudden praise of Stella.

'Have you ever told her that you think that?'

Eliza pressed the back of her hand to her eyes. Shaking her head in muddy confusion, the beer fizzing with the tablets in her stomach. She said, 'No, I don't think I ever have.'

Nicholas looked disapproving of her.

She wanted to counter him. Her voice slurring a little, she said, 'You won't go gallivanting off now with Roger and leave Forstall forever, will you?'

'No. Never. You know I will never go. For this is where Martyn lived.'

She saw then how raw her husband's grief remained and how close to the surface it lay, like a seam of exposed rock. And also how restrictive and intensely private it was.

'Do you think we've done all right?' he asked, a boyish shyness in the dip of his head.

'Nick, I think *you* have.'

Eliza slipped into the house, drowsily barging her shoulder into the door post. Night had fallen and Forstall was quiet. Morris and Mathilde had retired to their bedrooms. Stella was upstairs. The clock in the hall marked time to itself in its regular, hollow fashion.

She opened the door to the cellar, tensing at the creaking and yawning of the ancient oak, and crept down into the comforting, warm well of dankness. The whiff of earth down there was fresh and loamy; the frothy spiderwebs, the scurry of mouse feet, reassuring.

She bent to Morris's vast wine collection, pulled out a Merlot and wiped the dust off the label. She had no inclination to appreciate the vintage, but quickly climbed back up the steps with it. The upstairs landing was lit by a single lamp and she followed its beam, mounting the Jacobean staircase with the excruciating care of a drunk. She passed the half landing and the framed wedding pictures. As usual, she averted her gaze; could not look Sybil in the eye.

She stopped outside Stella's bedroom. The door was open a fraction and she hesitated before peering in, fearful of waking her daughter and yet desperate for one last glance. In the soft light from the landing she saw the faint glimmer of Mucha's artwork on the wall and the tousled head of her sleeping daughter on the pillow. What must Stella have seen at Haricot? What grim terror might walk through her dreams now and forever?

And it was her doing. What had she put her through? No one – certainly not her own child – should know of such things. Should see someone's bones.

In the darkness, she could make out the vase on the dressing table. It was empty.

Back in her room, Eliza slipped the bottle of tranquillisers from her pocket and emptied it on to her bedside table. The tablets rattled over the crumpled, damp, smudged, ruined map of stars. She swept them off into a little pile and took up her pen. She wrote along the bottom of the map, squeezing her words in under Lewis's handwriting. Oh, how beautiful and fine was his hand, even though he had been crouched in desperate fear in a French pasture, bloodied, broken; the enemy just a breath away. She wrote:

Stella, Maman, Nick, Morris. You all must know how much I loved Lewis. I tried so hard to get over it, to get better after the war. And now I want to give up trying. There are things that I did that I cannot face up to. And if you knew what I have done, you would no longer love me. Like the moon, I have only ever shown one face to you, to you all. And it is not me, not real, not my own.

She broke off and hissed to herself, 'But I am still a coward. Always a coward.'

The wine, she knew, would not be enough. She needed brandy.

Fearful of waking the sleeping house, she crept back down-stairs to Morris's study and felt her way into the dark room where the light reflected from the landing found its way to highlight the leather chair and framed photographs lined up on the mantel. She remembered them all, then, so very well: the Christmases around the tree; the summer picnics by the Stour; the sledging with Nick; she, with Martyn, leaning together and laughing.

She reached like a blind woman for the drinks tray, fingering the lid of the heavy decanter, pouring out the pungent liquid, clutching the tumbler in her vibrating hand. Thank God, she thought, I have a lock on my bedroom door.

Back on the half landing she stopped, her breathing tight and her heartbeat flickering in her throat. She shifted the tapestry curtain to one side to peer through the window. The short, light night was not able to hide much of anything, for the garden was a misty grey, the shapes of the trees emerg-ing; the orchards in the distance identified by linear rows. The eastern horizon was already a strip of pale yellow and within the deepest part of the sky was the embryonic morning star: the bringer of light. She found it, stared at it, understanding it, utterly transfixed.

A sudden explosion of gladness, a pure rejoicing in her deepest parts made her shiver, made tears spring from her eyes. She turned from the window, and her hair crisped over her scalp.

On the stairs above her, taller than her, stood Martyn. He was wearing his flight suit and his boots. He was grown-up, steady and confident; no longer the stroppy lad, no longer the cocky new pilot. He was perfect.

Shock cascaded down her body, stripping her to the bone. She remembered seeing him, oh, so briefly, as a boy watching over Stella on the doorstep when she returned from London. It'd seemed so perfectly natural, then. He had kept Stella safe while she was away. And now, it was so completely wondrous and agreeable that he should return.

Jessica's friend had said she'd heard the pilots scream as they burnt to death in their cockpits. The thought of it made her guts crawl, even now, twenty-five years on. But what did that WAAF girl know? There was not a mark on him.

He was angry with her. She could see. Furious. His expression was a duplicate of the way he'd looked when she'd teased him on their long walk to Forstall for Sunday dinner, the day war was declared. *I think it's time you grew up, Martyn*, she'd said. And, in the way the dead must do, he was looking into her, right into her. He saw everything about her.

Here you are again, she told him without speaking, gripping the banister with a stiff cold hand. *But, this time, you are no longer the boy.*

She cocked her head, squinted, tried to get a better look at him. She challenged him.

How do I know it is you? How do I know you are not a figment of my wild imagination? The result of the drugs I've been taking. The drink. This terrible state I am in.

He was as immobile as he was in his photograph. It was as if he was carved into the dark air of the staircase. He continued to stare at her, his silence beseeching her; his anger at her plans and design for her own death was tangible, inescapable. His mouth did not move as he spoke to her. She heard him only in the part of her that was deeply, truly her.

You know it's me, because I'm as quiet as mices.

She blinked and, as if a light had been switched off, he was gone.

Eliza knelt at the hearthstone in her bedroom, holding the map of stars in her hands. She ripped it, and folded it, and ripped it again. She turned it, bundled it and scattered the flakes of paper into the grate. She scooped her tablets from the table into her palm and tossed them on top of the shredded map, following with chunks of apple wood cut and seasoned from the orchard and piled so neatly by the hearth. She struck match after match, blowing on the kindling. It rustled and cracked as flames blossomed and swelled, the thin, blue smoke licking its way up into the darkness of the blackened, ancient chimney.

She snatched up the ring and tossed it in, watching the rose-gold blend with the fire, to tarnish, to blacken, to disappear, to be raked up with the ashes in the morning. It would be unrecognisable; it would be thrown into the dustbin.

She crept to her bed and drank a long, cool draught of water. As her tears washed down her face, she licked them off with her tongue. She blew her nose long and hard, at last feeling able to breathe again. Lying on the bed, she pulled the quilt up to her chin. Her mother had pieced it for her when she was a girl; it used to cover her bed at Nunnery Fields and had survived the car crash. She remembered this, inhaled its smell, drank it in and curled up underneath it like a baby, numb at last to the very worst.

As the flames in the grate settled into a comforting, pulsing rhythm she took a deep breath and waited for morning.

Chapter 30

Stella

There was curious smell around the house; it lingered on the landing and settled down the stairway. Stella had first noticed it after the night, a week before, that Mum had decided to light a fire in her bedroom grate. She'd woken that morning to the bitter, sweet and spicy – and far from unpleasant – scent that reminded her of burnt herbs and which had tarried, even when the windows and doors were opened to the summer air. It was a new aroma, but could have been ancient, the very incense of Forstall that came from its dark corners and dense beams, its dank cellar and warm, dry attic.

Dad had commented, half-jokingly accusing Mum of smoking marijuana in her bedroom like a right-on student. Mum had laughed and told him that chance would be a fine thing; after all, she had no idea where to buy the stuff. She said she had, on a whim at midnight, lit a fire in her bedroom hearth. It had been like a ritual, she explained, to watch the flames. Quite cathartic, and wonderfully primitive. It had helped her sleep. At last, to sleep.

Stella noticed, since that morning, that Mum had visibly brightened, taken a step out of her despair. For she was up, bathed and dressed before the rest of them. This morning, which was particularly glorious, she was outside already, sipping breakfast tea under the tree with Grannie. They'd carried the table from the terrace and set up home in the balmy shade.

Stella spotted them from the landing window on her way back from the bathroom and realised that the new smoky fragrance was here to stay: organic and comforting – and adding to the unchanging immemorial scent of her home.

Grannie had left some post on the bed for her. She opened the envelope and pulled out a cheque from the *Kentish Gazette*. The edition with her story about the pigeon in the chimney, just a couple of paragraphs on page five, had come out the day before. Sitting there yesterday with Mum at the kitchen table, she'd pushed the newspaper across to her with trepidation, warning her, frightened of what she had done. Had she gone too far, brought it all back *again*; wrecked her newfound peace? But Eliza had read it quickly, once, and then again more slowly. She had looked up and smiled.

'You've done very well, my dear,' she said. 'Very well indeed.'

Disarmed by the praise, by the new warmth in her voice, Stella had pressed her. 'Really, Mum?'

'If I'm ever to be myself again, I must let things go. I have learnt this the hard way.' Eliza's voice had been soft and sad but wonderfully barbed with potency. She'd brightened. 'When are you going to finish your novel, Stella? Because I can't wait to read it.'

Stella dressed now, picking out denim shorts and a white smock. It was so warm, she'd go barefoot today, she decided, as she tied her hair back with a long scarf. Perhaps she'd get the bus into Canterbury tomorrow to pay in her cheque. Her typewriter sat idle, the stack of typed pages no higher than it had been the week before. But the day was luminous, the air from the orchards sweet; she'd see if she could catch Gramps and go with him on his morning constitutional.

She heard the car long before it pulled up, and rushed to her bedroom window. A low-slung little sportster in childish red, its engine roaring deeply, pulled up in the lane beyond the gate with a middle-aged man in sunglasses and cravat in the driving seat. When he shut off the engine, the whole world was startled back into peace again.

Gramps, at the garden gate, greeted the fellow like an old friend, leaning into the car to pat him on the shoulder, nodding and gesturing back towards the house. The visitor eased himself out of the low, bucket seat with more than a little difficulty and leant against the bonnet while fumbling in a top pocket for a handkerchief to wipe the top of his balding head. Gramps walked off, whistling and calling cheerio.

'Dammit, Gramps, wait. Oh, for goodness' sake!' Stella muttered.

She wanted to hurry down the stairs to catch him up, but could not take her eyes off the car and its occupant who had inserted a pipe in the corner of his mouth and was fiercely stoking it. The woody scent of the smoke reached her as she leant on her windowsill. Then she heard Dad's voice as he emerged through the front door below her.

'Roger, old fellow,' Nicholas called, clearly elated as he bounded down the path and up to the car.

The men shook hands, their free palms clasping each other's shoulders, their equally balding foreheads coming perilously close to touching.

'How long have you had this thing, Rodge?' Dad asked as he threw a small suitcase into the boot and sank carefully down into the passenger seat.

The man's animated response was snuffed out by the revving of the engine and the little car zipped forward, hugged the lane low, disappeared around the bend. Once more, the countryside of Kent settled back to its realm of order and Stella's parents' relationship fell as swiftly into place. She burst out with bright, relieved laughter.

Mum and Grannie were lingering over their late breakfast under the tree at the bottom of the garden. Stella took her toast and jam from the kitchen and went to sit with them. The sun was warm already, but hiding behind a blanket of milky cloud, its hazy light stippling the angles of the manor house. The garden, the whole world, seemed to be half asleep.

'So he's away then,' Mathilde commented.

'Said he'd be back Sunday night. Now, Stella,' said Eliza, pouring her a cup of tea, 'how is your writing going?'

'I've had a few false starts, to be honest,' she admitted, cautiously. 'But what I really want to do, is write what happened to you. What happened in the war? About the map you created, how important your work was.'

Eliza's hand froze. Tea spilt over the edge of the cup into the saucer.

'It's amazing that no one knows about any of this, Mum,' said Stella, grabbing a napkin to help with the spillage. 'Do you think I could tell your story? Would you mind?'

Stella saw her shudder briefly, privately, but then turn on her a lovely generous smile.

'I can't see why not.'

Mathilde reached across the crockery and pressed Eliza's arm, her clear blue eyes glimmering with understanding. Stella watched Mum's strength, garnered by her own mother's touch, floating just beneath the surface of her skin and was hit by overwhelming love for them both.

'You really don't mind me writing about it?' she urged.

'No. I have told you, it's OK,' Eliza said, memory glinting in her eyes. She gave a soft tinkling laugh. 'But would anyone really be interested?'

'Of course they would, Mum.'

Eliza gazed at her, surprised and trusting. She suddenly looked incredibly young, as if the years and the pain had drifted away.

Mathilde looked over her shoulder. 'Is that the door?' she asked, cocking her ear. 'I thought I heard the bell.'

'Not the postman again, surely?' Eliza said.

Stella went to find out, hearing the gently chatting voices of Mum and Grannie fading behind her. She darted between the open French windows into the drawing room and through the house to the front door.

A man stood on the threshold with one foot poised on the step, covering the motto carved there. He opened his mouth to speak and then drew back a fraction to stare at Stella, quizzical and wary, as if he had just opened a door to find her there.

Stella held the door half closed in front of her like a shield. In his youth, he had been tall, but now there was a gentle stoop to his shoulders, the normal legacy of middle age. His hair was full and quite luxuriant around his collar. Once quite dark, Stella guessed, and now luminous with silver-grey. An open neck shirt was a little crumpled beneath a fresh linen jacket. His eyes were an extraordinary clear green and sparkled in his tanned, worn and quite lovely face. The startling irises darted with apprehension, his smile twitching politely.

Stella gasped, her hand flying to her cheek. 'I think I know who you are.'

His face brightened momentarily, then fell back into a frown of worry.

'Is she here?' His voice rasped.

'She is.'

Stella pulled the door back wider and he slipped into the hallway, glancing around him, assessing the space.

He waited for her to close the door. 'And,' he said, 'I know who you are.'

The hallway was dim, the dark beams and stone floor soaking up the light, but she could see clearly that he was trying to smile despite deep, dredging memory distracting him. His face was fixed and almost frightened; his eyes wide. He coughed, cleared his throat.

'The last time I saw you, and your mother, was in Hampstead.'

'In *Hampstead*?'

Stella took a step back and held onto the newel post at the bottom of the stairs. She wanted to touch the old wood of the house, something solid in her hands.

'You were all arriving together.' He stood quite still in the centre of the hallway, as if stunned. 'Nicholas, Eliza and you. You were tiny, a little poppet. Nicholas was carrying you. You were clinging to his neck. I watched from the edge of the Heath. You all stood and looked up at the house. Eliza looked around. Didn't see me. I'd taken a short cut from the station.'

'I vaguely remember the visit.' Stella recalled sour rejection but dismissed it. That time had now passed. 'I remember a strange place, tall houses. The terrace. Mum stayed.'

'You were a family,' he said. 'I could see that. Or I convinced myself of that. I could not break you up. The three of you, standing together. She must have got my message from France a long time before. A whole year before. And this, *that*, was her choice. Her family. I loved your mother, I confess. I only wanted her happiness.'

Stella watched regret manifest, flinching over his face.

'I walked away.'

'But why were you there, on the Heath? Outside Angela's house?'

'Who?'

'Angela Stratton. She gave the house to Mum. Such a generous old friend. I stayed there, recently,' Stella said. 'It's lovely.'

Lewis Harper's smile was sudden, wide and dazzling, his teeth bright in the subdued light.

'She's a clever puss. Making that one up.'

Stella shook her head in confusion, her mind muddling. She brushed his answer aside, bent on following her own course.

'But why were you even *there*?'

'Where? Oh, at Hampstead? I'd been dumped in London by the Secret Service; debriefed, checked over, sent on my way. The war in Europe was over. They had no more use of me. I thought I'd pop back home. The house, you see, is actually mine. I gave it to your mother.'

Stella nodded vaguely, trying to keep up. Still not understanding.

Lewis said, 'I'd been in France since D-Day. Shot down behind enemy lines. Injured, but taken care of by the Resistance. Managed to lie low until the Allies reached me.'

Stella sat down on the bottom step and gazed up at him, open-mouthed, unable to begin to imagine.

'But that's a whole other story,' he said, quickly, sensing her distress. 'Perhaps I shall tell it to you one day.'

She rubbed her hands together; the sensation was comforting amid the realisation of the absolute importance of the man standing there. She glanced towards the drawing room, where the French windows stood open. A drift of voices lilted through the air.

'She's only just got your message,' Stella spoke quickly. 'The pigeon. It fell into my fireplace.'

'I know, I read your story in the *Gazette*. That's why I am here.'

'Of course.' The prickle of satisfaction, of a job well done, lasted mere seconds. 'But there's another thing: we found a body, Dad and I. And the whole thing spun Mum out of her mind. It's been bloody awful for her. It was connected to the past, to the war. This person was local. Mum and Dad knew her. Oh –'

She put her hand over her mouth, remembering his message on the map of stars. Jessica had been his wife.

'Mum has been quite unwell.'

'Oh, God, has she? I see, oh, dear.'

'I think she is getting better, though.'

Lewis glanced back to the front door, and pointed, gesturing towards the motto on the threshold.

'Do you think, then, Stella, that the journey is over?'

She agreed, smiled at him. 'She's home. She's in the garden,' Stella said, and stood up, ready to lead the way.

He stopped her with a hand gentle on her arm.

'You know who I am, don't you?' he asked. 'To you, I mean.'

She looked at his extraordinary eyes, at the same peculiar green that she had known and wondered at from the very first time she had ever looked in a mirror.

Yes. She nodded but could not answer him. Maybe she had known for a while. *Yes*.

'You know that I have been in Deal, not ten miles away, the whole time?'

Stella dipped her face to hide a sudden spurt of tears.

'Follow me,' she whispered, wiping her eyes.

At the bottom of the garden, the women were chatting, Eliza pressing her hand to the side of the teapot, wondering about its temperature. Mathilde was biting into a slice of toast, touching crumbs delicately at the corners of her lips; Eliza laughing gently.

Stella stood to one side of the French windows, leaving the way open for Lewis. He paused on the step. His hands, held loosely at his sides, suggested nonchalance, but she saw they were trembling.

At the bottom of the garden, simultaneously surprised, both women lifted their heads. Mathilde shielded her eyes and squinted. Eliza kept perfectly still, her face pale in the shadow of the tree.

Lewis took a hesitant step forward, paused and then began to walk across the lawn. Stella watched the lifting of his head, the determination in his departing back, the set of his shoulders straightening.

Mathilde stood up, pulled back her chair and with another incredulous glance towards Lewis, walked away from the table, away towards the river. Eliza, too, rose unsteadily to her feet, but stayed exactly where she was, raising a hand to her face.

Stella glanced at Grannie. She was not alone. Beside her walked a young man, or rather half of him, like a dark moving reflection in water, a suggestion of shadow. He was the young man from the photographs on Gramps's mantelpiece, the man in uniform in the picture on the stairs. He was Martyn, her uncle. She took a breath, realising. He had grown up. He'd been the boy she'd left behind in her childhood. Her Tintin.

But Mathilde did not notice him. She had no idea that her son was there, walking beside her, accompanying her as she made her way across the garden and down to the river.

And Eliza and Lewis, a step apart and reaching their arms wide for each other, did not notice him either.

ACKNOWLEDGEMENTS

I have known and loved the Isle of Thanet for nearly twenty-five years. So much so that in 2014 I upped sticks from Buckinghamshire and made my home here, ten minutes from the sea. East Kent and Thanet's proximity to France, its vulnerability and outstanding bravery during the Second World War had always intrigued me and I wanted to write about what it was like to live here on the front line in plain sight of the coast at Calais.

It was a strange case of having the title of the novel before I had the story. A map of stars came to me while I was doodling with words one day. Then a newspaper report of a mummified carrier pigeon falling into someone's hearth, complete with unopened wartime message, sparked an embryonic idea. I looked into the vital work of war-time homing pigeons and, when I dug deeper, I unearthed the Auxiliaries – our very own British Resistance – and the deadly secret tasks that they had been poised to do. To discover that they had been sent into Normandy behind the Allied invasion took my story to another level. I wanted to portray the incredible skills of the War Office men and women, the map makers, and the code breakers who changed the course of the war. And around all of this, of course, write a love story.

As for Forstall Manor and the Map of Stars itself, they are entirely figments of my creative mind. Or are they? In the words of Picasso: Everything you can imagine is real.

I'd like to acknowledge the information and insights I collected from the fascinating RAF Manston History Museum, the Spitfire and Hurricane Memorial Museum, Canterbury Museum and the British Resistance Archive (www.coleshillhouse.com). And thank you to Darren Jones for taking me to Deal and for setting me straight about a potential historical faux pas concerning the castle.

Thank you to both Joel Richardson for seeing the potential of the novel when it really was in a bit of a mess and to Claire Creek for her brilliant editing. And thank you, Judith Murdoch for still believing in me.